AMBASSADOR 6: THE ENEMY WITHIN

PATTY JANSEN

GET FREE EBOOKS

Visit pattyjansen.com
or scan the QR code below with your phone to get four series starter
ebooks for free!

DID YOU KNOW?

Ambassador 6 is also available in audio. Visit https://pattyjansen.com to find out more.

1

THE DELEGATION from the Thousand Island tribe was definitely the strangest party to ever have graced the hall of my apartment.

We'd been expecting them, even if they had never let us know what day and time they would come—lacking, as Sheydu would bluntly say, the means to tell the time with any measure of accuracy. Not that I believed for one moment that Pengali didn't have an accurate timing scheme, but I suspected that they, being Pengali, didn't think notifying us particularly important.

Because there was always someone at the apartment, right?

So they had arrived at a slightly inconvenient moment, when I'd been in the middle of a prearranged call that I couldn't end based on the activity in my hall, and I'd spent the rest of the call—to my accountant at the Trader Ledger of all things—listening to the various sounds in the hall with one ear.

I didn't like talking money at the best of times—I'd put off doing the budget for long enough already—let alone when there was stuff going on in the house that I should attend instead. Admittedly, the budget was important, especially when it concerned over twenty people and provisions for off-world trips; and the bottom line made me cringe with its stark revelation that our household would go in the negative unless I found another source of income. Although I was no stranger to finding funds, it was one of my least favourite activities and one I had—wrongfully—assumed I'd been relieved of by signing on as a special envoy to *gamra* for Ezhya Palayi. But now our team had grown so much that expenses outpaced income and I was going to have to do something to get additional income, because shedding people was out of the question. That was what the accountant wanted me to do, but she was Kedrasi and had no concept of Coldi associations and their loyalty networks, and some of the other staff had been at the apartment longer than I had. Did she really expect me to toss them onto the street?

When the call finally ended, and I came from the dark hub into the light-filled hall, I found the Pengali delegation in the middle of the pretty mosaic tiled floor.

The group consisted of at least twenty Pengali, bunched together with the young males facing outward, ready to protect their elder who stood in the middle of the group.

That elder was Abri. I knew her and was expecting her. I hadn't *quite* expected so many others.

All of them looked splendid, with intricate, traditional hairstyles with many plaits full of glass beads and little trinkets made from fish scales, teeth or lizard feet. The male guards' torsos were naked, displaying the typical giraffe-like skin patterns of the Thousand Island tribe. They had even applied paint to their skin to bring the patterns out more. Their attire consisted of little more than a belt, on which most of them carried stonking great big knives of the type that would make the guards on the *gamra* island nervous.

Two of those guards had come into the apartment with the group, and they stood near the front door, which was still open, and through which I could see my faithful guards Evi and Telaris on the walkway, both looking on in a bemused fashion—dare I say *laughing*?

My eyes found another familiar face in the group: the young male Ynggi, who was going to be the group's translator into Coldi. The Exchange would provide a certified Coldi to Isla translator.

I remembered I should never bow to a Pengali, not even to greet someone, and I waggled my hand in front of me, lacking the tail that they used for signalling greetings.

In fact, those black and white banded appendages were waving in and out of the group, signalling their feelings. The young men at the front appealed for calm. An older man behind them was unsure about the members of my team who stood in the hallway and looked very threatening. His tail waved at shoulder height.

Abri—good old Abri—elder of the tribe, waved her tail around her knees and the younger woman next to her, who had to be her daughter, made zigzag patterns in the air, whatever that meant.

And that thin, wildly waving tail from the arms of the daughter, was that really a young child?

What was a child doing here in this group? The Pengali were here because we were going to a court hearing, on Earth no less.

· For that matter, why had they brought all these fighters with knives that made the *gamra* guards nervous? That was not part of our agreement. We'd agreed on Abri, her daughter and Ynggi.

As I approached, Abri came out of the group. She carried a low basket made from seaweed holding a glistening, smooth fish. She held this out to me.

Behind her, the young male fighters took up positions in two lines so that they all faced me. Their faces were very serious.

The offering of food was a traditional Pengali custom. As traditional custodians of the islands and the land around Barresh, the Pengali had welcomed several waves of newcomers—and had usually become worse off for it to the point where one rarely saw tribal Pengali in the city anymore. Yet they continued doggedly with this custom. Thousand Island Pengali were very traditional, scoffed at even by their own kinsfolk who lived in the poorer parts of the city and who had adopted notions like wearing clothes and working during the day.

I took the fish from her. It was quite heavy and didn't yet have the fishy smell that always hung around the markets.

"Welcome to my house," I said to Abri.

Thousand Island Pengali were more likely to speak Coldi than the local keihu language, because they had never been welcome in town and, in times past, their settlement had dealt directly with Coldi visitors from Asto who came to buy their products.

Abri looked at the high vaulted ceiling in the hall to my apartment. "Your house is very big."

"Thank you. I hope you had a nice trip." These were all formalities that were part of a Pengali greeting. You were meant to reply with honesty, not with empty platitudes.

Abri lifted her tail to eye level and wriggled the tip. "The fishing was favourable."

And that was all that mattered. That fish in the basket had probably been caught on the way in.

"I can see that. It is a very good fish that will grace our gathering tonight."

She seemed pleased with that. Taking a meal together was another one of those formalities.

With the formal part of the greetings now over, I asked, "Did you bring any luggage?"

She gave me a puzzled look.

I explained. "Packs? Shoes, warm clothes?" Or just clothes full stop, because they were only wearing their traditional belts, and this level of clothing, or the lack thereof, would raise eyebrows even in Barresh, where it was warm. "You know, any personal things you'd like to bring?"

"We have that." She gestured with her tail to a small bundle at the feet of one of her companions. It was a net, containing a couple of fishbone hoops with a thin gauze-like material, a carved box with a glass lid that contained hooks, and rolls of wire.

Fishing gear. Sure, that made sense. That was all one needed on an interplanetary trip.

Oh, well, I'd have to get Eirani to pack all the clothes we had fortunately prepared in advance, since in my past interactions with the tribe I'd had a feeling that it might be necessary.

"I will ask the staff to show you your rooms." I eyed the members of the entourage. We'd only prepared for Abri, her daughter Kita and the translator Ynggi. I didn't understand what the rest of all these other people were doing here and whether Abri thought that they could stay here before going back to the tribe's territory. On second thoughts, she didn't assume that they were *coming* on the trip, did she? Did she even know how much the tickets through the Exchange cost?

It wouldn't surprise me if she thought they were coming, Thayu said through our feeder.

I hadn't seen her come into the hallway, but she had been in the office, and would have heard the commotion. She stood behind me and I could feel the bemusement dripping from her. She'd been teasing me about Pengali and their customs ever since we'd gotten the summons to turn up at the court. It was a playful teasing intended for my ears only, but I well understood the basis of it: the stiff formalities at the court and the Pengali customs that related to place, weather and items of food were not exactly compatible.

Get this: we were going to take a bunch of tribal Pengali to a highly formal session of the Nations of Earth criminal court, where Abri was to be a witness. That was going to be, in Thayu's words, *interesting*.

I decided not to immediately press the issue of the extra numbers, hoping it would resolve by itself. Problems often did when dealing with Pengali, and it was never productive to press for an answer when they were not ready to give one. Frustrating, but true.

Their thought processes were alien and opaque to many of us, but they were definitely not stupid.

I invited the group into the living room, where Eirani stood at the entrance, looking slightly alarmed, probably by the increased numbers. In her eyes, I could see the protest: *But I didn't plan for so many for dinner!* She became the recipient of the basket with the fish.

An appreciative nod. It was a very good fish.

"Will I cook this for dinner tonight, Muri?" she asked, glancing sideways at the group.

"That would be a good idea."

"Are all these people staying here? We don't have any—"

"Shhh. It will sort itself out."

"But the room I set up is too small. We will have to move everything to—"

"Shhh. Let's wait and see. I very much doubt they'll expect to stay."

A nod, still a bit uncertain. To be honest, I was by no means certain that they wouldn't expect to stay either.

Eirani had been *somewhat* conditioned to the presence of Pengali through a prior visit to my house by Ynggi, during which he had explained the concept of fish-giving. But I didn't think Eirani either liked or understood them, and she probably had not been present when he gave his explanation.

Wait and see was not her style. She wanted to get things *ready*, not run after everyone and panic about how she was going to feed and look after these people. She wanted to be prepared.

In the old keihu families in town, like the one where she grew up, if keihu people worked with any Pengali it was in the capacity of being their boss. The Pengali in question were always from the Washing Stones tribe, many of whom lived in Barresh and were used to the requirements of living in a town, including the wearing of clothes and being awake during the daytime.

But these were Thousand Island Pengali, *alien, tribal, wild,* and everyone knew that they were fierce, could be easily offended by the strangest things, and had very big and sharp knives.

We went into the living room.

The Pengali fighters solved the issue for us by staying at the door.

"Do they not want to come in?" I asked Abri, because now was the time to raise the issue.

"The tide is going out." As it would be at this time of the day. "The fishing will be good."

"All right then. Tell them to take care. Tell them that they can come here to pick you up when we're back."

Abri spoke to the men in Pengali, a rattling language with a distinct shortage of vowels. They snapped their tails and retreated into the hall.

"Give them the parcel from the table in the hall," I called after Evi, whose dark Indrahui figure I spotted through the doorway. Evi was partial to fish. He would give the Pengali the presents for the tribe—in this case a few sets of children's toys and a box of Asian prawn chips which I'd gotten from the Chinese restaurant owner Huang Le and which he semi-legally imported from Earth for his restaurant. They were extremely popular with townsfolk, including Pengali, and there were always some kids watching through the window into Huang Le's kitchen when he tossed the chips into hot oil and they grew into arm-length wavy sheets. You saw people nibbling on those everywhere in the streets. Some people even tried to make their own. That was a typically Pengali venture, because they always tried to figure out how to make the things they liked.

I sat down opposite Abri. Ynggi sat on the carpet next to her. One did not sit in a higher spot than an elder. Ynggi was the least traditionally dressed of all of them, although I didn't think the pale blue skirt he wore was going to do the job when travelling on the shuttle, let alone on Earth.

And what was that? Why was that toddler still here, in the arms of the woman who was Abri's daughter?

"The tribal council decided it was a three-generation matter," Abri said, picking up on the fact that I had noticed the child. "My generation . . ." She pointed at herself with her tail, and then at her daughter whose name was Kita, and then at the child. "My daughter and my daughter's daughter. Three generations to talk. Kasamo was a good person, happy to share his fish with others. We come so that they punish hairy face for killing him." Thousand Island Pengali never used the names of people they did not respect. Robert Davidson, gun-crazy rogue mining magnate, had never shown any respect to the tribe. Gusamo Sahardjo, the victim of the crime—or Kasamo as the Pengali called him—had been a friend to the tribe.

"Hairy face has come too often and taken too many of our young men. He promised them things that were not his to promise. Money! What use do we have for that? Just so that the young ones leave and never come back? So that they get in with the bad crowd, become rebellious and rude? Hairy face needs to be punished for killing Pengali also."

"I did tell you that the issue of Pengali victims will need to be raised later. This trial will be about Robert killing Gusamo."

I hated telling Abri this when she asked, and she had asked every time I'd seen her: how can we punish him for what he did to *us*? I had no answers for her. People on Earth were not going to be interested in punishing Robert for crimes against non-humans.

Besides, I was pretty sure that without legal framework, which we didn't have because Earth was not a member of *gamra*, it would be almost impossible to charge someone from Earth with the murder of non-Earth people in the absence of a formal accusation, or, for that matter, much evidence.

I had asked the lawyers about it, because it felt like the right thing to do, but the Nations of Earth prosecutor, Conrad Martens, who specialised in cases like this, had said that the first step would have to be the current trial.

The little Pengali youngster peeked from over the top of the cloth bundle that her mother used to carry her. She crawled out. She was stark naked, completely covered, like all Pengali young children, in skin patterns which would become less prominent as she grew. Thousand Island tribe patterns were most commonly giraffe-like.

Her hair was still down-like and fuzzy.

She held her tail straight up to convey alertness. People on Earth spoke about "monkeys" but Pengali were nothing like that. They always walked with a straight back. Their back legs were strong and their arms were quite short. They used them for holding on, but I had never seen a Pengali older than a baby walk on all fours. They didn't look like any kind of Earthly animal at all. But her huge eyes and her little hands made her incredibly cute.

"Introduce the little one to me."

"This is Idda." Abri picked the youngster up. Huge dark eyes met mine. I could see my reflection in them. "She was born in the season of the rains."

The previous year, I assumed. That made her almost two, about the same age as Nicha's son Ayshada, who had gone out with the nanny and should be back home soon. "I understand you want her to come on the trip?"

"It is a three-generation issue." I guessed that was a roundabout way of saying yes.

"A lot of the places where we're going will not be welcoming to children." That was the understatement of the century.

"Do they not have children?"

"They do, of course, but children cannot come into a great many places where adults do business. They don't consider it appropriate."

She gave me a blank look. Even when I visited her at the tribe, when I had first heard of the impending trial and the fact that the prosecutor wanted to call Abri as witness, I had never felt that Abri came even close to understanding what sort of society she would be visiting.

And we were coming in with a bunch of people who didn't like wearing clothes, and two two-year-olds—because Nicha was bringing Ayshada. I guessed I could ask the nanny to look after this Pengali youngster as well. It would give Ayshada someone to play with.

One of the junior domestic staff showed the Pengali their room, and all became quiet for a while.

———

When the Pengali had left the hall, Nicha, Thayu and I reconvened in my office, which overlooked the marshlands that surrounded Barresh.

"It *will* be interesting," Thayu said.

"I just don't understand what the lawyers at Nations of Earth are hoping to achieve and whether we can deliver it," I said. "It would help a lot if we knew what they expected to get by dragging a witness like Abri into court, when it would be just as easy to record a testimony and deal with it remotely. There has to be a secondary purpose for our visit."

They both nodded. We'd been through it so many times, looked at political situations on Earth, and considered motives, but we had no answers.

Melissa Heyworth, who had been shot and wounded by Robert, and who was Earth's *gamra* representative, was already at the court. She had also been explicitly told not to discuss particulars of her testimony with Abri—and with me by extrapolation—in the interest of fairness of the trial.

We had stuck to that. We wanted Robert convicted of his deeds, and we didn't want to risk that he got off on a technicality. I also knew that if there was anything particularly controversial to share, Melissa had emergency ways of contacting us that wouldn't be picked up by Nations of Earth, so I guessed that everything was fine and there was nothing to worry about.

It was just that it took a huge chunk of time and effort out of my regular job to essentially be a chaperone to a group of Pengali.

But Ezhya Palayi, Chief Coordinator of Asto, who was my direct employer, had said to me, "Take the time you need. I don't know where it will take us, but the situation is very curious and I'll be watching. One way or another, we'll learn something from it."

And this was where I was glad to work for him, and not a rigid Earth-based employer who required me to work against set benchmarks and work only on certain projects and justify my time spent away from those projects.

I'd often watched Melissa deal with this. She'd had to apply to take time out from her job as Nations of Earth representative to testify. Nations of Earth hadn't liked it. They might even take her off certain projects and that would set back her career. I knew Melissa still hoped to get a job at Nations of Earth headquarters in Rotterdam at some point and she needed her brownie points.

Nicha said, "Karana can look after the Pengali child." In the silence, he'd clearly been thinking about practical issues.

"Yes, I thought the same. She can keep Ayshada entertained."

Then he said, "We need to press the issue of clothing on them. Can you imagine the news when the Pengali turn up in full tribal outfits?"

I *could* imagine the sensation. I could already hear the words *primitive* and *natives* and all the judgement that accompanied them. "We'll have to make sure they dress appropriately at all times."

Thayu snorted. "They'll be stubborn until they get there and realise it is *cold* over there. Then they'll wear the clothes no problem."

"Yeah, we better take some extra just in case. I know Pengali are not stupid, but they're going into this pretty unprepared for what they'll face."

"Yes, it will be very interesting."

I agreed.

Nicha said he wanted to bathe Ayshada and went out, leaving me alone with Thayu.

"How are you feeling?" I asked her.

"Tired."

She *looked* tired. I wished I didn't have to drag her into this. Not now.

After postponing my fertility treatment in order to wait for *a better time* we decided that there was never going to be a better time, and started with the easiest and least invasive genetic treatment option. It was not without discomfort. It had involved poking needles into my . . . you get the gist.

But it had worked, and Thayu was *pregnant*. We had not announced it to anyone since it was early days, but my household knew. And Thayu was *different*. Moody, emotional.

I took her in my arms and kissed her on her forehead.

"We'll be like a travelling sideshow," I said. "Every news service on Earth will be full of stuff that Pengali get into, what they look like, what they wear, or don't wear."

"Maybe that's the point of it, putting them on display."

"That would make sense if there was an election going on and

Margarethe was pushing for Earth to join *gamra*." But the election had been a few months ago, Margarethe had been re-elected with the narrowest of margins, and the last time I'd heard anyone at Nations of Earth speak about Earth joining *gamra* was years ago.

It looked less likely to happen than it ever had in my lifetime.

I let out a breath and registered the delicious smells coming in from the hall. "Let's go and get ready for that great fish. I'm looking forward to it."

But when I went into the hallway, we met Devlin coming the other way with a reader in his hand. His face carried an expression of worry.

"Muri, this just came for you."

He handed the reader to me. There was only one type of communication that would come this way, and sure enough, on the screen was a message from the Nations of Earth court. The first few paragraphs rehashed the details of the hearing. I skimmed over those, because I was already familiar with them. The last paragraph said,

Please ensure that you bring a translator acceptable to the court. Acceptable persons include any such certified, who must, in addition, not be a member of the group that the witness belongs to. Please resubmit your proposed official translator.

Crap. Holy crap.

I stared at Thayu, who had read over my shoulder.

I asked, heart thudding, "Does this mean they're not approving us to use Ynggi?"

"It reads that way to me."

"They *have* to be fucking kidding!" We were all ready to go. I spent months sorting this out, getting Abri ready, getting the permits, the new IDs, the health checks, everything.

But Nations of Earth had less humour than a dead fish. There it was in clear letters: *please resubmit your proposed official translator* and *not be a member of the group the witness belongs to*.

They weren't going to accept Ynggi as translator.

"Where do they think I'm going to get someone at such short notice?" Ynggi was one of the few Thousand Island Pengali who had lived in the city and had enough knowledge to translate official terms.

You couldn't take anyone from the Washing Stones tribe to translate for the Thousand Island tribe, even if people from the Thousand Island tribe rarely spoke keihu or trusted people who did; and you couldn't find a translator who translated from Pengali into Coldi who was available and was happy to work for Thousand Island people without being from the tribe. Dog, meet tail.

Well, wasn't that just awesome?

I snorted. "I'm going to take him anyway." I *trusted* Ynggi. I'd been in contact with him for months. He did a good job and was probably the Thousand Island Pengali with the most gumption about other worlds. He was *not* staying behind, even if I had to pay for his trip.

Thayu said, "We'll still need someone else."

Yes, I knew that, and when I met Veyada in the hall just before dinner and explained the situation to him, he agreed, after uttering a few strong words. "Just to appease their conditions. I don't think we'll be able to find anyone who is any good in that very short time."

We might not, but I could see Nations of Earth cancel the trial over this trivial issue. They were bureaucratic enough for that, and I didn't know if I could organise Abri to come here a second time without both her and me losing face with the tribe. Losing face was a big thing with Pengali. Promises had to be kept and failures to do so were chalked up to a person's social standing over that person's entire lifetime.

I shook my head. "I'll have to try."

But then I remembered the talk with my accountant. Who was going to pay for one extra person? I could not leave Ynggi behind. Three adults was a small enough group already. As we'd seen, Pengali travelled in bigger groups, usually with a few young male fighters. I couldn't leave him here. But if I overshot my travel budget before I'd even begun, the accountant would eat me alive.

Well, damn it.

2

———

ONE COULD SAY that it put quite a damper on what was otherwise an excellent meal taken with all the members of my association, as well as Evi and Telaris and the Pengali.

When Eirani brought in the fish, there was further ceremony to be performed.

The Pengali came in full tribal gear, with painted patterns on their skin and elaborate ornaments in their hair that included the famed blue diamonds that were the start of this whole affair.

Eirani brought the fish on a platter, steamed with a tangy sauce made from lily flowers. The meat was pure white, divested of the tough skin and drizzled with bright orange berry pulp.

I, the official householder, needed to cut the fish and divide it into equal portions for all the members of our group. The fact that they were all Coldi and that Coldi on Asto grew up not eating the meat of any animal higher than a slug did not compute with them. Veyada had developed a taste for fish. Having lived on Earth, Nicha would eat oysters and prawns, but was iffy about vertebrate animals, but the others were staunchly vegetarian. Reida looked like he might want to try it, but he was unsure if Nicha, his superior, agreed with it. His *zhayma* companion Deyu *had* tried fish on a previous occasion, but didn't like the taste nor the thought of eating an animal. She was interested in animals, but not in that way. Being pregnant, Thayu was definitely not going to try it. She was in general not particularly adventurous about food. Sheydu had spent most of her sixty years in a rigid military environment and would probably eat the fish if I told her and would never tell me how much she hated it, but she *would* hate it, so I wasn't going to. I appreciated Sheydu very much.

So we were left with the slightly awkward situation of having far more bowls than people who were actually going to eat this fish.

First, I was meant to taste it. I cut a piece of the pure white flesh and put it in my mouth.

The creamy taste was heavenly.

"It's a very good fish."

This was met with waving tails and serene, slightly smug expressions from Abri, Ynggi and Kita. The little child sat on a high table that normally stood in the corner with a vase on top. Ayshada occupied the apartment's only high chair, and he eyed this little intruder in his domain with curiosity.

Now that I had approved of the fish, everyone could start eating it. Veyada did not see the fact that so many of our association were vegetarian as a problem. Neither did Evi and Telaris, who were from Indrahui and had no reservations whatsoever about eating fish. Fortunately, the three of them were big muscled guys, with healthy appetites. The Pengali also seemed capable of devouring much larger quantities of food than their size suggested.

The little Pengali toddler Idda got a bowl and ate with both fists. Strapped in his chair, Ayshada protested loudly that Nicha would not let him eat fish. While everyone ate, Idda picked up her bowl, slid down one of the legs of the tall table, ran across the floor holding the bowl under one arm and climbed up Ayshada's chair. She slapped a piece of fish on his table and scampered off again.

Ayshada put it in his mouth but spent the rest of the meal rolling it into a ball with his tongue, dribbling sauce down his chin.

He always did this with his food, and I didn't think Nicha noticed.

After the official part of the meal, the Pengali retreated to the room we had allocated them downstairs. I thought they were getting changed out of their official gear, but they did not resurface. I asked Eirani what they were doing when she came in to collect the plates and bring fruit, and she said they had gone out, presumably to look around and get breakfast, or maybe see fellow Pengali, or whatever it was that Pengali did.

This gave us the opportunity to talk about the interpreter situation. We moved to the hub, where I sat between Thayu and Nicha, with Veyada on the other bench. The only light in this room came from the circular bench of communication equipment in the middle. It would normally display a holographic projection of whatever Devlin, who was in charge of the hub, was doing.

But Devlin had stopped work for the day. He was nervous about travelling with us tomorrow, and had gone into town to pick up additional items that his mother thought he might need.

We sat down, looking at each other in the semidarkness.

Thayu said, "Surely Nations of Earth wouldn't be so dumb to cancel the case over such a trivial technicality."

"You don't know Nations of Earth," I said, and Nicha nodded. "We absolutely have to find someone, or we will lose a lot more time and effort and we'll all have wasted a lot of resources."

Would the trial even go ahead if Ezhya said I needed to do something for him here and I couldn't go at a later date and therefore Abri wouldn't go?

But where could we find an acceptable interpreter? The Pengali office had already let me know that I would find many local Pengali unwilling to translate for people from the Thousand Islands tribe.

I thought the whole issue was petty and childish but, apparently, the feud between the Washing Stones and Thousand Islands tribe was about a lot more than rivalry and fishing grounds, although I couldn't claim to understand the source of the conflict. Each Pengali tribe seemed to be like this with all other tribes. There was a third tribe in the area, the Whitesand Creek tribe. They lived mostly in the forest and were equally hated by both the Washing Stones and the Thousand Islanders.

As translator, a Pengali person from *any* other tribe wasn't going to work. But Nations of Earth insisted that the interpreter couldn't be from the same tribe.

Thayu asked, "Would there be any non-Pengali? The keihu families have Pengali housekeepers and cooks. Surely some of their kids have grown up speaking Pengali?"

That was an option, albeit a far-fetched one, so I contacted anyone I knew who worked with Pengali. I even sent a message to Clovis Keneally, the tour guide whose falling out with Robert Davidson was the stitch that brought all of Robert's secret diamond smuggling business undone.

Clovis and his wife had a lot of health problems these days, and lived as virtual recluses. They didn't do tours anymore. I was sure that the affair with Robert had something to do with it.

His ferry company with all its inherent feuding over route rights was run by a manager. I didn't think Clovis worked a lot with Pengali anymore. Maybe just the domestic staff. I couldn't help but feel a bit sorry for him.

He got back to me quickly and said he knew no one. His reply suited the way I pictured him: reluctant, and always a bit shifty, even if he didn't mean to be.

I contacted Huang Le, who had recently bought a second restaurant in Fountain Street, the overflow of the hugely popular shop near the airport. I had to admit that he made a mean stir-fry and that the local fresh produce in Barresh suited Chinese cooking well. Even Thayu and I ate there sometimes.

Never let your dislike of the cook get in the way of a good fish. If that wasn't a Pengali proverb, it should be. Except Pengali didn't do proverbs like Coldi.

Huang Le did *not* like Pengali. His kitchen staff and waiters were all keihu. His children had keihu names and spoke no Isla. I guess that showed us what he thought of Earth.

Predictably, he knew of no one either.

We put requests on notice boards and local employment markets and sent out messages to several people who had contacts in the Pengali community, hoping against better knowledge that they would send us back all these amazing offers tomorrow morning.

We found nothing. Decent interpreters had their schedules full. We were *leaving* tomorrow. Was this issue going to scuttle the entire expedition?

I leaned my head in my hands. "We're not going to be able to find anyone."

Veyada gestured wordlessly at his screen.

I looked as he held it up. It said, *Hire any professional, any task. Guaranteed.*

There was no name. Advertising business names was considered tacky in Barresh, but I thought I recognised where this was coming from: Jasper Carlson, shady figure extraordinaire. He was, like Clovis, like Huang Le, a refugee from Earth for all the wrong reasons. He differed from those two by being smarter, richer and much less transparent in his goals.

"Really?" I said to Veyada.

Veyada shrugged. "It's your decision."

But at the same time, signing a contract with one's competitor to suss them out was very, very Coldi thing to do. He would jump at this opportunity.

I said, "I wonder what they can offer that the Pengali office can't."

"Maybe this is bluff. Maybe it isn't. But we can try." He was in favour, clearly.

"All right, then."

"You were planning to take Ynggi anyway, weren't you?"

"He at least knows the Thousand Island dialect and can translate it correctly."

"So we'd be taking this extra person to appease Nations of Earth."

"Yes." And pay for an extra person, too. Grrr. I really needed to solve this budget issue. "Contact him at least. See what he can do."

Veyada did. He would not use my name, but I had no doubt that Jasper would work out where it was coming from soon enough. I still didn't like it, but it was not to be helped.

We received a message back almost immediately that a translator would be available for us in the morning. There was no information about who this person would be, just a price tag that made me gulp.

Well, if it solved the problem . . . and surely cancelling the trial now would be more expensive than the interpreter could be. Or would it?

Oh damn, I could already hear the complaints from my accountant.

But funding was primarily *my* problem. My association did as I said. I made sure they had all they needed, including money.

We moved from the hub into the living room to share some tea.

A pile of luggage and boxes was starting to appear in the hall. Boy, I would look like an idiot if I couldn't find a new interpreter.

Deyu and Reida already sat in the living room. Sheydu was just coming out of the corridor, carrying two black bags with straps, her contribution to the pile of luggage. I bet they contained lots of weaponry. She came into the living room, too, and we all sat down on the carpet, where Thayu put out my projection sheet: a thin flexible screen that displayed a map of the Nations of Earth complex in Rotterdam.

Veyada shook his head, "Uh-uh. The court is in a different town, one called The Hague. It's affiliated with the *International Court* which is one of the oldest official institutions that survived the wars."

It always disturbed me to hear them using Isla words and knowing things about Earth, as if that part of my life was private, as if Veyada's knowledge implied that Asto, including Ezhya and Asto's secretive army also knew everything he knew. And yet I appreciated their knowledge.

Thayu pulled a face and swiped the map off the sheet. It was replaced by a question asking what she wanted to look at next. Veyada brought up another map of the town in question. It lay close to the ocean and, like Rotterdam, was surrounded by a sturdy dam that kept the water out. Beyond that lay seasonally inundated marshland dotted with agricultural communities, each also surrounded by dams and connected to each other by roads and train lines over further dams. Not dissimilar to Barresh, actually, if a lot colder.

Thayu looked at me. "Have you ever been to this place?"

"Not that I remember. I only lived at Nations of Earth as a child for less than two years."

"Do we have any information on this place?" She sounded annoyed. As if someone should have told her that she had the wrong town, or as if she berated herself for not having realised. I hadn't realised either. Coldi women had a reputation for being grumpy when pregnant. She was no exception.

Veyada said, "We do, but we'll distribute briefs a bit later. I'm still waiting on some information from Amarru." Amarru at the Exchange in Athens. Her information would be *very* useful, because it would include the latest intelligence.

Veyada then explained about the situation with the interpreter. My association were all Coldi, and so his version of events, that came down to, *We don't trust this man, but we're hiring him anyway to provide a vital piece that determines the success of our expedition,* was met with appreciative nods. They *understood* this action better than I ever could. We should have pulled Jasper in closer a lot earlier, I guessed.

"He doesn't like it," Sheydu said, looking at me.

"Never mind me. I'll trust your judgement." More like: I trusted that they had it all under control. I just provided the money.

Most of the people in my association had received official spy training in Asto's Inner Circle and this tactic—engaging your enemies—was probably a classic intelligence-gathering procedure. My team probably also considered this trip low-risk since it did not involve any of our regular enemies, and from their point of view, they were probably right. What did I know? Shut up, Mr. Wilson.

The discussion turned to more harmless things such as the weather. Reida wanted to know if it was going to be as cold as last time. It had been February then, so I said not. It was May, so it would be quite nice.

He asked if it rained, and I said it did, and that rain would be nothing like on Asto but more like in Barresh. He didn't seem convinced. Coldi did not like rain.

Then there was a commotion in the hall, accompanied by Pengali voices, followed by thunks and thumps and clangs and then Eirani said, "But I'm sure Muri does not like you leaving all these things here."

What things?

I rose from the couch and met Eirani at the door, coming in with the food trolley full of cups. "Tea will be ready very soon. Don't go too far away."

"Just seeing what's going on."

The front door was open and something was being delivered to the hall.

"Oh, Muri, these people will be the death of me." She shook her head and continued into the room.

The Pengali had indeed returned. Ynggi and Kita were carrying in a giant eel-hide covered drum. Idda sat on Ynggi's shoulder waving her tail in his face. The front door was still open and through it I spotted the building's concierge with a trolley carrying the hollowed-out tree branches of an instrument called an *irrka* which was the vital component of a betanka orchestra. The concierge's face carried a bemused expression, like he wanted to say, *Having a wild party in here?*

I'd been to a betanka party a few times, because if you lived in Barresh, you could simply not get away without going at least once, but those were the sanitised tourist versions of it. They were orchestrated, staged shows where one paid to see the orchestra and they each had arranged parts of drumming, playing pipes or singing, and none of the songs contained any rude words or gestures.

There were also the keihu-influenced city versions, where Pengali played in seedy, airless cellar bars and keihu men gambled and got extremely drunk and would embarrass themselves trying to sing or dance to the music.

Betanka proper was a community performance, where the leader played the five-beat rhythm on the *irrka*, tuned drum, and people improvised their parts.

This *irrka* drum was a huge thing, made up of a central barrel constructed from a huge hollowed-out tree trunk covered on one side with eel-hide leather. There were holes in the bottom half of the drum, for slotting in hollow branches of different diameters so that the whole thing looked like a giant spider. The betanka leader would sit near the top of the barrel perched on two platforms on the side of the drum for his feet, hitting the branches with a set of drumsticks with a rubbery resin head. The different pipes produced different notes.

The instrument came apart for transport, because Pengali measured their possessions by how easy it was to transport an item in a boat.

"They're not wanting to take that thing, are they?" Sheydu asked next to me.

"I think they are."

Sheydu hadn't spoken quietly, and now Abri turned to Sheydu, and, as a Thousand Island Pengali, she understood and spoke Coldi. "How else can we solve disagreements? We sing. We play betanka."

Veyada's eyes met mine. I could see he was thinking the same as I was: *And we thought we had it all sorted out?*

Sheydu scoffed. "You can't expect us to take this much luggage. Besides, these people we're visiting don't sing their disagreements. You're asked to give a testimony and answer questions by a bench of formal people. It has to do with *their* laws, not yours."

Abri was not as easily put off by Sheydu's curt tone as most other people. "It does have to do with our laws. Hairy face killed tribespeople. We are going to put in an official protest about that. We will do that properly by putting it in a betanka."

Put like that, it made perfect sense. The Earth lawyers had been waiting for a formal claim in *writing*, but while the Pengali had understood very well what they wanted, they responded in their manner. These people never disappointed with their last-moment surprises.

Ynggi and Kita proceeded to stack the *irrka* tubes next to the pile of luggage in the hall.

"There," Abri said when the door shut and the building's concierge had left with his trolley. "Now we have *luggage*."

They did, indeed.

But still no clothes.

———

Thayu, Veyada and I travelled into town the next morning to meet our interpreter. We were leaving in the afternoon, but most of the remaining work would need to be done by the staff: Eirani and Devlin —who were both coming—and Sheydu with Deyu and Reida, who were looking after the "hardware", meaning guns, explosives and spy equipment, however they thought to smuggle those through customs.

We took Ynggi with us, because I wanted to check the ability of whatever interpreter Jasper was going to produce, and also make sure that this person would not cause friction in our group by virtue of being from the wrong tribe.

Ynggi had visited us before, and out of all the Thousand Island Pengali, he seemed the most approachable. He even knew how to dress appropriately for going into town, even if only to cover his distinctive giraffe-like patterns that would raise ire from the local Pengali.

He was not afraid of trains, either, which was always a bonus.

He sat on the seat opposite me when I explained what we needed to do in town. The situation puzzled him, as it puzzled me.

"But why do they say that they need someone not from the tribe? People from the tribe will be fair because they have to speak the truth or they will lose face. People not from the tribe do not."

"It is what they ask. Their system works differently and their values are not the same. They say that someone from the tribe is more likely to give an unfairly favourable translation."

"With my elder watching?" He sounded horrified. "I could never do such a thing."

"I know, but that is not the way their system works. They need someone independent to judge whether a statement is true."

"No one is ever independent."

True also. "I can only try to do as they say. But whoever this person is, you will still come, and I will trust your translation before anyone else's."

Trust was a big thing in Pengali tribes.

I thought he looked mildly put out.

"So, this interpreter, do you know who it is?"

"I have no idea."

He snorted. "I say it is bluff. We can't have a Washing Stones translator and we know who in town speaks our language. There is no one else. This person will either be no good or from another tribe, like Whitesand Creek." And those were possibly even less liked than the Washing Stones tribe.

We got off the train at the airport and walked up the hill to the main square.

It was early still, but today promised to be one of those rare virtually cloudless days at the end of the dry season. It would get very hot today.

The message about the employment service run by Jasper Carlson had told us to come to an office in Market Street. It was located above a shop. The building was uncharacteristically new for Barresh, where everything was always just a little bit worn and slightly behind the times. Not this building. It looked fresh, with straight walls instead of ones set at odd angles, as was customary in Barresh. The windows had rectangular frames instead of triangular ones, and it was all very solidly made. Not by a local company, because the building style was too far removed from the local type. On second thoughts, I had heard people on the train talk about this building while it was being built last year. Eirani had called it a monstrosity and had told me how everyone was talking about how ugly it was. In Barresh, the keihu abhorred symmetry and straight lines and I could understand that this building offended their tastes.

It resembled, most of all, an *Earth* building. It must have been purposely designed by a Damarcian master builder and have cost a fortune to put up. I presumed it belonged to Jasper.

The shop on the ground floor sold security equipment. In most places in *gamra* worlds, businesses like that would not bother with a shop front anymore because most of the business was done electronically, but Barresh seemed to make a point of being nostalgically behind times. It was a trademark that was honoured by all, including people who had just moved there.

The funny thing was that, no matter how good the electronic displays, people *liked* shops, and as far as I understood, there were even businesses offering trips to Barresh for that reason: old fashioned markets and shopping. Smell the fish, see the food being cooked and wrapped in front of your eyes, try on clothes, have a live human comb, wash and cut your hair, have a dress made.

We climbed the stairs that led past the ground floor shop to the first floor. The building even had a lift. That was a rare enough thing in Barresh that I wondered if Clovis Keneally with Juanita, in her wheelchair, often came here, and that line of thought went off into unsubstantiated allegations.

The upstairs area was a cooled office with an open plan design. At this early time of day, the desks were mostly empty, but an olive-skinned man crossed the floor, carrying a plank of wood into a side room, where someone was hammering.

I recognised him. "Hello, Puck."

He stopped and gave me such a blank look that I wasn't sure I had recognised him. But I thought it was Puck, the Tamerian who had saved my life by donating his blood when I needed it.

"Mister? You know me?"

"You remember me from the hospital?"

He frowned. Like most Tamerians, he had thick bushy eyebrows, and frowning made the dark hair stand up like bristles.

I continued, "You told me that you liked to ski and I said that I prefer to surf, which is like skiing on water."

The eyebrows lifted. Apparently the concept of surfing had made a bigger impression on him than my appearance.

"Surf," he said.

"I can still teach you, if you like."

His eyes met mine and widened, as if he suddenly realised what direction the discussion was taking. He turned away and continued to the side room with his plank of wood without a further word.

Thayu gave me a puzzled look. *What was that about?* She asked through the feeder.

You do remember him, don't you?

He's the one whose blood you got? No, I didn't remember him from that, but I remember that there was a Tamerian. They all look very much alike.

They did, that was true.

I wasn't sure what to make of the conversation. In the past year or so, I'd seen the odd Tamerian in the street in Barresh. They no longer started gossip or turned heads when walking in the street. They were still as taciturn and impenetrable as ever but, in the end, they were people and had the right to be treated fairly.

A keihu man sat on a chair in a corner where chairs stood in rows along the walls. It reminded me of a doctor's waiting room.

He was in that age group where he could no longer be called young but wasn't middle-aged either. Keihu men tended to go grey quite early, and he had a good supply of white flecked throughout his glossy black hair, especially at his temples.

He rose when we came in and bowed. He was unusually thin for a keihu man. Even the fleshy bits on the tip of his nose did not have enough "meat" to them to form the characteristic keihu grooved nose tip.

I said, "We're here for the interpreter."

"That would be me." In perfect Isla.

He said something in Pengali to Ynggi, whose eyes widened.

Then he continued to me in flawless Coldi, "I guess this is why you brought a Pengali: to check my command of their language?"

Well, that was . . . something.

I honestly hadn't expected Mr Carlson's company to be able to pull it off.

He said something else to Ynggi, who still didn't respond. I met his eyes and he signalled *yes* with his tail.

The man continued in keihu, "I speak the Thousand Island dialect, too, as well as the Washing Stones dialect."

Ynggi said, "It's quite remarkable."

And it was. I disliked the stereotype of the keihu that they were fat and lazy, but unfortunately many of them lived up to the stereotype. Not this man.

"My name is Jemiro Pakiru. I'm at your service." He bowed.

Was this guy even for real?

I was unaware of his family name and should look it up. The abilities and inclinations of a keihu person were often directly related to their family's business activity. Pakiru must be a family of scholars.

A door opened in the back of the room and someone I knew came out: Jasper Carlson himself. He was a tall, lanky man with long dark hair similar to keihu hair. The dark stubble on his chin definitely marked him as coming from Earth. Virtually no *gamra* men needed to shave.

"Ah. I see you've met." His Coldi was also impeccable. He glanced sideways at Veyada and a cautious expression came to his face.

I had no doubt he knew who Veyada was and that he had worked for Asto's Inner Circle. He probably wondered if Veyada still reported to Ezhya Palayi, and he probably figured that yes, Veyada did.

We were all playing games here.

"Thank you for helping us out on such short notice," I said.

He nodded. "It is what we're here for. It's my business. Whatever type of employee you need, we'll find one for you. That's our guarantee." He smiled and then his face turned serious. "I believe you're going to attend the Nations of Earth court?"

"Yes." Again, it was all a game. He knew exactly where I was going and why I needed an interpreter. If it was his business to find just the right person for the job, he might even have alerted the court to the fact that the interpreter we wanted to bring was a member of the Thousand Island tribe.

"Melissa is over there at the moment, isn't she?"

I was sure he knew perfectly well where Melissa was. "I really don't know, and even if I did, I wouldn't be at liberty to discuss the particulars." Yes, Melissa was at the court and no, I didn't know what she was going to say. The court had instructed us not to communicate with each other until after giving Abri's evidence.

Jasper nodded. "I understand." Oh, so cool. "Well, good luck then. I would wish you a nice trip, but appearing in court is not the nicest thing to do, so good luck is all I can say."

"Thank you." Oh, I did not trust that man as far as I could throw him. "By the way, where did you find the interpreter?"

"Jemiro here came up in our system as matching the requirements you set."

"How did he learn Pengali?" In fact, how come he knew it, *and* was registered with the Interpreters' Guild and we had been unable to find him? The Guild had let us know that there was a shortage of Pengali interpreters. Why didn't they know about this one?

Jemiro answered the question himself. "My father had a business and employed Pengali workers. I spent a lot of time with them."

"They were from the Thousand Island tribe?"

"No. I met those later, when I worked on the fishing boats."

What a keihu man from an old family did working on fishing boats was another question, and his whole presence hung together with questions, but I guessed that was the whole point of this exercise. His sole function would be to appease Nations of Earth's regulations, and for my team to find out more about Jasper's activities.

I said to Ynggi, "Can you ask him to tell you in Pengali what he thinks he's going to be doing for us?"

Ynggi did. I listened to the rattling sounds of the language, and Jemiro's reply. I couldn't understand more than a few very basic words in Pengali, and those I probably pronounced all wrong.

His reply sounded confident and Ynggi asked something else, to which he also replied.

Ynggi turned to me, a sightly disturbed look on his face.

"I have no idea where he would have learned this."

"His Pengali is good enough?"

"Yes." He made it sound as if he wanted to add something, but those words never came. He just continued to give Jemiro a blank look and signalled his cautious approval with his tail. I wondered if the keihu interpreter would know about tail signals. I'd heard they varied a lot between tribes and groups within tribes.

"All right, we'll take him, if Nations of Earth is happy with him."

Jasper said, "They will be."

I turned to Jemiro. "Are you ready to go?"

"I am."

"I hope you understand that your employment depends on Nations of Earth approving your status as interpreter."

"I understand."

"And that you will have to provide them with all the details they may ask for."

"Yes."

"Can we see your documentation?"

He showed it to us on his reader. His paperwork was impeccable. He was an accredited member of the Interpreters' Guild. He also had *gamra* credentials and had worked in four different languages.

It was almost too perfect to believe. I met Veyada's eyes, sure that he would check out the authenticity of the documentation.

I asked him, "Do you need to pack anything? Do you need to go home to prepare? It will be a long journey."

"No, I'm fine."

"It's going to be cold there."

"I know. I have my things." A small bag rested on the floor next to the chair where he had been sitting. I judged it was rather too small for everything he needed, but we'd cross that bridge when we came to it.

On our way down the stairs, I sent all the details to Devlin, who shot back at me, *Is this guy for real?*

Which pretty much summed up my feelings about it.

We'll just have to run with him. See if Nations of Earth will approve him as our official interpreter.

Devlin did, and we had approval from Nations of Earth even before we had arrived at the *gamra* island. So Jemiro was going to come with us. Silent, watching, soft-spoken. His dark eyes looked like a sad puppy's. He sat next to Veyada on the bench opposite us on the train. He folded his hands and when he noticed me looking at him, unfolded them and leaned against the backrest.

He looked out the window, not meeting my eyes.

I did not trust him one bit and yet I could not find one single reason why.

At lunchtime, in my apartment, he sat next to Abri, who appeared to have just woken up. They spoke a few sentences in Pengali.

"I just told her that the fish is nice," he said when he noticed me looking at him.

"The fish *is* nice," Abri said. She pursed her lips.

I had not told her of the new silly requirement by Nations of Earth for an interpreter and she was probably puzzled by his presence.

"We're definitely relying on Ynggi," I said to Thayu when we were in our room to pack our personal things. "I don't trust this man at all."

Thayu said, "I looked up the Pakiru family. It seems they fell on hard times and have been struggling to make ends meet since a feud put an end to one of the businesses they ran. Their council seat is not currently occupied, and it hasn't been for a long time."

Interesting. The old keihu families—the Semisus, the Damarus and all those who lived in the stately houses in the quiet ends of Market Street and Fountain Street, to the east of the airport—lived in each other's pockets and would not let a chance go by to poke in another family's business, which was the primary purpose of the council.

One would think that for a traditional keihu family, their council seat was an instrument of power and influence. Why not use it?

3

____

W E GATHERED UP the last-moment things we needed. Personal items. Medication.

Thayu packed a small bag with her toiletries, which included the capsules she was taking to keep her normally variable Coldi body temperature even, so that the child had a better chance of growing. She smiled at me when she tucked those into the bag. A burst of warmth went through me. Damn, I loved that woman so much.

I added two additional lots of adaptation capsules. One set to keep the temperature down, and one to raise one's body temperature. I'd been stupid enough to go without the ones I ended up needing a few times. I was taking no more risks. I was going to take all of them, including the ones I thought I would never need.

"Ready?" I asked Thayu, with my hand on the door.

"I think so." She snorted. "I didn't think we'd ever make it this far. I mean with all the ridiculous rules and quarantine regulations and now this business with the interpreter."

"No, I was starting to have my doubts."

Preparing to travel with the Pengali, who had no documentation, no health checks, no *gamra* ID, had been a major undertaking. We'd spent months getting all the right paperwork in order, finding records of birth for people who kept none, making official translations of declarations, sorting their health checks, and then, because we'd been to the tribe's land, redoing our own.

But we had made it and now there was a giant pile of luggage in my hall, and a whole host of people in dark blue *gamra* security uniforms carrying guns. Nicha was there, Sheydu and Veyada, and Reida and Deyu. The latter two looked very dapper in their official gear. It was the first time since qualifying for *gamra* security that they wore it on an official trip, and they appeared keen to prove every bit of their worthiness.

At the door were Evi and Telaris, looking very threatening, their belts bristling with weapons. They were sorting out some sort of issue with electronics and the men who would look after the apartment's security while we were gone.

The source of all the fuss—Abri, Kita and Ynggi—sat on the little ornate bench that no one ever used in the hall. They wore clothes, no less, and having heard Eirani complain about that this morning, I understood that it was a Herculean victory in a battle that had been fought over many bathrooms and bedrooms.

Devlin kneeled on the floor, nervously checking his bags and his pockets. His travel had been limited to one trip to Kedras for his training. I had decided to take him so that he could be our liaison contact with *gamra* while we were in the courtroom, because there would be many things that Amarru at the Exchange would need to know. The prosecutor Conrad Martens had agreed that he was an acceptable addition to our attending team, because it was important that we keep *gamra* informed about the proceedings.

I had paid to bring Eirani, because I felt sorry that so many of us were going and she wasn't, and that she always had to stay home. Once the court session was done and Abri and her family, plus guards, safely delivered to Athens for the return trip, I was hoping to tack on a visit to my father on the farm in New Zealand, which had plenty of room. My stepmother Erith was Damarcian and she would make everyone feel at home. Eirani, of course, had never travelled and she had packed a host of soft bags full of warm clothes. She even wore some of those clothes. She had taken the warning that it might be cold *very* seriously, and appeared to have packed her entire wardrobe.

Apparently, Eirani hated cold. She also hated being unprepared.

And then there was Jemiro Pakiru, prim-faced. He stood by the door holding his small pack. During lunch, all I'd been able to get out of him was that he worked as translator for *gamra* and the council, and that he had recently specialised in the Thousand Island dialect of Pengali. So recent that the Pengali office didn't know about it? I asked. He said the Pengali office was a charity run by volunteers. They did not know everything.

No, the office was paid for by Pengali, and Pengali paid each other in favours and in food and lodging. They had no use for money. I wouldn't call those people volunteers, but I guessed it depended on what definition one used.

The whole situation with him was very strange, and he seemed defensive when we asked questions about his skills. And when Nicha asked him where he had obtained his certification, he said Kedras; and then Nicha said that it was unlikely he could have learned Pengali on Kedras.

"No, no." His face grew red. "I learned that here, but I became an interpreter at Kedras. Coldi and keihu and Damarcian."

"And then you tacked on Pengali?"

"There seemed . . . a demand. I'm good with languages, you know."

Oh, I didn't doubt that, but I wished I knew *why*.

Finally, the group included Nicha's nanny Karana Semisu—definitely from a well-respected keihu family—who had also agreed to look after little Idda.

But Pengali toddlers, as it appeared, were impervious to commands, angry words in any language, threats or bribes.

The little ratbag had taken off her clothes and had climbed on top of the pile of luggage, where Ayshada had been told repeatedly he couldn't jump. So he stood squealing at the bottom of the pile, and she danced on top displaying her giraffe-patterned skin and swinging her black and white banded tail for all to see. The nanny was too short to reach her, so that job fell to Evi who had developed a particularly good relationship with Ayshada, even if only because Evi's name was the only one Ayshada could pronounce.

So he yelled, "Evi, Evi!" and he pointed at the pile of luggage and the Pengali brat on top.

Evi reached out his very big and very black hands—even the palms were black in Indrahui people—and nabbed the youngster off the pile of suitcases.

She let out an almighty squeal and tried to free herself, kicking and snaking her tail around Evi's hands. When Evi set her on the ground, she scurried across the hall under the bench where her mother and grandmother sat and paid her no attention. Ayshada followed her.

Karana, the poor girl, ran after the pair of them.

Thayu gave me an apologetic glance. All of a sudden, I wanted to take her in my arms. I wanted to tell her that no, I didn't mind the noise and I knew children made rather a lot of it, and that she would do infinitely better than the Pengali in raising her child—*our child.*

Something else to tell my father when we got there. I was looking forward to spending some relaxing time on the farm.

Reida had opened the door to the apartment and was talking to someone on the gallery outside.

A man's voice drifted into the hall—the concierge. Apparently, the train was ready and waiting for us.

So the great exodus began. People picked up their packs and gathered up children, and the party started moving towards the door. Sheydu and Veyada already stood in the hall. Devlin was giving last minute instructions to the young man who would be looking after the hub in our absence, and whose job it would be to relay and file the correspondence we would send him.

Jemiro had picked up his little bag and stood on the gallery, looking impatient and prim.

Karana picked up Ayshada—giving up on the Pengali brat—who sat triumphantly on the luggage trolley.

Eirani walked past, chatting to Karana about how much she had hoped that working for me meant that she could travel one day. Pearls of sweat glistened on her forehead from wearing all those clothes.

Jemiro followed them.

Then Evi and Telaris, Deyu and, finally, Thayu and I.

I waved to the remaining staff, looking a bit sad in that big hall.

There would be fewer of us left in the apartment than ever before. The staff would probably play games in the hall and eat in the hub with the plates on their knees while talking to their friends elsewhere or watching whatever vids youngsters liked to watch or games they liked to play. And we would come home to a house that was neat, clean, no matter the mess they would make in the intervening time.

We walked as a big, chatting group across the gallery, where our voices echoed in the atrium and brought one or two curious folk to open the front door to check what was going on. We went down the stairs—or in case of the drum and the trolley, in the lift—and then out the building's entrance, past the uniform fitter, and into the court-yards and avenues of the *gamra* island. People stopped to let us through, or watched us from the eating-houses or balconies of their apartments.

Thayu said nothing, and I caught some cautious thoughts through the feeder, which I had turned down since so many of these people were connected to me and it was getting very noisy inside my head.

"What are you thinking?" I asked in a low voice.

"Can't hide anything from you, can I?"

"Nope."

She let a small silence lapse. "Well, what I'm thinking is that it's really strange that any government is happy to pay for us all to come to deliver a simple testimony that could be given remotely."

"Yes." In the end, Nations of Earth had paid for all of us, even Eirani. Devlin had told me that Nations of Earth had refused to take my payment. Thayu was right that it was strange, and I had no answer for the reason for this other than the ones he had given me: that they wanted to treat the case properly, whatever that was supposed to mean.

I strongly suspected that there was some other motive, but we wouldn't find out what that was until we got there, or maybe not even then.

We made it to the train station without too much hassle. The train waited for us with an entire carriage dedicated to our consider-able party with our luggage that included the big drum and the bundle of pipes of the *irrka*.

The moment she saw the train, Idda jumped off the luggage trolley and ran, squealing, into the carriage, flying from backrest to backrest like a squirrel. Apparently, Pengali kids were particularly fond of crawling into hollows, like cats, and the train had all kinds of hollows within hollows: the luggage racks, underneath the seats, the emer-gency compartment—

"Oh, no, you don't, you little brat!" Karana ran after her, hair flying.

Idda squealed and scurried to the far end of the carriage.

Ayshada ran after her.

Karana tried to catch them, gave up in Idda's case and scooped Ayshada from under a bench. He didn't agree with the sudden restriction of his freedom, and let that be known in a loud voice.

"Really." Eirani sat down, with a withering glare at Idda's mother Kita, whom I had not once spotted trying to control her daughter's behaviour.

Everyone else came in and found seats. The luggage trolley was secured and the train was off.

I stared at the window while Reida chatted excitedly to Veyada. It was not Reida's first trip with us, but the previous one had been very short. The wonders of Earth were often discussed in the circles of security where he and Deyu had trained for the past two years.

"You're quiet, too," Thayu said softly next to me.

"I think everyone else is already making enough noise."

She smiled, and my heart melted. I loved that woman so much.

"What are you worried about, then?"

I blew out a breath. "I'm hoping that Abri giving evidence is all we're going for. With these kids here and . . ." I didn't need to say more. I wanted to *protect* her, not let her protect me.

This morning was the first time I'd happily packed my new gun, although I fully intended to leave it in the hotel room as much as possible. "We're vulnerable. We can't move fast if we need to. I'm even hoping that those kids won't make too much trouble for us in our accommodation. These people are not very accepting of children in public places and there are hundreds of ways for toddlers to injure themselves or get lost. And I do not like that interpreter."

She nodded.

The man in question had taken a seat on his own and, while everyone chatted, he stared out the window. One could pose that the whole issue with his inclusion in the party was ridiculous, designed to drive up our costs and line the pockets of service industries. There was always plenty of that going on at Nations of Earth.

Bureaucracy. Coldi had a fairly low tolerance for it. I would almost say that the scheming at Nations of Earth was more foreign to me than Coldi associations.

Thayu briefly flitted through my thoughts about that.

She briefly touched my hand, that subtle Coldi sign of solidarity.

Right at that moment, I would a thousand times rather take her on a trip somewhere than drag my entire household to Earth for a court case that, by all the signs, had the potential to be highly political. There would be hundreds of ways in which we could stuff up, say or do the wrong things.

My team chatted around us, but Thayu looked at me and I looked into her gold-flecked eyes. The sun peeped between the clouds and made her eyebrows and eyelashes glitter, peacock-like. She was oh so serious, and gorgeous. And I wanted to put her in a protected room and bring her breakfast while she left the running and shooting to others and she grew big and round and her breasts full and firm.

Veyada glanced at me from across the carriage. He knew. He had no children, despite my frequent reminders that I would be happy for him to take time off to look for a mother, but he appeared uninterested.

Not much later, the train slowed and slid into the airport station.

Because the train lines between the islands of Barresh went over the water and never crossed the land, we had to make our way up the slight incline—truly the only hill in Barresh—and around the side of the complex.

I walked at the front with Thayu and Nicha, but the rest of the party spread out over a long distance. I could see Idda trying to climb the fence behind us.

"I don't know how we're going to manage to keep that one out of mischief," I muttered.

"I still don't see why she should come, Pengali habits or no."

"But then we wouldn't have been able to take Ayshada." And he was part of the family.

But the Pengali were also a family, and apparently, Thousand Islands tribe law said that if a senior tribe member were consulted, all generations under her should also be involved. Hence the daughter and the daughter's daughter.

We finally entered the building when everyone, including the toddlers, had caught up with us or had been retrieved from the bushes. Idda didn't like being restrained. I wondered if Pengali babies ever slept.

We lined up for the security point, where a cheerless guard in a black uniform checked our passes and bags.

Someone shouted behind me. I turned around. Idda had escaped from the nanny's arms. She ran past the line, climbed up the guard's leg like a monkey and perched on his shoulder for a split second before he yelled out. She jumped—onto the luggage conveyor belt, up on somebody's bag, which was at that very moment hoisted to the ceiling rails by a mechanical arm. Idda hung on, squealing her lungs out.

"Stop the conveyor!" Nicha yelled. The guard seemed too stunned to do anything. Of course one could never find the emergency switch when looking for it, and so as not to waste time, I jumped up on the belt—an alarm started ringing—and ran over it, while all around me, bags and cases were being picked up by automatic arms. One missed my legs by a hair's width.

I got to Idda, couldn't quite reach her, and pulled her by the tail—the worst thing you could do to a Pengali, but it was the only part of her within my reach. Thankfully, she let go. I jumped off the belt, meeting a couple of guards who came running to help me.

The belt and the automatic arms stopped moving. The alarm fell quiet. Everyone in the hall was looking at me with a Pengali youngster clinging onto my shirt.

I said, "Move along, nothing to see. It's all good."

I rejoined my group, muttering to Nicha, "That starts well."

Nicha grinned. "I think she likes you."

I unpeeled the youngster's little hands from my shirt and lifted her up. "How about you join your mother and keep out of the way for a while?"

Her huge dark eyes blinked at me. Pengali eyes had almost no whites. They reminded me most of the eyes of the possums that would sometimes sleep in the tree in our back yard when I was a kid in New Zealand. During the day the irises would be brown, but at night their eyes would be almost entirely black, and the eyes would flash like a cat's when you shone light into them.

I didn't know if she understood what I said, but when I set her on the ground, she scurried to her mother's chair and hid underneath.

Maybe there was hope yet.

I also sat down with the rest of the group. I met Veyada's eyes across a pile of luggage. He restrained a chuckle. Coldi were equally free with the raising of children and he probably found my efforts very amusing.

This was an important work trip, not a family holiday.

"Calm down," Thayu said. "If this is the worst we face . . ."

I knew, and I shrugged. I didn't think it was the worst we faced. I worried much more that the youngster would be harmed than that she would embarrass anyone. Because by taking Abri, her daughter and granddaughter, I had the obligation to the Thousand Island tribe to bring them back safely. And, because none of them ever travelled, that wasn't a responsibility I took easily.

A man called behind us, "Delegate, the vehicle is here for you and your party."

He was a stiff-faced airport guard, no doubt glad to see us go.

The bus stood outside the building. We filed out the door and into the cabin, more closely resembling a family trip than a diplomatic mission. I waited outside with Thayu while Nicha and Ayshada took the bench in front of the bus. The Pengali went to the back.

I was about to get in when a man came running up. He was dressed in the carmine red of the Trader Guild employees. A courier.

"Delegate Cory Wilson?" He held out a red envelope which bore my name in official Coldi, handwritten by one of the Guild's calligraphers.

Well . . . that was unusual.

I took the envelope from him. It was highly unusual to get a message delivered through the Trader Guild couriers, and I honestly couldn't think of anyone who would have needed to talk to me with this urgency.

But when I opened the envelope and glanced inside, I knew.

President of Nations of Earth, Margarethe Ollund.

One time when I had seen her, I had warned her never to send anything through the Exchange that she wanted to keep absolutely confidential. The Exchange staff could see your correspondence, and they did sometimes listen in. Others could listen in, too.

I had told her of the only method of delivery that guaranteed that no one else would see what you'd written: the trader Guild couriers who would deliver a written message on paper. I'd given her an account with enough credits to get a message to me. For emergencies, I'd said, because I didn't want to end up as I had earlier in my time in

Barresh, when obstructionist elements at Nations of Earth prevented me from accessing information I needed, and were blocking my accounts.

This was clearly an emergency. And I should probably not open it right here but wait until I was on the bus.

4

____

I **TUCKED THE ENVELOPE** under my arm and climbed into the bus, where laughter and chatter filled the air.

I chose a spot towards the back and sat right next to the window. Thayu sat next to me. While the rest of the team chatted, I opened the envelope again, took out the inside envelope with Margarethe's writing, ripped it open and unfolded the single sheet inside. The very plain sheet gave no sign that it came from Margarethe's office. There were only a few lines on the page.

It said,

Cory,

You are probably on your way here by the time this note reaches you, but I am not sure in whatever way it will be delivered. I want to warn you that you will be coming into a volatile political situation too intricate to be explained in a few words. As soon as you arrive here, before you see anyone else, insist on having a meeting with me.

Margarethe

I stared at the text and that loopy signature that had become quite well-known over the past few years.

Well, that confirmed all my suspicions. This trip was not about the court case. Through a roundabout way, she was paying for it, and I wouldn't hear what the real issue was until I faced her in her office.

Ezhya would pull that sort of stuff on me. She must have learned from him.

My frazzled senses registered that the bus had stopped, but not in the usual spot.

What was going on?

I'd been under the impression that we were to travel on the regular shuttle. That craft, however, used a different part of the airport. I could see it there, in the distance, and it hadn't opened its doors yet. The craft in front of the bus was smaller, one of the private variety.

Someone had sent and paid for a craft just for us.

Definitely something going on.

And here I was, with a huge entourage, which Nations of Earth had *encouraged* me to bring, because I needed to look *official*, but which included people with no political, weapons or travel experience who were on a holiday, my *pregnant* wife and two *children*.

Well, damn it.

The door had opened. A crewmember in the uniform of the Pilot's Guild stood at the door. Everyone was getting up and leaving the bus, and I was sitting there, not sure what to do. I was starting to get that ominous bad feeling about this. Who was I to lead all these people, mostly defenceless and innocent, into what might be a dangerous situation?

They—the Pengali, Eirani, Devlin, Karana, Jemiro—thought they were going on a work trip that might even be fun, and I should know better and stop this, while I could—

On what grounds?

Just because Margarethe wanted to see me?

"What does it say?" Thayu said in a low voice, indicating the envelope.

I showed her the letter.

She read—she understood Isla quite well these days—and frowned. "Maybe she wants to tell you what Abri should say at the trial."

"I don't think so. Or if she did, it would be wrong. The court is separate from the assembly. Margarethe has no power over the court."

Her frown deepened.

It was so easy to think of Ezhya Palayi as a friend, but the truth was that people on Earth would use only one word to describe his rule on Asto: that of an absolute dictator. Ezhya had a huge hub which he used to control every aspect of the huge network that could be described as "government" on Asto. Not that it looked anything like the form of government on Earth, or, for that matter, most other worlds. It was a vast informal spider, controlled by the instinct Coldi called *sheya* that, when two unfamiliar people met for the first time, determined which of them was superior. In Asto, there could only be one person at the top. That person was Ezhya. There was nothing on Asto that he didn't have a say over.

Coldi didn't use trials. They served legal writs, to which the accused party had to give a satisfactory response within the given time frame or risk an assassination squad. They did have mitigation hearings, where the accused party could ask witnesses to explain the situation.

If this were Asto and any of us had to appear in such a hearing—which might be against a challenger or a minor leader who might make a challenge—Ezhya would call me in and tell me what to say. I would be required to do as he told me, and the hearing would go the way he wanted, or, if it didn't, the accused would face severe retributions, frequently including the dispatch of a death squad.

Someone at the door of the bus called, "Delegate, the craft is ready."

Yes, yes, they were waiting for us. The pilot had a departure slot that needed to be filled. Having come this far, I didn't have an option but to go ahead with it, and given the information I had, that was the choice my association would want me to make. Plunge in, see what was going on, but remain alert.

I pushed myself up, still looking at Thayu.

"Well, you'll just have to go and see her to ask her what it's about then," she said.

"Yes." And that was a sort-of-definite reply, a "What else can we do?"

Thayu gave the letter back to me. I folded it and inserted it back into the envelope, which I tucked into my shoulder bag. I handed the red Trader Guild courier envelope to the driver on my way out of the bus. It would somehow make its way back to the Guild office.

Then I was out of the bus and up the ramp into the craft.

The rest of the group had already settled on the craft's plush seats.

I didn't have to look hard for the Pengali. They sat towards the rear end of the craft. The little brat had climbed on the backrest of her mother's seat and reached for the luggage rack. I thought of the power of the engines on take-off and those moments of weightlessness prior to transfer, when loose items became projectiles. People needed to be wearing a harness, absolutely.

"Don't," I said when walking past her, and to my surprise, she scurried down and sat on the seat next to her mother, eying me.

"Make sure you strap her in," I told Kita, who gave me a hard look. Apparently, one did not strap in little ones.

"For her safety. You don't want her flying around the cabin when we take off. Please do it, because I don't want her to get badly hurt."

"Yes, Delegate."

I didn't know how much more Coldi she spoke than that, or even whether she had understood anything I'd said. All of my communication had been with Abri, who merely watched the conversation, but then said something quietly to her daughter after I'd continued down the aisle. Hopefully something was getting through to them.

I joined Thayu and Nicha at the front of the craft. Nicha had given Ayshada a little puzzle to solve. An old Kedrasi man sold these at the markets. They consisted of pieces of wood that you had to fit together to make a shape. Ayshada loved these and was far better at them than I'd expected a two-year-old to be. He babbled and cheered when he completed the cube, then pulled it apart again, dropped one of the pieces and squealed for Nicha to fish it up, because he was properly strapped in and couldn't jump off the seat to get it himself.

Veyada and Sheydu sat on the other side of the aisle. Sheydu fixed her attention on the reader in her hand. I didn't miss her pursed lips, which indicated her annoyance. Sometimes it was hard to believe that Sheydu had once had children. She usually ignored Ayshada or rolled her eyes when he made too much noise, so I could only imagine what she thought of the Pengali brat whom I couldn't see anymore, but who was squealing at the top of her lungs.

While the crew loaded our luggage and prepared the craft—I lost count of how many times Idda escaped from her harness—I told Nicha, Veyada and Sheydu about Margarethe's letter.

Like Thayu had done, they frowned.

Veyada asked me, since I said it probably didn't have anything to do directly with the court, what I thought it was about.

I said, "I'm thinking it might have something to do with the fallout from the *election*." I used the Isla word, because Coldi didn't have elections. I could have used the Coldi word for *voting*, but it in no way captured the politicking and backstabbing that came with an election.

"Margarethe won, right?" Thayu said.

"Only by a very small margin."

She spread her hands. "I don't see any problem. She won. People chose their leader. Now they have to do what the leader says." The whole concept of low-ranking people voting high-ranking people into power was alien to her.

Veyada said, "The political *parties* are like associations, except they fight with each other on all levels, and they fight within themselves for who will be the leader all the time."

"So they're nothing like associations. It's a silly and wasteful system. They spend huge amounts of time and effort on making themselves look popular so that the low-ranking people, who have very little clue anyway, will vote for them."

That was not entirely how the president was elected, because that was done by the assembly, but the assembly members were voted by the people in their respective countries. Thayu, and most Coldi, didn't believe common people should vote, and Thayu had a very low tolerance for "idiotic systems" in her current state.

Nicha said, "Did Melissa mention anything about political issues in the assembly when you last visited her?"

I had to think about that. "Yes, but she always talks about lots of political issues. Melissa is a very political person." Melissa had mentioned some of the issues that played in the assembly. The usual arguments about the divide between the poor and rich countries, and the allocation of the inadequate aid funds. Nothing that stood out to me as particularly unusual. But I admitted to not having followed Earth politics recently.

The crew finally finished all the preparations, the door shut and the pilot turned on the downward jets. The cabin pressure turned on with a hiss and popping of my ears. The floor vibrated with the low hum of the engines. The Pengali sat quietly in their seats, and I spotted no wayward children.

I glimpsed Deyu's face, looking out the window. She had developed into a most loyal member of my association. So young, so utterly serious. She had been quietly excited about this trip for weeks—when she permitted herself to be, which was mostly when she thought I wasn't looking.

Somehow in all this mess, I had to make the time to show her some of the sights. Not cities—her native Asto did big cities much better than Earth—but animals. I'd promised horses and dogs and cats. It wouldn't be too hard to rustle up some of those. If we managed to get to my father's place—and I would do my utmost best to make that happen—there would be camels and ostriches as well.

Then the hum of the engines increased and increased, and grew into a whine. The craft lifted with a shudder. The ground and then the buildings slid from view. The pressure increased.

Veyada and Sheydu were looking at their readers, probably catching up on some work, but Reida sat stiff-faced, looking at the back of the seat in front of him.

Deyu touched his hand, and they exchanged that intimate look that could only be shared between *zhaymas*—equals, partners.

Everything was all right. And it would be. How exciting could a *court case* get, for crying out loud? I should stop worrying and enjoy the trip.

———

Exchange travel tended to mess with time. I'd never been able to accurately measure the time taken from Barresh to Earth, but I believed it to be about half a day; at least that's what it felt like to me. It involved three or four anpar jumps, depending on how busy it was, but if you tried to take any kind of time-measuring device on board the craft, it usually went backwards between fifteen minutes and an hour.

The trip was quite uneventful, though it involved Idda escaping from the harness several times.

We arrived at the Exchange when the eastern sky was turning light blue. As the craft flew low over the hills behind Athens, and the city lay spread out before me, I couldn't remember how long ago I had last been here for a visit that *wasn't* work. Probably when Thayu and I had a mock wedding ceremony at my father's beach house, but then that had turned into a work visit anyway.

The Exchange's big circular arrival and departure hall was, as usual, a cacophony of light and noise. The Asto or Hedron-built craft favoured by transport companies were as noiseless as possible for craft of that size, but still, when a lot of them departed and arrived in that enclosed space, the whine of engines became deafening.

Noisier than the craft themselves were the giant turning platforms and the sirens that hooted before one of the levels was about to turn.

Coming down the gangplank amongst the flashing lights and screaming engines, we were met by Amarru herself, a stocky woman wearing unassuming maintenance overalls. She had cut her greying hair into a fashionable short hairdo resembling a shag pile carpet and wore glasses with pink frames.

It never ceased to amaze me how such a powerful woman could look so utterly like someone you'd just pass in the street without giving her a second thought. That type of behaviour was not Coldi at all.

But she was blunt like a Coldi, and didn't waste any words in telling me that she was going to do the formalities, and while my team went off to find breakfast, I went with her to her private office on the floor below the canteen, the second-highest floor in the building.

As soon as the door shut, she said, "I don't like this, Cory."

And good morning to you, too. I had a very nice trip, thank you very much. "What exactly don't you like?"

"The fact that they're paying for you to come here with all these people while the matter could easily have been handled remotely."

"All right, no, I don't like that either. I guess there are much better uses for the money." Ultimately, it wasn't *my* money, and while I couldn't say it hadn't bothered me, I'd had more pressing things to worry about.

"Exactly. Just recently, there have been a lot of scandals exposed in the assembly where representatives were taken on extravagant trips while aid agencies lost their subsidies."

Coldi didn't tend to care much about charities, so to hear her mention this was strange. "Anything that the Exchange was involved in?"

"Yes and no. We're not involved in anything directly, but we're accused of being involved a lot. Recently, a couple of refugee crises have originated from conflicts fought with what seems to be off-Earth weaponry and maybe people."

"Originated from the Zhori mafia?" We'd seen that before. Kazakhstan and Ethiopia were two of the hot spots that sprang to mind.

Wherever there was trouble, members of the Zhori clan of the Coldi were usually not far away. Those families were often third or fourth generation refugees from Asto and often utterly out of Amarru's control.

Amarru blew out a breath. "I don't know who they are and where those weapons are coming from. The local governments are not even making formal complaints against us. Most of the trouble is in dangerous, lawless areas with a long history of unrest. Southern Africa, mostly. If you have some time, look up Freedom State and you'll get the gist of it. There were a lot of refugees. A lot of them died, too, and to top it off, in the middle of that crisis, a major aid agency lost financial support from Nations of Earth. They had no option but to withdraw from the area, or stay and die with the refugees. They left. A local authority was going to supply water and food, but they didn't have the resources. They stopped coming. People in the camps died. Some people walked for days through the searing desert. Many more died along the way. Then the Zhori mafia sells weapons to the survivors and you have a rebellion. And *gamra* gets the blame, because there were 'alien weapons' involved. Frankly, I'm sick of it."

I'd heard this story in its many variations before, too. It all came down to the same thing: the Exchange, and through it, *gamra,* had no authority to act because there was no agreement between it and Nations of Earth, because Earth was not a member of *gamra.* It was not the sole reason that these problems kept cropping up, but it was the sole reason that very little could be done about them.

We both knew it, and we were both powerless to change it.

We got into the administration side of the matter. She sent me all the information we needed: travel passes for anyone not in possession of *gamra* ID, mainly the Pengali. Also weapons permits for anyone who wanted to carry a weapon. She handed me mine with a look of appreciation. "I bet Thayu has had something to do with the selection of this piece."

"She has."

"Very fine choice."

When we finished all the documentation, we spoke a bit about the court case, which had already been going for a few weeks. She had heard no shocking revelations recently. "Basically, this vile man travelled under false ID through the Exchange. He came back, sold the blue diamonds that his company had been advertising for exorbitant prices, and used gullible travellers to both carry the loot for him and help him find it. Then when one of his clients started questioning his methods, he brought out the guns. That's how I understand it. You may correct me if I'm wrong."

"Something like that."

She spread her hands. "This vile man, this Robert Davidson, did a lot more than kill one single person from Earth. Someone who, I should add, shouldn't have been where he was either. Yet this murder of this rich guy Gusamo Sahardjo is the only crime he's being accused of committing, and it's not even a very good accusation, because we have no body and no solid evidence. But who looked at the examination reports of the Pengali bodies they found of Melissa's trackers? Who looked at all that evidence for smuggling that was much better than that for the murder of Gusamo? When are *those cases* going to come before the court?"

She met my eyes. The answer, of course, was *never* and we both knew that. As long as Earth was not a member of *gamra,* these types of crimes would go unpunished.

Amarru continued. "Meanwhile, I recently sent one of our people to attend a court case for a Coldi man accused of murdering a local, and he is now in jail. The unwillingness to bring justice goes one way. If a *gamra* person had been the victim, no one would have cared. Because, supposedly, we have no legal status on this world. Rubbish. We had legal status, but they took it away in the citizenship case. In those days, they were open to us and interested in collaboration. You remember that Ezhya visited Nations of Earth, gave a speech and officially met the president?"

I remembered that. I had been four or five.

"These days, everyone is afraid of us. I barely leave the enclave anymore. For all that they espouse fairness, this world is terribly biased in the way people are treated. Look, some of us—not me but many—have lived here all their lives and have no other homes. Yet they are not allowed to call themselves citizens? And worse, if someone commits a crime against a Coldi person, that Coldi person has no right to legal protection? No right to get valid ID, no right to insurance. No right to *exist*."

Amarru was one of those people who spoke more slowly when she was angry, and she pronounced each word with exaggerated sounds.

"I worry about where it is all going," she said. "We are lucky that at the moment, stability is in the hands of a few sensible people, one of them being you. You are friendly with Ezhya. You are friendly with Margarethe. Hell, they are friendly with each other because of you."

Friendly with each other, huh? Well, let's not go there. Also, I didn't think it had anything to do with me. I just happened to have been present at their first meeting.

Amarru continued, "Margarethe damn near *lost* the election. It's her last term. Ezhya is not a young man. What is going to happen if either or both of them lose their positions? Nations of Earth is going to vote in some hardline puppet president, who will be nothing but a mouthpiece for commercial interests! Those multinationals have steadily bought up government debts of small, poor and insignificant countries that no one in Rotterdam cared about. Now they have this empire of very angry, mostly African states, who are furious about the way Nations of Earth has constantly ignored and screwed them and milked them dry and spat them out, and they want their revenge. At the Exchange, we have traditionally supported Nations of Earth, but I'm finding that harder to justify in the face of their recent unwilling-ness to cooperate with us. For example, if we have a really busy day, we can't even reach the proper authorities who give us permission to extend the operating hours of the Exchange anymore. Last time I opened the Exchange during daylight, I did so unauthorised. We're reaching a breaking point, and something is going to explode."

I toyed with the idea of mentioning Margarethe's letter, but she had sent it to me in secret. "I'm listening. I agree with you. I will need to see how I can build your concerns into my future actions. For now, though, there is the court case. Is there anything specific you want me to do?"

Amarru snorted and briefly lifted her hands. "Not much you *can* do there. The trial is about one Earth citizen against the family of another. They *should* have included the murders of the Pengali, because the evidence that Robert killed them is much stronger, but they didn't do that. They should have invited you to give evidence, but we all know why they didn't do that either."

"Conrad Martens said it was because Melissa already covered everything I could say."

"He's a nice man, and honestly one of the fairest you could get, but do you believe that?"

"Not necessarily, but I'm just glad I didn't get drawn into this any further than necessary."

"That's it." Amarru pointed at me. *"Drawn into*. This trial is not about the murder of one man by another and their whole sordid business fought out over the heads of thousands of decrepitly poor people in Jakarta. It's about who controls the justice process. You are an inconvenience because no one can control you. You don't work for any of them, and don't rely on any of them for protection. You have nothing that they can threaten to take away from you. They've had to call Melissa. She works for Nations of Earth and her family lives in Germany. If she says something they don't like, they can threaten her."

Boy, she rarely got as riled up as this. "Well, I think that's taking it a bit far?"

"You think so?"

"I do. The court is a fair institution and the judges are sworn to impartiality. And besides, they're inviting Abri. They didn't need to do that at all."

Amarru let out a breath. "No. They didn't need to. It's the one puzzling aspect of this case: why did they invite Abri and you?"

This, finally, brought us to the practicalities of the court case.

She said, "Nations of Earth have sent a hover jet for your party. I understand that there may be particular reasons why they don't want you to talk to certain other people that are involved in the court case, but I feel they are taking control over your witness a bit too seriously. I think the situation would benefit if we could disturb their plans a bit."

"Yeah. I have to admit that I'm not comfortable with this all-expenses-paid trip either. Someone is bound to want something."

"We're in agreement, then. No need to make a lot of noise, though. We'll create a diversion. I'm not going to tell you what it is, but there will be some suggestions made by people during your travels. You might want to follow them."

Hmm, she clearly had something planned. I would probably do well to listen to her. Not only was Amarru an extremely smart woman but, right now, she knew the political landscape of my home world much better than I did.

"As for the case, I'm sending two legal experts with you. I know you've got Veyada, but these people are specialists in Nations of Earth and international law. They should be able to assist you and Veyada, and they'll be the official *gamra* observers which we are allowed every time any *gamra* citizen is involved in court. We have an agreement with Nations of Earth that we can record the proceedings, as long as the recordings are not made public."

Here was another problem: the Thousand Island tribe's territory wasn't technically under the jurisdiction of the Barresh Council and Abri wasn't a *gamra* citizen, because that was something you needed to apply for and pass tests in order to be granted.

But I appreciated Amarru's assistance. "I hope Nations of Earth isn't paying for their fare?"

"No, we are. I'm also sending two more security staff with you. They're aware of the latest developments and risks to look out for. Right now, your security staff will receive an update about the team I'm sending with you to assist them. They will expect to be subordinate to your team at all times." That was a typical Coldi remark if ever there was one.

So, four extra people. This party was rapidly expanding into a full diplomatic mission which, I realised, it was. A mission representing *gamra* on Earth. And I didn't belong on the Earth side. That was an odd thought.

The lawyers she was lending me were both Coldi. The man wore the blue earrings of the Azimi clan. His name was Reya and he was very prim and proper, greeted me subserviently and managed to bow without dislodging a single hair in his ponytail. The woman . . . She squinted at me. Her hair hung loose over her shoulders. It was *curly* and fell over her ears, so I couldn't see her earrings, but I would bet they were amber.

Her gaze flitted to my Domiri earrings, and a faint puzzled look went over her face. Coldi clan membership by non-Coldi was extremely rare.

She did not perform any kind of traditional greeting, and looked me straight in the eyes.

Then she introduced herself as Mereeni with the oddly rolling *r*, and I no longer needed to see her earrings. She was Ezmi, from Hedron.

"We will be travelling on from here immediately," I said to them. "Are you both packed and ready to go?"

They said that they were. The two security guards were ready, too. They waited in the hallway, each with a small pack. As with almost all of Amarru's security people, they were from Indrahui. Although both were older than the brothers Evi and Telaris, they reminded me of the pair and how Amarru had allocated them to me years ago, when I just started my job. She seemed to have an endless supply of people.

Not interpreters, apparently.

I asked her before we went out, "Nations of Earth did not approve our choice of interpreter and they only let me know the day before we left. I was forced to use a local service to hire someone, and against my expectations they could supply someone. I don't trust the man in question. Would you happen to have anyone?"

"Pengali?" She chuckled.

I guessed that answered that question.

Her face turned serious. "Why don't you trust him?"

"Because of his employer. Because he behaves oddly." It was hard to pinpoint why Jemiro's behaviour was odd. "Do you have any data on this man? He speaks Isla."

She frowned but shook her head. "I saw his name on the passenger log, but he has no records."

"Any records from people with the same family name?"

She shook her head. "He or his family have never been here."

Jemiro was destined to remain a mystery.

It also struck me how, when you needed to know something on Earth, there was no better person to ask than Amarru. Not only did she have an encyclopaedic memory, she knew how to connect facts and decide which ones were important. In the years that I'd known her, I'd been constantly amazed at her power, and feared that one day she might use it.

When I finally left the office in the company of the four new people, I realised that people here could take two things from me: the NZ tag on my ID card that allowed me to come to Earth, stay as long and I wanted and travel unrestricted—and the other, even more important thing. My father.

5

____

INTRODUCING **TWO** unrelated groups of Coldi to each other was always a risk, so when we came to the canteen, where the rest of my team sat, I let the two guards walk at the front, and positioned the Coldi lawyers behind them.

The Coldi *sheya* instinct fired at first meeting between two people who didn't know each other and it informed both parties which of the two was superior. This was a physiological reaction, and Amarru had seemed overly confident that the lawyers would be subordinate to the members of my team. I didn't understand why she thought that. Because of the position they held in relation to her? All I knew of the instinct was that you could never be sure, especially when there had been an upset in relationships or when two people had no inter-meshing loyalty networks, such as when they lived on two different planets.

Coldi from the Ezmi clan from Hedron, like Mereeni, were said not to have the instinct; but some of them did, and I had heard that forced repression of the instinct only made it surface more strongly when meeting complete strangers.

Fights to establish position were uncommon, but they still happened. It was considered to be extremely embarrassing for an association leader to let a fight happen.

This kind of thing made me nervous. I supposedly led this association, at least according to everyone on the team. Me at the top, Thayu and Nicha as *zhayma*s on the next level and then Sheydu and Veyada as *zhayma*s under Thayu and Reya and Deyu as *zhayma*s under Nicha. Coldi leaders of associations would know how to handle a situation like this, but, lacking the instinct, I was a pretender, flying by the seat of my pants and making it up as I went.

My group sat at a table near the window. Plates and cups, a half-empty jug of orange juice and a plate with a few crackers were on the table.

The window overlooked the messy jumble of apartment buildings of the city. The sky was hazy, blocking the view to the ocean.

Thayu saw me first, then she looked at the two Coldi lawyers. By the way she straightened and stiffened her back, I knew there was going to be trouble, because at least *one* of the lawyers triggered the fight instinct.

I pushed myself between the two Indrahui guards at the front— and faced Veyada, who had sprung up and approached faster than I'd noticed. He was tall and solid and there was no way that if he put his mind to confronting either of the lawyers, I could stop him.

But he did stop. True to his position under me, he did not meet my eyes. He looked down, and let his arms hang down his sides, palms facing backwards.

Veyada very rarely took up a subservient position and I found it embarrassing to see him like this. Reya had the grace to turn away, his expression disturbed, but Mereeni looked on with interest.

I put my hand on his shoulder. "I'm sorry. Amarru insisted we add him to the team." I should have suspected it. Veyada had no love for Reya's Azimi clan, especially since they had attempted to infiltrate our group several times in the past few years and had managed to get Ayshada into our household.

"Come, greet each other and agree on where you stand." This was a formulaic expression that I'd heard leaders use for the purpose of resolving tension in their associations.

Reya came forward, head down, his arms by his side, with his palm facing backwards. *That* surprised me. I had expected him to be the source of the trouble, but he was completely demure.

I said to the rest of my team, "These are Reya and Mereeni, lawyers with knowledge of local laws as they relate to us." *Us* being our Coldi association.

Veyada touched Reya's shoulder. Reya looked up to the level of Veyada's chest, making sure not to meet Veyada's eyes.

"Well met," Veyada said.

Reya nodded, still looking at the ground.

Both of them ignored Mereeni, so did this mean that she was not part of this silent working of Coldi instincts? I wished I knew. I wished I could *feel* it like they did.

"Make sure you eat something," I said.

Reya bowed, and sat down at the table. Veyada sat down, too. He didn't seem entirely happy.

My heart was thudding. Phew. Did this mean that the danger was now over?

"Let's have breakfast, then, if there is any left." I hope I didn't sound as fake-cheerful as I felt.

I found a seat in between Thayu and Nicha. A waiter was already on the way to bring a new tray with fruit and rice balls. I pulled over the jug and filled a glass with orange juice. My hands were shaking.

Mereeni had sat down opposite us. "Well, let's just work together then. I'm ready." Her Hedron dialect was very strong.

What was more, she acted innocent, but I didn't think for one moment that she didn't know what had happened. She probably understood it better than I had.

"What business is that to you?" Veyada asked, glaring across the table. And oh, that was a downright denigrating pronoun form. "Who are you, anyway?"

"I'm a lawyer." Hedron didn't have as many pronoun intricacies. The form they used was the colloquial type. It sounded wrong to my ears in every aspect. "I'm trained in local law and I'm here to assist you."

"Is that right?" Veyada breathed in deeply, nostrils flaring. He glanced at me, his cheeks red, as if he suddenly realised that I was there. Looked down. "I'm sorry, I . . ." Breathed in deeply. "I'm sorry."

Sheydu, next to him, put her hand on his upper arm. "Come on, knock it off. She's not worth the trouble."

Veyada's shoulders slumped.

Mereeni snorted.

I knew better than to apologise to her. Rude as that exchange had seemed, it was a completely normal Coldi interaction between two people who were not linked through loyalties. The only troubling issue was that, because Mereeni didn't have the instinct, the matter of superiority would never be settled.

Great.

Why couldn't Amarru have included a proper Coldi lawyer? She knew who was in my association and would have known that including her would create friction.

My reader buzzed with the message that a bus had arrived for us downstairs. I grabbed a handful of rice balls and gulped my juice before letting the team know that it was time to go.

The whole party moved to the ground floor. The Pengali wanted to try the lift, and those who didn't fit in the lift, including me, walked.

Our luggage had arrived in the main hall and stood behind the reception desk, two trolleys full of bags and one trolley with the components of the *irrka* drum.

The latter drew some strange looks from fellow travellers.

Nations of Earth had sent a minibus to take us from the Exchange to the airport. It was a regular taxi, with a civilian driver rather than a military employee, so it was allowed into the grounds and up the long driveway to the entrance of the building.

Someone at Nations of Earth had obviously had an optimistic view of how many people their bus could take, and how much luggage it held. Or they had not been notified of the extra people Amarru had added to our group, in itself a rare slip in her usual impeccable organisation.

Indeed, all these people with all their luggage wouldn't fit in the bus, no matter how we tried.

I told the driver, "Just get a second bus."

But there was some reason that he couldn't. His Isla left a lot to be desired and none in our party spoke Greek, so I wasn't sure of the issue there.

I proposed, "How about we just order another taxi for the people who don't fit?"

But he couldn't do that either. I didn't understand the issue. Maybe the problem related to taxi companies and how they carved up their business?

The driver then began an argument with the Exchange guard

about moving the bus away from the entrance, where it was blocking traffic during our futile efforts to stack our luggage in the luggage compartment. It was really the *irrka* drum causing most of the problems.

Could we put some of the luggage in the cabin?

Apparently not. Also the bus didn't have the required number of seat belts. In addition, our group included two children who needed special restraints, and he had only one of those.

The guard at the front door told him repeatedly to shift the vehicle. I asked why the driver couldn't take us anyway, or if he really was that fussed about road rules, take half of us and come back for the rest later?

The driver spread his hands in frustration. "The hover jet is waiting. Do you know how much fuel those things go through when they idle?"

I was tired and didn't have the energy for this. My team was tired of travelling as well, and I still had to make that meeting with Margarethe before I could go to sleep. "Look, either your bosses want us to come, or they do not. Take your pick and act accordingly. We know our way around here and we can make our own way to the court. I would much prefer to go on the train anyway. If you can't take us, we'll go back inside and arrange transport to the station ourselves."

He gave me a wide-eyed look. Yes, that was my past ten years of living with Coldi speaking. Bluntness was catching. Us getting on the train was clearly not part of his orders. He relented and let us into the bus.

It was very cramped indeed. The Pengali, with little Idda, all sat on one bench that was meant to hold two people. Amarru's two security guards, very black and very Indrahui, sat on the back bench with Reya and Mereeni and with Jemiro jammed in the middle, looking very put out about being squished. Evi and Telaris had to sit on the floor in the aisle, both using their backs to hold in place a stack of luggage, including the bag with the Pengali *irrka* pipes inside.

I was one of the last into the bus, and found there was no room to sit other than on the steps next to the driver, until Reida decided that was not on, and gave me his seat next to Deyu.

The driver was packing as many of our bags in the luggage compartment as he could, but when that was full, several extra bags had to be stacked in the aisle, handed to Evi by Reida, and added to the heap between them.

Idda was bouncing off the seats. Nicha held Ayshada, who was out cold with his little face scrunched into Nicha's chest, mouth open and drooling onto Nicha's shirt. Seriously, did those Pengali youngsters ever sleep?

Finally all the bags were in, the driver slammed shut the door and we were off.

By now it was midmorning, and there were a lot of buses on the road, as well as taxis. Deyu stared out the window. She had been here before, very briefly, at night. To someone not used to road traffic, this place must seem like absolute chaos.

I tried to think if I'd seen any private traffic in Athyl, but I'd been so stressed out by the heat that I didn't remember. Certainly the place was too crowded for most regular citizens to own private vehicles.

Many cities on Earth had gone that way, but there was still a lot of commercial traffic.

To Deyu's great delight, a man with a donkey cart toddled along the side of the road. He was one of the tourist taxis that you could hire for a day and he would take you to all the good spots, the ancient sites, the restaurants, the shops, wherever you wanted.

The animal pulling the cart was a horse, Deyu was convinced, having put some study into the subject of Earth animals. I had to explain the difference between a donkey and a horse, and then it turned out she had apparently seen some images from Africa as well, and I had to explain that those "black-and-white striped horses" were not the same as either of them, and that you could ride a horse and use a donkey to pull a cart, but that a zebra was good for none of those things. Her eyes were wide. "So many creatures."

When the meteorite had struck Asto fifty thousand years ago, only plants and lower creatures had survived, and a limited subsection of those at that. I'd heard, now that the climate on Asto was becoming cooler and wetter, that people were considering reintroducing larger animals, especially those from Ceren, since many of those had originally come from Asto anyway.

We hit a really busy patch of traffic where progress halted completely. From my position behind the driver, I couldn't see what the holdup was, but there seemed to be some people on the road, directing the traffic into a single lane.

Sure enough, a couple of police had blocked off the road and flagged vehicles, taxis, buses and driverless cars to the side.

We inched up to the roadblock, and of course the bus was taken aside.

The driver was muttering in Greek. Swear words, I guessed. A police officer knocked on the door and the driver opened it. A bout of yelling in Greek ensued.

"Is this it?" Deyu asked. She glanced at the monotony of blocks of apartments that lined the road.

"No, we're not at the airport yet."

The police officer came into the bus. He glanced over all of us squished into the seats, counting. Oh, crap, it was a traffic cop. Seriously?

He spoke to the driver, but my limited knowledge of Greek did not cover the subject of traffic infringements. There was a lot of waving of hands involved.

Thayu gave me a sideways glance. "What's going on?"

The others in my party were also looking on with suspicious glances.

I said, "Some sort of problem. I think he doesn't like that we have too many people in the vehicle." The notion of *police* roaming the streets pulling up citizens for minor infringements was abhorrent to a native of Asto.

"Do you mean they make these silly rules and then send people into the streets to check if others obey those rules and charge them money if they don't?" Sheydu had asked when I'd tried to explain.

And when I said that was the gist of it, she started laughing.

Veyada, who had studied various kinds of law, had said that it was similar to the Damarcian code of behaviour.

Sheydu had objected. "Yes, but that applies to a person's standing. It's not a money-making scheme."

So it was a fair statement that most people in my party were not favourably disposed towards police officers, especially those of the traffic variety. And here was one arguing with our driver, and people on the bus were becoming impatient.

I rose because we couldn't afford this little issue to become a bigger problem than necessary. I stepped over Reida, who sat in the aisle. "Is there a problem?"

The police officer met my eyes. He seemed almost glad.

The issue was, as I had already suspected, that we had too many passengers on the bus, and that many of us weren't wearing seat belts, and that our luggage was not secured, unless you counted those items weighed down by the sheer bulk of Evi and Telaris. Fortunately, Idda appeared to have finally run out of energy and sat quietly on her mother's lap, cuddling her tail. She was not in a child seat. Ayshada was not in a child seat either.

At this point, Sheydu rolled her eyes and muttered in Coldi that if we wanted to kill ourselves in an accident, it was our freedom to do so. I should have known that as Ezhya Palayi's former guard, she had access to the best translating gear and could understand us.

I apologised to the officer, but this fellow was a particularly petty individual, and in addition to a fine, he wouldn't let us go on in an overcrowded bus. The driver agreed in Greek, which elicited a barrage of Greek comments from the officer.

I could argue that we had a flight to catch, but at that point I remembered Amarru's talk about a diversion. She had said, *There will be a minor diversion along the way. Follow the suggestions made in the diversion.*

So this was the diversion?

I wasn't terribly keen on the hover jet, and it looked like she might not be, either. The suggestion seemed to be: split the party.

Sheydu pushed herself up from her seat. She must have picked up what I thought through the feeder, although I wasn't sure that my link was open far enough for her to listen in.

She said to me, "If you want to reduce the size of the party . . . I've been here before and know my way around. I could take the young-sters and provide them with some more interesting training than being shuffled around by minders. Telaris might want to come."

Her words were full of suggestion and belied her casual tone. For starters, Sheydu rarely offered to do something if there wasn't some ulterior motive to it, so I guessed this was indeed the diversion, and she had received some communication about something that Amarru wanted her to do.

I said, also casually, "Yes, do take Telaris, because otherwise we'll still have too many people."

I told Sheydu to make an independent copy of all our meeting details and catch the train to Rotterdam. Veyada and Thayu shared a feeder with her, so would stay in contact.

She agreed and went to gather the small group; and a moment later she, Reida, Deyu and Telaris left the bus, each carrying a small bag. Security staff always travelled like this, I realised, prepared to travel light when the necessity arose.

To the bystander, this looked very casual, but there was nothing casual about it. Every moment of this operation, including the surly Greek policeman and the traffic holdup, had been planned, just like Nations of Earth had attempted to control our movements by sending vehicles to pick us up. Amarru inserted one snag: order a bus that was too small, or maybe she misreported our numbers.

It would look like an honest mistake, but oh, no, the battle to control what we saw, heard, and who we spoke with had already started.

For now, Amarru held the winning cards.

6

———————

P REDICTABLY, ONCE SHEYDU, Reida, Deyu and
Telaris had left, the police officer left the bus without
imposing the fine, and we progressed to the airport without a
further problem, which let me know that this had indeed been Amarru's diversion and I felt happy to have reacted in the way she would
have expected. Separate the party; spread the risk. Keep all the lines
of information open.

Sometimes I wondered how these people thought I could keep up
with them. Amarru Palayi was one of the smartest and most powerful
Coldi I knew besides Ezhya. Had she lived on Asto, she would definitely have occupied a position very close to him, possibly even in his
primary association.

You should ask her how she ended up here, Thayu said through the
feeder where she was following my thoughts.

I wasn't sure if my position allowed me to do that.

It does, rest assured.

That was always quite frightening, when Coldi who possessed the
sheya instinct told me that my position was different from how I
would have perceived it. I would have thought that Amarru was in a
much superior position to me.

You are just being stubborn, Thayu said, through the feeder again.
*That's the problem with you people. You are conditioned into behaving at a
lower station than you really are, as if being low-ranked and powerless is a good*

image of yourself to project. You call it "humble". She used the Isla word. Now that I thought of it, I wasn't even sure a proper translation for "humble" existed in Coldi. A word that both indicated lower station and positivity. *You talk as if acting according to your position is "bragging" and is not good. You know that you can ask her. You're Domiri, and Domiri clan does not invite people as members unless they're highly ranked.*

Yes, I knew that, too, but it was frustrating not to *feel* it in a natural way as Coldi did. I always ran one step behind everyone else, because I needed to have these relationships explained and needed to be reminded that I should use this power, that I was even expected to use it.

Insecure, one might call it, and yes, I would love to feel the instinct, but instead I had to resort to affirmations like this to make sure that I made the correct decisions.

We reached the airport and went into the building through the usual VIP lounge entrance and the counter dedicated to people from the Exchange.

The hover jet waited on the tarmac. When we climbed up the steps, the scent of lunch drifted from somewhere at the back of the craft. Abri, Kita and Ynggi had been rather quiet on the bus ride, and Idda had finally curled up on top of one of the bags and gone to sleep. She stirred a bit when her mother carried her into the plane and put her on a seat, but did not wake up.

This craft was quite small and had a couple of groups of seating along the right-hand side—couches and soft leather chairs grouped around low tables—while the aisle and row of low cabinets ran along the left side.

The Pengali chose the couches near the door. Ynggi looked around, sniffing the air.

"Smells like fish," he said.

I joined Thayu, Nicha, Veyada and Evi at the next group of chairs, and Devlin, Eirani and Jemiro headed for the last group. They were talking in keihu about the weather, I thought. Just Eirani being her usual self, trying to talk. Jemiro had been very quiet during the trip. I didn't think I'd heard his voice once.

Karana walked along the aisle carrying Ayshada, who was fast asleep, his arm dangling down her tunic. She sat on a bench against the front wall of the cabin, away from the others, holding him on her lap. The remaining people—Amarru's security guards and the lawyers Reya and Mereeni—went into some kind of security station next to the door, where they spoke to a man who was part of the craft's crew. I kept an eye on Veyada, but he appeared to have finally relaxed.

The soft cream-coloured carpet had roused the curiosity of Ynggi. He knelt and ran his hands over it and pulled the fluff to see if it came loose.

It was easy to mistake the almost childish Pengali curiosity for naivety. Even I had fallen into this trap until delving more into Pengali culture for the sake of this trip.

That was the trouble with Pengali: they never drew attention to themselves. They were always silent, in the background, beavering away, often in the dark, because they were nocturnal.

I knew no people who had ever been inside the traditional Pengali settlements, but I'd heard people use the word *hive* for it. They were big structures crafted between a couple of the huge rainforest trees. Each settlement would have several floors with living spaces and dorms. Truly traditional settlements would only use local materials and Pengali technology, which included extensive equipment to cut and polish glass-stone—that is, diamond, the source of all this trouble. Some of the upwellings and caves on the edge of the escarpment yielded solid chunks of diamond that required two people to lift them. The Pengali chipped, cut and polished these into windowpanes, ornaments and eating bowls and drinking glasses. They had even made eyeglasses prior to the advent of eye correction treatments, because there was a market for them, and Pengali had the skill, maths and precision to produce them. Pengali had been exporting their products to Miran at the time when there was still a land route between Barresh and Miran. Their farming practices had been adopted by what was today the food bowl of Asto: the Mirani western plateau centred around the farming community of Bendara. It was as easy to underestimate the Pengali as it was to be intimidated by Coldi bluff.

More recent studies, including the human tree project at the hospital in Barresh, had found that Pengali possessed extraordinary practical and spatial skills, and this made it logical that Pengali often worked as operators of machines: usually boats, but lately also aircraft. The Pilot's Guild had a big office in Barresh. Many of their freight pilots were Pengali. But all of those were from the early urban families, and had worked their way up out of the mires of Far Atok, the largest island of Barresh that was *still* the home of the poorer communities.

Pengali were a very interesting people, much older than any of the other humans, thought to have split off the human tree much earlier.

I knew it would create some friction with my existing household, but I wanted a Pengali on my staff. I was toying with the idea of asking Ynggi. He was an adaptable sort, who didn't seem prone to doing strange and unexpected things. He was sensible; he had done some study and lived in town, and when he lived with the tribe, he used to speak to the Coldi couriers who came directly to the tribe.

Thayu didn't agree with having a Pengali on the staff. I could feel that. "Eirani would have a fit."

"Since when do you care about what Eirani thinks?"

She pulled one corner of her mouth up and grinned. She and Eirani had spent a lot of time bickering when I first came to Barresh.

The crew shut the doors to the craft. Engines whined and we started moving.

The craft came with a steward, who came to me and told me that lunch would be served once we were in the air, and did any of these people need anything special?

I resisted telling him that many of "these people" could understand his question just as well as I could, because he happened to have addressed us in the proper Coldi manner: when speaking to a group, always go through the leader. Although I didn't think he'd done it by design.

So I just answered the question, quietly already annoyed that the same old attitude had still not shifted here, that people on Earth were still reluctant to speak to *gamra* people. The steward went off to a little cubicle at the front of the cabin, where I assumed a mini-kitchen to be.

Amarru's two Indrahui security personnel had found something to talk about with Evi. Both were of the nameless, faceless mould that had once produced Evi and Telaris, security personnel one addressed as *mashara* and never asked for their names or anything personal. I'd since learned that at Indrahui, not giving out personal information and not getting attached to people was a way of protecting one's emotional state, when, as fighters, it was likely that the person who had become your friend would not survive. Neither Evi nor Telaris were forthcoming with emotions, but I hoped the two brothers no longer felt faceless in my household. I had not used the word *mashara* to address them for a long time, and then only on the most formal of occasions.

The jet taxied over the airport. I looked out the window at the city where I'd lived for four years in a cramped apartment at the Exchange with Nicha. I hadn't spent any more time than a few hours at a time in the city since, and it had changed a lot, I'd been told.

When we lived there, the world had come out of a deep depression and the vibe was positive. There was hope that Earth would join *gamra* and that new markets would open up and all the refugees would find homes and there would be technology to turn countries that had turned into deserts back into their former agricultural regions.

None of that had eventuated. There were more refugees than ever before, giant tracts of Africa and the Middle East were wasteland and the home of bandits, and no one had any money for any of the beautiful projects that, if they had been started at all, were woefully behind.

That was fertile ground for radical movements.

Athens was tired of being in two worlds. It was tired of receiving a constant stream of refugees both from *gamra* and North Africa. It kept on plugging along, because it had done so for over four millennia, but the mood had turned grim.

It showed in the greyness of the vista over the city as we took off, tainted brown with the haze of smoke from people burning rubbish to fuel their cooking stoves. So many people were so poor. So few people were disgustingly rich. It was a sad world, and not one I could fix and one I *shouldn't* turn my back on, but I had no idea what I could do to help.

The jet levelled out.

A glance over my shoulder revealed that the Pengali were looking out the window, softly discussing the things they saw.

Reya and Veyada had definitely sorted out their superiority and were talking about legal things. Everything about their behaviour showed that Reya was the subordinate. He did not look Veyada in the eye, and kept studiously out of Thayu's way, because she was Veyada's superior. When I came past, he cast me uncertain glances. Likely, he was getting mixed messages: from Veyada, that I stood at the top of the association, and from looking at me that he didn't *feel* any of this.

Mereeni sat on the corner of the u-shaped bench. She was looking at something on her reader, ostensibly avoiding Veyada's glances. Thayu was glaring at the lot of them from her seat next to me, or maybe she was just staring into space.

I didn't like this new taciturn Thayu, but it would be temporary, I'd been assured.

Sounds of clinking cutlery and plates came from the door at the front of the cabin and, not much later, the steward appeared wheeling a trolley that contained a tray of snacks for each table.

Fruit, pieces of cheese, little square sandwich cubes with various fillings.

Nations of Earth was already laying on the favours. They had even gone out of their way to offer some Coldi-style food. Not red-coded, because little of that was imported, but Coldi-produced locally.

Not for the first time, I wondered who was paying for this, and why Abri's testimony justified the expense.

At the first sight of food, the Pengali had abandoned their study of the world outside and attacked the tray like a bunch of starved dogs. Bread, cheese, salmon sandwiches all vanished at record speed. Abri was highly amused by the concept of a strawberry, and, when she bit it, gave a startled look that made the other Pengali burst out in snorting laughter. Maybe she had expected it to be some kind of fish.

Veyada got into the salmon before the Pengali could start on the tray from our table as well. Reya looked on with a *you eat that stuff?* look on his face.

Being a Coldi from Hedron, Mereeni did not have a problem eating meat, and she tried the fish as well.

"It's good," she said, and then the Pengali started asking her about the food at Hedron, so she joined their table. There was a lot of laughter.

Thayu watched her with narrowed eyes. I felt her discomfort through the feeder.

"Are you annoyed because she is from Hedron or because of the way she behaves?" I asked her when I sat down next to her.

I was wading into deep water here, because much of the interactions between them would be determined by the *sheya* instinct, and hostile as they seemed to me, they might not even see anything wrong with them.

She snorted. "I'm not annoyed. Veyada is. She is rude to him, even if he is her superior."

"I thought they didn't have *sheya* at Hedron."

"They do. They just force their people to suppress it."

"Same as people in the Outer Circle used to force people from the Ezmi clan to fake it?"

She gave me the stink-eye. Thayu hated politics. I teased her with it sometimes. The pregnancy made her grumpier than usual. She was probably tired. We all were.

I reached out, briefly touching her hand.

"I'll handle the politics, right?"

"Then you must do something to settle the issue between Veyada and the Hedron lawyer, because it won't resolve without your interference."

This was the part about Coldi associations that frightened me and that had kept me for so long from accepting that I was part of one, let alone at the head of it. When these types of pathological disagreements happened, I didn't *feel* what I should do. Speak calming words and smooth it over? Take both aside and give them a talking to? Or, in line with typical Coldi behaviour, should I burst in with all guns blazing and issue threats? Not that I would ever say anything threatening to Veyada anyway. I respected him too much.

"That is your problem. You're afraid to act because you think that he will be angry. He will *not* be angry. He will do as you say and respect you."

Boy, she was cranky.

"Do you want anything to eat?" I asked her. "Before it all disappears."

"I'm not that hungry."

More likely, she didn't trust the food on offer, but I knew better than to press the issue, even if she was pregnant and even if it worried me. Weren't pregnant women supposed to be always hungry?

Damn it, did Thayu really have to go like this on me now? "How about you have a rest until we arrive?"

She shrugged. I saw in her eyes that she would love to sleep, but thought she couldn't until we had arrived in a safe place. Because protecting the association was her ultimate job.

I decided to solve the problem for her. I undid my seatbelt and pushed myself up. "I'm going to have a chat with a few people."

Thayu could be really stubborn when it came to the matter of sleep. I was tired, too, but felt the same about sleep and safe places, and I was really bad at sleeping in transport, besides.

I thought Thayu hated for other people to watch her sleep, and the pregnancy made her inability to sleep more of a cause of grumpiness. Maybe something else bothered her. I didn't know. It worried me. There were so many things going on that if she really had a problem, she would need to be clear about it and speak up or no one would notice.

I crossed the cabin and went to join the Pengali table.

Not a crumb of bread was left on the plate that stood in the middle.

The Pengali had gone back to studying the landscape outside the window—the snow-covered Alps. Mereeni looked over their shoulders, but they all turned to me when I sat down.

"Did you like lunch?" I asked.

"Food is good," Abri said, and Kita and Ynggi both waved their tails as sign of agreement.

"Tell me," Ynggi said. "I see no water. Where do these people catch their fish?"

"There are oceans, just not in this part of the world."

"Yes, I saw the oceans. The one we saw when we took off, or the bigger one over the horizon?" He pointed with his tail. "Or the one on the other side of the continent?" He pointed his tail the other way, and it missed Mereeni's arm by a hair's width. She raised her eyebrows.

"So, which ocean? They are different, yes? Cold, warm, deep, shallow, rough, rocky sandy."

"Basically."

"What sort of ocean does this fish come from?"

"I'm not sure." Where *did* people catch salmon? If it had even been real salmon, not that artificial stuff, which I didn't know either because the salmon had been so popular that I hadn't gotten any.

We talked about the mysterious strawberry. Yes, it was a fruit, not a sea creature.

Kita wanted to know, "But what about the specks on the outside? Those are for disguising itself, are they not?"

I said that they were seeds and also that fruit disguised itself to avoid being eaten by birds.

"Birds?" She repeated the strange Isla word.

"They fly like bats, but they have feathers." And there was no decent translation for the word *feathers* because Barresh had no birds, only lots of very large insects and flying crustaceans, and bats. Lots of them, too.

And then they wanted to know about the cheese, and were slightly horrified by the idea that one *stole* the mother's milk from another animal to make *little yellow squishy cubes*.

Did they think the cheese tasted bad? I asked.

Ynggi rolled his tongue over his front teeth. "No, but . . . it's strange."

We dissected the entire contents of the snack tray.

Mereeni watched, but said little. Her expression was intelligent and attentive. I found her quite attractive. Many Coldi could have really flat, emotionless faces, but hers had more angles than the typical Coldi. Then there was the curly hair, which made her appearance unusual.

I glanced over my shoulder to see Thayu lying down over two seats, fast asleep. I really had to give her a bit more space to rest and recover.

Food was always a great point of conversation with Pengali and it occupied us until the plane started to descend and I had to go back to my seat and had to wake up Thayu, because there was nowhere else for me to sit. She was grumpy about that, too, and wiped her face, even if the impression of the seatbelt buckle in her cheek did not disappear immediately. I didn't have to ask her, and bringing attention to it would only make her grumpier, but I didn't think she was feeling very well.

The craft descended over flat fields where water glistened between dams that surrounded villages. It was midafternoon, golden light streaming into the cabin. Below us the odd clouds looked like fluffy balls of cotton wool, coming ever closer. Their shadows drifted over the water and occasionally I could spot the shadow of the jet.

The tapestry of dammed-in islands and water was extremely pretty, helped by the fact that it was tulip season and those islands of habitation—lower than sea level—were painted in stripes of red, yellow, purple and white. The surrounding orchards and grass fields were extremely green, dotted through with farmhouses.

"It's very pretty," Thayu said next to me. She still sounded a bit woolly from sleep.

Yes, it was pretty. In the distance I could see the white sand dunes across the marshy delta.

Rotterdam was an island with tall buildings surrounded by a couple of additional islands and linked by raised roadways. The airport floated outside the city. Here and there rose additional tall buildings of other towns, including the sleeper cities and industrial estates and the older, flood-prone suburbs where the lower classes lived.

The craft went ever lower and, not much later, we touched down. Not at the main terminal, but the VIP lounge to the side, where we had to walk down the steps onto the tarmac. The sky might be clear and the sun bright, but the breeze was cold. Thayu wrapped her arms around herself and pulled her shoulders up. The look in her eyes was feral.

Again, Nations of Earth had sent a bus for us—the right size this time—and the stiff-faced airport personnel loaded our luggage on board. The bus was a driverless vehicle so I asked the baggage handlers about the details of where we were staying. I had to see Margarethe.

"I don't know, Mr Wilson," was the reply. "I can have a look." Every time I came here, I had to get used to hearing this proper Earth version of Isla. What I had learned to speak was technically the off-Earth colonists' dialect Cosla, and there were a good number of differences between the two.

The man climbed the steps into the bus and touched the screen on the control panel. He frowned. "It doesn't give an address, only a code."

"It does that sometimes," his colleague said, halfway through taking a bag off the airport trolley. "Security reasons."

I asked, "Any way to find out? We're a bit late, I have a meeting to attend and I want to make sure I can arrange to get there on time."

He touched the screen a few more times, but shook his head. "I'm sorry. I'm sure you could find out, but I don't know how."

Well, damn it.

"Is there a problem?" Veyada said.

"I was supposed to meet . . ." I glanced at the luggage handlers, who had gone back to operating the machines. I could never assume that people wouldn't speak Coldi, and I definitely didn't want them to hear Margarethe's name. "It's going to be hard because I have no idea where we're staying."

"It can't be too far away."

That was true. "Somebody will be waiting for us when we get there."

"It would be unwise to take everyone to the meeting anyway."

True, and we only had one bus. In fact, I'd much rather use the train. We'd just dump our stuff, get on the train and go.

We all piled into the bus, and the bus started moving. Instead of right, to the island which had the main Nations of Earth buildings, it turned left.

Damn, that meant we were going to be staying somewhere close to the court. Veyada was right, we couldn't turn up at Margarethe's office with this entire entourage, but damn. How could I tell the driverless bus to stop and let us off?

The panel at the front said *job in progress* and not even when I leaned over would it show me information.

I could of course make enough of a fuss to make the bus stop, but then we'd be in more trouble, because they'd know that I was up to something, and my visit to Margarethe was supposed to be a secret.

There was nothing I could do.

I sank into my seat, looking out the window with an increasing feeling of unease in the back of my mind.

On the other side of the aisle Veyada was keeping an eye on the map, logging where we were. I guessed he was sending this to his mother. I wondered whether he had heard anything from that group.

There was green land with cows on one side. It was spring, and yellow flowers bloomed in the grass.

On the other side of the raised road was a channel full of reeds and another field behind it, this one with precision-straight rows of green plants and furrows in between. An agricultural robot of some kind crawled across the field. Not a building to be seen.

Mereeni and Reya were talking about some legal thing; Thayu stared absent-mindedly out the window; Nicha had fallen asleep with Ayshada, awake but very quiet, on his lap; the Pengali, including the little ratbag, had also curled up and the only thing I saw from the bench where they sat were dangling tails.

Amarru's security guards were reading.

Eirani and Karana were talking animatedly, probably about something related to clothing or cooking.

Devlin sat next to Evi, and they were both fiddling with devices.

Veyada looked up from his map. "We appear to be headed over there." He pointed at the horizon, where, through a pale haze that hung over the water, I could just make out a bundle of surreal tall buildings that rose from the field.

Amarru's nameless, faceless Indrahui guard spoke up. *"Mashara* advises that the Nations of Earth court is not at the compound. It is in a city called The Hague."

"I know that, but it's not far from where we normally stay." Jemiro was sitting at the very back of the bus, looking straight at me with his vacant, hollow expression. Listening? Recording everything that happened?

Don't be silly, Mr Wilson.

The guard continued, "The court wants the Delegate in the vicinity. They booked the accommodation."

"Why not the Exchange?"

"There was an agreement. The court is fickle and does not like surprises."

"But they spring extra requirements on us about interpreters?" I was thinking that someone from the court was getting way too controlling.

"Mashara does not know about that."

No, it was their job to protect me, not to ask probing questions.

Nevertheless, I asked a few more questions, but the guards didn't appear to know any more about where we were going than I did. They assumed we'd be staying somewhere close to the Nations of Earth court building, which, according to information I found, was only a few years old and only a block away from the famous Peace Palace, the home of the International Court. A lot of legal services had their offices in that area.

Not long after, the green paddocks along the side of the road were replaced by suburbs. In places, walls blocked the view on both sides of the road. These were really old constructions designed to shield the suburbs from the noise of motorised vehicles when those vehicles still ran on petrol. And one such wall had been turned into a monument, inscribed in huge letters with the text *We will survive*.

Visiting only the Nations of Earth compound shielded me from a lot of the painful history of this area. The text on the wall went back to the terrible flooding disasters that had killed more people than the much-publicised conflicts that were fought last century. I remembered watching the vids when I was a student at the Nations of Earth compound school. I'd been seven or eight, and the grainy images of cities, farms and factories being ground to bits by pounding waves had made for harrowing viewing. At night in our safe little townhouse in the compound, I'd asked my father to assure me that we were safe, because all of Rotterdam was below sea level, with only walls of earth and grass and pumps protecting the city. He had told me we were safe, and I still had nightmares about walls of water washing through the streets.

It was odd that it had frightened me more than travel in a long-haul space ship ever had.

We now entered the city proper, where canals and quaint old houses alternated with glass and concrete towers.

Something was familiar about the broad street with glass-and-steel buildings on one side and quaint old houses and a canal on the other. I must have been here before, but a lifetime spent in many different places had buried the memory. There was an old, old tram, I remembered, a red one with a bell that went ding-ding-ding, and it went to a place where a wide boulevard looked out over a grey and featureless beach. It was windy there, and seagulls had been very keen on my chips. I remembered sitting at a table at a cafe or a picnic table, protecting my plate with my arms. My father had to chase the seagulls off.

Gosh. Disturbing how one could be hit in the face with long-forgotten memories like this.

7

———————

THE BUS TURNED OFF the main road and crossed a canal where a white swan paddled across mirror-like water.

When we turned the corner into the street that ran along the other side of the canal and the display on the bus said, *Arrival in three minutes*, the ever-present sounds in my head winked out. Thayu noticed it, too, and Veyada and Evi both stirred at the same time. We all looked at each other.

I raked my hand through my hair. My feeder's legs pulled loose from the skin and resettled when I dropped them again. It made no difference. The transmission was dead.

"It's a dead zone," Veyada said. "All communication is blocked."

"Whose dead zone and why?"

"The court's, I presume. They really don't want us to talk to anyone while we're here."

"They told us we couldn't speak to Melissa or anyone else involved, but isn't this a bit ridiculous?"

He shrugged. "It's their rules."

I remembered talking to Conrad Martens about the practicalities of the hearing. He had told me, "Various kinds of technology may be used." I just hadn't expected anything so drastic. I bet there was going to be surveillance, too.

There went my plan to easily contact Margarethe.

The bus stopped in front of a stately white building. The entrance was directly on the street, by way of a glass door through which I could see a foyer where water burbled in a fountain with a bench on one side and plants on the other.

Several of the hotel staff came out of the entrance in their prim uniforms with grey jackets. If they were perturbed by our alien group members, they didn't show it. Except they were all, "Yes, Mr Wilson, we'll do that, Mr Wilson."

They didn't attempt to speak to any others on my team, even if some of my people spoke to the staff in Isla. It was a bit disturbing to see this attitude survive for so long and it made me doubly annoyed that we couldn't stay at my regular hotel. At least the staff there were used to people from off Earth.

The porters took our luggage out of the bus and loaded the mountains of bags and cases on trolleys. They were baffled by the hollowed out tree trunks that were components of the *irrka* drum.

The porters wheeled the tottering piles through the entrance, to be taken to our rooms. We filed in after them and, while the others sank on the couches, I went to the reception counter for room numbers and other details.

Veyada and Thayu wandered casually through the foyer, looking at the fountain and the artwork on the walls, but I didn't miss the fact that the scanner on Veyada's belt was on.

I had almost forgotten that people had the strange habit of tossing coins in ponds. Idda spotted the glitter and she lay on her stomach next to the water, sticking her arm in to fish the coins out. She soon figured out that those coins were not edible, but there were also a couple of lazy, fat goldfish in the pond, congregated in the part of the pond where Idda wasn't.

Ynggi also watched the fish. They were quite large, and maybe he was wondering what they tasted like.

Were these fish supposed to be alive by the time we left?

I insisted that the Pengali were allocated a room first. "Just out of curiosity, there are no aquariums in the room?" I asked the receptionist.

She raised her eyebrows.

"The little one is fascinated with fish."

"Oh." She eyed Idda on her stomach at the edge of the pond, her tail in the air. "They are very pretty, right?"

More like, *They look like good eating.*

"Don't worry about the little one. There is no water in the room other than in the bathroom." She smiled. The badge on her chest said *Odette.* "That little kid is so cute."

I wondered if she'd still be saying this after we left. But I had to admit that the little yellow romper suit looked good on Idda, even if she was now getting it wet—

"Enough. Leave the fish alone, Idda." I scooped her up. She felt soft, flexible, like a bag of loosely-connected bones in my hands. I gave her to Ynggi. "Those fish are not for eating."

"I'll keep an eye on her," he said, but Kita gave me a look that said *What else are fish for if not for eating?*

Finally, the Pengali were directed off to the relative safety of their room—a big apartment at the end of the hallway on the first floor.

Getting out of the bus had woken Ayshada. He was cranky and keen to let everyone know. Nicha took him from Karana. I made sure that I allocated his room next so that he could put his son to bed. Thayu and I were to get a room next to his.

The hotel was not very big and didn't seem to be busy at all.

Most of us ended up on the first floor and some on the second floor. Most people shared rooms between two, except the Pengali.

Thayu and I got a suite above the entrance with a view over the street, the tramline and the canal—so that I could see any wayward Pengali youngsters. There was a dedicated driverless bus lane on the other side of the canal and a kind of park, beyond it, of the type I suspected to once have been a median strip in a busy road. Now, it was full of trees and a shed with a solar roof—which was probably a waste-processing station—a couple of windmills and a water-purifying tower. A row of glass-and-steel constructions rose from the other side of the park.

Veyada had the room opposite us, and he would share it with Sheydu when she turned up, and of course Evi and Amarru's guards had the first rooms at the top of the stairs, next to a small conference room suitable for use as a security station.

The rest of the people were on the top floor.

Ayshada had completely crashed, so Nicha left him in his room and came to share tea with Thayu, me and Veyada.

"You haven't heard from Sheydu yet?" Nicha asked Thayu.

"Not a thing."

That might not mean anything. They were probably on the train. They might be doing a little side project, although I had no idea what that could be.

Neither Nicha nor Thayu seemed to be terribly concerned and so I resolved not to be either.

"We missed making our contact." I kept it deliberately vague. "I'm not sure what we should do about it. This place is likely to be bugged."

Nods. Yes, that went without question. Within the next day or so, we'd get a much better idea of who was listening in and where they were.

"Have you found anything yet?"

"We've not located any devices in the rooms yet. The dead zone covers this street up to the corner, the canal, the other side of the canal and the entire block at the back of the hotel. The court building is in that block. There are likely to be transmission-cancelling devices in the courthouse and on the roof of the hotel or the building behind it. They've probably got a surveillance post in one of those towers over there." He pointed out the window, where I could see the glass towers behind the park.

It never ceased to amaze me how quickly he could establish things like this. "Is there anything we can still do to make our contact?"

"Yes, but not without drawing attention to the fact that we're doing it. The transmission block is nonspecific and untargeted. We would need some brute force to break it. Unless we repurpose our visit, I see no reason to do this and upset a lot of people. We came here to get Robert Davidson convicted. This block is unlikely to be about us or pose any threat to us. I guess it is standard court procedure."

As usual, Veyada was the voice of reason. I just didn't like being in a communication-restricted area. And I still needed to establish contact with Margarethe.

He continued, "I have to admit, I'm used to a greater degree of directness in trials and legal matters, but this is not my system. It is not *our* system. They don't want us to talk to anyone in relation to the trial, so they house us here, where we can't communicate. I don't think that is an unreasonable request."

Ultimately, that was the crux of the matter: it was not *our* system. Even if I had grown up on Earth, its systems and governments were no longer mine. Veyada was right, and Conrad Martens had warned me that the court might use technology.

I said, "I guess we can leave the dead zone and establish contact from there?"

"We could do that once we get a chance, and when we know the details of our meetings and we know why and how we are or are not permitted communication with others."

"But I'd really like to get in contact—" *What about Margarethe?*

"There is little we can do about it without using blunt force and risking disturbing the legal process."

It was getting late and everyone was tired. I couldn't blame them for not caring much about our missed appointment. I just wished to hell I knew what Margarethe wanted to talk to me about. But I had to accept that I'd missed the opportunity to see her, that I'd failed and that there was little I could do about it, especially since offices were about to close. The best thing we could do was to start fresh tomorrow.

Only one thing still bothered me.

I had expected that someone from Nations of Earth would meet us here and give us our schedule, and no one had contacted us.

I went to the hotel's reception, where the receptionist sat alone. She smiled when she saw me. "Dinner will be ready soon."

"Thank you." I didn't think many people would come, but that aside. "Do you have any messages for us about what is going to happen tomorrow? I'm a bit worried that no one from the court has contacted us yet."

"They said they'd give you a day to recover. I've been told Mrs Trnkova will be here first thing in the morning to explain everything to you."

I hadn't heard that name before, but she was probably one of Conrad Martens' assistants.

"What would I need to do if I wanted to talk to someone now?"

"Someone in an official role within Nations of Earth?"

"Yes." I guessed Margarethe qualified as such. "But it's not about details covered in the court case."

I didn't *know* what Margarethe wanted to talk about, but she wouldn't be so stupid as to risk Robert getting off on a technicality because she spoke to me beforehand. Certainly she wouldn't have funded my trip here only to thwart it. Maybe she was going to tell me what the point of this extravagance was.

"If you want to talk to someone about matters unrelated to the trial, you will have to do it from outside the hotel. Be aware that when you leave the building, you are likely to be monitored."

"I am aware of that."

"Also beware that a horde of activists and journalists are permanently camped at the steps to the courthouse. I would strongly advise you to avoid that area."

"Activists?"

"Yes, the trial has attracted a lot of attention locally. The court has even had to draw a lottery for people to get tickets to the public gallery."

Activists, well, I began to see reasons for the dead zone and the strange arrangements for our arrival. "Why are those people there? What's the interest for them?"

"It started because there has been a bit of fuss about Robert Davidson's company Execo and the way they treated their workers. The board is reclusive and has been avoiding questions about it for years, and when Robert Davidson went on trial and actually had to appear in court, a lot of people lined up to question him publicly about the company's dealings. The journalists were attracted to this drama like flies." Then she grinned. "And I guess a lot of people are curious about the tailed monkeys."

What the actual fuck . . .

I put both my hands on the desk and leaned forward. The receptionist leaned back in her chair, her eyes wide. "I suggest, if you want to avoid nasty situations, you stop calling them that."

She laughed, uneasily. "They don't speak Isla, anyway."

"You assume."

"Well, yes."

"Don't."

I glared at her. Her cheeks had gone red.

"Don't—ever—assume anything when it comes to Pengali. Don't even assume that they won't be using their diamond knives to stick in your ribs. Because they are not dumb, they are not backward. And they're armed and can harm you in hundreds of other ways besides."

"Whoa, I didn't mean it like that. It was just a joke. Light-hearted, you know."

"It's not funny."

"All right, I'm sorry."

I held up my finger. "No more 'monkeys'."

"No, no. I understand."

But I doubt she did and it didn't matter anyway, except that I was so terribly sick of these attitudes. And what was worse, in the past years, nothing seemed to have changed in this respect at all.

"I also suggest that you do something about the fish in this pond. You saw how the kid was eying them when we first came here."

"Yes, yes, sure."

I turned away, but not before catching her muttering, "No sense of humour." It was true; a lot of people in our party had no sense of humour that she would recognise.

Pengali, in fact, were the most humorous of people in our group. Try tickling Thayu's sense of humour, or Evi's. This was how diplomatic incidents started. "Humour" and rudeness were not interchangeable, and "humour" was not an excuse for being rude.

I went back upstairs, angrier than I should have been. Damn it, why did these people keep doing crap like this? They were not the farmer next door to my father's house, or random people in the street, who could be excused for trying to be funny while making insulting statements. These people should know better.

Thayu had gotten changed into informal clothing: the same fluffy pants and big jumper she had worn when we last stayed at my father's farmhouse. And that was—oh—far too long ago.

Her eyes widened when she saw me.

"What's going on?"

"It's always the same with these people. They think none of you can understand them and they think that is their license to make insulting comments under the guise of a joke."

"Humour is a mask for fear," Nicha said. "They're afraid that these strange people will drive them out of their homes."

I knew, but that didn't make this behaviour any less annoying.

"How is the room?" I asked and I gestured under the table to Nicha, making the security hand signal for "listening bug".

He signalled, *Can't find any*.

That didn't mean none were there. It was worse than *We found some* because that would mean that they had been disabled.

At that moment, Veyada came in. He had that *I've got news* look on his face.

I gestured, *Bathroom?*

When suspecting that people were listening in, all security guards had their meetings in the bathroom where they could mask speech through sounds of splashing or running water.

As it was, the bathroom was a lot smaller than any we'd had the necessity to meet in previously. Nicha turned on the tap. Water splashed in the bath.

Nicha sat on the edge of the bath, Veyada sat on the floor and Thayu leaned against the cabinet. She looked tired, I thought, and then I felt guilty. I should let her sleep, in her condition.

Evi must have had a sixth sense that we were about to have a meeting, because he came in, shut the door and leaned against it. I'd had no indication that *their* feeders to each other were working either. In fact I was pretty sure they weren't.

There was no room for me to sit except on the toilet. I shut the lid and sat on top of that. "You got news from Sheydu?"

Veyada shook his head. "Nothing yet, so we've contacted Amarru."

"How can you contact her if you can't contact Sheydu and we're in a dead zone?"

He raised his eyebrows. "We have our ways."

Of course, he was unlikely to explain it in case someone *was* listening in, and also to protect Amarru, whose secret systems this message had probably come through—those little routines that, over their one hundred and fifty years as part of Earth society, the Coldi were rumoured to have built into ordinary electrical equipment, and that should only be used in emergencies.

I'd never liked the possibility of the existence of such routines, but I'd seen too much solid evidence for their existence to deny it. "What news does she have to report?"

"She told me that she sent Sheydu to Rotterdam."

"Why?" My heart skipped a beat.

"I think you know. To honour a meeting that we can't attend."

Damn. It suited us because I really couldn't see how I was going to see Margarethe without being noticed, but damn Amarru. "That message to me was meant to be *private*." Sent through the Trader Guild and all that. I'd told Margarethe that it was guaranteed private, and if Amarru had obtained the message without Margarethe's knowledge, I . . . I guess I wasn't going to be very happy about that.

Shit. This thing was getting away from me. For years I'd argued to people at Nations of Earth that *if* the Coldi had built their secret routines into Earth technology—and in all seriousness, there was no "if"; they had done it, loud and clear—the surveillance was going to be benign, because the goals of Nations of Earth and *gamra* aligned. But spying on the president fell squarely outside what was acceptable even to me, and if it was true, I was going to have to face Amarru.

She held a higher position than I did, but because I was the leader of an association, she might view it as a challenge to her position. *That* was something I needed to avoid, but oh, I was becoming increasingly uneasy with her power.

I let the subject rest, because I wanted to risk exposing Amarru to whoever listened even less than I wanted a confrontation with her. The main reason I'd never raised the issue of Amarru's power before was that she acted in everyone's best interests, right?

A chill crept over my back.

"Are Sheydu and the others coming here to the hotel?" They would be monitored when they came in that way, and they couldn't slink into our party.

Veyada said, "We'll have to arrange a meeting place and they may have to stay outside this area. If they come into the hotel's front door, they'll be photographed and profiled, and people will start wondering where they've been."

That was my thought, too. "On the other hand, it's not a secret that a couple of people in my party went on the train, is it?"

"I don't know. Amarru added four people to the party. Four people went on the train. The size of the group that arrived at the hotel was the same as the number we told them were coming."

Damn, Amarru's interference again. That woman was starting to scare me.

I thought of that moment where Sheydu offered to go on the train and casually remarked that she'd take Reida and Deyu, and Telaris. There had been nothing, *nothing,* casual about it.

So, it was likely that Nations of Earth *didn't* realise that four of our party had split off.

Well . . .

A chill crept over my spine.

Disturbing.

"So what can we do now?" I asked. "Wait until they turn up and see what Sheydu has to say about the meeting she's had?" I still had trouble envisaging Sheydu in Margarethe's office. I guess that was why she had so casually suggested taking Telaris: he knew Isla.

Veyada made a hand signal that I interpreted as: *Be quiet.*

He listened.

I glanced at Thayu, who was yawning so much a tear ran over her cheek. A pang of guilt went through me. I'd meant to let her rest. Never mind the time; never mind dinner. She should go to bed.

"Anything going on?" Nicha asked Veyada after a while.

"My feeder was getting a very weak signal just now. There is a large public meeting going on in the building next to the court."

Yes, I remembered the receptionist mentioning it. "Someone trying to contact us from there?"

Veyada shook his head. "I think it's just some spillover from local data overload in that area. I suspect it's coming from just outside the dead zone. The transmission block is crude, and there would be limits to its strength."

"I wonder what all those people are there for, then, especially at this time of the day. The court would be closed by now."

Veyada spread his hands. "The ways of this world are a mystery to me."

I had to admit that they were a mystery to me, too.

I wish we had paid less attention to documentation and regulations before coming here. Clearly, there were issues going on that went beyond Robert's appearance in court, and clearly someone at Nations of Earth had wanted to shield us from those events and they had done so by putting lots of bureaucratic roadblocks on our path. And we had let ourselves be distracted.

"We need to find a way to get a picture of the issues surrounding this trial or whatever else is going on. All we hear is that it is a criminal trial, but the issues that surround it are obviously much bigger."

Veyada said, "Agreed. Let us make some investigations."

"First we have to get out of this information trap," Thayu said. "We can't communicate effectively without anyone listening in."

"What about Amarru's secret channels?"

Veyada said, "Once we start fully using them, they won't be secret anymore. They're only for short messages and emergencies."

Nicha said, "We need to see what the court schedule is."

I agreed. It was hard to plan without knowing when Abri would appear.

I asked, "So the communication dead zone covers this building and most of this block?"

"Yes, it's not terribly big," Thayu said. "They'd probably get too many complaints from local businesses every time they turn it on."

"So we could 'casually' wander outside that area, since we haven't been told about it, or haven't been told that we need to stay inside."

"Why don't we take Ayshada for a walk after dinner?" Nicha said. "Someone put a *pram* in my room." He used the Isla word, because Coldi parents mostly carried their children in slings. Mostly also, the children were pretty good at keeping up with the adults soon after they started walking. "We'll stay away from the courthouse or any other sensitive areas. You might even ask the reception if there is a nice park for him to play in or something."

"We'll be watched," Thayu said.

"That goes without saying. We're not going to do anything except listen."

A walk was a good idea. This far into May the evenings were long.

We went to the dining room, a light-filled room at the back of the building, looking out into a courtyard with clipped bushes. One side of the room was all glass, with double doors into the courtyard that might be open when the weather was nice. A path led through the courtyard to a gate in the back fence. There was a security lock on the fence, but I suspected that it led into the alley behind the building.

As predicted, dinner was a quiet affair. We shared it at the big table in a very lonely dining room where there were no other people. Just Thayu, myself, Evi, Veyada, Eirani, Karana and Devlin. Amarru's people had some other job to do. The Pengali didn't turn up. Jemiro didn't turn up. I asked Devlin if he'd been notified that there was dinner and Devlin said that he had.

Everyone was tired. Devlin was going back to bed himself and looked at me as if I were nuts when I said we were going for a walk.

I had heard people say that your body got used to travel through the Exchange and I'd always laughed it off as old wives' tales, but here was the proof in front of me.

So, we got ready after dinner. Nicha went upstairs first while we remained at the table, drinking tea. He had secured some hot water to make Ayshada's favourite instant porridge, and went to feed his son before we left.

Thayu wanted to come. Veyada asked Evi, but he was going to stay to check out the hotel and report on bugs.

I went upstairs and met Ynggi in the hallway carrying a stack of blankets—had he been to reception to get those? He declared that Abri and the other Pengali couldn't possibly do anything in the daytime, so they were going to bed. Good. Asleep was the best way to be for them for now. I guessed we'd pay for it later, but it gave us some downtime.

I found Jemiro moping in his room from having nothing to do, but I managed to find a news service that wasn't banned by the block. I thought it was boring but he said he found it interesting.

"There are so many nuances to the use of the local language," he said.

Sure. If that excited him.

I went back to our room.

Our copious luggage had included sets of local clothes. Thayu spent some time choosing an outfit, wondering whether it was going to be too cold, and when she came out of the bathroom with her hair loose, wearing a pair of tight jeans, a short knitted top and a long trench coat, she almost blew me away. That was a woman who would turn heads.

The coat contained various types of weapons and spy equipment, I was sure of that, but it also wasn't out of place, because the wind was quite chilly.

Nicha looked like a very laid-back dad dressed in black trousers and black leather jacket—no doubt also with guns and listening devices. Ayshada wore a cute set of overalls with a train on the front and a red jacket. He had woken up cranky, not wanting to eat, but had calmed down at the sight of the pram and found it enormously interesting—to zoom around the hotel's foyer by pushing it backwards, missing vases and furniture by a hair's width.

In the hotel foyer, I also found the hotel staff's solution to the fishpond issue: they had put a childproof fence around it. It would be useful for all of the five seconds it would take the Pengali youngster to climb over it, but we'd solve that issue when we came to it.

I asked the receptionist for directions to a park and she reminded us to stay away from the court building, and that we would be monitored. "For your safety of course."

Yes, sure. "Do you know what sort of people these protesters are and what they're doing there?"

Her cheeks coloured. "Oh. It's all about politics. I'm not terribly interested in that stuff."

"Where can I see any news feeds about it?"

"I'm not sure. I'll look it up for you." Spoken much too fast. Then her cheeks went even darker red. "Oh, I'm sorry. I meant to tell you that someone will be contacting you tomorrow."

"You did tell me. The prosecutor's assistant."

"Oh, no, this is someone else. He wants to talk to you about business. He asked me to tell you to make some time."

Business? Make some time? "Does this person have a name? What kind of business does he want to talk about? Just so that I can prepare?"

"He said he'll introduce himself."

"How is he going to contact me? This is a dead zone."

"We have a hardwired line from our office. You can use that. I will come to get you."

"What about the court representative?"

"They will come here."

Once we left the building, Ayshada wasn't so happy sitting in the pram, but standing was another matter, even if it meant that we couldn't do up the harness and we had to make sure that the pram didn't topple. He was clearly enjoying himself, clapping and singing at the top of his voice while standing on the pram's seat.

Nicha joked about setting a precedent. Ayshada might from now on expect to be wheeled everywhere. But he was a delight to us, very Coldi, exuberant and incredibly cute.

I noticed Thayu's tender glances as him and could not restrain a smile myself. So much was changing for us, and it was all for the better.

It was indeed quite fresh outside, if sunny. The wind that rushed through the streets was bitingly cold. The signs of spring were everywhere: in the fresh green leaves on the trees that lined the street, in the tulips that grew in planter boxes outside people's doorsteps, in the mother duck with a long trail of yellow and brown fluffy ducklings that paddled across the canal.

We walked along the street, looking at houses that must be close to a thousand years old. All along the sides there were places to leave bikes and scooters, and charging stations for those scooters. We'd come past the wind farms that harvested the power for them.

We'd arrived at the end of the street when suddenly my feeder burst into action. It always amazed me that I never missed it when it was out, but found it so noisy when it came back.

Did that mean that Nations of Earth had blotted out communication in a whole city block just to keep us from talking to anyone about the trial? Did that mean that none of the businesses we'd just walked past had wireless connectivity?

"I said their methods were crude," Veyada said. "Although a lot of houses and businesses have hardwiring so they wouldn't notice."

After I'd made certain that there wasn't anyone desperately trying to contact me, I told them of the second meeting I was supposed to have the next day, the meeting with the businessman. Predictably, Thayu and Veyada were more interested in whether they would be able to use the hotel's hardwired connection to contact Sheydu. To be fair to them, business people did contact me sometimes when I was here, so they couldn't see what was unusual about it. Except for the fact that I wasn't on a visit related to Nations of Earth and that they had managed to circumvent a communication block.

I explained that the wiring used to be an old telephone network, that newer buildings relied on wireless transmission—which was subject to the communication block—and that some parts of the wired network were likely defunct.

My team, and especially Veyada and Thayu, found it very interesting.

"We must locate those wires," Veyada said.

There were clearly none in our room, otherwise he would already have found them.

Nicha judged the wind too chilling for Ayshada to play in the park, plus there was a family with two kids already at the swings and he wanted no trouble caused by the fact that Ayshada as a Coldi toddler was stronger and mentally more developed than those children, so we kept going. Thayu and Veyada were silent, presumably checking out the news. I didn't have that level of connectivity. I preferred to use my reader, because I hated the noise in my head.

We found a quaint little cafe on a street corner. A bell rang when I opened the door and stepped into the warm air that smelled of coffee and sweets and was filled with talk, the hissing of coffee machines, the whine of blenders and the clinking of cutlery on plates.

Our presence didn't attract a lot of attention, although one or two patrons glanced at Thayu. She really was stunning. We sat down near the window and ordered when a waitress came to our table. I found that the little EXO tag on my Nations of Earth card absolved me from restrictions about what I could order. Seriously, since when did authorities think they could be so meddlesome as to dictate what and how much people could eat?

While we waited, Veyada declared casually that he was going to find the bathroom.

He opened his feeder and I could sense him walking down a set of stairs into a semibasement where sounds were hollow.

And, suddenly, Sheydu was there. They were indeed in Rotterdam. To Veyada's question whether they had what they needed, she said they did, whatever that meant. They would stay in Rotterdam overnight and we'd try to meet up with them tomorrow once we knew the court schedule. I asked them about information surrounding the trial, especially in relation to the protesters outside the courthouse, and if there were major issues.

Sheydu said no.

But what about protesters outside the courthouse, I asked her.

She seemed surprised that I wanted to hear about them.

Just some people unhappy with what they've got, she said and couldn't see how it was related to the case, or the Pengali, or us.

To appease me, she sent me one of the news items. They were poor people from Africa, a quick skim revealed.

I'm not sure that this is terribly relevant to us, she said.

At this point, lacking further information, I cautiously agreed.

I was wondering how to bring up Margarethe, and the action of thinking about it sent a signal to Veyada and he let me know both to shut up and that it had been taken care of.

So I shut down the link, not being as good with controlling my thoughts as they were. The waitress had arrived with a tray full of goodies. She unloaded coffee, tea, a plate full of pastries and a sippy cup of apple juice for Ayshada.

He squirmed in his high seat, worming his legs under him so he could reach the pastries. Thayu gave him one and he took a huge bite, spilling pastry flakes and powdered sugar all over his face and the front of his cute overalls.

He was so much better behaved when that Pengali brat wasn't running around.

"It is really hard not to tell the mother to teach the kid some manners," Thayu said, having followed my thoughts.

"Feel free to tell her."

"It's not my place."

Meaning it was *my* place, and yes, it might well come to that. "I can try, but I doubt she'll listen."

Thayu's face turned dark. "I'm getting really sick of their poor behaviour masquerading as Pengali culture. They want us to accept them? Then let them start behaving politely."

Thayu, having grown up in a military household and trained as spy, was about orders, responsibilities and promises. Lack of structure and clear authority annoyed her even more than it annoyed most Coldi.

Veyada returned and we drank and talked about the weather and tourist things. Nicha was quite interested in the beach suburb I'd mentioned and, apparently, a tram still went to it.

We finished our coffee. Ayshada had reduced two whole pastries to a set of crumbs. He had crumbs all over his face and sticky little hands, which Nicha wiped down. Fortunately, he was also getting tired, and he let himself be strapped into the pram before cuddling up with his blanket.

Thayu gave him a tender look. It was hard to believe that we would have a little brat like that, and somehow, I still couldn't believe that it had been so easy.

We walked back to the hotel. By now, the sun was sinking, the light turning golden, and people on scooters and bikes were filling the streets on their way home from work.

Ayshada would have enjoyed seeing that two-wheeled traffic, but he was fast asleep.

We had a security meeting in the conference room at the top of the stairs, where the oval table was barely visible under all kinds of equipment. Evi and Amarru's guards had completed a thorough scan of the hotel. They had located a few listening points and had established that we were being monitored from the second floor of an office block across the canal.

Again, I had no idea how they knew this, but security was security and they did what they did best. In those types of conversations, I was a fly on the wall and I didn't ask questions. I just let my security do their work.

After the meeting I spoke briefly to Jemiro, too, and asked him if he needed anything, but the young man was painfully shy and he looked like a stunned rabbit every time I asked him a question. I wondered how much good he was going to be in the courtroom. Enough to satisfy the court's demands, but I was sure going to rely on Ynggi for translation, and so I went to check with Ynggi to make sure that he'd be up and ready tomorrow morning for when the lawyers were going to turn up.

The Pengali all sat on the floor in their room in a very serious-looking meeting. I asked if there was an issue, but apparently, they were deciding "the order of statements", whatever that meant. Yes, Ynggi would be ready. He'd make sure the others would be ready, too.

Then I spoke to Devlin, and he told me that because Jemiro was not from one of the major keihu families, he would live in constant fear that people with higher social standing would come and take his job away if he drew too much attention to himself.

It was an odd thing to say, but little surprised me about the keihu anymore. On the surface, they looked civilised and polite, but that veneer wore off quickly when you started poking, and it revealed a nasty world of rivalry and backstabbing between the major families.

"The old Pakiru, Jemiro's grandfather I'm guessing, got badly into debt and the family couldn't pay their creditors. They had to move to another part of town. They now run a handful of eateries."

Not the most glamorous business in Barresh.

"How did he even get his education then?"

Devlin shrugged and spread his hands. "I guess we all lost track of the family."

I felt a little more favourably disposed towards Jemiro after that. He must be a very determined man to have climbed this far out of that hole.

I went back to our room and did some reading, but I spotted Thayu's eyes falling shut a few times, and we decided it had been enough for today. The shower was hot, and the bed big and comfortable, and Thayu's arms soft and warm. Before I drifted off to sleep, Thayu said, "Have you noticed that we're the only guests here?"

8

THAYU WAS RIGHT, we *were* the only guests in the hotel.

I'd noticed that the place seemed unusually quiet and wondered about it. Now it seemed that *someone* had gone all out on the expenses. I guessed they really wanted to convict Robert Davidson of murder.

Or they *really* wanted us to remain out of contact with the rest of the world until Abri had presented her evidence.

I guessed it was the court's right to order that, but just what was going on outside the courthouse that somebody didn't want us to see and that the receptionist had so casually mentioned to me? On second thoughts, how casual had that mention really been? So the protesters were "dangerous", right? They were so dangerous that we needed to be warned off and steered in the other direction, just in case we saw . . . what? That the police were lacking in control? That some people didn't like Robert Davidson's companies? We already knew those things.

And what did Margarethe want to tell me and was the fact that I'd been unable to contact her really an unfortunate congregation of events?

That question kept going through my mind while I lay there staring into the dark after having woken up in the middle of the night, unable to go back to sleep.

Years of living at *gamra* and living with several people who were highly trained spies had given me a sensor for when something was off. That sensor was firing at full strength right now, even if I had no idea if there was a threat, where it came from, if it was directed at us or who we could confide in to talk about it. In fact, I wasn't sure we *had* much to talk about.

Our communication was being blocked—but that was understandable because of the court.

We were warned not to meet with the protesters outside the courthouse—but that might be out of genuine concern for our safety, never mind that we were well equipped to look after ourselves, although being outnumbered could be a dangerous factor.

We needed to know more before we could ask for any help, but the thought of sending my team out to investigate made me feel ill. Out of all of them, only Nicha was confident in Isla. Thayu was breathing softly in her sleep next to me, and I didn't want to put her in *any* danger.

As soon as it started to get light, and I could hear someone talking downstairs at the entrance of the hotel, I got out of bed.

Thayu was still fast asleep, on her stomach with her face scrunched into the pillow. I took care not to wake her, dragging all my clothes into the bathroom to get changed there. That was more difficult than it sounded. *Gamra* people put a lot of stock into signals sent through one's clothing, and I'd spent some time considering what I'd wear. My regular outfit, including the shirt with the gauze-thin sleeves and embroidered vest over the top, was out. It was much too cold for that here. So I had asked Eirani to procure me a slightly thicker shirt that I could wear under the vest. I'd been tempted to discontinue my adaptation medication that made me more comfortable in the humid heat of Barresh, but sudden changes in adaptation tended to cause severe nausea, and I could certainly do without that. So I had taken the temperature retaining suit that a manufacturer on Asto had made to my measurements and I put that on underneath all my clothes.

From the bathroom, I quietly slipped into the upstairs hall. The Pengali were up, or at least the door to their room was open. Through the opening I could see a mess of blankets on the floor and wished good luck on the cleaners who would have to sort it out. The door to Nicha's room was closed, but I met Nicha downstairs in the foyer, where a few of the others also hung around waiting for the breakfast that was already spreading delicious smells through the foyer.

Nicha was reading something; Ayshada ran after Idda, zigzagging between the couches in the foyer, both of them making far more noise than was comfortable at this early hour.

Reya was talking to Amarru's guards; Mereeni sat on her knees next to Eirani, who had dragged over a display table and was looking at advertising displays of cooking utensils. The two women were pointing and laughing, and making movements with their hands as if demonstrating what each unfamiliar appliance on the display might be for. Karana sat on Eirani's other side. She thought it was extremely funny. Her high laughter echoed through the hall.

I thought I understood my association's issues with Mereeni: because she was from Hedron, they didn't know how weak or strong the *sheya* instinct was in her, so they had no idea how to treat her.

But seeing her sit there, I could understand why Amarru had sent her. Would any Coldi so easily talk to Eirani in this way? The members of my association spoke to Eirani, but never without inhibition. In our household, *I* interacted with the staff, because that was my task, being the leader of the association.

Mereeni just talked to everyone regardless of position, the way she talked to a bunch of keihu people now and had talked to the Pengali yesterday. What was more, she acted genuinely *interested* in everything, from fish to cooking utensils.

And Veyada didn't like it.

He sat on a bench across the hall, arms crossed over his chest, glaring at her. And she *didn't* have the *sheya* instinct or she wouldn't have so utterly, pathetically *ignored* him.

Which probably pissed him off even more. I knew I should go to him and show solidarity, but a big part of me wanted to slap him in the face and tell him to stop it and loosen up.

Except he couldn't and, knowing Veyada, that probably embarrassed him immensely. I sat down next to him, and utterly failed at finding something meaningful to say. So we ended up talking about the weather—the fucking *weather*—while avoiding the subject that made him so uncomfortable, and while that subject's laughter echoed through the hall.

After the sunny weather yesterday, the sky was bleak, with low clouds chasing each other over the city. No rain, fortunately, but it didn't look or feel warm.

But weather wasn't a very interesting subject, so we did swing around to work.

"Are you happy working with Amarru's lawyers?" I asked before I could spend too much time worrying about the wording.

"They are very knowledgeable. My understanding of local law is not nearly as extensive."

That was not really what I asked, Veyada. "But there are no problems? I noticed that you seemed to have an issue settling your *sheya*."

"She is from Hedron. They don't have *sheya*."

Did he believe that? They had it, or at least some people had it, maybe not as strong, but they definitely had it. If nothing else, she definitely had an effect on him. But he obviously didn't want to talk about that, either.

And then, before I could muster up the courage to call both of them to me to get this sorted out, because that was what I would have to do, some commotion broke out.

Karana sprang to her feet, yelling, "No, Idda, no!"

She ran across the hall, where the Pengali brat sat atop the "child-proof" fence that stood around the pond. She would have jumped into the pond had not Ayshada gotten hold of her tail. He was pulling it, and she squealed, and Karana shouted for them both to stop it. She pulled Idda off the fence.

Ayshada laughed.

Idda wriggled loose and jumped from Karana's arms onto the carpet. She scampered across the foyer. Ayshada took off after her. She jumped onto the stairs, and ran up to the upstairs landing, jumped on top of the banister and then—

"No!" I ran forward, but it was already too late.

She jumped—

—sailed across the atrium—

—into the pond in the hall.

Splash!

Water went everywhere. People yelled. The receptionist—a prim woman I hadn't seen before—copped a fair bit of it.

Her mouth was open in utter horror.

That was enough. In a few steps, I was across the hall. I shoved the useless kiddie fence aside, fished the youngster out of the water—where she was already chasing the terrified goldfish—and carried her up the stairs two steps at a time. I charged into the Pengali's room, where the door was still open and handed the brat, dripping and all, to her mother.

"Keep her with you or make her behave, or I'll lock her in a room."

Kita gave me a shocked, wide-eyed look.

"You want her to be safe, don't you?"

"She must learn." She sounded defensive.

"Yes. She must learn to listen and stop making people angry. I want you to help me stop her getting into trouble. I want her to return home safely."

She held the youngster to her chest, the first time I'd seen her even touch the child in any kind of protective gesture.

Idda looked shaken, shoulders hunched, head low. She was shivering in her wet clothes.

"Go and dry her. Hey." I patted Idda on the head. Her coarse hair felt rough against my fingers. "It's not so bad. I just want you to keep out of trouble. Get dressed and come down to breakfast. Wear appropriate clothing."

I went back down the hallway.

Ayshada stood at the top of the stairs, imitating the snorting Pengali laughter.

I had to bite my lip to keep a straight face.

In the foyer downstairs, Karana and Eirani were already helping the poor receptionist clean up the mess. Because that was what they did: clean up and do the thankless jobs. I should make sure that Eirani got out of the trip what she wanted.

We went into the dining room, which looked pristine with its cloth-covered tables with gold-rimmed cups and white plates.

Thayu had come down, looking much better and healthier than yesterday, and the Pengali were just coming into the dining room as well.

At least all of them had put on adequate clothing in the form of the clothes we had made for them. Normally, in Barresh, both Pengali men and women wore exceedingly short skirts that allowed free tail movement, and most of the time they went without shirt or wore tiny singlets that were loose to the point of being purely ornamental. No one in Barresh had an issue with it. Pengali had patterned skin; it was not uncommon for women to go bare-breasted, and clothes were superfluous in that climate anyway. But it was cold here, and people got upset with nudity, so we had some more formal clothing designed based on the uniform worn by the Pengali who worked for the Trader Guild and the single Pengali Trader.

I explained the menu choices to the Pengali. They were disappointed that there was no fish. I'd definitely have to talk to the hotel about that, if the goldfish in the foyer were to hang on to their fragile goldfish lives.

But there were eggs, and this, apparently, was another thing that Pengali enjoyed. They also understood the concept of eggs, and agreed that it was food. They wanted them cooked, fried, poached or raw, and they each piled huge tottering mountains of eggs onto their plates, containing enough bad cholesterol to give a normal person a heart attack in five seconds flat.

I didn't know how much they had slept overnight, but I had warned Abri that any meetings and the court proceedings would take place during the day, and she seemed to have understood that. Or so I hoped. They were chatty. They laughed, and ate with their fingers.

Veyada sat with the security people, and Mereeni was attempting to talk to Jemiro. I had no idea how successful she was, but he listened to her, and nodded, lips pressed together.

He wore his dark hair slicked back from his forehead, with curls tickling the collar of his shirt.

He must have finished eating; he sat straight like a rod, clutching his reader. He wore—of all things—an earthly business suit. It was a dark grey number, made from the smooth and slightly shimmering fabric that I had seen men in the street wearing yesterday.

Where had he obtained that? Then another thought: his family was in the restaurant business. If he was involved with Jasper Carlson, it could be that his family was involved with another slightly dubious character in Barresh: Huang Le, who owned the first-ever interplanetary Chinese restaurant, who was not favourably disposed towards *gamra* and who wanted nothing to do with any of us.

Hmmm. Another tick against Jemiro.

So far, Jemiro had not *acted* in a suspicious way. In fact, he seemed rather thick to me. Maybe I was wrong. Maybe he was putting on an act, but if someone *did* want to act so as not to draw suspicion to themselves, then they would not portray themselves as a person as weird as Jemiro, would they?

Sheydu, Reida, Deyu and Telaris hadn't turned up yet.

I felt nervous throughout breakfast and let the chatter of our company wash over me. Thayu and Nicha were probably the only ones who noticed, and they didn't say much either. Both ate a lot more than I did, which wasn't unusual.

Towards the end of breakfast, when I sat sipping tea, a member of the hotel staff came to tell me that someone was waiting for me.

I rose and went to Abri. She, too, seemed a little quiet, her hands folded on her knees. It *had* to be intimidating to her, knowing that she was appearing as a witness in a process she didn't understand, while also carrying the expectations of the tribe, to get justice for crimes against the Pengali, on her shoulders.

I had to admit that the prim dark blue shirt, albeit very proper, didn't look natural on her and she kept pulling the sleeves as if the fabric irritated her. Veyada came with me as well, and Mereeni.

He glared at her.

She glared back at him and said to me, "Why does he need to come?"

Veyada said to her, "I'm a lawyer just as much as you are."

And she addressed me again. "He knows nothing about local laws."

"That is not for you to decide," Veyada said. "I know all laws well enough that I can make all legal notes for our association, and none of this is any of your business anyway."

I called out, "Stop it, stop it!"

Veyada looked down.

"What is going on? Just settle whoever is superior, and stop acting like this."

"I'm sorry. It is unprofessional of me. I will try not to let it happen again."

That reply disturbed me. That was not the measured, well-educated, emotionally stable Veyada I knew, and it disturbed me, because this went into that deep secret area that I could never come close to understanding, that governed Coldi relationships to each other: the all-pervading *sheya* instinct. In this case, it kept misfiring for Veyada, since Mereeni didn't even have the instinct.

Well, this meeting with the lawyer was going to be interesting. I made sure that on our way out of the dining room, I walked in between those two.

We gathered in a little group in the hallway.

I said to them, "I hope you are all ready to start today."

"I am," Veyada said.

"I am," Mereeni said at exactly the same time.

And then they eyed each other over Abri's head.

Abri pursed her lips, oblivious to the uneasy exchange. "This is a strange place." Her eyes were so large they were like mirrors, showing me my own reflection.

"Are you unhappy about anything?"

"People tell us not to do so many things. People ask strange questions."

"Yes, but answer them truthfully, and they will be happy."

"They don't want to hear our story."

"They do. They just have their own processes in dealing with it."

"I need to ask my daughter to come. I need to get Ynggi with—"

"This is not the official trial yet. Today, we're just meeting a person who is going to tell us how the process is going to work."

She frowned. Her tail wriggled behind her. I thought it indicated a state of uncertainty.

Kita came to the door to the dining room, looking into the hallway. Ynggi was there, too, and Idda, wriggling her tail as well.

That was evolution in action. A black and white banded object attracted attention, even in dim light. Fast movement indicated distress. Others were cued to act on it.

Damn. Clearly this morning's episode with the fishpond had shaken them more than was evident on the surface.

I attempted to put them at ease. "This won't be the official meeting. I will make sure that you can all come to the court hearing. I will promise that." They might have to hide Idda and give her something to make her sleepy, but I'd make sure that the tribe's customs would be adhered to. That was the very least I could do for them. "Today, I will take just Abri and Ynggi. I want Ynggi to check how well Jemiro translates."

They agreed with solemn faces.

Veyada and Mereeni had gone ahead to the foyer and already

waited there, each on a different couch, keeping as far away from each other as possible. Jemiro stood at the edge of the pond with his hands in his pockets.

There was also a woman in a long pale coat, standing in front of the window. That had to be the assistant to Conrad Martens. She had been looking at the street or the canal but turned around when we came in.

She was tall, slender, perhaps in her late thirties or early forties. She had straw-coloured hair, hanging down in two straight curtains on both sides of her head. Her eyes were pale blue and unusually far apart.

Her face showed no sign of emotion when she spotted Abri, although her gaze lingered on her longer than me.

"Mr Wilson, I presume?"

"That is right. This is the witness, Abri, her assistant, Ynggi, and my legal team, Veyada and Mereeni." *Team*, ha, ha, ha. "And this is Jemiro Pakiru, our official translator."

She glanced at Jemiro and her eyes widened briefly. I made a guess that Jemiro's outfit did not pass the *acceptable* test.

"My name is Lenka Trnkova, assistant to the prosecutor. I'll be running you through the court procedure and witness account today."

"Do you work for Conrad Martens?" I had hoped to finally meet the man. He seemed a reasonable person and could help us get some issues sorted. That of communication, for one.

"Dr Martens is no longer assigned to this case."

What?

"No one told me about this. I spoke to him only. . ." It would have been a couple of days ago, a week at most, and there was no indication that he'd leave. "Why did no one tell me?"

"Just an internal clash of commitments. It shouldn't affect you or the witness."

"But why?" There went my hope to have someone represent us who had experience with off-Earth people.

"Just a rescheduling, nothing major."

"Does this happen a lot?" I was trying to gather the pieces of my rattled mind. Conrad Martens had told us that not many other lawyers had his level of experience.

"A bit."

Not half as often as she said it would, I bet.

"So who is the new prosecutor?"

"Dr Timothy Cross. He is extremely experienced and fair, and I'm sure that if Mr Davidson is to get convicted, he is one of the best to put together the case. He has received all the notes Dr Martens has made and will be carrying on with the work in the same manner."

"Why hasn't he contacted me?"

"The work *will* be continued in the same manner. You are a very busy man, and he will be following Dr Martens' notes, so he probably judged it better not to disturb you."

Rubbish. "I'm not particularly happy about this. Let him know that when you see him. We'd also like to see him as soon as possible."

She nodded, her lips pressed together.

Damn it, Conrad Martens was known as having represented *gamra* people fairly in previous cases. He appeared to have some understanding of the different customs.

Ms Trnkova took us to a small conference room on the ground floor of the hotel, which contained only an oval table surrounded by chairs and a light board on the wall, which was off.

We sat down. I ended up facing the window, which looked out over a courtyard at the back of the building. A delivery truck was unloading bags of laundry.

She turned on the light board. It displayed Abri's statement that I had taken in Barresh and recorded in the presence of an official *gamra* observer. She went through every word and sentence of the statement, asking if Abri had anything to add, and trying to find ways to disprove what Abri had seen.

Ynggi, listening through a translation device that allowed him to understand the rough meaning of the speech, signalled a few times that he thought Jemiro did a competent job of translating her words and Abri's replies.

Abri fidgeted through much of this and glanced at me several times.

Then Ms Trnkova asked how well Abri knew Gusamo Sahardjo, and asked if she knew the value of sky stones—blue diamonds—on Earth.

Abri said that she knew but did not understand why people made such a fuss over the stones. "They are only valuable in the land where they have grown. Kasamo knew that. He did not take stones. He taught our youngsters funny tricks."

Ms Trnkova went through the effort of explaining why blue diamonds were of so much value. Months ago, in Barresh, I had tried the same, but had given up. Abri would not understand why people would attach so much value to something that had lost its value by removing it from its place of origin and that was good for nothing except decoration. When you thought about it, that attitude held a good deal of common sense and also said a lot about Pengali. They became emotional over *people* and *places*, but cared little about property.

Then Ms Trnkova went into how Abri had not actually witnessed the killing of Gusamo Sahardjo, so how had she concluded that he had committed the crime.

Abri grew agitated.

"You talk about this man. You talk about Kasamo only. Hairy face kill several of our people. No one ask about that. We did not see that he kill Kasamo, but we know he kill Pengali people. We saw it. We can prove it." Robert's victims had been Washing Stones Pengali, and I found it satisfying that in the face of a bigger enemy, Pengali banded together, even two tribes normally hostile to each other.

"But the trial is not about that," Ms Trnkova said.

"It is what we saw. It is important that story is heard," Abri insisted. "It proves that hairy face is a bad man."

"Well, I can ask." Ms Trnkova's voice sounded awkward.

At this point, I probably should have reminded Abri that she had agreed to answer the court's questions. I had already explained that the case would be about Gusamo Sahardjo and not about the murdered Pengali, that the story of those murders was not particularly relevant to the case in question, and that an additional case might well start later, if the Pengali could negotiate it with Nations of Earth.

But what was the value of this trial anyway?

The prosecution's case was weak and they clearly knew it. They did not want to consider evidence that was stronger based on technicalities—the victims were not citizens of Earth and no Earth-based investigators had heard that evidence.

So I asked why the murders of the Pengali were not included, and Ms Trnkova grew flustered. She said something about Dr Martens wanting to do that, but running out of time. It didn't sound terribly convincing.

Abri was unhappy, glaring across the room, her arms crossed over her chest. Her tail stuck out of the hole in the back of the chair and waved at waist height, occasionally producing a little snap.

She spoke to Ynggi in Pengali a few times, and neither Ynggi nor Jemiro offered a translation. I thought I picked up the word "out" in their speech.

This was not going well.

I said to Ms Trnkova, "At least let her tell their story and record it."

Ms Trnkova agreed to do that.

I felt sorry for her. I would have liked to ask her what she thought of the new prosecutor, but I guessed she wouldn't be so unprofessional as to reply to that question, therefore I probably shouldn't be so unprofessional as to ask it.

So Abri described how young men from the tribe had seen the murders of the Pengali trackers. Apparently, when Melissa had gone looking for Robert because his wife had reported him missing, and a search of satellite footage had turned up the location of his boat, Thousand Island Pengali had been watching from a distance because the trackers were from the Washing Stones tribe and they were trespassing on tribal land. They had witnessed that Robert had shot the trackers as they were trying to escape.

I had heard this story a few times before, and it had never varied. Pengali were known for their storytelling as means of communication.

"To tell the story properly, we need betanka," Abri said. "Only then can the truth be heard."

Ynggi nodded sagely.

"We put it in betanka. Hairy face can respond. We will report truthfully to the Washing Stones elders. It will give us much *karrit* points that we need so that our craftspeople can come to Barresh again to sell our wares."

Wait—*karrit* were points that every Pengali, indeed every person, built up during their lives. There were points for good deeds, points for being honourable, for repaying favours, for always telling the truth.

Word went that when the Pengali Office in Barresh had accepted electronic data systems, this was the first thing they'd done with it:

make an intricate system of all the *karrit* points that every citizen of Barresh had. It, more than anything, determined how keen Pengali were to do business with a person.

The Pengali themselves built up huge reserves of these points in their lifetimes, because the more points, the better the position in the tribe. The more points, the better the tribe would look after you when you were old and needed help.

I'd never realised that not just individuals, but also tribes built up these points.

Ms Trnkova said that she'd try to get the story covered. Clearly she had no idea what betanka was. I didn't think she was unsympathetic, just hamstrung by the rigid process.

The meeting was finished, and the delicious smells of lunch wafted into the room when Jemiro opened the door and was the first to leave. The Pengali left after him, followed by Veyada and Mereeni.

I remained alone in the room with Ms Trnkova.

"Unfortunately, we cannot cover crimes against non-Earth citizens," Ms Trnkova said, her voice low. "I'm sorry, but we can't. We're not set up for that. I thought you would understand that."

"I do, and the Pengali probably understand as well." At some level, maybe, hopefully. "But they want their grievances heard."

Those light blue eyes met mine in a brief moment. One human to another. She nodded. "I will see if I can put a word in. But do understand that if the story is told, it may not have any influence on the hearing."

"I understand. Thank you. I'm sorry about the trouble we are giving you."

A tiny smile crossed her face. "I've seen much worse. To me, the case is quite interesting."

She didn't know by half how interesting.

Then I asked, "One thing I've been meaning to ask. I was on that boat that came to the island when Robert shot at us and later at Melissa. I also saw the beisili throwing around Gusamo's body, and I saw the camp where Gusamo spent the last days of his life. Why didn't the prosecutor call me to the court? Make no mistake, I wouldn't have been keen to do it, but it seems to me that I should have been called."

She looked at me with those pale eyes, and then looked away.

"Between Abri and Ms Heyworth, the prosecutor must have considered that he had covered all the angles he needed."

"*Must have?*"

A small shrug. "I don't know. I'm a legal assistant. It's his case and he makes decisions and has no obligation to discuss them with me beforehand."

"I understand, but if it were your case, wouldn't you have called me, especially since I was going to be coming here anyway?"

"Time in the courtroom is very expensive. We're not encouraged to bring in witnesses who double up stories, and that's to put it mildly."

So it was all to do with the bureaucracy of funding? I found that a bit hard to believe. "It wouldn't have had anything to do with the fact that I don't work for Nations of Earth anymore, would it?"

"That certainly makes things harder."

"But not impossible?"

"Of course not. We've got Abri here."

"Or would it have been because I tend to say inconvenient things?" I could never say "convenient" without being reminded of its sexual double meaning in Coldi.

"You would have been questioned on the case only, so I can't see how that would have been a consideration." But her cheeks flushed with red, which had to be a disadvantage of being as pale-skinned as she was.

"Well then, thank you. Will we see Dr Cross before the hearing?"

"Oh yes, but the next step is to wait for the witness to be called."

"Will that happen this afternoon?"

"No. You'll get notice on the afternoon of the day prior to the hearing. Tomorrow maybe. If you haven't heard by five this afternoon, then it will be the day after. We will send someone to pick you up from here and take you to the courthouse. When you get there, I will be there, and Dr Cross will meet you there, too."

"All right."

Ms Trnkova rose, turned off the light board and gathered her reader and put it in its case.

But I wasn't finished. I asked her, as casually as I could, "I heard that there is a large crowd gathered outside the courthouse's entrance.

Is that going to affect our ability to get in? The Pengali are not terribly fond of crowds."

She gave me a startled look. "Oh, the protesters? You don't need to worry about them. You'll have access to the back entrance of the building and you won't have anything to do with them."

At least she didn't deny that these people were there.

"But what do they want? Why are they there?"

"They are political activists, and they're protesting about a matter unrelated to the court case. Mr Davidson and the Execo board run several mines of rare earths in various countries in southern Africa. Strange rumours are flying about the company's involvement in the government debts in various countries, and controversy about the treatment of their workers. A collapse occurred in a poorly built mine in Namibia last year and a lot of people died. Their families demand answers and compensation. As I said, it's got nothing to do with this case, but Robert Davidson is a recluse and this is the only way people can get a glimpse of him. They're in for the publicity, but the whole area has been declared a dead zone for that reason. I guess you have noticed that."

"We have." And was that really the main reason?

But I didn't ask further. She seemed cooperative and I didn't want to put her in a spot about matters that had nothing to do with us and that she might not even know anything about.

"Dr Martens said that the hearing would be completed in a day and half. Is that still the plan?" I wanted to take the Pengali and Jemiro and Amarru's people back to the Exchange and then get a flight to New Zealand for the rest of us. I'd like to book that as soon as I could.

"Probably. Look, I can't promise anything, because it's up to the judges. They may have additional questions, or may want to hear additional testimonies—"

Someone knocked on the door, which stood ajar.

Ms Trnkova whirled around.

I said, "Come in, it's open."

The door creaked open letting in Odette in her receptionist uniform. "I'm sorry to interrupt, Mr Wilson. I have Mr Kluysters waiting to talk to you."

I guessed this was the business contact that the receptionist had told me about.

"Can he wait a moment until I've finished this meeting?"

Ms Trnkova pushed herself up from the table. "No, you should talk to him now. We've pretty much finished anyway. I'll see you tomorrow, probably."

She smiled at Odette, picked up her bag and left the room. Too quick, too nervous. She was so keen to get out of here all of a sudden. Did she know who this person was?

9

———————

I **FOLLOWED ODETTE** out of the room through the hall to the reception area. She opened a door for me behind the reception counter. It gave access to a narrow hallway with store rooms on both sides: cleaning equipment, laundry bags and surplus items of furniture all stood crammed into the small and darkened rooms.

Odette took me to a room that was bigger than the others, at the end of the hallway. It had windows near the ceiling. I guessed it had once been a laundry, but now it had been turned into the hotel's communication hub. A cabinet against the wall contained all the on-site data storage and a long desk against the other wall was filled with equipment for surveillance and communication. It disturbed me that most of it was unfamiliar to me.

A screen at the far end displayed the interior of a light-filled room. A man sat in front of the camera, speaking to someone out of view. He was perhaps in his fifties, with short salt-and-pepper hair, a short beard and sharp eyes. He wore a neat business shirt. I had never seen this man before, but his face was pleasant and intelligent.

The person off-screen in the room with him—a woman by the sound of the voice—said something; I guessed it was about me having appeared on the display. He turned to the screen.

"Mr Wilson?" His voice sounded pleasant.

"Yes, that's me."

His eyes scanned my appearance while I sat down.

My hair was long enough to fit into a Coldi-style ponytail. I'd treated my face so that I no longer had any facial hair. I wore Domiri clan earrings with red gemstones—a different earring in each ear because I had a partner. I wore *gamra* blues, and even my thicker shirt was much more ornamental and flowery than was customary for business attire on Earth.

Often, when meeting with Earth business people, they seemed confused about my appearance, or they would think that I was part of the creative design community and would be taken aback when they heard who I was. But he showed no sign that he disapproved of it.

"My name is Minke Kluysters, CEO of Sandowne Pharmaceuticals. In case you are unfamiliar with the company, we specialise in nanomedicine and bioprocedures."

"I have heard of the company." It was one of the largest and most powerful in the world. CEO? I had never seen this man before, nor heard his name.

"That's good. It makes my life easier." He smiled.

His accent was unfamiliar to me, short and clipped, but it suited him and the businesslike demeanour well.

"Well, then, let me start with the reason why I'd like to talk to you: my company is interested in establishing a presence in Barresh. Our research team is interested, in particular, in some of the medicinal components that can be found in highland vegetation in Miran. They would like to establish an office or research post in Barresh, because I understand that Miran is not an easy place to do business."

He had that right, but his reasoning appeared to have missed several crucial steps. "Forgive me for saying so, but that will probably be the least onerous consideration. It's next to impossible to establish a formal business presence in any *gamra* entity without being a member."

"I understand that there *are* a couple of businesses owned by people from Earth."

"True. In two cases, the business owners have cut all ties with Earth, and in both of those cases, I couldn't vouch for the legality of their activities." Those were Huang Le and Clovis Keneally. There was also Jasper Carlson. "In another case, I'm not sure of the person's affiliation. There is also an academic."

"Ah, Benton Leck."

"You know him?"

"We've met."

"Apart from Leck, whose employment is governed by the knowledge exploration agreement, all the others don't have a formal framework for their interaction with Earth. They don't import or export legally, because Earth is not a member of *gamra*."

He reached out of the field of view of the screen, and set a bowl on the desk in front of the camera. I recognised the style: it was a Pengali artefact from the Washing Stones tribe's diamond cutting facility.

He said, "Of course people import and export *illegally*."

He picked up his reader and held the screen to the camera. On it was an official Trader Guild transfer sheet, covering a box of these bowls, from Barresh to Athens.

Well . . . damn it.

"I want to know how they did this. I will send you the document, but I can verify that it's not falsified. There must be a loophole that allows him to do this."

I checked the name on the document . . . Clovis Keneally. "Well, I don't know that this was done legally. . . ." Knowing Clovis, my guess was not, but that Trader Guild transfer sheet . . .

"Whether it was or not, I want to know. This is a consulting job for you. I am prepared to pay well if you can find out how he did this. If we know and it's done legally, we can establish an office Barresh, which would benefit all involved. I am certain that we could import these components under the exemptions to the import restrictions. The medicinal components we are looking at are to treat diabetes and certain types of cancers and they will classify as humanitarian."

True, humanitarian substances could be imported under Earth's law, but that didn't mean they were exempt from export under *gamra*, because they didn't like things leaving the system and going to nonmember entities. Miran, Barresh's agricultural and quiet sleeping-giant neighbour, was more precious about it than most. I guessed he was right in that if Clovis did this, and he had a proper Trader Guild document to prove it, his process warranted investigation. Never mind that I didn't think there was anything legal about it. "Do you have this proposal in writing?"

"Sure. I will send that to you as well. I'd like to move on this soon."

"I would like to have some time to think about it." I should mention this offer to my association to see if they had any issues with it before accepting it as a consulting job.

"That is fine. As long as we get an answer within the next few days."

As soon as he signed off, the message with both documents appeared on my reader. The Trader Guild document looked genuine to me. As far as I knew Earth had an import and export code with the Trader Guild, but the status was "restricted". Maybe Clovis had found a way of circumventing the rule, possibly to have the cargo classified as "humanitarian". Pharmaceuticals that saved people's lives could be governed by exceptions, except *gamra* would not want the material exported to a nonmember entity. The Trader Guild was its own entity and maybe it had its own agreement with Earth. I had no idea about things like that.

I'd pass this to Veyada, to see if he could find out what was going on or if it was wise to take this consulting job. Hell, I'd like to know how that permit came about, and I was sure some other people would like to know. And I could use the money to plug the hole in my budget, and we'd all be happy.

But I was suspicious.

Unfortunately, if things seemed easy, they rarely were.

It was lunchtime and, when I walked back to the dining room, I met Abri standing in the hallway, as if she was waiting for me.

"Is there a problem?"

"We need to go fishing. We have all the fishing gear, but we need to know where the best places are."

"That's not necessary. You smell that? The kitchen is already cooking lunch."

"We need fish."

"But there will be fish. I asked the cook. He said he'd get us as much fish as possible."

"But . . ."

"Don't worry. There will be plenty of fish."

"We need fish," she insisted. "Tomorrow we have our story heard, the lady said. We need to bring a fish to please the claimants, Kasamo's family and other associates."

Oh damn, I saw now. They wanted to present the court with a fish as they had given me one. "The customs are different here. You don't need to do that."

"You misunderstand." Her eyes were intense. "These people may not think that it's necessary. But *my* tribe thinks it is."

Karrit points again.

I sighed. "All right. Let me look into it. I'm sure we can get a fish for you somewhere." Maybe I should pay a visit to the kitchen. The cook might be able to help.

"No, you still misunderstand. *We* must catch the fish."

"But . . ." I spread my hands. I'd wanted to say *But we're in the middle of a city,* and *We have no time for that,* but that would not hold any water with the Pengali. I let my hands sink. "I'll think of something."

She nodded, her face prim.

Damn it, damn it, another thing to worry about.

We arrived in the dining room, where some of the team were already seated around the tables awaiting lunch. Thayu—busy with some kind of device—Veyada and Nicha, the latter with Ayshada. Jemiro, at a table by himself. Eirani and Karana were in the hall; Devlin, the guards and Reya were probably upstairs. Mereeni was just coming down the stairs.

Also missing were the other Pengali. Surely, they were interested in lunch—or had they gone to sleep after someone had told them that the court didn't require them until tomorrow? I'd ask Abri about it, but she was now talking to Mereeni, and then she went upstairs.

I sat down with Veyada and Amarru's two lawyers, meeting Thayu's eyes across the room. It was work time, and her work was security. Mine was the trial and Abri's witness account. We'd have a proper holiday once we got to my father's place.

Readers were put on the table and plates pushed aside.

"What are your thoughts about this morning?" I asked, looking around the table.

Mereeni said, "I don't think Abri's witness account is strong."

We'd discussed this several times already, while we were still in Barresh, but of course Mereeni had not been there.

She continued, "There is plenty of evidence that Robert is a real piece of work, but none that he killed Gusamo specifically, although it wouldn't surprise me at all if he did. I don't know what evidence

Melissa will have presented that we don't have, but I don't see how the judges could conclude that he is Gusamo's killer."

"On Asto, a case like this would never stand up as writ," Reya said. "There is just not enough evidence."

They discussed that for a bit.

I said, "I'm wondering what the trial is really for."

Frowns.

"What could it be for except to get justice for Gusamo's family?" Reya asked.

"I'm not sure. That's what I wish I knew." Why would Nations of Earth go through all this expense for a trial that was unlikely to deliver the justice they wanted? Why would they replace the prosecutor who had a decent chance of getting it for them? Was this what Margarethe wanted to talk about?

Veyada snorted. "I thought I understood this world, but the ways of these people are mysterious to me."

"That makes two of us, then."

He grinned. "You should really take Asha up on celebrating your formal induction into the Domiri clan."

Yes, I should. I understood that induction into a clan happened upon turning adult, or whenever needed in the rare cases where some of the clanless Coldi were assigned a clan. We would be a one hundred percent Domiri family. Thayu was Domiri and our child would be Domiri, regardless of the gender.

I mentioned Minke Kluysters to my team. I had not expected Veyada or Nicha to know his name, but even Reya and Mereeni came up with a blank.

"He says he's the boss of Sandowne Pharmaceuticals."

Reya's mouth from a soundless O.

"You know him?"

"Well, if he's the same one, he's also on the board of Execo."

Robert Davidson's company. Right. "So, what should I do? Trust this as an honest job?"

"He's probably trying to make you see the business favourably."

"So you think he's dishonest?"

"Not based on this, but you don't need his money," Veyada said.

"Actually, we could use it. The budget is going to be interesting this year."

"Then just ask Ezhya for more."

"For people *I* have employed?"

"Why not?"

Because silly humans found it crass to ask for money. I blew out a noisy breath through my nose.

I guessed Veyada wasn't in favour of the job.

The waiters came to serve lunch, which, for our table, involved vegetable patties with mushrooms and salad and toast. I had to commend the cook for having made an effort to understand Coldi tastes.

When sitting with Coldi, it was rude to eat meat of vertebrate animals, so I also got a vegetable patty, which turned out to be just a "little bit" spicy.

This cook definitely understood Coldi. I hazarded a guess that they hired a Coldi cook. There was also the promised fish for the Pengali, beautifully steamed white fish in a giant tray.

Except the Pengali themselves still hadn't turned up.

Nicha said, "Well, they got their fish, now where are they?" He sounded a bit annoyed. Ayshada was standing on the seat of his chair, wanting a piece of said fish.

"Why don't you give it to him?" Veyada said, eying the fish himself.

Nicha made a helpless gesture. He'd grown up in a fairly orthodox household with his mother in London, where she had drummed into him that Coldi were *not* like those disgusting humans from the very moment that he could understand. Some of the habits he found hard to shake. He didn't like fish, he'd told me, but I'd never seen him try it either.

Veyada rose and helped himself to a chunk of fish, and brought one for me. He gave a small piece to Ayshada who put it in his mouth with both his chubby hands.

"Abri said that the Pengali need to catch a fish to bring as a present for the court," I said, cutting into the soft flesh.

Where *were* those Pengali? Surely they could smell the fish from upstairs?

Veyada nodded, in thought. "I was wondering if something like that was going to come up."

"What should we do about it?"

"We can buy a fish," Nicha said.

"But they need to catch it. Abri wants to go fishing."

"Some of the fish markets let you catch your own. I presume they still do that?" He glanced at Mereeni, who nodded.

"It's a good idea, but is there time to find a fish market?"

"We can try this afternoon—uh-oh."

I turned around. Devlin had come into the room, his trousers dripping wet.

I thought of the poor goldfish in the pond in the foyer, or the canal across the road.

I rose, heart thudding. "What's going on?"

"It is that brat. She managed to detach a piece of metal from the wall in the bathroom in the Pengali room and now there is water coming out and we can't stop it."

"Show me."

We left the dining room. I stopped at the reception on the way, and suggested that they might call a plumber because there might be a leak. I checked the status of the goldfish—they were still swimming around. Phew.

While the hotel staff scrambled to find someone to check it out, I followed Devlin upstairs. In the corridor I could already hear the sound of gushing water and voices.

Abri stood just inside the door. Her mouth fell open when I came in, fearful almost. I strode past into the bathroom, where Kita and Ynggi were trying to push the tap back onto the wall. Each time they pushed the metal against the hole, the water squirted everywhere. The floor was covered, the towels were dripping, the ceiling was wet.

I went back to the room's entrance where I opened the cupboard door. With a bit of luck—ah, yes, there it was. I turned the tap. The noise in the bathroom stopped.

At that moment, someone knocked on the door. I opened it, finding a man in overalls in the hallway. "Problem with the taps?"

"You can say that again."

Ynggi came out of the bathroom. He was soaked, and had seen the sense to take off his clothes. That was what people would do in Barresh.

But the technician's eyes widened at the sight of a slight, humanoid figure with giraffe-patterned skin and black-and-white banded tail who was otherwise completely naked.

Well, at least now I needed to field no more silly questions about whether Pengali were patterned *down there* because he could see that they weren't.

"He's here to fix it," I said in Coldi. Ynggi and Kita came out of the room, wet, shoulders slumped. They gathered around the table, where Abri sat on the tabletop, and avoided meeting my eyes.

I sat with Abri. "What's happened?"

Abri glanced up, but went back to staring at the table.

I was sure the table would not normally stand in this part of the room, where it blocked the way from the bathroom to the sitting area. The dining table chairs stood next to the window, with a blanket draped over the top of them to make a tent. I spotted a couple of pillows and sheets which had been pulled off the bed. It seemed that they had slept down there. Their bags stood in a neat row at the entrance of the tent. The *irrka* had been unpacked but not put together. The large central drum stood in the corner closest to the bathroom, where little depressions in the carpet indicated the usual position of the bed.

Abri said, "My granddaughter has not been very nice. Sorry."

"It's not your fault. You weren't even there."

Kita looked straight at me. *She* had been there, and it seemed she was finally starting to realise that we expected her to keep the little one's behaviour under control.

"Where is she?"

Abri pointed with her tail to the double bed—with sheets removed—in the corner. I dropped to my knees and could just make out something against the far wall at the very furthest point removed from me.

"Idda?" I stuck my arm under the bed, but couldn't reach her. "Idda, come here."

Abri said something in Pengali.

A little cold hand touched mine. I grabbed hold of it and slowly pulled the youngster out from under the bed. She climbed up my arm and clung onto my shirt, shivering. Once in my youth I'd had a friend whose brother kept snakes. He would get his friends to hold the mildly poisonous ones by putting the snakes in the fridge so that they grew sluggish.

Cold snake. That was what Idda's skin felt like. She wasn't even terribly wet after that adventure.

Obviously her clothes were not warm enough for her. She may have tried to turn the tap to get warm water. I remembered how stressed Nicha got if he was not warm enough. Pengali came from a warm climate and they weren't taking adaptation medication because adaptation medication didn't work on Pengali.

I should have realised this and should have made sure that they had plenty of warm clothes.

I was failing them.

"Mr Wilson, sir?" It was the technician, carrying his tool kit. "It's all fixed."

"Thank you for coming so quickly. I'm sorry about the mess."

He glanced at the tent in the room, but said nothing. He'd probably seen much stranger things that people did in their hotel rooms. "It's all right, Mr Wilson. The tap was probably loose anyway."

I saw him out of the room and then went back inside.

"Well, that's taken care of. Come down to lunch. There is a lot of really nice fish on the menu."

But my statement was met with sad looks from all three Pengali.

"That is *their* fish," Abri said. "It wouldn't be right to eat *their* fish. We should get our own fish to make this right."

10

THE PENGALI DID FINALLY come down to the dining room, and they did eat some fish, but they were very quiet. I told them several times that no one was asking them to bring food to make amends, and that people in the hotel understood that things broke when children played with them, but they kept talking about fishing.

"People here don't have that custom," I said to Abri.

"I am an elder. I must do the right thing, or I will lose *karrit* if I don't."

And *that* was an important consideration for Pengali.

There was no way around it except to take the Pengali fishing.

First, though, we had another problem to solve, and maybe we could walk past a fish shop to see if they had ponds where people could catch their own trout or lobsters. I didn't know if the shops around here were big enough. They probably got the fish from farms. Maybe customers went there.

I rose and explained to everyone that we had the afternoon off and that we were going to go shopping. People could come with us or stay here as they pleased.

The word "shopping" made Eirani's face light up. Evi wanted to come, as well as Amarru's guards, and everyone in my association. I suggested to Thayu that she stay here to rest, but she would have none of it.

I wondered how we were going to keep ourselves from attracting too much attention.

Most people on Earth were by now used to seeing Coldi without disguise. Coldi could comfortably disguise themselves as Chinese, if they dyed their hair black.

But most Coldi I knew who lived on Earth had stopped doing this years ago. Coldi hair had a strong metallic gleam, with highlights of purple, blue and green, a bit like the feathers on a peacock. Especially in sunlight it was quite distinctive. So many Coldi were on Earth now, and it was known who and what they were, so they didn't need to hide their hair colour anymore.

Pengali on a tram, however, proved to be an entirely different matter, which we found out when we got on the tram at the station in front of the hotel.

Not only were Pengali not familiar with the concept of trams—why was there no driver in the vehicle?—but more importantly, these types of people never came to Earth. In all honesty, I probably wasn't supposed to take them on a shopping trip, but if the court officials didn't want me to show them around, they should have given me orders to that extent.

There were a lot of us, too. Thayu and Nicha with Ayshada, Veyada, Evi and Amarru's two Indrahui guards. Jemiro and Reya and Mereeni chose to remain in the hotel, but everyone else wanted to come.

Because the weather had turned blustery and cold, everyone wore coats and jackets, warm jumpers and boots. Both Nicha and Thayu were wearing their temperature retaining suits.

Ayshada's pram had come with a soft and warm cover, and Amarru had provided us with a couple of jumpers and little jackets. Ayshada wasn't too excited about wearing them, because at home he usually ran around in singlets and shorts.

The passengers in the tram gave our mixed company wide berth. Some stared, some made an effort to look the other way. It was busy, there was not much room, and we were only going a few stops, so most of us stood near the entrance, laughing, chatting in languages these people had never heard before.

If Earth ever joined *gamra,* would that change?

In between getting on the tram and the next stop, we left the communication dead zone, and my feeder burst into life with thoughts from Thayu and Nicha. Veyada was there, too, and via him I even got a snatch from Sheydu who, apparently, had discovered something else she needed to do and might not be able to meet us today.

Security talk was always vague as hell and full of code, so I'd need to wait until Veyada explained what was going on, and there was no sign of him doing that. We were being monitored after all. In the central part of any city, there were security cameras on every lamp-post, in every vehicle, at every station. Cameras were also in almost all vehicles, including trams. Some of those were ours, but the rest was all controlled by Nations of Earth.

We got off the tram a few stops later and walked through the shopping district, which consisted of a whole city block of pedestrian traffic only, an open mall with quaint old shops. There was also an underground mall with all the modern trappings.

We found one fish shop, but it only had a sorry-looking aquarium with a couple of lobsters.

Abri wanted to know how long the creatures had been in the aquarium and was horrified to find that it was a couple of days. Then she wanted me to buy them so that she could release them, and they could be properly caught, but I explained that the canals were quite dirty and the water not warm enough for lobsters. Then she wanted to know where the lobsters came from.

"They *grow* these creatures? In ponds?" Her eyes were wide. "You don't need to *grow* them. They are wild animals. You catch them, and if they're big enough, you can take and eat them."

Trying to explain that the oceans were polluted and that lobsters otherwise couldn't live here at all was bound to fail, and it did.

And meanwhile the fish shop owner was looking at us, wondering when we were going to buy these lobsters, which I had no intention of doing.

The situation was uncomfortable, and I managed to get Abri out of the shop—still without fish.

Hopefully, finding better clothing was going to be easier.

Of course, this far into spring, all the clothing shops had long since sold out of winter gear, especially in the sizes we required. We wandered around a big multilevel store taking all the leftover items off the sales rack and dismissing them for being miles too big, when Idda came wandering through the aisle with a bright orange beanie pulled over her eyes. She bumped into things and tripped over the wheel of Ayshada's pram, but when I tried to take the beanie off her, or even just lift it so that she could see, she held it over her ears with both hands and her tail and squealed.

"Where did she get this?"

Kita pointed.

There was a rack with beanies, jumpers, jackets and scarves, all of them bright orange. Most items were adult size, but some were children's sizes. Many of the items displayed an embroidered logo that was also on the beanie on Idda's head: a black and white ball.

"This looks like some kind of sport supporter gear."

Of course that didn't translate well into Coldi, since the only word available for supporter meant both "army" and "gang" and Thayu gave me a strange look.

"It's for people who watch sports teams play."

"Like a race?" Racing things or obstacle courses was big on Asto. They raced on foot, running or carrying things, on bike-like contraptions and any type of vehicle you could imagine.

"Yes, like a race."

She snorted. "I think the colour is abhorrent."

"Idda likes it," Nicha said, appreciating, on behalf of another parent, that golden moment that a stroppy toddler found something to like.

Not much later I had bought the beanie, a little orange jumper that was still too big for Idda, and a fluffy zip-up orange jacket in adult size that could function as blanket to carry her. When you zipped it up, her head stuck out and the rest of her, including the tail, sat snugly in the body part. You could then use the sleeves to tie up the parcel or tie them around one's waist.

It was the first time since going on the trip that Idda looked genuinely happy. I felt sorry for her that I hadn't realised that she had been so cold, and carried her home. She rewarded me by falling asleep against my chest.

We were almost back at the hotel and were walking along the canal, when a man on the footpath in front of us decided to cross the road. That would have been fine had he looked over his shoulder, and even not having looked would have been fine if there hadn't been a taxi on the road.

It was a regular street bubble-car, moss-green, driverless. You told it where you wanted to go and it took you there.

It beeped.

The man froze. His eyes widened.

The taxi slammed on the brakes and screeched across the road like in the old movies, even if the new vehicles were no longer supposed to do that. Too late. The vehicle came to a halt with a sickening thud.

By this time, several people in my group were running.

The pedestrian was on the ground.

Veyada dropped to his knees next to him, and the man pushed himself up checking his arms, his legs. He had fallen in a puddle and was covered in mud. He had a few scrapes on his hands, but nothing serious.

Nicha retrieved a pack of moist towels that he always had ready to deal with Ayshada's messy eating habits. He helped the man wipe his hands and his face.

While all this was happening, the taxi's single passenger got out, ran to me, and pressed an envelope in my hand and ran off down the street.

What the. . . ?

I looked at the envelope.

There was no name or sender on the cover. The paper was thick and high quality, but felt like there was only one sheet of paper inside. I wanted to open it, but knew that the whole incident would be recorded and I didn't know where the cameras were and how good their resolution was, so instead I stuck it in the inner pocket of my jacket. I'd read it when we came to the hotel.

The members of my team had helped up the pedestrian, who assured that he was perfectly fine.

The taxi had already resumed its path, now without its passenger.

I glanced at Thayu.

We were already inside the dead zone, but the same question hovered in her eyes. *Did they just stage a mock accident just so that he could give that to me?*

It looked very much like it.

Everything would be monitored inside this area, and people who were not allowed to see us—and clearly there were such people—could not come in. Any unusual incidents would be logged, too, so even if the man in the taxi was an agent for someone, his identity would be known through the taxi, and any stoppage would be recorded. If there was no obvious reason for it, security forces could check out footage from various cameras. So he had created a reason to stop—an almost-accident.

Interesting.

The envelope burned in my pocket, but I resisted opening it until I was sure that no one on the street watched, and had reached an area that the guards had declared free of visual spying equipment. Also known as the bathroom.

And as I opened the enveloped and unfolded the single sheet inside, I knew that it was not from any of the people I would have expected to write: Margarethe, or Sheydu even.

The sheet was plain. The letter was handwritten in an unfamiliar hand, quite formal-looking.

It said,

Mr Wilson,

I wish to offer you my sincerest apologies that I was unable to continue to offer you my assistance with the witness' appearance in court. I don't know what the new prosecutor has told you about me, but I did not voluntarily step down from my involvement with the trial. As you know, cases involving *gamra* citizens have been my specialty for a while so it was natural that I was asked to look after it.

As the preparations for the trial progressed, I became aware that a lot of resources were being allocated to bringing you and the witness over. I argued against the exorbitant cost, and said that the witness could testify remotely. I've worked on a number of cases where this was done successfully, but the decision was made by the new Chief Judge that the testimony needed to be given in person. I put it down to her being traditional and new to the job. Because she had obtained funding to do so, I did not question this decision because it seemed in the interest of the fairness of the trial. In hindsight, I regret not spending the time to look into it.

I discovered the source of funding by chance, when doing administrative tasks for an unrelated matter. The court has a special account for sponsorships and donations, most of them political, and this is managed by Nations of Earth, because it should not be possible to trace individual donations to particular cases. But a lot of money suddenly appeared in that account prior to the trial and this was what was used to fund your trip.

I traced the influx of funding back to a company with known links to the Pretoria Cartel. I asked about this, and that's where things started to go bad for me.

Within days, I was contacted by several people with anonymous threats, and when I went to the Chief Judge with them, she suggested that I step down from the case. Even that was not an unusual request, because it is what would normally be expected, so I did, but I have since discovered a number of other disturbing things the nature of which I am reluctant to reveal to you in this manner.

I strongly urge you to contact me. I have paid a team of observers to keep track of your whereabouts. If you see an opportunity to speak to me, leave the dead zone and we will make contact. A warning: you may be curious about the presence of a crowd of protesters outside the court building, and you may feel that the people in charge of the trial are trying to keep you away from them. This is true. There are, amongst these people, certain individuals they would prefer to keep you away from. I have spoken to most of these people and, when we meet, I will inform you of their positions and opinions. It would be unwise to try to speak to the protesters yourself, as your minders will probably not take too kindly to it and may see cause to delay or even cancel the hearing.

The letter was not signed but I knew who this was from: Conrad Martens. And Robert Davidson was said to have been involved with the Pretoria Cartel, which was, from all I'd been able to track down, a group of very rich business owners, who were also said to have been behind the fielding of candidates against Margarethe purely to push through changes to further their businesses.

Make contact?

I was alone in the bathroom, because Thayu had met Evi in the hallway as we returned to the hotel, and he wanted to speak to her.

I glanced at the time. It was midafternoon. We had nothing to do for the rest of the day. People might have been watching us while we went shopping, but they also had not stopped us leaving the dead zone.

I guessed we could add in another tourist trip. I could even let the receptionist know that we were taking Ayshada to the beach and to let us know if anything came up. If Conrad Martens' people were shadowing us, they would follow and contact us when it was safe.

I went into the security room where I showed the letter to Thayu, Nicha, and Veyada. They nodded and said nothing, because we knew someone listened somewhere.

I asked, "That tram line to the beach, did you find out where it leaves from?"

Nicha said, "Not yet, but I can do that now. Did you want to go today?"

"It doesn't sound like we'll be needed until tomorrow. I want to spend a bit more time with Abri, but I can do that tonight. We can get that trip in now. I've always wanted to go back to that place where I came with my father."

And so we got organised.

The Pengali wanted to go to bed. I reminded them again that the court sessions would happen during the daytime and that this was when we were likely to be needed. They said they understood, and wanted to go to sleep anyway.

Amarru's lawyers had some job to do. I went to speak to Devlin and asked him to find as much as possible about the protesters at the courthouse: who they were and why they were there. He asked if he should establish contact.

"Is that even possible?" I asked him. "I mean, without attracting too much of the wrong sort of attention?"

"Everything is possible." He gave me a sage look.

I didn't know where he had gotten this smug confidence, but I told him that contacting the protesters wasn't necessary now. I'd want to see what Conrad Martens had to say about them, and then decide if I needed to take the risk.

I told Devlin to continue finding information about Sandowne Pharmaceuticals and Minke Kluysters, because a first probe had proven that information fairly elusive, and to help Reya and Mereeni, who were going to write answers to some of the potential questions that the prosecutor and the defence lawyers were going to ask Abri. They were unsure whether she would need to stand in the witness box alone—the consensus was that she probably would—and wanted to talk her through all the possible questions, including the ones about character that would mess with the *karrit* system.

They assured me that they didn't need my help, and told me to go to the beach.

I just needed to make sure that everyone was looked after. Seriously, the bigger my team, the long it took us to accomplish *anything* as simple as leave the house.

Eirani wanted to go back to the shops, and Karana wanted to come with her. I told one of Amarru's guards to go with them. That flustered Eirani.

"Oh, Muri, I can look after myself."

"I know, but how well do you speak the language?"

"Oh."

I clearly had a point there, so one of the guards it was.

Those guards, and Devlin and Evi, had a job to do as well, but the members in the party were their priority, so Devlin and one of Amarru's guards would stay here, while Evi would come with us and the other guard would go with Eirani and Karana.

While I waited for Nicha to get Ayshada fed, I overheard Eirani and Karana talking about places where they could look at kitchen equipment.

I couldn't restrain a smile. I might have started something by taking her a bowl from Kedras a while back. My staff was nothing if not dedicated to their task. I would have to organise the purchase of some gadgetry for Devlin, because he looked like he *might* want to come shopping, too, but he'd gotten roped into doing some monitoring work for Amarru's guards, whatever security personnel were doing. It looked like even Jemiro was involved. I took one of Amarru's guards to the hallway and warned him that Jemiro might be compromised.

"The interpreter is not one of our regular contractors, and I did hire him from one of the more dubious Earth citizens in Barresh. I cannot guarantee that this man does not work for dubious sources." In fact, I was fairly certain that Jasper Carlson did.

The guard nodded, his obsidian face solemn. *"Mashara* is aware of that."

Meaning: stop double-guessing our job, Delegate.

Oh well, at least I couldn't be blamed for holding back information. Also, I was extremely glad that I was no longer talking to Evi and Telaris in these highly formal terms.

I wished Telaris would come back, and Sheydu, too. I missed her no-nonsense dry and sarcastic comments. Maybe she could have made a decent guess at what was going on. I missed Reida and Deyu, too. Every time I saw a seagull or a duck, I thought of her.

By now, the Pengali had all retreated into their room, including Idda; Mereeni and Reya sat in the small conference room surrounded by readers and projectors; Devlin and Jemiro were doing something else in the security room; and Eirani and Karana had left with their guard, so Thayu and I, Nicha and Ayshada, Veyada and Evi finally left the hotel.

We had rugged up pretty well, and Thayu looked cute with her face buried in a fluffy scarf. The weather had taken a turn for the worse, with low-hanging clouds and a cold wind pulling at trees and hair and clothing. Gusts of wind blew ripples across the water in the canal on the other side of the tramline.

A few people were at the tram stop, but without the Pengali we didn't attract a lot of attention.

Thayu stood with her hands deep inside her pockets. Both Nicha and Veyada used their eye movements to scan the area. Veyada wore the tiniest of earpieces, barely visible behind his ear lobe. It would be connected to his feeder and the data would be shared with the others as soon as we left the dead zone. I was curious about what they were listening to and who they thought was watching us, but I kept quiet so that they could do their job. I trusted that they'd tell me if there was something I needed to know, but I was wondering if I should maybe try to contract Margarethe while we were out of the dead zone.

Maybe. Maybe not, if there were really that many people watching us. I'd been told in a roundabout way that Sheydu was already doing that.

The tram took us through the centre of the town, along tree-lined boulevards with historical houses that had probably not changed much in the last two hundred years. I did seem to remember that the streets were more open, but that could be because I had been so much smaller, or it could be because the trees had grown and a lot of roadways had been turned into lawns. At one point, the tram even went through a forest, where the trees burst with fresh green leaves and lush grass, and dandelions grew in open patches.

We got off at a little station with a shelter amongst multi-storey residential buildings.

The wind picked up considerably here.

We were in yet another shopping precinct, but we turned into a narrow alley that opened out onto a wide boulevard where, directly ahead, the white-tipped waves of the North Sea met the leaden grey sky. Not the greatest day for a beach outing. At least it didn't rain.

The beachside boulevard was pretty much as I remembered it. Dozens of cafes sat on top of the sea wall overlooking the beach. Most of the patrons hid inside, but some of the establishments had put up glass shelters so that they retained the outdoors feeling.

Gusts of wind blew sand drifts over the pavement. It was really not the most pleasant of days.

Ayshada didn't care. He wanted to be let out of the pram and let us know this by squealing and arching his back.

As soon as Nicha undid the harness, he climbed out of the pram, ran across the paving and bolted down the stairs onto the beach. He actually fell the last step and landed face-first in the sand, and then rolled around squealing and laughing.

Thayu went down the steps and set him on his feet, only for him to roll over again.

She laughed. "Oh, come on, Ayshada!"

There would be sand everywhere tonight.

Nicha also came down the stairs. "Come on, let's build a sand castle. That's what people do, right?" He smiled at me. He knew this very well, having lived most of his younger years in Europe. He showed Ayshada what to do, and found him some shells and a washed-up sea star for decoration.

"So, what did you really think of that letter from Conrad Martens?" I asked Nicha, while Ayshada started pushing heaps of sand around at our feet.

He glanced at the boulevard above us, and the windows of the cafes. Checking for listeners.

"I don't understand. He seems to say that our trip here was paid for by the group whose member we've accused of murder. Robert is in the Pretoria Cartel and therefore the Pretoria Cartel are paying for us to come so that the best witness can be at the court . . . to prove that their member committed a murder. I don't understand it."

"I don't think Abri's story is particularly convincing."

"Better than anything else they've got. That's what I don't understand. If they wanted Robert to get off, they could have just . . . been happy with Melissa's evidence, which proves that Robert shot at her, but doesn't involve Gusamo, so Robert could get off with a fairly light sentence, and that would have been the end of it. Instead they call out Abri, who makes a reasonably decent case that Robert has murdered Gusamo, and they're paying for it. What's the deal? Did Robert fall out of favour with the group? Is this his punishment? If he did something they really didn't like, why spend all this money on the court? They could have hired an assassin and be done with it. Would have cost much less."

That would have been the Coldi solution. A writ to the person in question, and, if no favourable compromise was forthcoming, an assassin.

Bang. Problem solved.

I let out a breath. "I can't say I understand it either. I agree that it does look like Robert fell out with them. Maybe he threatened to reveal their secrets."

Thayu snorted. "They would have been even quicker with the assassin if that were the case."

True. "Maybe it has to do with his wife."

Fiona Davidson had run against Margarethe for the presidency of Nations of Earth, but she'd been considered a lunatic fringe candidate and hadn't come close to winning. She had been able to run because she had formally divorced her husband, but few people believed that the divorce was genuine. But what if those people were wrong and it was genuine, and she was angry at him for something and, within the marriage, she was the one most heavily involved in the Pretoria Cartel?

There were way too many open questions and I hoped that Conrad Martens would answer some of them for us when he turned up. Which he was not doing right now.

Evi and Veyada remained at the top of the stairs, watching all directions, ready to deal with any people coming to us.

I asked Thayu what they were watching.

She said, "We are getting many signals, just trying to determine which one is of interest to us is exhausting."

"But do you know how many people are watching?"

"There are at least two groups."

"Two? Our minders from Nations of Earth and Conrad Martens' people?"

"We're not sure about that. They're very secretive and use highly advanced equipment."

"Equipment? Locally made?" With Coldi spy routines, of course, so that was why my team could know this at all.

She shook her head. "It doesn't look like it."

"What do you mean? That it's *gamra* technology?"

"It means that they have very effective shielding or their transmissions are highly targeted, either of those more so than we'd expect from locally made equipment."

"And what does that mean?" I asked her.

"It could mean anything. Mainly, it means that we don't know who they are."

Damn.

I wanted to speak to Margarethe. I wanted to ask people what the hell was going on. I wanted to be done with the trial where I felt like we were a museum piece, a display exhibit under the control of someone else, if only we knew who.

A lone fisherman stood in the surf wearing galoshes and holding a rod. Occasionally, he would reel in his bait and toss it back out again with a swing of the rod. He didn't seem to be catching much. I had considered telling the Pengali before we left that we would be going to a place where they could catch fish, but now I was glad I hadn't. Pengali fished with spears and nets. I didn't think they would catch anything here in that way. Besides, the weather was foul, I didn't have any wet-weather gear to keep them warm and they would just be miserable as well as unsuccessful.

Nicha, Thayu and Ayshada really got into the sandcastle building. They dug moats, shaped mounds, found sea stars and shells to put on top.

Thayu's cheeks had gone pink with the chill air. When she bent over, I could see the temperature retaining suit under her clothes, but for once, she utterly enjoyed herself. Evi offered to get drinks and came back not much later with hot chocolate—made with soy milk for himself, because Indrahui didn't tolerate certain proteins.

Ayshada had been fast to cotton onto the idea of hot chocolate, and he came running when he spotted Evi with the cups.

We gathered in a group on the sand, wind-blown, red-cheeked, covered in sand. It was a joy to see their faces.

"Is this as you remembered this place?" Nicha asked.

"Mostly. My father and I came on the tram and then we walked along the waterfront. I remember going to a museum about a pier that used to be here but that got so badly damaged in a big storm that it had to be taken down. The weather was a lot nicer, and it was busy. We had to line up for a long time to buy chips."

Fish and chips, apparently, were still a thing, even if the chips now had to be hot-air fried by law, and the blustery weather had closed most of the beachfront booths. We traipsed off to one of the eating houses, where Ayshada stood on a chair looking into the kitchen where the cook tossed a basket of uncooked chips into the chamber where searing air blew them around in little eddies until they were golden.

It smelled so good that we all attacked when the big basket, steaming hot, was brought to the table.

By now, the sky was starting to darken. I figured we had better start making our way back soon, because the others would wonder where we were. Nicha wanted to put Ayshada to bed. Most importantly, our Nations of Earth minders would wonder where we were, and that might include some people we did not want to alert to the fact that I was in contact with Conrad Martens.

But someone should have contacted us here, and if they were going to show up, they'd better get on with it.

11

———

W E HAD JUST ABOUT eaten all the chips and Ayshada was picking the last crumbs out of the fish basket when a middle-aged man entered the cafe.

He sat down at a table behind me. The waitress came to bring him water and take his order. I glanced at him over my shoulder. I had spoken to Conrad Martens on a vid link a few times and didn't think that this was what he looked like. I'd have thought he was older than this man, but maybe this was an agent. Or maybe they were playing a game with us and this was just a member of the public.

In the window in front of me—behind which the sky darkened ominously, and in which I could see the reflection of the interior of the cafe—I spotted him picking up a reader and flicking through a few pages before looking at something in more detail.

Thay'? Is that him? I asked through the feeder.

She didn't know. He didn't have any particular devices on him that suggested so. Devices? Since when did they tell people's intentions by the devices they carried? That was Amarru's information through the little Coldi built-in routines again.

One day, I was going to have to delve into exactly what information the Exchange in Athens had about people and their electronic devices with computer chips, and, most importantly, the level of control they had over these devices. I strongly suspected that I wasn't going to like the answer, much as all that knowledge suited me at times, and much as it had never been a secret that they *did* have a lot of information.

But by now we had finished our meal, and we should be heading back. Ayshada was getting sleepy, and even allowed Nicha to strap him in the pram, as long as he had his blanket. I went to the counter to pay for the meals.

The man behind me didn't move or look at us. A member of the public then.

On our way to the door, we walked past his table. First Evi and then Veyada and then me. As I passed his table, he said, looking up at me, "Be careful when you go out there, especially with the kid. A lot of police are in the streets, especially at the tram terminal. They're obviously looking for some miscreant."

"Thanks for the warning. We'll avoid the terminal." It was further to the north, not where we had gotten off, and I didn't think we needed to go there anyway. But my heart jumped. Had something happened?

We filed out of the cafe, into the biting wind that whipped along the boulevard. It was fast starting to go dark. The ocean was black and the crashing waves sounded like thunder.

"What now?" I asked Thayu.

I shrugged. Whatever had happened, we'd obviously missed our contact.

"We need to go back to the hotel," Nicha said. "Devlin says there are some developments."

Thayu snorted. She looked at her reader, flicking through messages and news services. "There has been a shooting not far from here."

She showed me the screen with the news item. It was most handy that she had learned to read Isla to a functional level, even if she didn't speak it.

The news item spoke about a broad daylight murder of a prominent figure. There was no name mentioned, but my blood ran cold. How much would I bet that this was about Conrad Martens?

"Yes," I said. "We need to go back to the hotel."

In fact, it might have been exceedingly stupid to come here. I didn't need to voice my concerns, because the others had already been informed through my feeder. They shared my concern. Thayu quickly confirmed through Devlin that this was indeed about Conrad Martens. He had been killed when leaving his apartment building. The police were investigating. The news said nothing about the type of weapon. They had no suspect and no motive. I could give them some suggestions.

But . . . the Pretoria Cartel? Really? These were rich, smart business people with a lot to lose. They weren't going around shooting judges about to reveal things they didn't like.

Unless they *really* didn't like what he was about to tell me. Which was about those protesters in front of the court building, right?

We started walking down the boulevard to the street where the tram station was. Veyada and Evi walked at the front, then me and Nicha and then Thayu. I didn't like having her behind me, but I knew she had a weapon somewhere, and I had none. Besides, she was much better with a weapon, and she'd be safer at the back of the group than the front. I still didn't like it.

We were dealing with very dangerous people and we had no idea who they were, and whether the Pretoria Cartel was involved in any of it, and if so, how. Had Nations of Earth set up the dead zone for our safety but neglected to give us the accompanying warnings about leaving it?

The only one who was truly oblivious to the danger was Ayshada, asleep in the pram.

The clouds that had been threatening for most of the day decided to discharge their rain. It was cold and horrible. Warm light radiated from the windows of eateries and you could see people inside, but all the tourist shops had closed and many were dark.

Hardly anyone still walked along the boulevard. I felt stupid and horribly exposed. There could be snipers in any one of those apartments, or on any of the roofs. They could shoot us and no one would ever know who did it.

We walked under awnings, close to the display windows.

We went around the corner into the alley that took us to the tram stop, and then we ran out of shelter. The large exposed area was designed to handle the big crowds that came here in summer. The pavement was gritty with sand.

We didn't see any police although a siren issued short bursts of sound somewhere in a nearby street.

The tram station was empty, if well-lit. The shelter faced the wrong way to keep passengers out of the rain, so we huddled at the back of it.

A pillar displayed the timetable on a screen that cast a blue glow over the wet pavement. The news scrolled over the top bar of the screen, including the news about the shooting and that it affected two tram services. None of the ones we needed.

No one said much. I knew Veyada and Thayu were listening to whatever signals they received from whomever was sending them. Nicha stood with his face hidden in the collar of his jacket, and Evi watched every tiny movement around us. When the wind made the trees wave, he glanced at them. When a man in fluorescent clothing came to empty a rubbish bin, he followed him with his eyes until he vanished, whistling, around the corner pulling his trolley with larger bins into which he emptied the smaller ones. Two automated police vehicles came past on what seemed to be a normal patrol. Somewhere in a control station, there would be people manning the moving camera on the roof. Neither found a reason to linger.

How long until this tram turned up? Should we perhaps get a taxi instead?

Evi froze, staring at the building opposite the shelter. Warm light radiated from most windows, and you could see people moving inside.

Thayu turned in the same direction. She held up her reader. It showed a yellow bar across the screen that became longer or shorter depending on the strength of some signal. It was the strongest when she pointed the device at the building.

"There," Veyada said in a low voice. His screen showed a 3D image of the building with a blinking dot that corresponded with a spot on the second floor balcony directly opposite us. A light was on in the unit, and the balcony was full of various items. I couldn't see a person.

"What are you seeing?" I asked.

He showed me the screen. A section of it showed scrolling text. I recognised some words, but it mostly consisted of code.

"Some form of communication?" I asked.

He nodded, his eyes still scanning the building, not looking at me. "Who is it?"

"I don't know. I'm not getting any data on the origin."

"Record it," Thayu said. "We'll have a look at it later."

"Already doing that."

A short period of silence followed, in which all the members of my team focused on the building. Thayu established that there were at least two spies.

And then Evi said, "Look at this."

He was pointing his reader to another building behind us. This one was not a residential building, but commercial premises with shops on the ground floor. He, too, had text scrolling across the screen. It was in Coldi, but I recognised a few Isla terms transposed into Coldi script: the words *unit* and *police* jumped out at me.

"Those are our Nations of Earth minders," I said.

But then who were the other ones? If they were the men hired by Conrad Martens, they would have been easily identifiable by their communication that would be similarly peppered with Isla words.

And it wasn't.

Most of what Thayu had on her screen was code of some type. What sort of people had Conrad Martens hired? Or who else was watching us? Who—or what—were they?

"Interesting," Veyada said. "Very interesting." By the tone in his voice, he didn't think it was a particularly *good* kind of interesting.

Another police vehicle showed up, this one with four uniformed officers inside. It stopped at the entrance to the building opposite us. Three officers went into the building, and one remained with the car.

"Someone is coming down the stairs," Nicha said.

"Do they know we're here?" I asked.

Neither Veyada nor Thayu answered that, but Veyada pushed me to the other side of the tram stop, behind the shelter, where I was buffeted by the wind. Ayshada in the pram woke up and protested against the onslaught of weather. Nicha picked him up and sheltered him under his jacket.

The shelter's back wall was made out of see-through plastic. I peered through the surface, scratched by the use by many passengers, bill posters and bored teenagers keen to let the world know who was dating whom.

Veyada reached under his jacket. He didn't pull out his gun, and that was probably a good sign.

I could now hear a shout drift from the building, a couple of loud bangs, at least one of which sounded like a gun shot, and then the sound of someone running down the stairs.

At that moment the tram came rumbling into the street. A young woman ran across the pavement at our back to the tram stop shelter oblivious to the goings on.

The tram stopped.

A man ran out of the building on the other side of the street from a plain door that looked like a fire exit. He turned left and took off at incredible speed. The police officer who had remained with the car shouted and ran along the front of the building. He was far too slow.

The tram opened its doors.

Veyada said, "You go, I'll catch up." And he was gone.

He sprinted across the street—and to see a Coldi man sprint at full speed is a truly awesome sight—and followed the escapee down the road. The police officer had already decided to call for help.

Since this was the end of the line, all the tram's passengers got out and we and the woman were the only ones to get on the tram. We sat down at the front. I tried to look down the street, but Veyada had already disappeared.

Nicha lifted the pram and jammed it in between the first bench and the cubicle where the driver sat. It just fitted in sideways. Ayshada was whining. He wanted to run around. Thayu attempted to distract him by letting him look at her screen.

He pointed a chubby hand. "There, there!"

Yes, the screen showed bursts of communication in code, alternating with lines that came clearly from the police officers, who now came out of the building.

"Very good," Thayu said to him and then continued to Evi, "Be prepared."

Evi was prepared, I had no idea what for. He sat sideways in his seat, following the progress of this running person through the building.

The tram doors closed and the tram set off. The lights dimmed, which made it possible to see out.

"There they are," Evi said.

The tram passed first Veyada and then the man who was running along the footpath.

The tram pulled ahead, but then it came to a stop where two

people waited. By the time we set off again, the escapee had caught up and I could see Veyada not far behind.

There was no one at the next stop, so the tram pulled ahead a good lot.

I thought we had lost him when the tram needed to stop at the station after that. Three young women got on, talking and giggling. They weren't very organised, and one had to look in her bag for her pass, and while the tram sat idle, he caught up again.

"Suspiciously excellent runner," Thayu said. Her voice sounded dark. "Very, very suspicious."

Yes, it was strange. The only people I knew who could out-run a Coldi person were—

Tamerians.

Really?

I asked against better judgement, "Could he be a messenger from Conrad Martens?"

"A Tamerian? I don't think so. If he was a messenger from Conrad Martens, or Margarethe, he would have come and introduced himself, not spied on us from a distance."

True. But still, a Tamerian? Who here used Tamerians? Tamerians didn't have *gamra* citizenship. How did they get them in through the Exchange?

The young women looked wide-eyed at our group and went right to the very back of the carriage. They didn't say anything while they found their seats and then only spoke in low voices.

The tram continued.

It didn't stop at the next stop, and didn't stop at the stop after that either.

"Do you think we've lost him?" I asked.

I imagined Veyada catching up with the man and tackling him to the ground.

But at that moment, the tram slowed and stopped, the door opened. The three girls got out.

Evi sprang up and bolted out the door.

"Come." Thayu pulled my arm.

Nicha carried Ayshada and the pram down the steps onto the platform.

"What are we going to do here?" I asked. But Thayu and Evi were already gone into the darkness.

"Wait here," Nicha said in a low voice. "There will be another tram later." He, too, vanished in the darkness, leaving me with the pram with Ayshada on the platform.

He blinked at me with big round eyes. The peacock purple sheen on Coldi hair was very prominent in newborns and faded slowly over the next few years when the underlying black pigment grew in. Ayshada's hair was still quite soft and thin and therefore quite strongly purple.

It glittered in the single light on the platform.

We were in a park where giant oak trees lined the tram rails. The shelter had a neon light that cast a bleak pool of light on the platform, but the surrounding area was dark. Thayu, Veyada and Evi had disappeared into the darkness, as had the three girls, although I could still hear them talking and laughing when the sound was carried in our direction by the breeze.

Then the sound of running footsteps resolved from the background city hum. It was too dark to see anything along most of the footpath, except for a couple of sparse lanterns, mostly obscured by greenery.

The runner was definitely coming closer.

Someone cried out. A dog yelped and started barking. A man's voice shouted, "Watch where you're going, idiot!"

A dark figure ran along the footpath through a pool of light cast by a street lamp, followed by a man with a dog pulling on its leash and barking. The first man ran into another area of darkness.

Then two people came into the light, both swerving on either side of the man with the dog.

That looked like Nicha and Thayu.

The man with the dog yelled and the dog went nuts, almost pulling loose.

Nicha and Thayu also disappeared into the darkness. There was a thud and a scuffle. A man shouted and then the footsteps continued. The first man pelted down the footpath faster than I had ever seen anyone run. Nicha and Thayu followed, but he pulled ahead. Thayu had to give up first. She stopped, out of breath. Nicha kept going for a while longer, but even he could not catch up.

They both came back, panting, in the company of Evi. Veyada also joined us, breathing fast.

"I could have caught him if I was in better shape," Thayu said.

The pregnancy was already slowing her down.

Veyada shook his head. "I don't know. He is fast."

Nicha said, "We might have caught him if it hadn't been for the guy with the dog."

"At least I got his jacket." Thayu held it up. Plain, made from dark leather with lots of pockets.

"Did you see anything of him?" I asked.

"Not much." She let a little silence lapse in which the unspoken comment went between us: not many people could outrun a Coldi. Coldi were much stronger and faster than any people on Earth, or even people of *gamra* . . . except for Tamerians.

Could there be Tamerians following us? Nicha seemed too think so.

Jasper used Tamerians. I thought of Puck and his puzzling answers. Tamerians were supposed to be super humans, but all I saw were semi-robotic people who were physically strong but with the mental capacity of a toddler. However, they were effective killers.

Was there a chance that these were the people who had killed Conrad Martens?

Tamerians, in the pay of someone else, of course. But who and why?

And look at my team, all of them on high alert, standing around me facing outwards, watching with their Coldi eyes unused to the darkness, listening to the sounds on their feeders. That man was out there somewhere. He was armed, and there were others, too.

Evi was communicating with someone, probably Devlin, asking for reinforcements.

He had to be unhappy that Telaris, his work partner and brother, wasn't here.

The next tram came into the station, and we got on. About ten people were in the carriage, and we got some strange looks. Both Thayu and Veyada had wet smudges on their clothes.

I sat down next to Thayu, who was examining the pockets of our pursuer's jacket. She found a transport pass and an old ratty earpiece that was probably broken.

In the other pocket, she found a very thin, lightweight reader. She held it up, grinning at Veyada, but didn't touch it otherwise, and Veyada didn't ask her to see what was on it. I guessed they assumed it had some sort of self-destruct mechanism that would destroy all the data if it wasn't accessed by the correct person. She slid it in the pocket of her coat.

She grinned. "Who needs a useless, annoying Tamerian when you can have his reader?"

The rest of the tram ride was uneventful. We got out at the stop in front of the hotel, where the dead zone had already gone into operation.

Dinner had passed by without us, but we'd eaten at the beach so that was not a problem. I was also informed that notice had come that Abri was required to appear in court tomorrow. Apparently Reya and Mereeni had become concerned about the requirement, written on the summons, that no recording equipment be taken into the courtroom.

I thought that was a standard provision, but they didn't seem to think so.

Thayu took her prize jacket and reader to the spare room at the top of the stairs, which had become a communication and tech hub, and where the table, dressing table and part of the bed were all covered in equipment and chargers and blinking lights. Evi and Amarru's guards were also in there, and they went into technical discussions that were very much over my head.

Nicha wanted to bathe Ayshada, who was covered in sand and sitting very quietly in the pram.

Tired, I guessed.

I was wet, windblown, cold and tired so I also had a shower. When I came out, Thayu had still not returned, and a peek into the security room showed them very much still at work. Thayu was yawning, but I knew better than to tell her to go to bed.

I found Eirani and Karana in the foyer, admiring their purchases, which included forks, a cheese slicer, a turban cake tin and an orange press. What did they need that for, I asked, since Barresh had no oranges?

"There was a woman demonstrating this in the shop," Eirani said. "She put half a fruit on top of this part here, and then brought down the lever. It pushed the fruit into a cup shape. I thought I could use it for other things that are not fruit. It has always annoyed me that the filled rolls take so long to make. This is easy. You put the dough in here, push down, here is your cup, put the filling in and seal the top."

"That sounds good."

I hadn't noticed Jemiro in the room, but there he was, sitting in the corner clutching a cup of tea. He wore a thick jumper that was much too big for him, with the sleeves rolled up. I asked him if he was all right and did he have everything he needed and he said he did. To be honest, I was getting annoyed with his one-syllable responses and his refusal or inability to engage with the group. It was not that we were terribly noisy, or deliberately kept him our of discussions.

"Have the Pengali woken up yet?" I asked him.

"Oh, yeah."

"Where are they?"

"They went that way." He made a broad gesture to the door.

My heart jumped. "That way? Outside?"

It was dark out there, and it was raining. On the other hand, Pengali were nocturnal, *and* they'd been keen to go fishing.

Oh, crap, oh crap.

I ran back to our room and put on my coat, which surprised me unpleasantly with its lingering salty dampness from the beach. I looked around for something drier in our suitcase, and found, at the bottom between my clothes, the case with my gun. I picked it up and weighted it in my hands. But I put it back down.

This was Earth. People here didn't solve things with weapons, at least not in a civilised town.

I went into the hall.

"Where are you going?" Thayu asked from the security station as I passed.

"The Pengali have gone outside. I'm afraid they may have gone fishing."

"In this weather?" She met my eyes. We both knew that Pengali often considered rain favourable fishing weather. She added, "Oh, shit."

Oh shit, indeed. Veyada and Evi jumped up. They were still in their work clothes.

Thayu said, "Let me come."

"No. We're just going for a look. We'll call when we want reinforcements."

"How? We're in a dead zone, remember?"

Yes, I remembered. I did not want her out there. "We will come back if it's going to take more people than just the three of us. You try to see what's on that reader. I'm useless at stuff like that."

I was right and she knew it. She sighed. "Do me a favour and take the weapon." She gave me a penetrating look. She knew me well enough to guess correctly that I didn't have it.

"But Evi and Veyada—"

"Take it."

She was right, too, so I went back to our room, took the weapon out of its case and strapped it on. In Barresh we would wear the weapons openly on arm brackets, but because the weather required jackets and coats and we could not openly wear weapons on the street, I had harnesses made that allowed a weapon to be carried against one's side underneath one's clothing.

We left the hotel. As soon as I was out the door, I remembered why I was so glad to have arrived back at the hotel. A biting wind threw ice-cold drops of water into my face. Veyada hid deep within the collar of his coat. Evi was doing up the buttons, with his gun on the outside of his jacket. I hoped that wasn't going to cause any problems.

12

<hr>

THE STREET OUTSIDE was empty. A row of bikes and scooters stood parked on the side of the street, as well as a van. The tram station was deserted, silvered in pale light from a single fluorescent lamp under the shelter.

We crossed the street, stepped over the low fence that separated the street and the tramline—apparently it was to keep ducks off the rails—and crossed the tracks.

The water in the canal on the other side was very dark and very empty. There was a tourist boat company a short distance to the right, and their low boats with glass cabins lay alongside the canal wall. The wind was quite fierce here and even the water in the canal was whipped into little waves that slapped against the concrete sides.

"I can't see how they could have gotten down there," Veyada said.

Evi took off in the direction of the boats, and we followed. There was no light anywhere along the quay. I wondered again if Pengali could swim. Then came the sound of a splash.

"There," Evi said.

Veyada pointed his scanner, because with his poor Coldi night vision, he could not see much in the dark.

A couple of tourist boats with glass canopies lay a bit further down the quay. There was a jetty and on the screen of the scanner, I saw a couple of small figures moving around.

We quickly walked in that direction. The rain lashed in our faces.

We couldn't get to the tourist boats because a fence blocked the way onto the jetty. Fences were not as much of a hindrance to Pengali as they were to us. I guess I could ask Veyada to kick it open, but that probably wasn't necessary. A small motion-sensored light came on when we got to the fence. It cast a small pool of light on both sides of the fence, showing the wooden planks of the walkway, wet with rain.

"Abri, Ynggi, come back inside!"

"We have to go fishing," Ynggi's voice came back through the drip-drop of the rain on the surface of the water.

"There are no fish at night."

"There are."

"In Barresh maybe, but not here."

He didn't reply immediately. He spoke to Abri and Kita in Pengali.

A moment later, he came to the gate. He carried a broken umbrella with a piece of string tied to the end. At the very end of the string he had tied a piece of ham that he might have saved from lunch.

"This is how people catch fish here, no?"

"Yes, but fish sleep at night." I was pretty sure they did. My grand-father in New Zealand had often enough taken me fishing.

Abri also came to the gate, carrying a net over her arm. Kita carried a bucket. Where had they gotten that? It looked suspiciously like it came from the hotel's cleaning cupboard.

Idda was jumping inside the bucket, a ball of bright orange, trying to look over the side.

"Believe me, there are no fish that you can catch at night," I said. "Come inside where it's dry."

Ynggi scaled the fence in two leaps, put his improvised rod down and took the bucket with Idda inside that Abri handed him over the fence. Abri and Kita climbed over as well.

We walked along the quay.

"It is a shame to us not knowing how to fish," Abri said into the silence.

The hotel management had an artificial open fire going in the foyer, probably fuelled with gas. The flames spread an orange light through the room. In the corner, the goldfish still swam around in the pond.

I should suggest to reception that they move the animals somewhere safe.

Abri said, "If we have no fish, we can't meet tomorrow."

"Look, I already told you that these people don't have that custom and don't expect you to bring a fish."

"But I have to—"

"You have to bring something so that you don't lose *karrit* points, I know. But no one says what you have to bring. You can bring something else."

Her expression brightened briefly, before darkening again. "We did not bring any gifts from home."

Yes. Had I realised how important this custom was going to be for the Pengali, I might have asked them to bring some Pengali-made artefacts. Glass-stone bowls would definitely have made an impact—although they were mostly made by the Washing Stones tribe.

Maybe a headdress made from fish scales—except people would view that as a trinket, while it was an important tribal item. Trouble was, Pengali cared little for personal possessions. Except their drums.

"Why don't you give them music? These people like music very much."

Abri shrugged. She let her shoulders slump, and her tail almost dragged over the ground. "We must have a meeting about this," she said.

Ynggi and Kita agreed.

They went straight up to their room. Wet, dejected.

I went back to my room, worry eating away at me.

On my reader I drew a diagram of how I understood the parties to be aligned. I put a circle with "Robert" in the middle.

I put another circle with "Gusamo" on the side. In truth I didn't know where Gusamo stood. I guessed that much of Abri's appearance would be trying to uncover a motive for Robert to kill Gusamo, because Melissa had told me that the two men hadn't known each other before coming to Barresh.

There were several possibilities:

It was an accident and Robert had not killed Gusamo deliberately at all.

Or there had been a disagreement on a personal scale, which had gotten out of hand. Robert Davidson had been unpleasant to me, so I could imagine that.

Or it could be because Gusamo aligned with the Pengali who didn't want Robert and his business to be on the island in their territory.

Or it was because of something on Earth, either something to do with Robert's diamond trade or something else.

Gamra's involvement was . . . I guess they were the least-involved party, as long as Robert didn't harm any of their citizens. They didn't care about the diamonds, because they couldn't see the value of diamonds and didn't care that they had a value on Earth, because Earth was not a member.

I drew the *gamra* circle on the edge of the screen.

Nations of Earth cared, because of the smuggling. The illegal trade in items from *gamra* worlds was one of the strongest arguments for Earth's closer involvement with *gamra,* and one that had both been systematically ignored by some and passionately argued by others.

I drew the circle representing Nations of Earth closer to Robert, but not close enough that I couldn't fit anything in between.

The Pretoria Cartel cared a lot about the trial, because this case could unmask activities that they preferred to keep out of the spotlight. Robert might have fallen out with some of the Cartel's members, so I drew the circle representing the Cartel half through Robert's circle.

Then the protesters outside the courthouse . . . they fitted in somewhere. They were there because of Robert, to protest against the conduct by Robert's mining operations or development projects.

I felt that those people might be more closely affiliated with Gusamo who had, strangely, not been much of a factor in the hustle so far, besides being the victim of the crime. I knew that he came from the self-made hip rich community of the educated and world-wise part of Jakarta. His business was graphic design and marketing and he counted many very large businesses as clients.

I also knew, from reading about him while I was still in Barresh, that he was passionate about nature and about justice for poorer communities with no voice.

Hmmm, there might be something in that.

I had not yet entered him on the page.

I drew a circle for Gusamo next to Robert's and a circle for the protesters next to it. The protesters had no relation to Nations of Earth, none to the Pretoria Cartel other than attempting to get justice out of one of the cartel's members, and had no relationships to *gamra*, at least I didn't think so. They appeared to be sort of isolated from the big stage, on their own in a corner, which was the point that Conrad Martens was trying to make, also illustrated by what we'd seen today: people were trying to keep us from talking to these protesters.

And then we had Tamerians, of all things. I drew a circle close to the edge of the screen.

Tamerians did not have opinions. They belonged to someone. Because they were not affiliated with the Nations of Earth guards, I judged it most likely that the Pretoria Cartel, or individuals within the cartel, owned them.

I dragged the circle over to the circle representing the cartel.

I now had Robert in the middle, with the cartel on one side, and the protesters on the other side. Both *gamra* and Nations of Earth were sort of on the sidelines, except where court judges had been bought by the cartel. I drew a dotted line between those two circles.

This was the central problem we were dealing with. The question of whether Robert killed Gusamo was secondary to that. Whatever the outcome, the case represented a conflict that was bigger than Robert and Gusamo.

So what was Robert's business doing that Gusamo might object to?

What did Execo mine?

Rare Earths. Strange metals like dysprosium and other elements needed for advanced technology, that the mines in southern Africa were producing ever less of.

Robert also dealt in city rejuvenation projects.

So maybe Robert was involved in a project in Jakarta, and Gusamo objected to this project, and maybe they accidentally crossed paths on the surfing trip in Barresh.

Maybe.

And now people supporting the cartel were trying to control the court.

Melissa had been called to the court. Clovis, Robert's guide and tour operator, had given evidence. He had probably pleaded ill health as an excuse not to appear in court. The fact that he actually was of ill health probably suited him fine. Clovis had many illegal projects, although none of them were large enough for Nations of Earth to worry about.

I hadn't been invited to give evidence, because I'd been considered as having too many strings attached.

Instead, Abri was considered to be a softer target.

All in order to prove something unprovable? *No one* had witnessed Robert killing Gusamo, not even Abri.

So, the court, influenced by people aligned with the Pretoria Cartel, wanted Robert convicted because he was a maverick, but they also wanted to shut down questions about their treatment of workers in the southern African mines and other bad practices?

Then Conrad Martens had been killed because he had been going to reveal something to me about those protesters, and had been trying to penetrate the shield placed around us by our minders who were employed by the court and were aligned with the cartel by extrapolation. And they used Tamerians to do it.

And Margarethe . . . had she been going to warn me about the very same things? And had her request to me been scuttled by overzealous guards and—damn, by my own actions for not realising how urgently she wanted to speak with me, or not realising that we were already in the hands of the people she wanted to warn us about?

Damn, damn and damn.

I checked the news.

Was there anything known yet about the motive to kill Conrad Martens?

A police statement, not terribly enlightening, had said that the police were investigating several leads which most of the news services interpreted as, "They have no idea." One news service said that he might have been mistaken for someone else, but didn't give a source.

According to the reports, the police had combed his apartment without much of a clue. There had been no threats made against him recently, although they acknowledged there had been previous threats. I wondered if I should tell them about the letter I had received, but letting the police know about this might hamper my team's investigations. Tamerians were very good at disappearing. It was not a good idea to make too much noise before Thayu had finished, and if Tamerians were involved, then I didn't want another bout of panic of the "Aaaaaahhh! Aliens!!" type.

Talking about noise, a couple of ominous thunks echoed through the hallway. I went to look for their source, and found that the Pengali had put together the *irrka* drum in the middle of their room. With all the pipes inserted in the slots in the main drum, it looked like a giant, many-legged spider and it took up most of the space in the room.

Ynggi sat on top of it, testing the sound of the bottom pipes with a stick that had a knob at the end. And impressive sound it was, too, hollow and sonorous.

"Er, I don't think that is such a good idea," I said, in the doorway.

All of the Pengali turned to the door, four sets of huge brown eyes with almost no whites. Idda sat on the bed, next to Abri, who gave me a "why ever not?" look.

"People will be going to sleep soon."

"We need to have a meeting of minds," Ynggi said, tapping one of the pipes at the top. It made a higher-pitched, hollow sound.

"Yes," Abri said. "We are much worried that these people don't believe us and cannot be appeased in ways we understand."

And of course, the traditional use for the betanka was a structured format to have discussions within the tribe.

What could I say to that? They were already stressed out about the lack of fish. "Just for a little while then."

Ynggi started tapping out the typical betanka five-beat rhythm, hitting the bottom pipes for two of those beats and the top ones for three.

Idda climbed on top of the drum and jumped around. She got so close to the edge that I was afraid she might fall off, but no one shared my concern.

Ynggi started chanting in Pengali, occasionally interrupted by Abri.

I let them be, much as the floor vibrated with the thunks and the sound annoyed me. They had looked stressed, and they probably needed to do this. I'd tell them to be quiet later.

Veyada had gone to join the lawyers upstairs and in the stairwell I met one of the hotel staff who came up the stairs looking alarmed about the source of the heavy thumps.

"It's just music," I said. "They'll be quiet later." Or so I hoped.

In Reya and Mereeni's room, the two of them and Veyada were involved in a very dry discussion that was far too detailed and legal for me to understand. I observed Veyada and Mereeni instead. He made an obvious effort to ignore his irritation about whatever irritated him about her. She interrupted and irritated him further. There would probably be some bust-up between them at some point, but I couldn't babysit Veyada all the time. He was old enough to handle his own issues. All I could hope for was that when the bust-up happened, there wouldn't be any blood; but even that was out of my hands. I had to let Pengali do Pengali things and Coldi do Coldi things. I couldn't lead their lives for them.

I was about to leave the room when Veyada called me.

"We've established that by the exact letter of the law, the court should allow us to bring recording equipment and allow someone dedicated to this task into the courtroom. Amarru signed an agreement with Nations of Earth. It covers all citizens of *gamra* worlds, and all courts under all jurisdictions that fall under Nations of Earth, and that includes the Nations of Earth court itself."

"Do you think these people know about that agreement?"

"If they don't, it might be prudent to remind them."

Indeed. I could have sworn I heard *point out to them that they are breaking their own agreements* in his words.

"Thank you for establishing that." I was already dreading tomorrow's events. There would be conflict from this and other issues. The Pengali were stressed and nervous. The trial was just window dressing, and a man had been murdered.

I was about to leave the room when someone downstairs shouted. I didn't recognise the male voice, but it sounded like a shout of distress. Had the Pengali gotten hold the hotel's staff? Had a cleaner unwittingly wandered into the security room?

I ran down, with Veyada on my heels.

Jemiro stood in the corridor, his back against the wall, facing Kita with her glass-stone knife pointed at him. Her tail swayed behind her, like a snake about to strike.

"Help, Delegate, help," he squealed as soon as he noticed us. His eyes were wide. He spoke keihu. Why? Coldi was the language spoken in the group and had been since we left.

I asked, "What's going on? Kita?"

"He interrupt our meet," Abri said from the door.

Jemiro squealed, "I didn't do anything!"

"You stop the betanka."

"You were making so much noise, I only asked you to stop. I couldn't sleep."

"Sleep!" Abri snorted. "Who sleeps in this time of the day?"

I said, "Some people do, and I also agree that it's a bit early, but that the drum is very noisy."

"We have to have a meeting."

"I understand. I told you to keep it short."

"We have not finished."

"No, I understand." And then to Kita, "Please put away the knife."

"*He* has to stop interrupting us. Yelling at us. Distracting us with other noise."

Yelling? I doubted Jemiro could yell.

"I only banged on the door to make you be quiet."

"You banged wrong rhythm. You disturb betanka."

"Look, sorry. I didn't know not banging the same rhythm was an offence. I've done nothing wrong."

Whoa, there was a bit of spunk coming from him, finally.

I said, "Abri, Kita, there is no need to worry about this. He won't bother you again. Come on, let him go."

Kita lowered the knife.

Jemiro let out a relieved breath, tucking his shirt back into his trousers. He came with me into the corridor, wiping the sweat off his face.

"Jemiro, it is important that the Pengali can do this. I have their word that they will finish as soon as possible. If we need to speak to them again, I will do this."

The door to the Pengali room closed, but I could still hear their voices through the wood, although I could only imagine what they were saying.

Jemiro met my eyes. His confused expression disturbed me. On second thoughts . . . he knew Pengali and he knew it rather well. How come *I* needed to lecture him on Pengali customs?

I said, "Just go to your room, shut the door and let them play for a bit. It's important to them. They gave me their word that they will stop."

Without a word, he turned and strode back up the stairs.

Now what the heck had suddenly gotten into him?

I went back to my room as well, where Thayu still hadn't returned.

I tried to ignore the drumming coming from the Pengali room, now joined by singing, and watched the news come in, but most of the mentions about the victim of the shooting were very sparse. I remembered talking to Conrad Martens. He was on the wrong side of middle age, with brown eyes and sagging cheeks. He reminded me of one of those sad-looking, loose-skinned dogs.

From all the articles I had read about him, he was a man with a high level of integrity.

I went over his handwritten note.

He said he had discovered that the Pretoria Cartel had funded my trip, but it was considered to be within the "fairness of trial" guidelines. He had received death threats. He had been asked to step down. Who was the Chief Judge who had asked him to do this?

Ms Trnkova's documents told me that it was a woman called Maaike Hermans, and apparently she had been appointed after the election, replacing an old but well-liked judge who was retiring.

I couldn't find much information on her, except a dry career summary. Her name sounded Dutch, but she and her family had come to Europe as refugees from the second American civil war, which resulted in the country's break-up into four contentious and ineffectual states. That was in the time before I had been born, when many people were on the move looking for hope and mostly finding none, unless they had lots of money. Her family might have had lots of money to let her study. I could see nothing about her personal opinions, but I bet she was of the protectionist mindset, like Sigobert Danziger, like Eva's father. Not because of anything she'd said, but people from her type of background often were, especially if their family had money.

I *could* be wrong about that, of course.

Thayu came back, letting in a blast of sound, and the expression on her face showed me that they hadn't made much progress on the reader. "It's got a lot of protection and we don't want to destroy the content with our probing," she said, in reply to my unasked question.

I made her tea, and she lay back on the bed with her feet up.

Exhausted. Yet, I had to ask her more, and hated it.

I carried the cups to the bed and sat next to her. "What about this Minke Kluysters guy? Did you find anything about him?"

Her face lit up with the delicious, devious passion that I loved so much in her. "He is a real interesting one. For one, we've watched that conversation between you several times, and had a lot of trouble finding out his location, but we found it. And here is the interesting part: he was speaking to you from what I presume is his private home, which is an estate next door to Robert Davidson's."

"In South Africa?"

I met her eyes, and I could see she was thinking along the same lines that I was: what's the chance this is someone from the Pretoria Cartel? We let the unspoken silence linger. Normally we would communicate via the feeder, but it didn't work inside the end zone. Sometimes, I argued with Thayu, I barely needed it.

I asked, "What do you want me to do?"

She smiled. "Veyada was hesitant to let me tell you, because he said you would go all conservative and want to minimise risk."

"He said that?"

"Veyada knows you better than you know yourself."

"But you didn't agree with him?"

"I think you *should* know, so that you can take precautions."

"You're not answering my question."

She smiled, her eyes glittering with mirth. "I did agree with him. I also told him that you almost always see our point of view in the end."

"Thanks, Thay'. That's a real . . . backhanded compliment."

She laughed, and I laughed, too, but then her face turned serious. "I also told him that by giving you the information, something excellent and unexpected may result, and he also agreed with that."

"You better be careful not to inflate my head too much."

She gave me a playful slap. "We let you deal with the problems. That will shut you up."

I hugged her. I remembered how Thayu had been mysterious and a bit aloof. Mesmerising, but always just out of reach of my understanding. Becoming Domiri, spending so much time with each other, and experiencing moments of danger together, had brought us both much closer together than we'd been when we accepted each other as partners.

I also understood that it was highly uncommon that security

personnel shared this much information with their association's leader. The workings of the intelligence departments of Asto's Inner Circle were a mystery even to prominent leaders. I had already been privileged to more information than most.

We finished our tea in companionable silence with, in the background, the five-beat rhythms of the *irrka* drum.

Just as I was about to remark that I'd tell the Pengali to shut up, the music stopped.

Phew. The silence was heavenly.

"I don't understand why they had to bring that thing," Thayu said.

"There is a lot about Pengali I don't understand. But somehow, they always manage to end up getting their stuff organised."

"Do they?"

"I think so. They work it out between them, and then they all get behind it, the job gets finished and everybody is happy."

"You must be talking about a different kind of Pengali from what I'm seeing."

"What do you see, then?"

"They never do what you want, they use everything for strange purposes and never in the way it was intended, and they have no idea how to raise their children."

"But they're ready on time, they wear clothes and just now I said that they could play for a short while, and they did."

Thayu snorted.

"You hate that they're unpredictable."

"Yes. That, too."

"You're grumpy."

"Yes. I don't want to talk about Pengali. I don't want to have anything to do with them for a while."

I leaned against the pillows next to her. "What is the problem? This is not about Pengali, isn't it?"

She let out a sigh. "Tamerian or not, I should not have let that man escape."

"You're pregnant."

"Is that an excuse to be slow?"

"It's an excuse to be grumpy."

"Oh, shut up." But she took me in her arms, and the tea was forgotten.

We were all tired and the best thing we could do was to go to sleep so that we could be fresh tomorrow when we went to court.

Sleep sounded easier than it was. Thayu was exhausted and fell asleep quickly, but I lay awake, listening to the rain lashing against the window, wondering if there was anything I could have done to save the life of a man I'd never met.

13

———

I WOKE UP WITH A SHOCK.

For a moment, I lay on my back, wondering where I was, trying to parse the unfamiliar sounds and smells. Then I remembered: the hotel, the trial today.

Faint grey light peeped between the curtains.

I hadn't intended to sleep for that long. I'd wanted to get up early to see if the Pengali—

Damn, the Pengali. I jumped out of bed and went to the window. Through the crack between the curtains, I could see grey sky and a misty horizon. It was still before sunrise. There might be a sunny day ahead, but for now, a low blanket of mist hung over the ground.

The water in the canal was perfectly still, like a mirror. I couldn't see the Pengali, but a lone fisherman with a rod stood on the side of the canal. Instead of peacefully gazing over the water—and his bait—he kept looking to the side.

What was the bet that the Pengali were out there where he could see them and I could not?

I got dressed. Thayu mumbled some unintelligible words, but I left the room before she could wake up. The door to the Pengali room was closed, and when I knocked, no one opened. That proved my suspicions.

Should I go out there by myself?

I was sure that my association wouldn't like it if I did, but I didn't want to wake anyone up for what might be nothing more than just a quick peek outside. I'd come back here if there was a reason to wake them.

There was no one in the foyer, except—wait. Jemiro. He was sitting on one of the couches in the foyer while the receptionist worked behind the counter. He just stared into the distance, not even looking in my direction when I greeted the receptionist.

So I said, "Good morning, Jemiro."

Now he looked at me, a slightly confused look over his face.

"Sleep well?" That was a bit of a silly question after he'd been threatened with a knife, but I was out of ideas for what to do about him, and through with tiptoeing around him.

"I'm going for a walk. Coming?"

He shook his head as if I'd suggested he'd come with me to the dentist.

Well, suit yourself.

I walked out of the hotel alone into the cool and misty dawn, crossed the road, walked past the bikes and the scooters, stepped over the fence that stopped the ducks crossing the rails and walked over the grass to the canal.

I expected the Pengali to be on the jetty or the quayside, but I didn't see them there.

A dinghy puttered along the canal a bit further down. In it was a man in a bright yellow rain coat with buckets, an icebox and a couple of fishing rods. What was the bet the Pengali were there somewhere?

Sure enough, they were on the walkway on the other side of the tourist boat operator, walking along the quay with the dinghy. It was not very fast, so they had no trouble keeping up. The fisherman seemed most uneasy about his unearthly following.

"Ynggi, what are you doing?" Apart from scaring the bejesus out of the poor guy.

"Do those . . . belong to you?" the fisherman asked.

"These are Pengali from the Thousand Island tribe of Barresh. They are very interested in fishing and want to know how to catch fish."

"Oh." He gave them an uneasy look. "It takes a bit to learn."

"Do you catch fish in the canal?"

"Here? Not really. There's a lot of rubbish in this water. You have to go out of town."

"Thanks."

I stopped, letting the dinghy pull away from us.

"There is no fish in this water," I translated to Coldi for the Pengali. "He says you have to go out of town, and we have no time for that, and I couldn't teach you how to fish there. I'm very sorry, but we need to go back to the accommodation and get ready for our meeting. You were going to talk about using music as a gift. What did you decide last night?"

"We found a solution," Ynggi said.

It was only then that I noticed that Kita carried a rolled-up towel from the hotel's bathroom under her arm.

When we were crossing the road, Abri said to me, "Our story will be heard today, yes?"

"Yes. Today and tomorrow."

She said nothing and I thought she seemed smug. Whatever was in that rolled-up towel? Had they actually caught a fish? With their bare hands?

We went back inside the hotel, where the news of the murder of Conrad Martens was everywhere. The receptionist was reading about it, the waiters were talking about it and the wall screen in the foyer showed an image of what looked like a news service announcement from the police.

I went to sit next to Devlin, who looked tired and dishevelled.

"Any news?"

"Nothing that concerns us at this point. The authorities are in the dark over who murdered the judge." The dead zone was meant to limit access to the local news, but Devlin and Amarru's guards appeared to have rigged up some workaround so that we could at least have access to some communication. "I kept an eye on the news feed as soon as we heard who had been killed. The authorities appear to enjoy putting up communication blocks for us to get around."

"Does that mean you can listen in on the *police* communication?"

He flicked his eyebrows. Yes, people were listening. Devlin was clearly enjoying himself, and learning lots of new and very useful things.

"We do have some other news. I managed to crack the Tamerian's reader." He'd probably spent all night doing it, judging by his appearance.

Like most people in the room, he came to the dining room with his reader on the table next to him. He dragged it over, hit the corner of the screen with his thumb and showed it to me.

It displayed, in Isla, a list of documents. The first was a list of locations, which Devlin had plugged into a map, showing our hotel, the shops we had visited yesterday, the tram line and the cafe at the beach. It included the cafe we had visited on our first day here.

Yes, I'd known that we would be followed, but it was a bit disturbing to see it in front of me.

The next document was another map that showed certain zones in red: the forecourt of the court building and the adjacent street, and another street that was unfamiliar to me. I guessed this was where we were *not* allowed to go.

There were a lot more notes, including details about each of us, what we looked like, what we usually wore. It pained me to see that even good old Eirani had a file, although they had rated her as "non-essential, harmless". About Jemiro, they said suspiciously little. Was this because he was their mole or because he was as impenetrable to them as he was to us?

There were a lot of other documents, and I didn't have the time to look at them all.

"Do you have an executive summary yet?" I asked him.

"We've studied a good number of them. It contains orders about what to do, a list of vantage points and a chain of command that goes to a couple of addresses in town, one of which is in the tall buildings over there." He jerked his head at the window where the tall buildings poked from over the treetops. My team had already established that people were watching us from there. "Also, there are external links to a place here." He showed me the map. Of course. South Africa.

"What is there?"

"A shed on the edge of a town, it seems." He brought up a satellite image with a yard that contained a couple of buildings, with concrete between them. The yard was tidy, almost empty, except for a single truck. There were trees and a strip of grass where the yard faced the street.

"What sort of place is this?" I asked.

"We don't know yet," Devlin said. "It seems a storage place but I have no idea what they could be storing. It belongs to a farmer."

"You said they were transmitting things from this place. What sort of things?"

He shook his head. "It's in code. We're working on it, but so far it looks like a repeat of the orders."

"So this place is where the orders come from?"

"It looks like it. It looks like someone here sorts the orders and decides who does what."

And Tamerians, of course, were nothing without orders.

I asked, "Did you check how far this is from Robert Davidson's house?" And from the house of Minke Kluysters, whom I hadn't yet contacted about his consulting job offer.

"It's not terribly close. There is an area of forest in between. Not many people live there. Thayu says it's rogue country."

I studied the images. There seemed to be a smaller shed where someone was walking across the yard carrying something. I enlarged the image of the yard, but it grew so grainy that I couldn't make out any more detail.

While I was looking at Devlin's reader, a message came in to my reader from Ms Trnkova. At the top it said *21 May 2121*, today's date, and then it said *western courtroom*. Then there was a code and underneath it said *Number: Admit 2*.

Surely that had to be a mistake. This was our admission for the courtroom. Were they only going to allow two of us in the public gallery?

I showed Veyada. He gave me a dark look. "We're going to have to talk to them about this."

"That is just ridiculous," Mereeni said.

Then she and Veyada gave each other a look, as if surprised they had agreed with each other.

Abri and the others had gone upstairs, and they came to breakfast fully attired in the official *gamra* clothing I had given them. Their expressions were morose and dejected. Even Idda sat quietly through breakfast, reducing a bread roll to hundreds of little pieces, but eating none of them. She only squealed a bit, not even very loudly, when a waiter came with a broom to sweep up the mess from under her chair.

In contrast, Ayshada was full of beans, and he even attempted to "help" the waiter by wheeling the trolley. Nicha had to intervene to prevent accidents involving the waiter's bruised shins.

It was an odd party, with a chunk of our association missing, and had anyone heard from Sheydu and the others? Weren't they supposed to have met us yesterday when we went to the beach?

Or did their absence have something to do with the attack on Conrad Martens?

A chill crept over my back.

Thayu had come to breakfast and sat with Nicha, Eirani and Karana; the latter two were both talking excitedly about things they still wanted to look at and buy.

Thayu, though, stared morosely at her plate. I briefly sat down at the table, wishing I had more time to spend with her.

She looked up, and those pretty eyes looked so tired. I wanted to tell her to go back to bed. Did Coldi women get morning sickness? I had no idea. They didn't tend to speak about pregnancy much. I wasn't sure if, apart from Xinanu, Ayshada's mother, I'd ever seen a pregnant Coldi woman and I hoped Xinanu's terrible behaviour was not typical. Did Coldi women in Barresh hide it, did they not go outside, or did they, once they were pregnant, go back to Asto?

"We'll soon be done here," I said to her in a low voice. "Then we can relax at my father's. Do you still want to go there?"

"Of course I do." She sounded as defensive as hell.

"All right. I just thought I'd ask." *Because you look terrible, but I won't dare ask if you think you can do your job.* Stupid me. I *knew* that Coldi women experienced wild mood swings and profound periods of crank-iness and hysteria when they were pregnant. Why did I still pretend that it wasn't happening?

Because it was a damn inconvenient time for it to happen, that was why.

I needed her, especially when Sheydu, Telaris, Reida and Deyu were still away. Strange how quickly I'd learned to rely on Reida's inquisitive mind and Deyu's quiet industriousness.

It seemed we were missing some people at the breakfast table. I counted them off in my mind. Thayu and Nicha were there. Veyada was there, with Reya and Mereeni, Evi was there and so were the other two Indrahui guards, who were talking to Devlin. The Pengali were all there, even Idda, who was starting to get cheeky again and I wondered how we were going to keep her out of harm's way at the court.

Jemiro.

Where was he?

"Have you seen Jemiro?" I asked.

Thayu shook her head.

Karana said, "No, Muri, I haven't seen him at all today." She had become a lot less timid during this trip.

"The door to his room was still closed when we came down," Eirani said.

But I *had* seen him in the morning, when I'd come down to check out the Pengali. "He was in the foyer early this morning."

I rose from the table and left the dining room.

Jemiro was no longer in the foyer. I asked the receptionist if she had seen where he had gone, but she had not.

I went upstairs to the top floor. I knocked on the door to his room, and there was no reply.

Well, damn. We needed him today. But damn, where was he?

I knocked again, harder this time. "Jemiro, open the door! It's almost time to go."

I *thought* I heard a sound on the other side, a soft moan.

Oh damn it, he wasn't ill from eating some compound unfamiliar to keihu bodies? Something in the food or the air, or some cleaning product. That did happen, and the possibilities were endless.

I ran back down two flights of stairs to reception.

"Do you have a key to room twenty-nine? One of our people has locked himself in his room and we think he is unwell."

"I can call an ambulance."

"Maybe later." *For an off-Earth person? Never.* "I'd like to check first."

She came upstairs with me, because she could not give anyone their master entry card, which was fair enough. So she opened the door for me, and remained in the hallway as I pushed the door open a fraction.

"Jemiro?"

The air the wafted out of the apartment smelled stale. It was dark inside. I pushed open the door further, so that I could look into the room. I had expected a big mess, but the room was neat, a pair of shoes stood just inside the entrance,. The door into the bathroom was open. It was dark inside.

I said again, "Jemiro?"

A soft moan drifted from inside the room, around the corner of the bathroom, where I couldn't see. I slowly advanced into the room, now wishing that I'd brought a weapon, but as usual, I'd left it in my pack that sat on the shelf in our room downstairs. Should I go to get it?

I picked up the metal wire rubbish bin instead. I didn't know what to expect, but if he was going to have a go at me, I wouldn't be completely defenceless.

I went far enough into the room to be able to look inside. The bed was neatly made—almost untouched. His little bag stood on the shelf against the wall. An empty glass sat in the middle of the table.

"Jemiro, where are you?"

Then I saw him, jammed into the corner of the room in between the bed and the wall that separated the main room from the bathroom. He sat with his back against the wall, and his knees drawn up to his chest. His eyes stared into the distance.

I dropped to my knees in front of him. "What's wrong?"

His lips moved but I couldn't make out the words.

"Come on, Jemiro, say something to me."

"Is he all right?" came the voice of the receptionist from the hallway. Of course she didn't understand keihu.

I said to her in Isla, "I think so. Thank you."

I toyed with the idea of asking her to tell the others to come upstairs, but they'd probably come up anyway.

Meanwhile, Jemiro wasn't unwell exactly. He was just . . . muttering.

"She's going to kill me. She's going to kill me."

Hang on. "Who is going to kill you?"

"She's going to kill me. She's going to kill me. She's going to—"

"Stop it!" I put both my hands on his shoulders. He was so thin that I could feel the bones under his skin.

"She's going to kill me. She's going to kill me—"

"*Who* is going to kill you?"

He fell quiet. He turned to me, the expression in his eyes bewildered, but at least he was properly looking at me.

A soft sound near the door indicated that various people from my team had come up. Thayu was there, as well as Veyada and Eirani.

Jemiro looked from me to them. He frowned. Almost as if he saw us for the first time.

"What are you all doing here?"

"We're about to be called to the court. You didn't come to breakfast, and I was worried."

His eyes met mine, bewildered for a fraction of a second before his face went into a neutral expression. "No, no. No reason to worry. I'll be ready."

"Even if we're about to leave?"

He took in a sharp breath, but then he pushed himself up. "Yes, yes, I'm getting ready. Just you wait. I'll look my very best. The court case, yes? It's finally on now?"

Once we were in the corridor, Thayu gave me a strange look. "What was all that about?"

I spread my hands. "He appeared to have some sort of fit, and now he's embarrassed and trying to cover it up."

"It could be a reason that no one talks about him much," Devlin said. "The old families are still very hesitant about people they consider to be defective." His voice oozed with distaste.

Just that word, *defective,* breathed old-fashioned attitudes of rich households with entitled sons, who thought they were the best. Devlin had grown up in that world.

"Did you noticed how he was speaking differently from his usual accent?" Eirani said.

"Speaking differently?" I might have noticed it if I hadn't been so concerned about him or if my keihu had been better.

"Yes, less formal. More like the young guys on the street would speak. Not the best ones either. The gangs and louts."

"Is that where he grew up? Maybe when he had his fit, he forgot how to speak properly."

"You ask me, Muri, that man worries me. There is something not right about him."

Yes, he worried me, too, but so far, we had not been able to discover any wrongdoing on his part.

14

———

JEMIRO TURNED UP dressed in his formal clothes in the dining room not much later. He grabbed a bread roll off the table, and I felt like asking him if he was sure that he could eat it without it giving him any strange spells.

He had gone back to his taciturn act and I had to admit that I was getting more annoyed with him than I should, and with Nations of Earth for having insisted that we needed another translator. I couldn't imagine he was going to do a good job. All this, while we had Ynggi, who was bound by the code of the tribe to translate truthfully to the best of his ability, and we had Reya who was a certified Coldi to Isla translator.

I got a message from reception that Ms Trnkova turned up while most of us were still in the dining room. I was ready to go, even if many in my team weren't, so I told everyone who needed to come to the courthouse to get ready while I went to see her.

I took special note of the Pengali, but they showed no sign of distress, and I hoped they had finally accepted that bringing a fish was not necessary.

Ms Trnkova was dressed in a long dark coat today. It was no longer raining, but it still didn't look warm outside. She greeted me with a silent nod.

"My condolences for you colleague."

"Thank you." She closed her eyes briefly, as if fighting back tears. "He was a good man. There are not many like him."

"I am truly sorry. Have the police made any progress in finding who did it or why?"

She gave me a piercing look, but then her expression softened. "No, they haven't."

"Was he married?"

"No, he lived alone. He divorced long ago."

"I *am* sorry."

A silence passed between us in which I felt that she wanted to say more, but didn't. Because she knew we were being watched? Because she wasn't sure where I stood? Because she didn't know if saying more was appropriate?

Then she changed the subject. "I've sent you the tickets to the courtroom."

"I saw that, but there must be a mistake, because there are only two."

"It's not a mistake. It's very busy in the gallery. There are lots of journalists, observers and other people who want to get in."

"Wait—the court went through all the effort of getting us here with a large group of people, and then lets only two of us into the courtroom?"

"Sadly, yes."

"But that is totally unacceptable. I negotiated for the witness to attend based on the understanding that she could bring what they consider a proper tribal representation into the courtroom."

"Dr Cross said that he only needs the witness."

He only needs . . . what the hell. Why should we care what *he* needed? We had an agreement. "What about the interpreter? The court made me go through millions of hoops to get someone they approved of. Do you know how hard it is to get a Pengali interpreter?"

"The interpreter can come, but I've been told there is room for only two people in the public gallery."

"But the witness needs her delegation, and she needs me, and we have the right to take an observer who will record the proceedings on behalf of the Exchange. There is an agreement between Nations of Earth and the Exchange. And we have to have at least one of our legal team in the room as well."

"Well, I'll have to ask—"

"Yes, do ask."

She looked sort of desperate , pleading. Tired, too. "But I can't guarantee anything."

"If these people can't be in the courtroom, the witness won't be there either."

She nodded nervously. "Yes, yes, I understand."

But did she really?

Then Thayu came in with the Pengali group, all of them neatly dressed, including Idda in her bright orange get up. Kita carried Abri's small travel bag, and by the look of things, the contents were quite heavy. I wondered what was in there, but then Veyada and Amarru's lawyers came down the stairs, followed by Evi and the guards and Jemiro, Devlin and Nicha.

"Here we are. Let's go."

A van waited outside the hotel's entrance. We could easily have walked, but I guessed being driven was safer and, besides, the weather still wasn't great. We all piled in. There wasn't enough room, and the driver complained about seatbelts—seriously, for a trip that would barely take us around the block? We managed to fit in and finally we were off.

The van went to the top of the street past the station and turned left and then left again, and then right, through a narrow alley closed off from the street by a forbidding metal fence that slid open at our approach. It led between two buildings into an underground parking area.

The lift into the court building wasn't big enough to take all of us up and walking didn't appear to be an option, so the Pengali, Nicha, Devlin and Reya went up with Ms Trnkova; I waited with Thayu, Evi and Mereeni until the lift came back.

Sounds of footsteps leaving the cubicle drifted from above, as well as the distant murmur of a lot of voices. Thayu was checking something on her reader. A map of the building, I thought. I looked over her shoulder. A map of the building indeed.

"The main entrance is here." She pointed to the other side of the building at the level above us. There was a superimposed image of the front entrance, with a glass facade, steps leading up to a forecourt and a fountain with a statue of arms sticking out of the water, all grasping each other. That was said to symbolise the equalising power of justice. An icon indicated that there would normally be a live feed, but the link had been disabled so that we couldn't see what happened there.

The lift returned, we got in, and it took us one floor up to the ground floor atrium, a light-filled hall, with glass on the far side where the rest of the party waited.

Through the glass doors at the other side, I could see the forecourt of the building, filled with a colourful mass of people and tents and placards. A group of Africans were playing drums, clapping and singing.

Abri was looking at them.

A burst of shouting broke out in the forecourt when people outside spotted us in the hall. People crowded in front of the glass wall, held back by security guards. They waved and cheered—at the Pengali, I presumed. Two Africans in colourful dress were hitting hide-covered drums with big rhythmic thumps.

Ms Trnkova took us around the corner, through a hallway with a smooth polished floor to a meeting room with a large table surrounded by chairs.

She found a jug of water and cups and, while we sat down, a man came in. He was extremely tall to the point of having to stoop while coming in the door. His hair was flecked through with grey, his skin olive brown and eyes dark. He had a flat nose and a deep groove in his chin.

Ms Trnkova said, "Mr Wilson, this is Dr Cross, the prosecutor."

The man nodded stiffly and sat down.

Well, he was not terribly friendly, was he?

The Pengali were all still standing near the door.

When they met someone new, they considered it polite to chat a bit. This was not limited to Pengali, save that most people would not talk about fish and fishing.

Kita now came forward with her travel bag.

Dr Cross looked up at her, frowning with a *why are you interrupting me* expression.

Kita placed the bag on the table in front of Dr Cross.

Dr Cross turned to me. He looked impatiently puzzled. "Whatever is the meaning of this, Mr. Wilson?"

"When meeting someone new, especially someone in an official position, it is a Pengali tradition to give a gift."

I didn't say that the gift usually involved a freshly caught fish for consumption by the group. I had no idea what was in the bag.

Kita pressed her hands together in front of her chest and stepped back, bowing her head.

Dr Cross pushed down the sides of the bag.

Inside was a big saucepan with a lid.

Frowning deeply, he lifted the lid—and oh, the poor seagull inside skittered around, trying to climb up the sides and failing to find any purchase with its webbed feet. Its wings had been tied down with a napkin that the hotel used at the table, but as Dr Cross pushed the pan away, it came undone, and the bird took off, leaving behind a greenish deposit over the inside of the pan and one of Dr Cross' hands.

Dr Cross yelled out, pushing his chair back. "Get that bird out of here!"

The seagull flew around the room, panicked and squawking.

Two security guards came in, and as they opened the door, the seagull flew out, into the hall and the foyer.

I met Abri's eyes.

"He let it escape." The tone in her voice was horrified.

I wasn't sure what to say. What had she expected people to do with a seagull? Eat it?

"We noticed that people here like live creatures. We thought it would be a good present."

"It was good thinking," I said.

"But now they have to catch it again. We didn't tie it up well enough. I don't think he liked it."

"It's not your fault. I think you did well." They certainly did well to catch a seagull alive in the first place.

"It is not well." She let her shoulders sag. Losing *karrit* points was a painful thing.

A cleaner had come in to remove the evidence of the seagull's presence from the table. They had a box of anti-bacterial wipes for Dr Cross' hands.

The Pengali looked on. I guessed they were perplexed by someone who considered an animal so dirty that he needed to wash his hand with stuff that made Kita wrinkle her nose.

Dr Cross asked the cleaner to bring a new jug of water, because apparently also the water was contaminated from the seagull flying over it. The cleaner said he'd bring a new jug, and left.

The security guards shut the door, cutting off the sounds of the guards shooing the poor panicked bird out of the foyer.

Dr Cross sat down again, his face prim. Without asking about further mention of the incident, he launched into the details of the questions he was going to ask Abri during the hearing.

Jemiro was hard pressed to keep up, because Dr Cross was quite specific in telling Abri how to reply to each possible question.

Abri listened to Jemiro, and occasionally made a remark like, "I saw him there and not there." And they would argue over Robert's precise movements at the time of Gusamo's death.

The discussion took me back to that time I'd found the bottle with Gusamo's note on the beach, at a time I could probably still have saved him, had I known where to look.

Robert was also in the area at the time, and they had both taken part in trips organised by Clovis Keneally, who lived in Barresh. Neither of them were there for the first time.

Clovis' tourist groups were always very small. What was different about this one was that both men had opposing interests not just on Earth but also in Barresh. Robert bought blue diamonds from the restless and disenfranchised Pengali youths who found themselves on the edges of the Thousand Island tribe. Gusamo was interested in the tribe's customs and taught the respected youths in the tribe to surf.

The tribespeople did not agree with Robert buying the diamonds, and didn't understand it because, according to their values, the stones lost their significance once taken out of the land where they belonged. But to them, this was an annoyance more than a point of conflict. Their main problem with Robert was that he drew the inquisitive youths from the tribe and led them down a path that the tribe considered harmful.

There was no evidence that Robert and Gusamo had ever clashed about this subject, although they had heated discussions about other things. But since only the two of them had been on the trip—Clovis had taken off because he found Robert annoying and rude—no one was left to recount what had happened in those days that the two men spent on the island.

Earlier in the hearing, Robert had apparently made a statement that Gusamo had "gone aggro" on him and had left the camp on the island's eastern beach, and that was the last he had seen of him. Abri said that Gusamo had camped on the western side of the island for five to ten days.

As we had also seen, the beach on the western side of the island was not all that far from the one on the eastern side, both being on either side of a fairly narrow peninsula.

According to Pengali trackers, Gusamo had barely moved from this area in that time. There was a fresh water spring at the far end of the beach, but he had not even made it to that point. Abri said that it was hard for him not to have known about the spring, because the stream trickled over the beach to the ocean and it always left trails, so she concluded that he had been ill or injured at that time.

He had written a note, put it in a jar and thrown it in the water.

Then he had waited.

The easiest way of accessing the western beach when coming from the eastern side was by boat, because the peninsula was rocky and rough, and the dense forest made it hard to climb the ridge.

Abri said that the tribe's trackers had found evidence that a boat had come to the western beach and that the only boat of that type in the area was Robert's dinghy.

Robert had claimed that he did visit the beach, because he'd become worried about Gusamo, but he found no one there.

Dr Cross doubted that, because Robert had never told the investigators about this visit to the beach and he would certainly have remembered it.

It was the prosecution's case that Robert had gone to the western beach, found Gusamo there, killed him and dumped the body in the sea.

I had discovered Gusamo's note in the bottle three or four days later, the Exchange had contacted me that Fiona Davidson was worried that her husband was missing three days after that, and Melissa Heyworth had gone to check on the island where a satellite image showed the boat on the beach.

By this time Robert had gone crazy trying to defend himself, because he knew he was in trouble.

When Melissa and her party arrived on the island, Robert had taken her hostage, afraid that she was a pawn of *gamra's*—or so he said. Exactly what he was afraid of, Melissa had been unable to determine. Robert had seemed "unhinged".

Melissa had not witnessed the killing of the Pengali trackers she had brought, and Robert's statement said that they had been killed by the Thousand Island people, because they were Washing Stones tribe Pengali.

Abri vehemently denied this.

The angry sound of her voice made Idda stir under Kita's jacket. Dr Cross looked at the wriggling bump a couple of times as if he wanted to say, *No pets in the courtroom.*

Robert's statement also said that he assumed that, lacking food and the skills to hunt or fish, Gusamo had tried to swim to the shore, where he had been attacked by the beisili—swimming lizards that looked like plesiosaurs—who were not friendly during the mating season. We'd seen them toss his body around and I could wholeheartedly attest to that *not friendly* part.

When we were at this point, I made a remark that I thought that the case that Robert killed Gusamo was not convincing. He might have died trying to swim to safety.

Dr Cross gave me a sharp look.

"I was there," I said. "I saw the beisili toss the body around. Who's to say that Gusamo didn't drown?"

"Mr Sahardjo would still have been fleeing Mr Davidson, because if Mr Sahardjo hadn't been afraid of Mr Davidson, they would have stayed together and gone for help."

"Do you think that will be strong enough to convict him, though?"

"We will leave that for the judges to decide."

In other words: shut up, Mr Wilson.

He went step by step over what had happened, what Abri had seen and what she hadn't seen; and he repeated himself two or three times to the point where Abri was clearly getting annoyed.

She vented to me during the morning break, which was served in a little room a bit further down the hallway, where I could hear the sound of the drums and many people talking and singing.

Abri said, "I try to tell him, and then he asks again, and I tell him and he asks again. I'm not stupid."

By now, Idda was no longer happy to stay under her mother's jacket. She ate from the cakes provided by the catering staff, but the cake had sticky coconut icing which ended up all over her and the surrounding part of the carpet. Idda grew upset about her sticky hands, and possibly a little agitated because of all the sugar in the cake and the attention she was getting. She raced around the room like a wind-up toy gone mad.

I grabbed her by the back of the shirt. "Idda, Idda, calm down."

She gave me an indignant look, while dangling in her shirt.

I gave her to Kita. "Do make sure that she keeps calm."

I was never sure if Kita understood me. In this case, she seemed happy to pretend that she didn't.

"Don't understand," she said in heavily accented Coldi. "They are not hearing our story at all."

No. Dr Cross was rehearsing her to tell the story as he wanted it.

I felt embarrassed for them and about the entire process. Some time soon, either Abri or one of the others was going to remark on the lack of fairness, and there would be nothing I could do to help refute their claims.

When we went back, I asked Dr Cross about the extra tickets to the gallery that we needed, and not only did he pretend to have forgotten about them, he said the court could not possibly allow all of us in the room when so many other people also wanted to get in.

Idda had escaped from her mother's jacket and had discovered that the display screen on the wall of the room could be turned on and off by tapping her tail against it.

Dr Cross glared at her several times. Once, Kita made an attempt to catch her daughter—in itself a rare occurrence—and she ran around the room squealing and almost upsetting the trolley with the water jug and glasses.

By now I was getting really annoyed. "So we've come all the way from Barresh and the court won't let us into the room? I don't think the Exchange will be happy with that."

"This is *our* courtroom, Mr Wilson, and it is *our* law."

"All right. Maybe I should walk out of here with your witness. In fact, I'm highly tempted to do that. I have nothing to gain or lose from this process and the witness is not bound by law to appear, because, as you pointed out, this is your law, and not hers. We are doing you a favour."

He knew I was right. His mouth worked, but no matter how much he might have liked to say, *We paid for your trip,* he knew he couldn't say that either, because the funding of the appearance of someone in the court should never be related to demands made of that witness.

He gave a stiff nod. "I'll see what I can do."

"Notify the court that there will be someone in the audience recording the session, as outlined by your agreement with the Exchange."

"Our protocol prohibits recording equipment."

"Then I recommend that you speak to my legal experts who have assured me that the Nations of Earth agreement with the Exchange takes precedence over that requirement."

"I will have to get advice on that."

"Please do."

He nodded, stiff faced. And all of a sudden, the tables were turned. He'd gone from his assured way of intimidating Abri to uncertain, stiff faced, defensive.

Ms Trnkova, seated next to him, kept looking at me.

Dr Cross said that he needed some time to check my demands, and he would do so this afternoon.

After he had left the room, Ms Trnkova informed me that this meant that this afternoon's session would be delayed and Abri would not appear today.

"So we came here for nothing today?"

"You came here to give yourself a better position from which to present your information."

Well, fuck that. "That's one way of looking at it."

"I'm sorry. I can get the driver to take you back to the hotel."

"What would happen if we went out that door instead?" I pointed to the front entrance where the crowd still camped and talked and sang and held up their placards and flags.

"It's locked."

"But if we went out the back entrance and into the forecourt. What could all these people tell us that we should be sheltered from?"

"It's for your protection. They might be violent."

"They're playing music. We have nothing that they want."

She met my eyes. Her expression was disturbed.

"Why are those people actually there and why is it that every time I ask about them, the question is deflected?"

"Whatever do you mean?"

"You know what I mean."

Her cheeks had gone red.

"Look, I will tell you a few things I should probably take to the police, but when Conrad Martens was killed, he was on his way to meet us. When he didn't turn up, and at that point we had no idea why, we noticed that we were being followed. We managed to capture one of the followers' jackets and we found a reader with some interesting information inside about how certain organisations are trying to manipulate us. The same organisations who tried, and failed, to manipulate the elections and the same organisations which apparently funded my trip here. Money I shall be repaying as soon as I get a chance. I would like to go on the record that I am not for sale for any kind of money."

She gave me a startled look. "No, of course not." And then she added in a low voice, "I worked for Mr Martens. I *liked* him. He was an honest man." Her eyes glittered.

"Good. Don't forget it. Now what are all those people doing there?"

A door clanged in the corridor and a man left a room and walked down the hallway, carrying a reader. Ms Trnkova glanced over her shoulder, nervously, with her flaxen blond hair fanning out when she turned her head. "I will accompany you to the hotel." She spoke more loudly than necessary, perhaps to mask the fact that I'd asked her a sensitive question. She said nothing more.

We went down into the lift, where the van still waited.

With all of us, it was quite squishy in there.

All conversations in the van, of course, were recorded as well so on the short trip to the hotel we spoke about the weather. I was trying to think of a place where we could speak freely and in safety. I hoped that Veyada had cottoned on to my thoughts in that direction and had come up with a smart location that did not involve the bathroom, because goodness knew what sort of equipment Thayu or Nicha or Evi had left in there. Besides, it would be suspicious to see one's legal officer in the bathroom. Questions would be asked and suspicions raised. From this point onward, everything we did would raise suspicions. Did one take a legal counsel for coffee? That might be an option.

At the hotel most people left the van. I gestured for Veyada to stay behind. Sensing that something was up, Evi stayed as well. Nicha came out of the hotel's main entrance, but I sent him back inside to go to Ayshada, and to ask for Thayu to come down.

"I'd like to have a talk about how we continue from here," I said to Ms Trnkova, for the benefit of the driver, who would no doubt report on any of our activities. "Can I buy you a drink?"

"Sure. I don't think I'm expected back at the office. We're done for today."

"Let's go then, after I drop off this gear." I indicated my case with my reader.

Ms Trnkova went inside the hotel's foyer with us. She looked over her shoulder to the van, which slowly drove off. Hesitated. The driver kept looking out the window. We waited, but he finally drove off.

15

O NCE WE WERE in the foyer of the hotel, I had no intention of going to our rooms. I just wanted to get rid of that prying driver. Thayu and Nicha waited in the foyer and I gathered them, Evi, Veyada and Ms Trnkova around me.

They were full of questions, but I put my finger to my lips and glanced at the hallway. "Out this way."

We went into the dining room, and from there into the courtyard and out the back gate. It led into an alley that came out in the next street. We walked in a group, collars drawn up against the wind.

It was only a short walk to the cafe we had visited on the first day. We walked in pairs or groups of three along the footpath. I kept an eye on the traffic, but didn't see the van. I had no doubt that we were monitored, but at least I hoped it would be hard to hear exactly what we said in a busy cafe.

My feeder burst into life when we crossed the wide median strip of the street, with its energy and recycling station. The windmill turned lazily in the soft breeze.

When we came to the cafe, it seemed that a parents' group had descended on the place. All the tables were occupied with young women and men with strollers and toddlers and babies. Well, that was a bugger. I looked over the room and couldn't see a single unoccupied table, but then an elderly couple left when they spotted us standing near the door. The table had only two chairs, but we managed to drag a couple over. Veyada sat on a little table in the corner and Evi offered to wait outside to keep an eye on any of our followers.

I ordered coffee for all of us. Ms Trnkova was making eyes at my restriction-free card, so I ordered some pastries as well, just because I could, and she had probably used up her daily allocation of sugary food with the snacks supplied at the court this morning.

"You worked for Conrad Martens," I started the conversation.

She sighed. "I did. I assisted him with his cases, as I do for Dr Cross. But I was assigned to the case by the judges, and I usually work for Dr. Martens."

"What do you know about things that were going on with Conrad Martens behind the scenes?"

"He was disturbed. He said the fairness of the court was under threat. He . . ." Her eyes glistened. "I don't know what I can say."

"Is anyone directly threatening you?"

"Not me so much. I'm only an assistant and they don't know that I was the one who found a lot of this information . . . I believe you might have received a letter."

"Mr Martens sent me a letter, do you mean that one?"

"No, that's not the one. Also, please call me Lenka."

Wait. Was she talking about the letter Margarethe Ollund sent me?

She said nothing, didn't confirm, didn't deny it, but I knew that this was precisely what she was talking about.

She said in a low voice, "You were asked to see her." *Her* being Margarethe, no doubt.

"I couldn't. Or at least not without raising suspicion. Do you know anything about what she wanted to say?" I lowered my voice further. "This has to do with the Pretoria Cartel, right?"

The waitress came to bring our coffee and a plate of pastries. Veyada, Nicha and Thayu each took one, reducing the size of the pile considerably. Veyada bit into one, spilling powdered sugar and pastry flakes over the table.

Lenka was a bit more civilised with hers, breaking off a piece and putting it in her mouth.

For a while, we ate and drank in silence.

All around us people talked and children laughed and cried. Just a normal day in a busy cafe. I hoped the noise meant that we couldn't be overheard.

Then I said, "So what is actually going on?"

"I don't even know where to begin." Lenka looked at the cup clutched in her hands, her shoulders slumped. Her steely demeanour and business-like expression had melted while I watched. She still wore the same clothes but abruptly seemed like a completely different woman to me. Haunted, worried.

She took in a deep breath and sighed. "I might as well tell you what I know, even though the court officials told me not to. There is nothing more to lose for me. I might as well resign, because . . ." She shrugged and sighed again. "I thought it was exciting when I was asked to look after Mr Davidson's case. I really did. This sort of thing was why I'd gone into law. To convict criminals." She gave a wry smile. "For years, I did my time looking after court cases involving breaches of employment contracts by large companies. I won't bore you with the details."

"Veyada here is a lawyer. I guess he wouldn't find it boring."

She eyed him. Veyada's appearance could be fairly intimidating to people who didn't know him. He was tall and broad, even for a Coldi. He eyed her back. He was not supposed to speak Isla, but I was sure he understood precisely what I said.

"Everything about this case is wrong. You know, even what I just said is wrong. 'The court told me not to tell you.' That's wrong. Nobody should tell court officials what to tell their clients unless it pertains to the court process, for example if the judge decides that people should not speak to each other until after the trial, in case knowing a certain thing will colour your witness account. That's all they can tell you." Her expression was hard.

"And I guess that's not what's been happening?"

She chuckled, not in an amused way.

"Everything about this case is rigged. From the way the judges were allocated to which media were allowed to cover the trial to which witnesses were called. Dr Martens raised his concerns and look at what happened."

"You have evidence that the murder is related?"

"No, but why else would he be murdered in cold blood? No, they won't be able to find any proof, as with so many of these high-profile murders. The killers, if they ever get caught, will be nameless, faceless men without any form of valid ID."

Damn, *that* sounded familiar. My heart skipped a beat. "What do you mean? Have you had more cases like this?"

"Not here, but in other countries, mainly in Africa. I came across all this when researching the influences of the Pretoria Cartel. You see, they've been buying up countries in financial trouble. They set up a shell company that takes on the country's debt to other countries or Nations of Earth. And then they put in place administrators and other people to manage this debt while using the country's resources to siphon off money for themselves. It started with the insolvency of the Solomon Islands. It has accelerated because Nations of Earth can afford to bail out a few small countries, but when you start talking about large countries, like Egypt, then there is no way they can afford it. Besides, it wouldn't be fair to all the other member states, so the private sector got involved."

As it had gotten involved in so many other things, not always to the benefit of the people.

"Anyway, the companies also demanded a high level of involvement in the governments of the countries they bailed out. You might say, 'Fair enough,' but this control went far beyond financial management. People who protested disappeared. Sadly, a lot of those countries are so poor and disorganised that there is little avenue for the families of these people to report the disappearances. Until there were many, and political figures got involved, and many of *them* were shot. Usually in broad daylight, usually when going somewhere for a private gathering. In the few cases where culprits were caught, they were always without any form of identification and no record."

"What did they have to say for themselves?"

"Nothing! They were all dead. None have ever been caught alive."

I saw Thayu and Veyada in the dark, running after a man who had followed the tram. A cold feeling crept over me. "Tamerians."

She frowned at me. "What?"

"Tamerians. That's what they are. On the world of Tamer, people create a type of artificial human stronger than existing human types, but there is something wrong with them: they don't communicate very well. You can't hold a real conversation with them. They are very good at following orders. We almost caught one the day before yesterday."

She stared at me. "You mean they are actually . . . from over there?"

Why did I have the feeling she'd wanted to say "aliens"? "We're not quite sure where they're from. The ones we've dealt with in Barresh came from Tamer. That's why they're called Tamerians. We're not sure what they call themselves."

Then she gave me a sharp look. "How did they get in? I thought they were really strict on who can travel through their Exchange."

Oh, she understood *gamra's* travel system well enough.

"We don't know. Now that it's clear that we're dealing with some form of Tamerians, we should find out as soon as possible." I was sure Amarru would have a thing or two to say about it. And that was, I realised, how *gamra* was involved in this case, through the implication that they didn't police the Exchange well enough to stop these nameless spies and killers coming in. That was part of Amarru's contract with Nations of Earth: that anyone coming in through the Exchange was known to them.

This was a *huge* implication that could blow the relationship between Earth and *gamra* right out of the water. I should contact Amarru about it as soon as I could.

"Have you seen any proof that these people work for the Pretoria Cartel?"

She laughed without humour. "Proof? These people don't exist, how are they supposed to leave proof?"

I put my reader on the table and touched the screen to turn it on. Lenka watched with keen eyes as I flicked through the menus, all in Coldi. I sometimes tried to imagine what my life would have been like if my father hadn't made the decision to apply for the job as Station Director at Midway Space Station, and I could not. Literally *everything* about my life would have been different, and I might have looked askance at Coldi text like Lenka did.

I found the maps that Devlin had made for me and showed them to her. I told her of the man Thayu and Veyada had almost captured and the reader we had found in his jacket. "These are the positions where they are spying on us, and these lines indicate channels of communication. This one here—" I pointed. "—goes to some sort of warehouse in South Africa."

I showed her the satellite image.

Her eyes widened and she raised her hand to her mouth. "I wonder if that's the same place . . ."

"What place?"

She pulled out her reader, and flicked through a number of menus. Then she held up the screen. The headline to an article said,

Execo storage warehouse linked to disappearances

Execo, of course, was Robert Davidson's company.

I skimmed the first few paragraphs.

. . . warehouse, which has been linked as potentially suspect in a string of disappearances of mine workers employed by Execo, South Africa's largest company for mining rare earths. It is not the first time that controversy breaks out over Execo's conduct towards its workforce. In June last year, one of the company's operations in Rwanda closed indefinitely. While the company cited poor returns, the closure came after continued protests by people from surrounding villages about exploitation of workers and mysterious deaths.

The article included a photo of a handful of buildings, two of which were quite tall. Nothing like the low sheds from Devlin's image. This operation, whatever it was, spanned more than just a single location.

"There is obviously a lot of fishy stuff going on with Robert's companies. The authorities could investigate and find something to pin on him. Why, of all things, do they choose to bring him to court over the one thing that's hardest to prove?"

Lenka looked up at me. Her eyes were really disturbingly light. "That is the question, right?"

"Do you have any idea?"

"First up, the court case was initiated by Gusamo's family who want justice."

"Understandable."

"They were told that the case had a very slim chance of succeeding, but as families often do, they became irrationally fixated on putting Robert in jail over Gusamo's death. The judges said the case shouldn't come before court and the family found no prosecutor to take it on for them. At that point, the case should have died, but someone came in with a lot of money and resources."

"The Pretoria Cartel, clearly."

"Yes, because they want Robert put away, but don't want to shine the spotlight on any of their activities, is my guess. They don't want us to investigate this building." She gestured at her reader. "Or that building." She gestured at my reader with Devlin's picture.

"Because fishy stuff is happening there, and I hazard a guess that it involves Tamerians. *Illegal* Tamerians." Highly illegal Tamerians, who Amarru would have a fit about if she knew. How the *hell* did they get Tamerians through the Exchange?

I blew out a breath. Amarru would be *very* unhappy about this. "By the way, I was contacted by a man by the name of Minke Kluysters. Do you have any idea who this is?"

She gave me a sharp look. "You're kidding, right?"

"No. He seemed quite kind. He has contacted me with a proposal that . . . does not sound unattractive."

"No one will tell you in so many words, but Minke Kluysters is considered to be the head of the Pretoria Cartel."

So my gut feeling about him had been right. "Why would he so blatantly contact me?"

"Whatever you say about them, the Pretoria Cartel are mostly not evil and are not criminals. It would make life a lot easier if they were. But no, they are shrewd businesspeople, the most dangerous kind, who walk dangerously close to the dark side, test the limits, but don't cross. They keep one foot in each camp until the world decides which way to swing."

"But they hired Tamerians who murdered Conrad Martens?"

"No one will ever be able to prove that. The members of the cartel as such probably don't know about it, and have not directly ordered this to be done. The militia who has done this will be owned by one of them, but this will be filtered through so many shell companies that it's impossible to trace. That's how dangerous these people are."

"Which people in the court are aligned with them?"

"It would be quicker to mention which people *aren't* affiliated with them."

"The judges?"

"What do you think?"

A feeling of horror came over me. And now he was trying to pull me into his sphere of influence by giving me an interesting proposal, and offering to pay for the information. All so that the cartel could have more power and money.

I also realised that if I didn't provide him with the information, the cartel might get Jasper or Huang Le to get it; and while they were not as high profile, they would do it. The cartel wanted an office in Barresh, and they would get it.

Lenka's pale eyes met mine. "The scale of this is enormous. It's been going on for many, many years, secretive and unhindered."

"No one has ever questioned it?"

"Oh, they have, but they were unimportant people, minor clerks and assistants who could be moved aside or given lucrative positions in order to shut them up."

She took another sip from her coffee.

"Or they were poor people from poor countries. The cartel has been very smart about building their influence. They started with places no one cared much about. Really poor countries all over the world. Then they gradually moved into bigger countries, and bigger businesses, until they could influence the assembly itself. And the court. There are not many people in the diplomatic circles who are not affected in some way."

"What about Margarethe?"

"President Ollund and the elected officials are mostly clean. Mostly, because some are likely not to be. We don't know which ones."

A chill went over me. This was a nightmare. What was *gamra* going to say? What defence was Margarethe going to put up? *Sorry, but the desire by Nations of Earth to balance our books has spawned an organisation that's buying itself political support not just on Earth, but everywhere,* probably wouldn't cut it.

How much did Jasper Carlson have to do with them, and did the cartel simply hire the Tamerians to conduct its dirty business or was it involved in promoting the use of Tamerians? Did they—and a further chill tracked down my spine—have anything to do with that giant Aghyrian ship that was still out there in the galaxy somewhere, lurking and plotting trouble or revenge on the society they viewed as inferior.

How did one even begin to disentangle their influence from all levels of public life?

"Do they have a philosophy or political bent? A political party? I believe Fiona Davidson ran against Margarethe in the election?"

"They want free business everywhere. No regulations. In the countries where they control the government, they favour their own businesses for government contracts, and they don't approve laws that would make those business interests more expensive or more difficult."

She took another sip of her coffee.

"Their core premise is that business interests should always take priority over everything else. If business is strong, the people will be prosperous and healthy."

"Except that doesn't work unless business profits stay in the country—or planet for that matter—where the work is being produced."

"That is right. Siphoning off business profits to other countries as a means to avoid tax is akin to exploitation. But they don't believe in regulation, or taxation or legislation to protect groups of people, income streams or economies. They believe in the ultimate free trade in everything, including weapons."

Oh, I could see where this was going.

She continued, "It is a grand scheme in a time when grand schemes have died. There is, in the cartel, an almost religious adherence to the free market trade principles as laid out last century by an economist named Lucas Wright."

"I think I've heard that name."

"His text books are still used in basic economics courses at most schools and universities. They're not that controversial, just the religious way in which these people are applying the principles is. They've analysed every letter, every article he has written—and there are a lot —and they worship what he says almost to the point of being a religious sect. These people are everywhere, Mr Wilson. They control everything."

For a very brief, utterly frightening moment, I became gripped by fear that the reason Margarethe wanted to see me was that she had her back to the wall and wanted to ask Ezhya for help.

Damn, no, she wouldn't be that stupid. Ezhya liked her, and he *would* help, too, because on Asto, democracy was an undesirable brand of activism and helping soulmates was what people did, even if it involved armies.

Holy shit, no.

I licked my lips. "It's interesting, and disturbing."

"Interesting?"

"Sorry, that's what my partner calls serious situations." Thayu met my eyes, and I sensed through the feeder that she would indeed have thought this serious enough to call it *interesting*.

"Very serious. These people must be stopped."

Was I overly anxious that I heard *at all cost* in her words and that *at all cost* involved *gamra* militaries?

Damn, no, I'd done that once, and was not going that way again.

This was a matter for Margarethe to sort out. I could talk to her, but I wasn't going to get involved.

Deep breath, Mr Wilson. Concentrate on problems you can solve. "Are there any things I should know that directly affect the court case? How does it relate to Robert Davidson? How far into the cartel is he?"

"You know that he bought the property next to Minke Kluysters, right?"

No, I didn't know.

"Well, they became friendly and a few years ago Minke made the mistake of allowing Robert Davidson into the cartel. Robert is a show-off loudmouth, gung-ho, anti-intellectual. He'd probably never heard of Lucas Wright and doesn't have any time for discussions about tactics and economics. Instead, he started drawing attention to himself and, within a year or two, had gotten himself embroiled in a disagreement about a redevelopment plan for a suburb in Jakarta."

"Wait—that's how Gusamo got involved, right? Is Gusamo in the cartel?"

"No, not at all. He stands for everything the cartel does not: openness, creativity and art, conservation and national traditions, people power—having grown up quite poor himself. Having those two on a trip to a remote place was a recipe for disaster."

"I thought you agreed that the evidence for murder is not strong?"

She snorted. "It isn't. I believe that the cartel secretly put Gusamo's family up to pressing for charges. I know that they paid for everything, including your trip."

"But why, if the case is not strong?"

"Why? Because the cartel, and the companies associated with them, have gotten the reputation of being human supremacists. The rumour goes around that if their political candidates get the upper hand, they will expel the Exchange and declare war on *gamra*. A lot of people find that scary, so now they're showing the world that, in the first place, they're interested in bringing some of their own to justice and, in the second place, that they have good relationships with *gamra*."

And damn, that was where I fitted into the scheme as well. "So, we're paraded out as show ponies." Blood rushed to my cheeks.

"Pretty much. No one is really interested in what Abri has to say. Her function is to be seen in conjunction with the cartel so that they can point at her when they're accused of being hostile to *gamra*."

I was highly tempted to get up and tell her that we were going home and forget about the trial, but at that point I was sure that I would be reminded that they paid for our trip. That wouldn't be such an issue had my accounts been healthy.

Damn, damn, damn.

16

____

I ASKED LENKA several times if she was all right going home by herself.

"I have my husband there," she said. "He's into boxing. He's very big and very Russian." She attempted a smile but I didn't think she was that comfortable.

I told her, "Do contact us if you need help."

She nodded.

We left the cafe, and we waited while she walked to the tram stop, lonely and vulnerable. There were murderers out there, people who stopped at nothing to prevent the truth coming out. She knew a lot.

"Maybe we need to devote some resources to protecting her," I said.

"Maybe when Sheydu comes back," Thayu said.

And yes, we were down in numbers. We could use Sheydu, Telaris, Reida and Deyu. They were close by, I'd been told, but my team had stopped making predictions for when they would join us.

Back at the hotel, it was dinnertime. The hotel staff had taken a delivery of fish, which was served whole on big platters with parsley and lemon.

The Pengali sat on the other side of the room, but from what I could see, they enjoyed it. They were talking animatedly between themselves.

Jemiro sat at the table with Eirani and Karana, but the two women did all the talking. He stared into the distance, and had not yet touched his food. It was as if every time I looked at him, he behaved more strangely. The more I tried to understand him, the less I understood. He was like a robot, a translating automaton, because there was nothing else to his personality. If there wasn't all this other stuff going on, I would have asked my team to spend more time checking him out. But as it was, he posed no threat and had done exactly as promised by Jasper.

The hotel staff came to take away the plates and bring coffee and sweets.

The sky outside turned dark.

After dinner, we convened in our bathroom.

Thayu, Nicha and Veyada might not have said anything during my meeting with Lenka, but they had understood everything.

In Coldi fashion, I put the situation to them rather bluntly. "I would very much like to withdraw from this farce of a trial, but we can't. What should we do?"

"You can't?" Veyada said, raising his eyebrows. "They can play with us, and you can't withdraw?"

"They paid for our travel."

"Then pay them back."

"It's not that easy."

"Isn't it? Give them the funds, tell them that they broke your trust and that of the Pengali, and leave."

"I agree with him," Thayu said, hugging herself while sitting on the edge of the bath. "They deserve to be sent a writ. *I demand that the truth be told and that everyone in the courtroom declare their interest. I demand that the Pengali be heard.* Veyada will write it up. I will gladly sign it."

"Me, too," Nicha said.

"It doesn't work like that." I spread my hands. "I can't just . . ." I *could* walk out, but I'd be pestered and possibly blackmailed by the Pretoria cartel. And besides, I wanted Robert to be punished in some way for the manner in which he had treated the Pengali. I didn't want to risk the trial being abandoned. And the Pengali needed to have their story heard. And my accounts were in a rather sad state.

I sighed, walked to the bathroom door and put my hand on the doorknob. I wished I could spend more time with Thayu. From the way she sat there, she wasn't feeling particularly well, and I wanted to know what was going on, but there was all this *stuff* going on that I needed to deal with. "Why don't I talk to the Pengali now and then to the court officials tomorrow. I have to make them understand each other. If this whole trial is a farce, the best *we* can do, for our group, is to make sure the Pengali get out of it what they want. If we're still not getting anywhere by tomorrow night, then you can write your writ."

They just stared at me, deadpan. They didn't like it. They were Coldi and they wanted blunt, decisive action. They wanted it now.

I blew out a breath.

Well, hell, so did I, but what would Nations of Earth make of a writ? Their history with Coldi writs was not too good. Writs needed to be responded to immediately. They were a *Coldi* thing. I was *human*. No, I pretended to be human. I was a Coldi mind in a human body. Whatever the hell I was, if I used a writ I might as well leave and never again be welcome on Earth.

I had to find a satisfactory end to this farce by using my mouth. And that, according to my team, was big enough.

Heaven help me and my big mouth.

I left our room and made for the end of the hallway. The door to the Pengali apartment was closed.

I knocked, and waited.

And waited.

Seriously, what were they doing? This was supposed to be their awake time.

I knocked again. "Abri? Ynggi? Kita?"

Nothing.

Damn it.

I turned around. The hallway was empty, and quite dark, with only a few sparse lights. Where were they?

"Did you call?" Nicha poked his head out of our room.

"Do you know where the Pengali are?"

"In their room?"

"If they are, they're hiding from us and not answering the door."

Nicha came down the corridor and pointed his scanner at the door. Scanning through the wood made for a poor quality picture, but nowhere in the apartment did it reveal anything that remotely looked like a person.

Shit.

"Looks like they've gone fishing again," Nicha said, his voice weary. He sighed.

Yes, I was starting to feel like that, too. "I suppose we better go and look for them."

Evi wanted to come, as well as Veyada. Thayu looked tired and for once didn't protest when I suggested she stay in our warm and comfortable room.

By now, the sky outside was almost black. It wasn't raining anymore, but low clouds drifted through the sky while the branches on the trees in front of the hotel swayed with the wind.

Unpleasant weather.

I donned my coat.

"Take the gun," Thayu said, while leaning back against a pile of pillows propped against the headrest.

"I'm only going out to the canal. The Pengali are probably fishing again."

"I knew you would say that. Take. The. Gun. This is why you have it."

I sighed. I reached into the wardrobe and retrieved it. I still shuddered at the thought of how Amarru got these things out of the Exchange enclave, but it would be fine as long as no shots were fired.

There wouldn't be, because we were only going to find a bunch of wayward Pengali.

Nicha, Veyada, Evi and I left the hotel a bit later, a couple of dark figures going into the night. Odette at the reception desk gave us a cheerful "Goodnight!" as we walked through the foyer.

Ugh, it was dark and windy outside.

We crossed the road and the tram tracks. The black water of the canal loomed on the other side. I peered into the darkness, feeling the hope that this was going to be easy seep from me.

"Can you see anything?" Nicha asked.

Veyada panned his scanner over the water, the other side of the canal, the bridge, the tram station, then back to the quay and the tourist boat jetty.

Nothing.

Damn it. What to do?

We started walking along the canal in the direction of the tourist boats. It seemed the most likely direction for the Pengali to go.

We were almost at the jetty and the dark shapes of the boats moored alongside, when there came a faint whining sound from the canal.

"There," Evi said.

I looked at the screen of Veyada's scanner. A couple of small figures sat in a dinghy that was moving in the middle of the canal towards the hotel. The scan also showed the outlines of improvised fishing rods and other items that I presumed to be buckets and Abri's net.

The fisherman yesterday had said that to catch fish, they needed to leave the city, so that was what they were doing. These Pengali were nothing if not determined.

I ran back along the quay to a place where I could see the dinghy. Ynggi sat at the engine. Give the Pengali any piece of equipment and they worked out how to use it. "Abri, Ynggi, come back here!"

Abri's voice drifted over the water. "We catch fish. The people will be friendly with us."

I walked quickly to keep up with the dinghy. Fortunately, it wasn't very fast. "Please come back. I will talk to the court about telling your story."

"No fish, no story."

"Please Ynggi. The boat isn't yours. You can get into a lot of trouble for stealing. You don't have the right to use it."

The Pengali didn't understand the concept of stealing because they didn't own property. But I was hoping to appeal to Ynggi's apparent sensible attitude. At least I'd thought he was more accepting of other people's customs than Abri.

But he probably had greater loyalty to Abri than his own opinions.

The dinghy kept going and we kept following it.

The engine whined louder when the boat disappeared into the tunnel that went under the road.

We ran up the stairs, crossed the road—fortunately there was no traffic—and waited for the boat to come out of the tunnel.

There they were, and they turned left into another tunnel. We ran back up the stairs, crossed another road. The canal on the other side went between houses.

We walked quickly along the side, following the dinghy. Ynggi steered the boat. Abri and Kita each sat on the sides trailing their fishing nets in the water. Idda held a line with a floater. How long before they'd get snagged by some piece of a broken bike or other rubbish? How long before Idda fell out?

But the boat kept going at a steady pace, and, being a simple dinghy, was slow enough that we could keep up with it while jogging. The rain became heavier, and I had to focus on where I put my feet in the dark. I couldn't keep track of where we were going. First, we ran along the street with old houses and then we came to a newer section with apartments along the water. Here, the quay had been turned into a recreation area, with cafes and restaurants—most now closed—and benches and little cafes in market stalls. There were garden beds and giant pots with trees and children's play equipment. We ran up a set of narrow stairs to a much older part of the quay. Ahead, the street opened into a square, where the wet pavement and the tables and folded sun umbrellas glistened in the light of street lamps. I wondered where the Pengali thought they were going. Coldi were much better runners than I was and I was going to have to bail on this running thing soon.

And then—

"Halt!"

A man in a long raincoat with reflective stripes crossed the road. When he came into the light of a street lamp, it turned out that he was a police officer. A second man stood under the shelter of an awning.

We stopped. I was panting, but neither Veyada, Nicha nor Evi were even remotely breathing fast.

"Can I see your permit?" the policeman asked.

"I . . . wasn't aware that we weren't allowed to come here." I eyed the boat with the Pengali, which puttered on in the canal, unnoticed by the police officers.

"Security, sir. Do you have a reason to be here?"

"Not really, other than going for a walk. The weather turned awful, so . . . we thought we'd take a shortcut."

The Pengali boat had now almost disappeared. I became aware of the sound of music and voices of many people singing and talking, drifting from the square ahead.

"What's going on there? Some sort of festival?"

"Just go back the way you came, please sir."

We turned around. No point annoying the officers, since they appeared particularly humourless.

We needed to find out where the Pengali had gone anyway. I had no desire to create a fuss by annoying police officers, nor did I want to draw attention to who I was. To be honest, the weather was pretty awful.

But I knew what was going on in the square ahead: this was the crowd in front of the courthouse that people tried to keep us away from. Conrad Martens had even told me not to try to contact them, since he was already in contact with the organisers.

We stopped in a narrow side street, hopefully away from spying eyes.

"What now?" I asked.

Nicha was looking at a map on his reader. "The canal runs in this direction, and if they keep going, they will go in a circle and end up in front of the hotel again. We can try to catch up with them here." He pointed.

"You're on. Lead the way."

Nicha set the pace and led the way through a maze of alleys and streets, most of them lined by old houses. One day, I should come here to have a proper look around. We came past cafes and eating houses where warm light radiated from the windows, past shopping precincts where evening shoppers went in and out of colourful stores.

"Whoa!" Nicha stopped suddenly.

We all scrambled into a porch niche at the entrance of a dark shop, selling, of all things, candles.

"Someone ahead," Nicha said.

I fought to keep my breathing quiet.

A couple of dark figures stood ahead in the alley. It was impossible to tell if they were police, although they probably were.

"How far from the courthouse are we?" I asked

Veyada pulled out his reader. "It's behind this row. Wait."

He flicked through a couple of screens with menus and found a different image, this one a live view, which displayed a crowd of people, seen from something like the first or second floor of a building.

"Did you just hack into the safety monitoring cameras?"

"Devlin did that."

With instructions from the Exchange, no doubt.

I studied the screen more closely. I recognised the fountain with the statue of hands holding each other that stood in front of the courthouse.

A lot of people stood in a circle surrounding something that was happening in the middle, something that involved a group of cylinders . . . drums?

My thoughts immediately went to the *irrka* drum, which I was sure stood safely in the Pengali room at the end of the corridor.

"Are there any other cameras in the area? Any along the canal?"

Veyada nodded, and flicked through a number of displays showing empty, dark water. No sign of the Pengali, until—

"Wait, is that the dinghy?"

There was no one in it, though. It lay alongside the canal, in deep shadow, and the camera's resolution was too poor to enlarge it enough for us to see what the bumpy things inside the dinghy were. But they *could* be fishing nets. Added to that, the camera was right in front of the square at the courthouse, not far from where we had been separated.

Well, damn it. "I'm guessing, and it's only a guess, that they heard the drum music, grew curious and went to have a look."

"That's not a bad guess," Nicha said.

"Do you want to check it out?" Veyada said.

"There are likely to be police. I don't think we should draw attention to ourselves."

"We can do this without attracting attention," Evi said. He didn't speak often, and when he did, people listened.

"Is there a way?" Nicha asked.

Evi explained about an alley a bit further back, and a fence we could climb that would let us into the yard at the back of a cafe that faced the square.

I said, "You've been planning this for days, right?"

He grinned.

"Well, let's go then."

Evi led the way back. We walked in single file, keeping to the shadows. He turned left into an alley with a couple of small quaint shops and a cafe. At the end was a small courtyard with a couple of recycling bins and a parked delivery van.

Evi made for a metal fence on the other side of the courtyard. He dragged over a bin, climbed onto it and looked over the fence. "The way is clear."

Nicha jumped up next to him and helped me up with a strong hand, while Evi jumped down on the other side. I swung my leg over the fence and dropped to the ground on the other side, awkwardly, because climbing fences was totally my day job.

Veyada simply vaulted the fence without using the bin, landing with a thud next to me.

"Show-off."

"One has to exercise one's muscles."

We had come out into another dark yard with a storage container and the obligatory recycling bins. A narrow thoroughfare led to a place where I could see coloured lights and a lot of people.

Indeed we were right outside the protester's camp at the forecourt. The fingertips of the artwork in the fountain were visible over the crowd and tents.

We sauntered into the square as if we belonged there.

On the perimeter, along the walls of the surrounding buildings, news reporters had set up their equipment. Some had even gone as far as setting up tents emblazoned with their service's logo.

We attracted some curious looks, mostly because of Evi, who was both really tall and really black without being African.

Veyada was looking at his reader.

"There, and there, and there, and there." He glanced at each spot: roofs, balconies, office windows. I saw nothing, but his equipment told him that there was electronic activity in these places. Cameras, listening equipment. Maybe automated, maybe with people in attendance. Tamerians or Nations of Earth special services, no one knew.

"Everyone, look out for Pengali," I said.

It was going to be hard finding them in this crowd.

A number of tents had been set up surrounding the fountain. Some of them were of the circus-tent variety; others were household camping equipment, some big, some small, interlinked with tarpaulins that flapped in the wind. People had set up campfire barbecues and a smell of cooking hung over the area. The protesters had left a path open from the street past the fountain to the main entrance of the court. Various hand-painted and more professional-looking placards lined the way. The ones I could see displayed text like "Execo = Murder" or "Where is my brother?" or "Rich people take. Poor people pay." There were also some photographs of people: a school picture of a teenage girl, a picture of a young man in a wheelchair, a picture of a scene of the utter devastation of an abandoned mining site, with poisonous yellow ponds, churned soil and not a tree in sight.

The drum band I'd seen play through the glass of the courthouse foyer had abandoned their instruments in favour of dinner.

And there, behind one of the tall African drums, I spotted an agile black-and-white banded tail. "There they are!"

17

———

INDEED, THE PENGALI were studying the drums.

Ynggi tapped the tightly strung hide surface of one. It made a big hollow sound. He grinned and tapped it again.

Abri had found a set of smaller drums, and rapped the surface with her knuckles to test out the different tones of each. Kita was interested in the xylophone. She had figured that the sticks with the balls at the end were for hitting the keys. She tried out one, and laughed at the clear "ting" it made. At her feet, Idda jumped up, her arms in the air, wanting to be picked up. Kita put her daughter on her shoulder.

By this time, a lot of people had gathered around to look. They were a colourful bunch, many of them in bright clothing.

The bright colours often disguised a darker truth. Most of these people would classify as "Blue," people who, through having the wrong background and genetics, would never qualify for any of the jobs inside the courthouse, because it was almost impossible for them to raise themselves out of poverty with the Blue tag on their ID passes that they could never shed. I hated this system. My father had seen it instated and hated it even more. I had no doubt that, had I lived on Earth, I would have been blue, too, just because my mother had died of cancer which was a stain on my genetic record.

I had never been able to share the White-class people's disregard for this group. Because there were so many of them, these were the people who would ultimately seal the fate of the world, I had no doubt about that. Even though they needed to prove themselves worthy before they could vote—and as a consequence most didn't.

But it would be a lie to say that the army of unfamiliar people watching us didn't make me a bit nervous. They weren't hostile at all, but they weren't overly friendly either, and we dressed and acted like White-class people even if we were not. If the White-class were indifferent to *gamra*, the Blue class were often openly hostile, even if only because they would never be able to afford travel off Earth.

And here they stood, mesmerised by a couple of curious Pengali.

Ynggi was still testing the drum, and Abri dragged one of her drums closer to him. Then he took off his coat. His tail came free and went up into the air. He took off his jumper, and his shirt. A couple of street lamps lit the area, and his giraffe patterns stood out in the neon light.

By now, people were calling for others to come and watch.

Lastly, Ynggi kicked off his shoes and stepped out of his trousers. He wore the traditional Pengali belt with the teeth and stones and other trophies dangling from it, with his glass-stone knife. It looked impressive, but I hoped he wasn't going to be too cold.

He picked up a pair of drum sticks from a bag near the xylophone and, watched by everyone in the square, hit the drum in the traditional betanka rhythm: one low beat, two high, one low and one high, three—two, three—two or the other way around.

Kita added to the rhythm by beating a stick on the keys of the xylophone.

Abri produced her dyenka pipe, which was a type of wind instrument with a mellow tone, where one could play two-tone melodies by humming into the instrument. She always carried one on her tribal belt.

Apart from the vital part of the betanka leader—the one who played the drum—all betanka music was improvised. It was traditionally how Pengali unwound and processed the happenings of the day. It could be how arguments were fought out, how new people were introduced and tasks assigned. Sung betanka was more formal than instrumental parts, and they had different rhythms associated with them. Washing Stones tribe betanka was different from Thousand Island tribe betanka, and both of those were different from urban betanka, especially if non-Pengali were involved.

The Africans in the forecourt watched, and then they started clapping, and dancing.

And I hadn't realised how much betanka and its five-beat structure was part of Barresh. Every official document, official building, every council uniform bore the five-pointed star. Nothing was symmetrical, and the three—two grouping was extremely common, from the way council committees were structured to the way houses were built.

Betanka as a form of music was everywhere in the background, like annoying muzak that you could not turn off.

One thing about betanka was that everyone took part. Idda jumped from her mother's shoulder—dressed in her bright orange gear, and climbed on top of the big drum, where she jumped around, producing an arrhythmic thumping.

Kita plucked her off the drum—where she was at risk of being hit by Ynggi's sticks—but she wouldn't keep off.

"Here, give her to me." I held out my arms.

Idda was happy to sit in the warmth under my coat, her little hands clinging onto my shirt. She was awake and alert, looking around with wide eyes at the goings-on.

Ynggi gestured for the African drummers to join him.

They took a bit to get used to the unusual asymmetric rhythm, but when they got it, others joined in, or they clapped or banged bottles and sticks together.

The group grew ever bigger. A couple of police officers came to have a look. They didn't clap and dance, but couldn't stand still either.

Kita gave me a big can to beat the rhythm and even Veyada took part. Idda escaped from under my jacket and danced on the rim of the fountain, her tail waving in the air. She clapped her hands. People laughed at her, and she did look silly in her orange beanie and too-big jumper. Her mother stood next to her, so I judged that she would be safe.

Without speaking a single word, the Pengali had the whole group dancing and playing.

I took the opportunity to do some sleuthing. I quietly slunk into the camp, into the darker alleys between the tents where the light from the lamps didn't reach. Here, people sat in little pools of light cast by solar jars, which produced an eerie greenish glow similar to the light pearls in keihu houses.

The people who had stayed behind, who were not clapping and dancing, were the very old and very young and the incapable.

An African man I judged to be in his thirties sat in the entrance to a tent in a ratty old wheelchair. His trouser legs were folded under him from the knee down. It was cold, but he wore a singlet and sleeveless jacket, which showed his healthy arms—black-skinned and rippling with muscles. A poster that stood next to him said: "Have you seen my brother?"

The photo showed a young man with smiling eyes. Judging by the collar on his shirt, he was wearing a school uniform and looked sixteen or seventeen.

The man eyed me sideways, and I felt terribly awkward. Here I was, incredibly rich in his eyes, a traveller of the universe. I claimed to care about the poor people of all worlds and I didn't believe that to be untrue, but I knew nothing about the harsh lives of these people and I was unsure of what to say to him, because I didn't want to say anything that would sound belittling, insulting or flippant.

"How long have you been camping out here for?" That was a neutral enough question.

He counted on his fingers. The black skin on the back of his hands had big patches of pink, lacking pigment.

"Two weeks now, mister."

"Have you spoken to the people you came here to see?"

He laughed. His mouth was missing several teeth. "They don't want to hear my story, mister. We come here so that the fancy news people hear what we got to say. That evil man is not going to end up in jail and is not going to be paying us any money unless we make a big stink, because no one here cares about us."

"I care about you. Tell me your story, then. Sorry, what is your name?"

"Charlie, mister."

"I'm Cory Wilson."

His eyes widened. "You're kidding. Mr Wilson who travels to all them planets and makes all them aliens listen to us?"

Well . . . not quite. Not quite sure where he got that idea. "I am here with some of the folk who are telling *their* stories of mistreatment to the court. I would like other stories to be heard as well."

He laughed again. "We should be so lucky. If we was aliens, maybe they'd listen to us. But we got no money and no other flashy things. We're just dirty old poor people. No one wants to know about us."

"You can tell me why you're here."

"See him here, mister?" He gestured at the photo of the schoolboy. "He's my brother. His name is Jacko. He was born with the skinny sickness and when he was ten, people came into the village and gave him medicines to make him better. You know of the skinny sickness, mister?"

I had to admit I didn't.

"It came from monkeys, they said. Like *we* were monkeys. Like there even *are* any monkeys where we live, mister." He gave me an angry look. "Anyway, my brother, he got better and he got to go to school, because they said he had to because they made him better. He wasn't really better because he still needed the medicines, but they were giving him what he needed the whole time, and asking him questions about it, and making him do things. They were always these foreign men who would pick him up from home and take him to school. I was asking what they wanted, but they said nothing. I don't know if they could even understand me. And then one day he never came home."

He looked up at me, spreading his hands.

"He just . . . didn't come home." His voice wobbled.

"I'm sure you looked for him?"

"Oh hell, yeah, mister! I knew there was a house in town where these foreign men would stay so I went there. I had to do favours for a friend who had a car because you know how hard it is to get around when you use crutches? They said at that place that they didn't know my brother. And I told them he came here a lot, and then they said they knew no such person. And I got really angry and pushed this nurse aside and went into the building looking for him. I don't see him anywhere, but there were lots of people in beds. They were all just sitting there, staring as if they were dumbstruck. I knew one of them, I asked what he was doing there, but he didn't even say hello. Some were attached to machines next to the bed."

"Like heart monitors with screens where you can see the pulse?"

"No, not like that. Big machines that had a thing that you can put on someone's head."

"Like a helmet?"

"Yes, like that."

I had no idea what sort of thing he could have seen, but I couldn't say I liked the sound of this.

"Did you see what they were using those machines for?"

"No."

"Did those people tell you?"

"They weren't saying anything. They were like dumbstruck, as if I wasn't even there. But I wasn't in there for long, because the guards threw me out. Broke my crutches and my hip, and then I had to get my legs taken off."

That was strange. And chilling. It reminded me of another situation where I had walked through an entire ship full of people asleep. Why would they do this for any reason other than to run some sort of foul experiment on people?

"Did those foreigners ever come back?"

"They haven't yet. I tried to go back to that house, and I took some friends because the police wouldn't come, but I couldn't use my crutches anymore and it's hard to go places in the chair. Not here. This is easy." To demonstrate, he wheeled the chair back and forth.

"Does it commonly happen that people disappear?"

"All around where I live, mister. They're always the people that have sicknesses. The foreigners come and tell them that they can get free doctors and free medicines and that's why they go. Because we have no medicines and no doctors. We have no money. People go with the foreigners because they're desperate. Then they disappear. Sometimes we hear that they've got to other countries, but mostly they just disappear."

While we were talking, another man had arrived. He was not African, but fairly dark-skinned, small and lean of statue. His clothes were clean and well-cut, his eyes clear and intelligent. Compared to the other people he looked, and I hated to say this, well-off and educated. Someone with a WHITE tag.

I acknowledged him with a nod.

"Mr Wilson, my name is Dharma Yuwono." He stopped as if that name was supposed to mean something to me. It didn't.

I was getting to the stage where I felt terribly embarrassed by these people. I was supposed to know what skinny sickness was and maybe I was supposed to recognise this man's name. Maybe I was even supposed to know the name of Charlie's village because it had been mentioned on the news that I never watched because I no longer belonged on this earth.

"I'm very sorry but I don't recognise—"

"Gus' husband."

Oh damn, make the embarrassment complete.

He continued, "That is the tragic truth in this story. Robert Davidson and the court have made this trial about Robert Davidson. A man was killed. His family—me, his sister, his mother and father— are not allowed to attend the court, because we question the practices of the Pretoria Cartel in attempting to influence the judges."

"I was told Gusamo's brother is here."

He snorted. "He let himself be bought by the cartel. It's silence money. He asks none of the important questions. The good prosecutor got taken off the case, and now he is dead. The other people are all puppets."

Except Lenka Trnkova. I hoped she had made it home safely.

"But you would surely want Robert in jail, which is what they want."

"Not if it means that our concerns about the cartel's treatment of its workers and corruption will be swept off the table and we will have to fight for years to get another cartel member to court again. That's what they want: sacrifice Robert and get him convicted quickly. Allow him to serve his sentence as house arrest, so that everybody can go back to doing all the things they were doing before—including performing medical experiments on people in Africa and buying governments of countries that no one cares about, until they own Africa and much of southeast Asia, and they control the numbers in the Nations of Earth assembly. Who knows, that may already be the case."

I looked from him—clean, well-spoken, healthy—to Charlie in his wheelchair and his missing teeth. My impression about Earth in one arresting image. I knew why the system of White and Blue classes had been instated: initially to help people after the war. To be given a Blue card meant that you qualified for greater levels of support services. The White card holders never qualified for any. It had gone from a simple classification to a deep rift in society. Rich and poor, divided across a deep gulf. There was no money, so the support services for the Blue card people dried up quickly. No one cared about the Blues, because they weren't seen as contributing much to the world economy. These people were angry, and they had not been sitting at home doing nothing for the last twenty years. They had made deals with whoever wanted to help them.

Now it came back to bite Nations of Earth in the butt, and there was nothing anyone could do to fix it quickly.

Dharma continued, "The members of the cartel don't want any of this to be revealed. Many people in affected countries don't want to hear it. Their lives have improved, and while they care a bit about the people who go missing and other atrocities, they don't want to go back to being poor and ill, so they're not speaking out. Only those who have lost family members and those foolhardy enough to believe in justice speak up. That's us, in this square here. There will be others across the city, across the world, but speaking out is dangerous, as Gus found out, as Dr Martens found out, as we could all find out at any moment." He nodded at me. "You had better get out of here soon. They usually send in squads to shut us up and conduct a roll call every night. You don't want to have it on your record that you were here." He reached inside his jacket and gave me a card. "You can reach me here. Use the passcode on the back and set up your own access pass. We're all there. Charlie and me and everyone here."

"Thanks." I stuck the card in my pocket.

A shout sounded behind me, and I noticed that while I had been talking, the atmosphere had changed. Where had all those police officers come from all of a sudden?

Some mingled with the crowd. Some stood in a line along the boundary between the forecourt and the street, where a handful of curious locals had come to look. It was not so much the regular police officers who worried me, but the people in armour with heavy-duty guns.

A group of them marched onto the forecourt, shouting for people to move aside. Many of the protesters grabbed their things and ran.

"I'm sorry. I'll contact you later." I pushed my way through the crowd to the fountain, where the music and dancing was still in full swing. I yelled, "Ynggi! Stop."

But he didn't hear me. Where was Veyada? Where was Evi?

One of the officers blew a whistle.

Ynggi gestured to him. *Come and play!*

I yelled again, "Ynggi, stop!" There were too many police here; this was going to end in trouble.

But he still didn't hear me.

The police surrounded him and Abri, who were still playing, but who was starting to look rather alarmed. While most Africans had abandoned their drums, a few remained defiant and stuck with Ynggi. Betanka was not only improvised, it was mood music. Rather than melodic, with a melody you could sing, it reflected mood and tone, and Ynggi was hitting the giant, noisy drum with increasing frequency and strength. The African drummers hit their bongo drums. The ground was vibrating with the thundering threat of a giant betanka orchestra.

"Ynggi, Ynggi!" I waved.

Finally, he stopped, and the Africans stopped drumming, too. They cast suspicious glances at the officers in armour, picked up their drums and took off.

A lot of other protesters had also retreated to the tents, where they formed a line of defence around their camp. Some carried sticks or brooms.

Whoa.

All of a sudden, the whole atmosphere had changed.

"Everyone calm down!" an officer called. "Line up starting here, so we can check your identification."

I spotted Veyada in the crowd, with his hand under his jacket, where I had no doubt he carried his gun. Mine suddenly felt heavy in its harness.

I gestured to Ynggi to leave the drum. There was not much point in turning this into a bigger conflict than necessary.

"What do these people want?" Abri asked me. She sounded half-puzzled, half-outraged. One did not barge into a betanka and stop it.

"They say people have complained about the noise."

"Pah! It's time to play. What else do you do after dark? Work and play. These people don't know how to live. I like the dark people."

Kita waved her tail in agreement. Ynggi did the same. They liked the poor Africans, who were also repressed and ignored like the Pengali.

The police were now herding people back to the tents. A scuffle broke out at the edge of the camp.

Someone yelled, "Keep your hands off me, man!"

A police officer stumbled backwards. I said to Ynggi, "Careful."

Veyada and Evi came through the crowd to join us.

Veyada said, "Devlin says there is a big group of these people in front of our accommodation."

"The *police*?"

"No, the protesters. They have come with vehicles."

"Cars?"

"No, they have two wheels."

"Bikes."

He gave me a blank look and craned his neck to try to see over the heads of the crowd. "We really need to get out of here."

A group of people on the street were yelling slogans. I couldn't hear what was being said, because the shouts echoed between the buildings. Veyada pushed into the crowd first, then Evi, then me with the Pengali followed by Amarru's guards who had quietly materialised out of the crowd. I was surprised no one had contacted the others yet, but I was sure there was some kind of plan.

The people in the street shouted. There was pushing and shoving, and sirens going off, a man yelling through an amplifier for people to go home.

The whole crowd in front of the courthouse started chanting the same words they had also chanted to the betanka music. When I saw it on a placard, I finally understood what they were saying: *Justice is right for Blue and White.*

The crowd consisted of Africans, a lot more than had been camped in front of the courthouse, as well as people in wheelchairs and others rejected from the White class.

People came in from a side street riding bikes, tens, hundreds of them, pouring into the square. They were all ringing their bells and the chorus of ding-ding-ding-ding was deafening. One of the men at the front—a big African with hundreds of plaits hanging down his back, wore a headset attached to a sound booster strapped to the back of his bike.

"Come and stand up with us!" he was yelling.

Part of me wanted to join them. I found the system of grading people according to their perceived "risk" and "intelligence" factors revolting. I had scraped into being classified White because I got my father to sign a declaration that said that my mother's cancer had been nonhereditary. Of course no one knew. Had I lived on Earth, this matter would have ruled my life and my ability to study and get work. Had I lived on Earth, I would have been there with them.

But we needed to get the Pengali to safety. I had *gamra* to think about. Thayu would be worried.

We pushed our way through the crowd.

Down in the street, we lost track of what was happening. People were pushing and shoving around us, mostly going in the other direction, *to* the unrest, while we were trying to get away from it.

Bright light flared behind us. Police voices gave orders in loud booming amplified booms of sound. Residents in the buildings facing the street came to windows, looking out at the chaos.

Abri, Kita and Ynggi were so much smaller than the rest of us that they could easily get lost in the sea of people. I checked that Kita had Idda, which she did; I could see the tail sticking out from under the jacket. The Pengali kept close together, in the middle of the group, all of them holding the trolley.

I hoped we were going to make it to the hotel unscathed.

I was just wondering if we should perhaps see if we could use the dinghy to get back when someone touched my arm. Someone tall and muscular with the familiar feel of the rubbery material that made up Asto-made body armour.

I looked aside into a grinning young face I had long hoped to see.

Since when had Deyu grown so impressive? Reida and Telaris were with her, too. I realised they had probably been following us, on the lookout for anything that might harm us in the forecourt to the courthouse.

And Sheydu was there. She greeted Amarru's guards with a stiff nod. I was so incredibly glad to see the rest of my team again.

I wanted to hug them, but one did *not* hug Sheydu. I wanted to ask them where they'd been and what they'd been doing, but this was not a time for talk. We needed to get out of here safely first.

With their help, we managed to make it out of the busiest part of the protest. The street was full of police vehicles. Lights flashed, people spoke into devices, loudspeakers crackled, screens flickered. A van that looked like a command post had a holo projector set up, displaying the whole area.

"What were you doing there?" Sheydu asked. "I can't believe that your people would have approved of this. Where is Thayu?"

"She wasn't feeling well." I hoped she hadn't worried too much about us. Although if she had, she would have come here, I was sure of that. She wouldn't let fatigue stop her.

We'd gone half a block before I realised we were going the wrong way.

I tapped Sheydu on the shoulder. "Hey, the hotel is that way."

"I know." She kept going without changing course. Veyada was behind me, and the familiar figure of Telaris behind him, and Deyu and Reida on either side of me, but I couldn't see any other members of our party. Not the Pengali, not Evi, not Amarru's guards.

"Then what is this about? Where are the others?"

"Going back to the accommodation."

"Where are we going?"

"You'll see."

I did see. We turned a corner and came to a main road, now empty. In the middle of the road stood a black bus with darkened windows, surrounded by at least a dozen guards on motorbikes. There were also two dark unmarked cars, one in front, one behind. A guard approached from the front vehicle. He wore the grey Nations of Earth uniform, with the small patch that identified him as a member of the president's guard.

That bus . . . could I hope that Margarethe was in there?

The presidential guard spoke briefly to Telaris and gestured for me to keep going, off the footpath, onto the road where, a block back, a few confused road users were being stopped, wondering what was going on.

The door to the bus opened at my approach. I climbed up the steps.

A small light burned in the back of the bus. In its pool of golden yellow sat a grey-haired woman I was well familiar with.

"Margarethe."

"It took some organising, but finally we meet. Sit down."

18

______

I **WALKED ALONG** the aisle in the bus and sat on the soft leather bench opposite Margarethe.

Alone. Sheydu stayed behind. Deyu stayed behind.

We had left the dead zone, but there was no communication noise in my head. The bus probably contained a different kind of communication block.

The door shut, and it was just us in a woolly bubble of silence.

Footsteps sounded along the side of the bus, a door slammed and we were off.

"Did you get my message?" Her face looked tired.

"I did. We were escorted out of the airport and had no opportunity to see you. I tried to see Conrad Martens the day before yesterday, because I had a feeling he was going to relay your message, but you know what happened there."

She nodded, her face grave. "It's the situation we are in. We can't trust anyone, especially those in positions of power."

"I spoke to Gusamo Sahardjo's partner. He told me that a number of the judges have been bought."

"A number? Pretty much all of them. The assembly appoints the judges every three years. The new bench are all choices that the cartel would approve of. They are also behind many political movements."

"What do they hope to achieve?"

"Get richer. Let commercial concerns run the world. Get rid of rules. Control people's decisions. These people are obscenely rich. Not even you or I have any concept of how rich they are. They have funded many scare campaigns, they own media, governments politicians."

"What about you?" I thought about last year's election.

"I'm reasonably safe, I think. Nobody has threatened to pull any of my funding if I didn't do certain things, and if there was anything fishy about the funding of my campaign, my office staff would have found that out a long time ago. Sadly, we all depend on private money to run for office. It's a fact of life. Also, because I'm not running any more elections, I am not an attractive target. These people want to buy power in the future. As for me: they want to turn me into a lame president because they control everyone around me, so that I can't do anything they don't like because I don't have the numbers."

"What can be done? Expose the rackets? Bring them to court?"

She snorted. "That's what they want. They own the courts. They make sacrifices out of single people—"

"Like Robert Davidson."

"Yes, like him. Getting him convicted satisfies people, but they never get to the big reasons behind big business. The whole process is designed to obfuscate."

"Any other alternative to stopping them?"

"There is only one that seems effective to me."

"And that is?"

She sighed. "There is some backstory to this. Do you want a drink?"

"Not an alcoholic one." I had been nearly killed while talking to President Sirkonen while having a drink, and Asha Domiri had tried to feed me zixas in a bar in Barresh, and I no longer thought having a drink while discussing important events with an important person was a good thing to do.

"I have tea or coffee, too."

"Tea would be nice."

She leaned over and pressed a button on a panel next to her. There was a soft humming noise and a door opened. Inside its lit interior stood a cup with steam rising from its safety lid. There was even a holder in the table next to me.

I clutched the hot cup with both hands. The bus was moving at a steady speed. Where to, I had no idea, but we seemed to be on a main road, one of those interconnecting ones that were raised over the water. The occasional light flashed past the window, and sometimes I could see reflections on surrounding water, but other than that it was dark outside.

"I guess you are aware that companies owned by Pretoria Cartel families have bought entire governments when they defaulted on their debts. At first they only did the small countries. The island states no one really cares about. I think Morocco was the turning point, where we started to get worried about it. Not that anyone could do anything. As soon as we helped one country, there would be a long list of others wanting the same level of help. We *could* help one country. We could not help twenty. A lot of the problems are systematic. The land can no longer support the population. It's too dry, or too wet. Agriculture that has sustained people for thousands of years has vanished. Governments are failing to provide help. They can't help, because they have no money. The citizens are powerless. They can't study because they have the wrong classification, and because they can't study, they're unemployable in the newer industries. Worse, there are plenty of people with education to take up whatever jobs are available, which aren't many because no one is spending any business capital in those areas. It's an ever deepening rut. I don't think anyone had the illusion that these debt companies would be altruistic in their aims, but at least they managed to get the issue of countries falling into anarchy off our plate. Most of this happened more than ten years ago."

I had been a student on Mars back then, full of politics and ideology. I remembered the alarm bells about companies buying the debts of countries. We had even debated it. To us, young students from well-off backgrounds, most of whom had spent much of our lives off Earth, the issue was distant and clinical, but of course it involved real people and real people's lives, and people reacted to things that happened to them, leading to unexpected outcomes.

"So the issue of insolvency of countries did go away for a while, but of course the underlying problems did not. The countries *still* can't support their own population, only now there are these companies that transport and provide food for the people. In return, the people are supposed to be grateful, vote for the right politicians or buy the right products. They have giant schemes of favouritism where people who openly support a nominated cause get more and better supplies."

She sipped from her tea.

"So where does all this take us?" I asked, clutching the warm mug.

"It takes us to how these people worked their way up to the assembly, to parts of the world where we are definitely *not* happy to let them exist, to how we almost lost the election to people affiliated with the Pretoria Cartel." She gave me an intense look.

I knew Margarethe had won by the smallest of margins, but had never heard the full story. "I didn't think Fiona Davidson came close to gaining enough votes."

"No, she didn't, but Ricki Guatierez definitely had a chance. In addition, if Fiona Davidson had simply been elected into the assembly, she would have taken a lot of supporters, and would have tipped the balance."

The president was elected by the assembly, not by the people. The assembly dissolved before the president was chosen, and prospective assembly members in each country campaigned on the basis of their support for a candidate.

"It was very close." She stared at the window for a short while, her face etched with worry. "These people have ended up in control of many of the important positions. The speaker of the assembly, the head of the Resources Committee, almost all the court judges, most of the representatives from Africa, I could go on and on. These people are everywhere. They're owned by companies."

"Surely there are regulations against that?"

"There are, but the ownership of these companies is so deep that you can't extricate it from the national interest. There is nothing on the surface that goes against our rules, and no covert relationship between the politician and the company; but when someone comes from a small town with only one employer, and all of their friends and family are employed by this employer, the person in question will have no demonstrable vested interest but will still vote against anything that harms the company. Their influence is engrained in these societies. Many representatives from those countries have already made it into the assembly. Next time, the vote will not go in our favour."

"What will the cartel do with this power? What is their aim?"

"Goodness only knows. There is one thing I know they will *not* do, and that is negotiate with the Exchange or any official *gamra* bodies."

"Why not?"

"Too many rules, according to them. Well, they don't put it like that. They say that the rules are all controlled by interests off Earth, and that most people on Earth haven't the financial resources to communicate with them.

I felt cold. I'd heard all those arguments before, out of the mouth of my then-fiancée Eva's father and out of the mouth of acting president Sigobert Danziger, all of whom wanted *gamra* to go away. "So . . . what can we do to stop them?"

Margarethe folded her hands, leaning forward on her knees. "This is why you're here. I know it's going to sound crazy, but I'm going to push for *gamra* membership."

What? In this political climate? What had gotten into her?

"Don't look at me like that."

I spread my hands. "Well . . ." And let my hands sink again. "Well, that seems like political suicide to me." Not to mention a whole lot of other things. A decision of this magnitude would require a referendum. That was a massive, expensive operation. If it failed, it would be many years before the assembly could afford to try again.

"Oh, it is political suicide, but it's my last term in office, and I can't be re-elected. Over the past few months, I've had a legion of people collect numbers for me. I think we might be able to pull it off. The cartel will fight it, but I think we're in a fairly good position to expose the foul schemes they've imposed on the countries where they have taken over government debt."

Well, that brought the protest outside the courthouse to a whole new level of importance. And, holy shit, what about all those people trying to keep me away from that forecourt "for my own protection"? Damn and double damn.

Actually, fuck on a fiddlestick.

A deep breath. And another one.

"All right. I'm guessing I'm here because you want me to do something?"

"No, you're here because I like to entertain people in this bus, driving around in the middle of the night in the middle of nowhere."

"Ha, ha."

She chuckled, but then her face turned serious.

"I'm guessing you want me to make sure Robert does not get off easily."

"No. You haven't been called to the witness box, and I don't want you to do anything. Let them think they own the trial. Let them put Robert Davidson in jail. That's probably where he belongs anyway. I want you to continue getting information about the people outside. I want to know who their leaders are. No, not on paper, because I can find that out. I want to know which people have the power and respect to make people act a certain way."

I remembered something, and produced the little card that Dharma had given me. I gave it to her.

"That's Gusamo's partner. He has a few things to say about the cartel in Jakarta. And there is a man in a wheelchair named Charlie. He has stories about missing children in Africa."

"I will get people on it."

"Can't you just send in some Special Services people to clear the forecourt?"

"I need a mandate to do that, and I have no strong reason to do it. The police have got the protesters surrounded, saying that these are dangerous subversive elements, but of course a lot of the police belong to the cartel and they've received hints that protecting your safety from those naughty unruly people is of utmost importance, and that is not untrue."

I was going to ask if it was really that bad, but I saw in her eyes that it was.

"The assembly is virtually under siege. I do have the mandate to disband any service that is performing gross transgressions of boundaries, but I will do my utmost best to avoid that, because a *lot* of data about the cartel and the technology to track them has been supplied by the Exchange."

Oh shit, I saw it now. This was precisely what I had so long been saying.

Coldi had been on Earth since 1961. Their technology was intermingled with everything, and, some people argued, every bit of electronics included spy routines that the Exchange could access.

I'd pushed the issue away, figuring that it wasn't my problem and that if it ever became my problem, I'd worry about it then.

I guess that time was now.

Margarethe held up her hands. "Don't even say the words, 'You should have joined thirty years ago.'"

Thirty years ago, when knowledge of *gamra* had first become public, when a much younger Ezhya Palayi had visited Earth in an official capacity—and had never done so since—when people were optimistic about the future relationship but had somehow not wanted to pull that trigger, because of some conservatives with particularly loud voices. Maybe they'd been genuine in their objections, or maybe, as I thought now, they had always seen it in their own interest not to join so that they could continue not to declare their interests in income made from other worlds. Because business could not possibly be put under any kind of restriction, right?

We both knew. It *should* have been done thirty years ago.

"Is there a realistic chance that it will pass?"

She sighed. "We have to try, Cory. That's all we can do."

———

By the time we came back to the hotel, it was very late.

The others had ridden with Margarethe's guards, no doubt exchanging whatever information security personnel exchanged while I spoke to their boss.

All the lights in the hotel were off, including the one in our room.

A pang of sadness and longing stirred inside me. It didn't feel right, doing so much without Thayu. I guessed I had better get used to this. She would not join me so often once the child was born either. Life was going to be different, and I had grown used to having her by my side.

The door into the foyer was shut, but the receptionist, seated in a pool of light in the dark foyer, opened it at my approach.

The young man on duty gave me and my heavily-armed party a strange look.

"These are the people we were still missing from our party," I informed him. "The rooms should already be allocated."

He produced entry codes, and everyone filed upstairs as they received them. Tired, glad of the prospect of a good night's rest.

Evi came out of the room at the top of the stairs when we came up and we all wordlessly filed into what had become the security station. They had pushed the bed aside, dragged the table into the middle, and covered it with equipment. There was also equipment on the bed.

The room's chairs—a couch, a lounge chair and three dining chairs —had been supplemented with some chairs from another room, and a table full of food containers and empty cups. I was sure that either the hotel staff were not allowed to come in here, or that they were, like me, astonished that so few people could produce so much stuff, including food debris.

We all sat down on the mismatched chairs. Thayu was there as well. Her hair was messed up as if she had been asleep. Damn, I felt sorry for dragging her here. She was too proud to admit that she wasn't up to it.

I said, "I'm not staying long. I'm tired." Because she would never admit this, I did it on her behalf.

Reya said, "Then let's get started. Lenka Trnkova has let us know that Abri is wanted again tomorrow. Apparently the confusion about support staff has been cleared and the witness account can now proceed."

"Are you satisfied that all our conditions have been met?"

"Yes. We got four additional passes."

That was good. That meant we could bring one of Amarru's lawyers and all the Pengali in, as long as we could keep Idda under someone's clothes. She had been behaving well recently, but I *might* just see if I could procure some sleep tablets.

Abri would be in the witness box with Jemiro.

I would go in the audience, and I wanted Thayu with me, but she said it would be much better for me to take Veyada. Which was true, and I hated how Thayu and I had spent so much time separated on this trip.

The three Pengali needed to come. Ynggi had said that he wasn't essential, but since I didn't trust Jemiro's translation, I wanted him there. My Pengali was nowhere near adequate to understand the nuances.

"Then maybe you should take Devlin so that he can record the proceedings," Telaris said.

Devlin shook his head. "I can easily teach Ynggi to do it, so that I don't occupy a spot that's better taken by one of the lawyers."

That was true, and, knowing the disagreements between Veyada and Mereeni, I, Devlin and Evi said at the same time, "Reya."

And Veyada said, "Mereeni."

And the others in my association said nothing. Nicha looked at me and started laughing. "Mereeni. Take it from me."

While we had been discussing who we would take, Thayu was listening to the recording I made of my meeting with Margarethe. I thought I could tell when Margarethe said she was going to push for *gamra* membership. Thayu's mouth fell open and her eyes widened. That pretty much described my reaction. Why did Margarethe think it was a good idea?

I guessed the answer to that was: it might not be a good time, but the next ten years or more might be impossible to try. And ten years down the track, who knew how much damage these companies would do to the fragile situation of relative peace between the major regions on Earth? Or how much damage to the reputation of Nations of Earth with *gamra* as an organisation in control of their citizens? Or, heaven forbid, how much damage to the peace between Asto and Nations of Earth. Because Asto was watching in the depths of space. They were always watching. Maybe even Kando Luczon and his band of entitled Aghyrians in their giant ship were watching. Maybe they were even behind the brashness of the Pretoria Cartel.

And now you're letting your imagination run away with your senses, Mr Wilson.

I needed some sleep. Tomorrow would be a big and important day.

I rose. "I think we should all go to bed and get a good rest. If we'll be finished here tomorrow, make arrangements to return to the Exchange. I plan to take my party to my father's place for a break, but everyone else can return home."

Evi looked up. "It will be arranged. We will book flights tomorrow."

"Good."

"Who do we take?"

"Just our association and staff. There is no need to take anyone else. The lawyers, the guards, the Pengali, the interpreter: they can go back to Amarru." And in Jemiro's case, home. The sooner we got rid of him, the better.

Thayu and I went back to our room, where I gave her a very

cryptic description of my meeting with Margarethe, in case someone was listening.

She had no great knowledge about matters that concerned Nations of Earth, so she only remarked that it seemed risky to her. Coldi, of course, didn't really understand the concept of elections either.

Then she smiled. "You really didn't get the situation with Veyada, did you?"

"No. He's spent most of this trip arguing with Mereeni and carrying on like he hates her guts, from the very moment they met. The only reason they haven't had a fight is because she's from Hedron and doesn't have the instinct. Then I suggest keeping the two separated, and *he*, of all people, wants to let her come."

"Do you remember when I first came to you, how much we argued? Do you remember that big bust-up we had after you visited Ezhya?"

I nodded. I remembered that well. It had been one of my more stupid moments, before I realised how the situation stuck together, and that I was fighting my own attraction to Thayu—wait.

"You're not suggesting that Veyada . . ."

Her smile widened. "Everyone else seems to be in on the deal. We're counting the time until he makes his move. I believe Nicha and Sheydu have already made a bet on it."

Someone knocked on the door.

When I opened it, I found Devlin in the hallway.

"I wanted to tell you one more thing," he said in that way he would speak when he was about to upset all our plans.

"Yes?"

"I managed to get a message through to the Pakiru family in Barresh. They were most upset and told me that their nephew Jemiro was killed in a street fight a month ago."

19

───────

SO JEMIRO—the real Jemiro—had died. Then who was this person we had with us?

I looked from Thayu to Nicha and Veyada. And then Devlin.

I asked the latter, "Did you ever know Jemiro? Is this the same person?"

Devlin shrugged. "No one ever had much to do with the family."

"What should we do about him?" Nicha asked. "Interrogate him?"

I glanced in the direction of the stairs, the way to Jemiro's room, thinking of how I found him in his room huddled on the floor after Kita had threatened him with a knife.

"Let's wait until the trial is done. He may not be stable enough to continue as our translator if we put too much pressure on him tonight. I don't want the trial to be cancelled because of something *we* did."

They nodded, but I didn't think they were entirely happy.

"I said we'd learn something from having him with us," Veyada said. "I think we're about to learn that lesson."

That was one was of looking at it. But I definitely wanted this investigated when the trial was over, and I'd put pressure on him regardless of how he reacted.

We went to our room and got ready for bed.

I was tired, but did not sleep well. As usual, when there was trouble or I had something big coming up, strange dreams plagued my sleep, in which we were chased through the corridors of the court building by a group of black-clad guards banging the *irrka* drum in the most unrhythmic fashion.

I woke with a shock, to find that Thayu was up, rummaging in her pack. It was early enough in the morning for the light to be pale blue.

I asked, "What are you looking for?"

"The infusor capsules."

"But you're not supposed to . . ." I sat up.

"I know, but I can't live with this anymore. I'm frozen to the bone. I can't think, I can't move. This can't be good for me *or* the child. I'll take just half and see if that helps."

"Do you want to see a medico?"

"Maybe when we're back at the Exchange."

I processed that for a moment. Here was Thayu admitting defeat. "You're really not feeling well, aren't you."

She didn't meet my eyes, pressed her lips together and shook her head.

"Was it like this . . . last time?"

In general, we avoided talking about her son, because after his father had been killed in the attempted coup at Asto, we had no idea what had become of the boy. It was on my endless "should do this one day" list, even if Thayu never spoke about it.

"I didn't have the requirement to keep my body temperature low."

In other words: no. Damn, Thayu. Why hadn't she said anything before?

She found the capsules and the band and disappeared into the bathroom carrying them and her clothes.

I lay back on the pillow, listening to sounds she made in there: the tap, the flushing of the toilet, the rustle of clothes as she put them on.

Down in the street, a rubbish truck came to empty the recycling bins with clangs and thuds and the rumble of plastic bottles tumbling into the truck's compactor. A tram zoomed past, the wheels whining as the vehicle turned the corner. Those were sounds of my youth.

Thayu came back dressed in her security outfit.

"Feel any better?" I asked.

She shrugged. "Lets go to breakfast."

At least she was hungry. That was a good sign, right?

While I got dressed, a door in the hallway opened and fell shut. A moment later, someone knocked on the door. "Muri?"

Devlin.

I got out of bed and opened the door.

Devlin indeed, already in his work clothes.

"What's the matter?" The inside of my head felt fuzzy. How could he look so alert—wait. Had he even slept at all?

"A message came for you."

I took the reader he held out to me. I thought it might be something from Barresh, but the message had been sent through reception downstairs.

It was very short and said, "Please confirm our deal."

There was no name, but there was only one person who would contact me in this way: Minke Kluysters.

Deal?

I'd made no deal.

What sort of dirty trick was this?

If I replied, was he going to use it as proof that there was a deal?

Thayu came behind me and read over my shoulder. "Who is this person?"

I told her. "I don't want to reply to this. He wants me to find loopholes by which he can have an office in Barresh. Well, I don't actually want his office in Barresh. We should find ways to make sure that doesn't happen."

"Then you just tell him."

"I have no intention of doing so. If I do, he can use my message to prove that I've agreed on a deal. I haven't agreed on anything."

Thayu gave me a wide-eyed look. "Really?"

"That's the dirty trick he could be playing." For Coldi, doing something like this would amount to a serious transgression against their loyalty.

A few people were coming down the stairs. Veyada and Sheydu, judging by the sound of voices.

I was right, and Mereeni was with them.

We soon followed them to the dining room, where most others were already filling their plates.

Fish had become a standard item on the menu, and my team had made a big hole in the pile of crumbed fillets and the Pengali were only just arriving. All of them were dressed in their official outfits with the blue stripes and pearl buttons. But what was with the anxious faces?

They came straight for me. Kita carried a blanket with a little tail dangling out, limp. Pengali tails were always moving. My heart jumped.

"Something wrong?"

Kita opened the blanket for me. Idda lay limp amongst the folds of fabric. Her eyes were half open and her gaze unfocused.

I met Ynggi's eyes. "What happened?"

"She opened a door in our room and found some things inside. She drank some smelly water from a little bottle."

Damn it. "Have you got the container?"

Ayshada sat in his chair next to Nicha. He stared, open-mouthed at Idda. He pointed. "Idda. Idda! Idda!" His face distorted with distress. His shrill voice cut through the gentle sounds in the dining room.

Everyone was looking in our direction.

Nicha lifted his son out of the chair, telling him to be quiet, but Nicha's face also displayed deep worry.

Ynggi had taken a little bottle out of his pocket. The label said "Vodka".

Well . . . I couldn't help laughing. "That explains it."

"Is it harmful?"

"No. She is drunk. She'll sleep well and won't annoy anyone. Just carry her under your jacket and make sure she drinks water when she wakes up. She'll probably be very unhappy for a while. Have some breakfast."

They still looked a bit unsure, but sat down anyway, rather subdued, still holding the limp bundle on his lap.

Ayshada looked on with wide eyes. "Wha. . . ? Idda?"

Nicha stroked his head. "Shh. Idda is fine. She's asleep. Have some bread."

"Fish!" Ayshada slammed his hand on the table.

Nicha gave me an *it's your fault* look, but gave his son a piece of fish anyway.

Talk in the rest of the room resumed.

I went to get breakfast at the serving counter, and stopped at Eirani's table on the way back.

Jemiro sat at the table with her and Karana.

"Any plans for today?" I asked Eirani. But I looked at Jemiro, who ignored everyone.

"We're going to take Ayshada to a park. Apparently it's a custom to give the children bread and let them feed the animals."

"Ducks," Karana said, using the Isla word. "They swim, and they fly, like ringgit."

"They're not like ringgit at all." The closest animal that came to ringgit were probably crickets, although those were a lot smaller. Ringgit were a type of crustacean, the size of an adult person's hand, that could be a menace in the older and more boggy parts of Barresh. They tended to invade houses and had a particular affinity for the pantry. "Ayshada will like the ducks, though. Make sure you keep an eye on him." For the safety of the ducks. I was afraid Idda had taught him some bad habits, including the desire to catch everything that moved.

"We are going to be spending most of the day in court. Devlin will stay here and can get a message to us if you need us. I really hope that we're going to be finished today, and I need you to be ready and packed to return to the Exchange tomorrow morning. All of us here from our household will be visiting my father." And when I noticed Jemiro watching me, I added, "I'll be providing everyone else with travel codes so that they can go back to their homes."

He nodded, nervously, and looked away.

Eirani glared at him, too. She might have said, "You can at least say 'Thank you,' " but he wasn't a child and I guessed she had said this a few times already.

Karana snorted. She was taking her cues from Eirani, and becoming more confident by the day.

In the awkward silence, I rose; and when I walked past the back of his chair, I hesitated. Part of me wanted to yell at him, "Isn't it about time you told us who you really are?"

But I wasn't sure that he knew, so I said only, "We leave soon. Be ready." I'd make sure I'd question him in between when we finished here and when we delivered him back to the Exchange.

"I'm already . . . ready."

I left the room via a detour past Thayu. She would spend much of the day in the security station, doing stuff for Amarru or Ezhya or whatever security people did.

I squeezed her shoulder. "Don't work too hard."

"I don't think I can be accused of working hard."

"No, and you shouldn't."

She pulled a face at me. She hadn't done that for a while, not since she'd confirmed her pregnancy. Her cheeks were red and her eyes clear and it occurred to me just how sick she had looked over the past few days. Hopefully she would now feel better. Once we got to my father's house, we'd laze on the beach and go for walks. I was really looking forward to it.

Veyada and Mereeni were already waiting in the hall, as usual in heated argument about some legal thing. It struck me that Mereeni argued in an atypical manner for Coldi people: she used her hands a lot. Her face was also unusually expressive. When Veyada said something, he remained more subdued, but he watched her with an intensive expression. I remembered what Thayu had said about the two of them yesterday, and with all the will in the world, I didn't see it.

Then the Pengali turned up.

Ynggi pushed one of the hotel's luggage trolleys with the barrel and pipes of the *irrka* drum on top.

What was this?

"Today, we tell our story," Abri said.

She seemed content, and I wondered what had happened to the requirement to bring the fish. I hoped she finally understood that it wasn't necessary, but I didn't hold much hope. I glanced at the fish-pond, and could just see two goldfish in the corner.

Why did I get a feeling I didn't want to know what sort of animal they were bringing today?

Ynggi followed me, wheeling the trolley with the drum; and Abri and Kita came in after him, followed by Jemiro.

The van waited outside the hotel's entrance. The driver helped us open the door and manoeuvre the drum and the pipes inside. It fitted —just. We were lucky that police weren't checking on silly things like seatbelts.

The streets were quiet, but we passed several groups of police, some in riot gear, mulling around in strategic places. Some of those police waved at the driver.

I glanced at Veyada. He was looking at something on his reader.

"Anything happening?" I asked him in a low voice when we got out of the van in the underground entrance.

"There is a lot of interest in the court case."

To his other side, Mereeni said, "There is interest from parties that normally wouldn't have interest." Every time I heard her speak her accent startled me. Hedron Coldi was as different as one could possibly go within the same language.

Veyada nodded.

There was a message in their words. It was not good, I didn't think. But they couldn't tell me what or who they thought was watching. Spies from the cartel. Tamerians possibly. Others maybe, I didn't know. People in orbit, even?

That was a disturbing thought.

None of us were armed. I'd gladly taken off my gun last night. Weapons were not allowed in the court building and everyone entering the courtroom was subjected to a body search.

If Thayu were here, she would still find a way to conceal a weapon, but when Veyada said he wasn't armed, he wasn't armed. And it felt disturbing and naked. I hated guns, but I found their presence on the belts and arm brackets of my team comforting.

Because there were fewer of us than yesterday, we all fitted in the lift, including the trolley with the parts of the drum. Idda was wriggling under Kita's jacket. I would have expected her to be fast asleep for hours.

Lenka Trnkova waited in the ground floor hall. She looked a lot more formal today, in a blouse with the buttons done up to under her chin.

She said, "Dr Cross is waiting for you."

Through the glass wall at the front of the foyer, I could see that the crowd had swelled. All the empty space between the tents was filled up with people.

The Africans were there again, playing their drums. I recognised the distinctive *boom-toc-toc-boom-toc-boom-toc-toc-boom-toc* rhythm of informal betanka. The Pengali had taught them this yesterday?

People cheered when they saw us.

A couple of guards stood near the door, and a few others were setting up a security checking station with a scanning machine for bags.

There was also a guard with a dog.

It turned around and sniffed the air when we came in.

Ynggi stiffened next to me. "Why is the animal inside?"

"It's a dog. It smells what people carry in their pockets."

"People can smell it just as well."

"They can't." Then a thought. "Can you smell if someone is armed?"

"Of course we can. We can smell everything."

"Everything?"

"I can smell that you had fish for breakfast and also that you had sex last night."

Really, could he smell that?

"It has a distinctive smell."

Veyada's back was shaking with his laughter. Mereeni rolled her eyes.

We went into the small meeting room where we had also met yesterday. Dr Cross came in while we were finding seats. He sat down and looked around. "No seagulls today?"

What sort of remark was that? Had he no concept that other people might have different customs?

He again went through his questions. He explained that he would ask questions and then the lawyer representing Robert Davidson would ask questions.

"Is he actually going to be in court today?"

"He will be."

I guessed this was the reason for the heightened security.

"Yesterday, we didn't get a definitive answer on our request for the Pengali to put their statement in music. This is a traditional custom. All their hearings of justice are set to music."

His face remained blank. I guessed he had deliberately avoided speaking about it yesterday in the hope that we would forget and it would fall between the cracks.

He said stiffly, "The case is not about their claims."

"No, but Dr Martens agreed that they could be heard anyway. I have that agreement in writing. And the Pengali put their official claims in music."

He nodded, stiffly. "I'll have to ask."

He rose and left the room. He didn't come back for quite some time.

We waited and waited.

Even Veyada and Mereeni ran out of legal arguments and sat glaring at each other.

Jemiro sat stiff as a rod, pretending he wasn't there. I didn't want to discuss anything in his presence.

The Pengali kept looking at the door. Idda was asleep inside her mother's jacket, but her tail kept wriggling as if she were about to wake up.

Abri said several times that she didn't think they were being taken seriously. To be frank, *I* didn't think they were being taken seriously.

I went to the door and opened it a fraction. A man in a suit stood outside.

"Sir?"

"We'd like to know what's going on." I could hear the hum of many voices. It seemed people had been let into the foyer, which meant that the hearing today was going ahead. "Dr Cross left an—"

"He's here now."

He was, too, striding along the corridor in quick steps.

"So," he said when he entered the room, still breathing fast. "The judges object to unrelated material being brought into the hearing—"

"But—"

"—*But* they have agreed that the witness and her family can play in the tea room in the lunch break."

What? Was he serious?

I was about to jump up and give him a piece of my mind, that this was not how the Pengali should be treated, but I realised that this would have much more impact if I saved it for when press cameras were watching. Bursts of anger were much more effective when they were uncommon.

I explained the situation to Abri to the best of my abilities in the most neutral tone I could manage.

Jemiro bumbled through the translation for the benefit of the official transcripts and Dr Cross, who did not understand any of our conversations. Jemiro seemed even more confused than he had been yesterday, or maybe I was just impatient because I was seething inside.

We could add nothing to this process they were interested in. The trial might drag out for weeks, months, years. Ultimately, we were nothing more than window dressing. This was not about us. I just wanted to get out of here.

Abri was not impressed and I couldn't blame her. She bypassed Jemiro, and said to me, "We have to make our claims in front of hairy face. He needs to hear our story."

"I know, but it's *their* process. They determine how we can appear."

As I said this, I realised that the Pengali story would probably be of greater interest to the spectators than to the lawyers anyway.

Lawyers could not make any money from the Pengali, but the public loved a good underdog story. The public outside the building in the forecourt would love their story. Not only that, it would give Margarethe something she, and other Nations of Earth politicians, had never had before: an in-road into the Blue faction of the population. We knew pretty much how the Whites would vote. There were hundreds of studies. Margarethe had said that her number crunchers said there was a chance she could push the referendum through. The *real* difference was going to be to get as many Blues registered to vote, and win their sympathy. Because they were being ignored. Because the Pengali represented *gamra* and *they* had suffered at the hands of the Pretoria Cartel.

We had everything here for a formal betanka: the drum, Abri, someone who could translate Abri's words into Isla so that the crowd of protesters could hear them. So that Dharma Yuwono could hear them, and he could keep in contact with Margarethe.

I said to Abri, "Let them have their way. I think we will be fine."

I said to Dr Cross, "Abri doesn't like it, but understands it's your call. They will play at lunch time."

He nodded stiffly and rose. "I'm glad they understand. Let's go then. The first session starts at ten."

"What do we do with the drum?"

"Leave it here. You can come back for it later."

I relayed that to the Pengali. They were still not happy, but came with me anyway.

We left the room to a great buzz of voices. The hallway was relatively empty, but the foyer was full of people.

We could only see them in the distance, though, because Dr Cross led us in the other direction. I wondered who they were. Certainly, they would not let any of the protesters into the courthouse, or at least not the ones whose identities they knew from checking their presence every night. But what about other people affiliated with the protesters? They couldn't possibly check the political bent of everyone they admitted onto the public gallery.

Dr Cross took us to yet another room, where chairs stood in rows. A couple of other people were there, none of whom I recognised. They gave us curious looks.

"Wait here," he said. "You will be called."

We sat and waited.

To my horror, Idda woke up and wanted to be let out of the jacket. She jumped from her mother's lap and zoomed around the room, to the amusement of the strangers who also waited there. Well, the effect of the vodka hadn't lasted very long. Kita made a few attempts to catch and calm her, but Idda had never been controlled that way at home, and she did not agree with it now.

"She has to be kept quiet," I said to Abri, exasperated. "I'm pretty sure that the lawyers won't allow children in the courtroom."

"I don't understand these people. They invite us, and then they don't want to hear from us at all."

"You'll get your time to speak," I said. "I will make sure."

The door opened, and Lenka came in. She was in her stiff work clothes, her hair tied up in a very legal-looking bun. Her eyes met mine briefly. "Abri, come with me."

Both Abri and Jemiro got up.

"What should we do?" I asked her.

"You can go to the public gallery."

We left the room.

Even though we were a distance from the building's forecourt, the sounds from the crowd outside were prominent. The drums were going, and people were clapping and chanting, still in time with the betanka rhythm.

A great deal of yelling broke out when the people in the hall spotted us going up the stairs to the public gallery.

A large group of varied, colourful people stood waiting there, and some waved at us. There would be a good number of supporters in the building, and even on the public gallery.

The guard at the top of the stairs wanted to see our passes before we were allowed into the courtroom.

The public gallery held at least two hundred people, and it was packed, so all those people outside would not be able to get a seat. They'd be impatient. Or they might watch the proceedings on screens.

A young woman ushered us to a row of seats at the very front.

I ended up between Veyada, doing something on his reader, and Ynggi, who was fiddling with an earpiece and reader, checking if the recording facility worked as it should.

The court building was modern, and the courtroom was equally spacious and light-filled, with a wall-to-ceiling window on one side that looked out into a courtyard garden with a burbling fountain and more damned goldfish.

The long table where the judges would sit, with a couple of micro-phones, was still empty. A jug of water and a couple of glasses stood on the corner.

The floor area, a few steps down from the public gallery and sepa-rated from it by a glass barrier, contained a couple of rows of seats to the left, in front of the window, and to the right. There were desks, too, and two witness stands, both consisting of a single chair in a boxed-off area with waist-high walls. At the corners of the box, there were slots for posts where I presumed police could put up a cage for dangerous criminals—or ones needing protection from the other people in the room.

A door opened at the back. A line of people came in, most of them carrying devices. They sat down at the tables to the left. Then another group came in, surrounding a man in a bright yellow jumpsuit.

Robert Davidson had aged terribly since I had last seen him. He looked tidier, and had shaved his beard, but his hair had gone grey, his skin looked sallow and his arms were thin and ridden with sores. He didn't look up when he was being led across the floor, wearing wrist braces and ankle braces.

The three guards with him pushed him down on the chair in one of the boxes, and attached a device to his braces. Probably something that would deliver an electric shock when he tried to get up. The guards shut the little door to the box, but remained on the outside. They wore Nations of Earth uniforms with an insignia I didn't know, and were visibly armed.

Another group of people came in, which included Lenka Trnkova, Abri, Jemiro, and Dr Cross wearing a long, grey gown.

A murmur went up when people saw Abri. Cameras zoomed and I picked up a few remarks.

She's really small, isn't she?

She's wearing clothes. They said she would be almost naked.

A lot of people had noticed us when we came in, but many more had entered the gallery after us and would not have noticed us in the front row.

A bell rang and everyone rose.

The three judges filed in, also in grey gowns, and found their places at the long table facing the audience. There were two men, and a woman who I guessed was the notorious Judge Hermans. Her hair was more grey than brown, and cut in a bob. She produced glasses and put them on her nose. "Please be seated." Her voice was stern and prim.

After the rumble of everyone sitting down had faded, she explained the agenda for today, and gave the floor to Dr Cross. He introduced Abri and her tribe. Apparently the judges had previously seen images of the area where Robert had made his camps and where he stored the diamonds. I didn't know there was more than one cave, but it shouldn't have surprised me. Apparently the photos were Robert's, and they were all slightly overexposed as photos taken in Barresh with Earth equipment tended to be. The light was different.

He showed images of Pengali kids on the beach. The light on the sand was bright and warm. The forest was so incredibly green, the water azure blue. It looked like a setting from a dream holiday destination.

Damn it, I wanted to go home.

According to Dr Cross, the Pengali lived peacefully—and they didn't. Neither were they primitive, or, for that matter, innocent; and those were all words he used.

Ynggi was listening to this in Coldi through a translation device. Jemiro translated for Abri, and she glared at us.

I knew I was asking a lot of her, and right now, she probably didn't think much of me, because I hadn't told her of my plans to let her speak.

Then he asked for the statement to be read. Abri did this, even if she didn't read. She had memorised the whole thing. Jemiro translated to Isla. Faithfully, Ynggi said, still listening to his translation device.

Then Dr Cross went into the questions. Exactly what Abri had and hadn't seen, where Robert had been, which tribespeople he had subverted. How she knew that he had killed Melissa's trackers and about the significance of blue diamonds.

Dr Cross then asked Robert to confirm or deny her words. He confirmed everything, looking at his knees.

The whole thing was anti-climactic and scripted. Veyada was fiddling with his reader. Abri was getting annoyed with having to reply to a couple of variations of each question.

Eventually she burst out, "I said all these things before. Do you not believe me? When are you going to ask about Pengali? Do you need to wait until after we present you with the gift?"

I couldn't understand her words, but this was how Jemiro translated them, in a halting way.

"Why do you not ask the other people with us for what they saw. I told you what I saw. I didn't see that he killed Kasamo. He killed Pengali. We saw that. Why don't you ask about that?"

Jemiro translated. Now his voice sounded positively dead and robotic. What was going on?

The sound of Abri's voice brought Idda out of her mother's jacket, where she had been wriggling around for a while. Now she came out and jumped—

From her mother's lap to the banister in front of us. She wore nothing except her orange beanie. The giraffe patterns on her skin were accentuated under the room's fluorescent light.

Kita lunged for her and missed, and then she ran past Ynggi who was concentrating on the trial and me. I tried to grab her tail, but she had worked out that I had a habit of doing this, so her tail flicked up and out of my hands. Then she ran in front of Veyada, who was listening and didn't notice her until it was too late.

The woman who sat next to Veyada gave a little squeal when Idda ran in front of her, balancing on the banister with her tail waving in the air. The man next to her gave an outraged shout.

Idda squealed and jumped down on the other side of the banister. There was about a metre drop between our level and the courtroom floor.

The judge noticed her then. Her eyes widened. "Whatever is *that*? Get that animal out of here, please."

Abri had also noticed Idda. She said something in Pengali.

Idda looked sharply at her grandmother, ran across the floor in the other direction, looked again.

One of the clerks had risen from his desk and came for Idda.

She jumped up the next banister—which was the one surrounding Robert Davidson's box.

"Hey!" one of the guards tried to grab her. At first it looked like he was successful, but Idda wriggled from his hands, fell on the carpet and ran, squealing, to where we sat. She tried to claw her way up the wood panelling that separated the gallery from the floor, but her little hands found no purchase on the smooth surface. I leaned over, but couldn't reach her, and then, because she was still squealing, I jumped over. I picked her up and handed her to Kita. Then I found myself surrounded by guards.

"You can't come in here, Mr Wilson."

"I'm just getting—" What the hell did they think they were doing?

Someone grabbed me under the arms—Veyada—and hoisted me up into the gallery. The seriousness in his eyes chilled me. Something was about to happen, something that I had not planned and had no control over.

A commotion broke out near the door to the hall, which opened, and a group of people came in: Sheydu, Deyu and Reida, Thayu, Evi and Telaris, all of them in *gamra* security gear and visibly armed.

20

REIDA PUSHED the hotel trolley with the *irrka* drum into the middle of the floor.

Judge Hermans yelled at the guards to get these people out of the room, but the security guards hesitated, which probably had something to do with the guns on my team's arm brackets.

Then she yelled at me to control them. I had no inclination to do as she said.

I stood at the front row of the public gallery, a position from which I could see over the floor. A lot of other people had come into the courtroom after my team had let the door open and distracted the security. They were some of the people who had been waiting in the foyer, a lot of colourful Africans, journalists of minor and unapproved news services and anti-Execo activists.

Ynggi slipped from his seat next to me and jumped over the banister, followed by Kita.

I presumed the courtroom's cameras were still broadcasting this to the screens in the foyer. All around us in the public gallery were journalists. There were more reporters in the foyer, and in the tents outside.

Here was our chance to inform the masses.

Ynggi undid the strap to the bundle of *irrka* pipes and inserted the large bottom pipes into the central drum.

People had noticed him, and a relative hush came over the courtroom.

I spoke up, raising my voice. "These are the Pengali of the Thousand Islands tribe. When I first spoke to prosecutor Conrad Martens about Abri being a witness in this trial, I was given the understanding that there would be space for her to air the tribe's grievances against Robert Davidson. With the changes to the prosecutor and other people from the court working with us, that agreement appears to have been forgotten. We remind you of it. The Pengali will now perform a betanka: the official ceremony that they use for formal negotiations. Our translator will tell you their story in Isla. He is a certified translator, approved by Nations of Earth, so you can faithfully report it to your news services."

Jemiro looked at me wide-eyed. His face had gone pale. I guessed that doing defiant things was not in his orders.

Reida and Deyu now lifted the completed drum off the trolley. As it turned out, there had been something underneath: a package wrapped in a colourful cloth.

Abri climbed onto the railing surrounding the witness box, and, under protest of the uniformed Nations of Earth guard, jumped to the floor.

She picked up the object from the trolley and carried it to the judges' table. She set it down in front of Judge Hermans, and stepped back.

The judge frowned at me. "What am I supposed to do with this?"

"It's a gift from the tribe to you," I said.

"What sort of gift?"

"I don't know. Open it." I hoped it was not another seagull or some other creature.

Judge Hermans unwrapped the cloth and unveiled . . . an African-style statue, cut from ebony wood. It depicted the statue in the fountain outside, with the hands. The fingers on each of the hands bore rings made from colourful African beads that depicted national flags. The meaning might be lost on the Pengali, but these flags represented all the countries that the cartel had bought: Morocco, Egypt, Sudan, a whole bunch of other central African countries, as well as the Vietnams, Burma and other sections of Asia. Also Bolivia, Venezuela and South American countries. In the middle of the circle of hands stood a colourful fish fashioned from beads. It stood propped up on its tail, its wide-open mouth gasping at the judge.

Abri had no doubt been attracted to the statue because of the fish, but as a gift, it was perfect. The fish with its open mouth symbolised the people outside, trapped by the private ownership of their countries by companies that supposedly conformed with Nations of Earth's rules.

The Pengali did not know this, but everyone else in the room knew. Including Judge Hermans.

Her cheeks went red. She licked her lips, opened her mouth and licked her lips again. Then she looked at me. "Mr Wilson, will you kindly remove these people from the court? They are disturbing the course of justice."

I had no intention of doing so. The guards could not "remove" my team either, due to their impressive weaponry, but I had no doubt that backup had been called, and we only had a short period to make our mark.

I gestured to Ynggi.

He put his foot on the step on the side of the drum and pulled himself up until he perched on the footrests that came off the side just underneath the rim.

The people grew quiet; the African drums in the hall fell silent. Everyone watched us. They listened.

Ynggi took the sticks and tapped the betanka rhythm, hitting one of the big low booming pipes every third and fifth beat.

Sung betanka was slower and resembled droning a lot more than the instrumental variety. The song represented a statement of importance or an argument and needed to be understood by all.

While Ynggi was getting ready, Reida reached over one of the unoccupied desks next to the judges' table. He pulled out an earpiece and tossed it across the courtroom to me.

Abri started to chant to the slow and heavy five-beat rhythm.

I turned towards Jemiro, who looked petrified. I tossed him the earpiece. "Translate what she says."

He shook his head vehemently. The colour of his face suggested that he was going to either faint or vomit soon.

"Translate! Make yourself useful for once."

"I can't. I can't! People are watching me."

"Of course they are watching you. I've had enough of this rubbish. Who are you? Why are you using Jemiro Pakiru's name, when he's dead?"

"Please." He clamped his hands over his ears. "Please. I don't know."

"What are you? Who are you?"

"Please, please. I don't know anything."

"What do you know? How did you even end up with Jasper Carlson?"

But Jemiro could only give incoherent replies. His eyes were unfocused, and Abri was chanting and someone needed to get on with the translation.

So I shouted to Ynggi to translate into Coldi for us, which he did while drumming. I retrieved the earpiece and put it on.

And to Veyada, I said, "Record it." Which he was probably already doing, as were a lot of other people.

It wasn't easy to hear Ynggi's voice over the racket, but I translated his—and through him, Abri's—words as faithfully as I could.

Abri sang about how Robert came to the tribe for the first time, how he promised the young people shiny things but didn't deliver on his promises, how he had rebuked protests delivered to him by tribe elders and how he had refused to leave the tribe's territory. Also how he stole artefacts from the tribe and threatened tribe members if he felt he could intimidate them. She sang how he lured the young tribe members away to work in his caves to clean and polish the blue diamonds and how he would chain them to their seats. She sang how he would not allow them to speak to others and would not allow them to leave their work spots, instead bringing their food to them and forcing them to sleep under their work benches on the filthy floor full of dust.

At this point a loud cheer broke out from the crowd at the door of the courtroom. A lot of the people there were Africans and a man with a very loud voice yelled, "Down with Execo. Take them to court!"

People cheered.

"Do they want us to stop?" Ynggi asked me.

"No, they're saying that the business owned by Robert has done the same thing to them as he did to the Pengali."

A look of comprehension went over his face. He hit the drum with increased intensity.

Abri continued singing and Ynggi translated.

The atmosphere in the room and adjacent hall was tense. People crowded around the screens and the door. Every now and then, someone would shout a slogan.

The Nations of Earth guards were alert and talking on their devices.

My team was alert, highly armed. Sheydu carried lots of pockets on her belt. Normally, the guns went on the arm brackets and the explosives in the pockets.

I had no idea how this standoff was going to end. Not well, probably. I wished Thayu were not here. I wished she—and Nicha, with Ayshada—were somewhere out of harm's way, with Eirani and Karana. Preferably somewhere in a vehicle that we might use to quickly get out of here. If we could get to the front door before a riot broke out, or before the guards took control of our movements "for our own safety", because if they did that, I might need to involve *gamra* security and it would get ugly.

Like, *really* ugly.

Abri continued. She sang about how Melissa had come to the island to look for Robert and how he had imprisoned her and killed her Pengali trackers, putting the blame on the Thousand Island tribe. The tribes might not get along, but it had been a long time since anyone had been killed for trespassing on another tribe's land.

"They gave us the blame for killing our president!" another man shouted.

"They put Johnny Moko in jail. He's done nothing!"

"Down with Execo! Justice to the people!"

Several people took up the chant in time with the betanka rhythm. Within moments, the courtroom vibrated with the voices of hundreds chanting. The guards were starting to look really nervous. More people wanted to come in. About five or six guards stood there, inadequate numbers in case that crowd decided to push.

A man behind in the gallery yelled through a microphone, "Please calm down. Please leave the building in orderly fashion. Please let's keep this civilised." He had to crank up the volume to ear-splitting levels in order to be heard.

"It might be a good idea to start packing up now," I said to Ynggi in a low voice, keeping one eye on the crowd that the line of guards in front of us was struggling to contain. The betanka stopped.

Then Dharma came out of the crowd. He smiled at me and simply said, "Thank you."

The words carried a hint of the meaning that he couldn't mention in public. I guessed Margarethe had contacted him and had informed him of her plans.

He said, "People, friends." He wore a small, high-tech earpiece and someone in the crowd must have amplifiers that projected his voice through the hall.

There was a lot of cheering and clapping.

He held a reader above his head.

"I have here on this reader a document I'm going to present to the Nations of Earth assembly. I will read something from it." He lowered the reader and looked at the screen. "We demand a fair inquiry into the conduct of Execo and its executive, Robert Davidson, in all parts of the world and elsewhere, and of affiliated companies and people. We demand that the inquiry be conducted by people who are judged independent by acceptable standards. We demand that affected people be paid compensation for injury or loss of income to ease our pain or our grief for missing family members."

A huge cheer broke out in the courtroom and a bit later, in the hall.

"We demand justice for the poor as well as the rich. Justice that includes the miners of Africa like Charlie Awaba and his missing brother, that includes the people who were evicted from their homes because of building developments. Justice that includes the people who are ill because of their experiments, and the widows and widowers and the children left orphaned. Justice that includes all the people who have been denied justice."

People cheered. Someone hit the African drum with big thumps.

"But right now, I want all of you to calm down. We will fight our fight and we will get our justice. If, however, we fight with our fists, we will give them a reason to call the riot police on us, label us law-breaking protesters and beat us down harder. Whatever weapons we have, they will have more powerful ones, and because we're poor and because we're Blue, they will beat us and put us in jail and no one will care or stand up for us. But give us some time, and we will forge stronger connections that will make us grow, not through scheming and fear, but through knowledge and honesty."

And oh, he came so close to mentioning the referendum and joining *gamra*, yet he didn't, and no one who didn't suspect that this was what his words were about would suspect. No one knew of the referendum. He did, I did. The planning had begun.

"Now kindly leave the building before these armed guards here become too nervous. The evidence has been given. Whether or not Robert Davidson goes to jail is up to the judges. They want us to forget him and his company, but we will not. Over the past days, you have given me lots of information to continue the fight. Now let's take the fight to the places where we can win: the media, the campaigns and your local governments. I will keep all of you updated. Thank you and be well."

A great cheer went up.

The mass of people started moving towards the doors, both on the ground floor and at the back of the public gallery. Things were peaceful, for now.

A commotion had broken out in the middle of the hall, where several uniformed officers knelt over someone on the floor.

Damn, that was Jemiro, curled into a ball. He was yelling at the carpet.

"Let me speak to him," I said.

Guards moved aside, and one of them pulled Jemiro up. His face was red and tears were running down his cheeks.

"I don't understand," he sobbed, in keihu. "What have I done?"

There was something *different* about him. He looked confused, but the emotionless mask he'd worn ever since he joined us was gone. "I don't know any of these people. I can't understand them. Please, tell me what I'm doing here. Please!" The raw tone in his voice made me shiver. Something had broken in him.

"What do you remember?"

"Nothing. What am I doing here?" His dialect was of the type spoken by workers in Barresh, like the builders or the warehouse workers, or the maintenance crew at the airport.

Veyada, who had some medical skills, sat next to him and examined his pulse and his eyes.

I asked Jemiro, "Do you know your name? Do you understand anything of what people are saying?"

He shook his head. His face shone with sweat. "Please, tell me what I'm doing here."

Veyada looked at me. He said, in Coldi, which Jemiro was unlikely to understand, "I have no idea what's going on or who he is, but his temperature is high, his heartbeat is irregular, and he needs care now."

The Pengali had packed up the drum and put it back on the trolley. There was a little bit of room at the front, and Veyada and Nicha lifted Jemiro up there. He was swaying so much that I was afraid he would fall off, but he managed to steady himself.

I was getting a really awful feeling about him. Was he some poor keihu young man picked up off the street by Jasper and given a false identity, who'd had his brain infused with language knowledge when I advertised for a translator? Was that how Jasper created people for jobs on demand? Obviously, the system wasn't working very well, and the changes became unstuck.

The Nations of Earth guards had managed to get a lot of the protester-gate-crashers out of the courtroom, leaving only the people who had already been there in some semblance of order, although the crowd had left debris of leaves, rubbish and the occasional pamphlet, which Idda was running around collecting.

A bell rang and a female voice said, "Everyone, sit down and return to your positions. Our interpreter is all right, I see. Now that everyone has calmed down and intruders have left, we will resume our proceedings."

I met the judge's eyes. "He is not all right. He is unfit to continue his work."

"Then have him taken to the hospital. We will continue the court session. Also can I ask these people to please remove the animal from the courtroom."

At that moment, something snapped in me. Idda was *not* an animal and Jemiro was *not* all right. I was supposed to protect them and I had failed. It was my task to make sure that the Pengali were heard fairly and I had agreed to come under those conditions, which were now not being met. I was through with dancing to their tunes.

I jumped over the banister, strode across the floor and scooped up

Idda. She let out a protesting squeal. "Come." I gestured to Abri. "Come, everyone. We're leaving."

People gave us wide-eyed looks. I'd spoken Coldi, so they had no idea what was going on.

Judge Hermans asked, "What is the purpose of this, Mr Wilson?"

I met Lenka's eyes across the hall. "We're leaving. I'm withdrawing my agreement to cooperate with this court. As you have already noted, the witness is not from here and is bound by no laws to appear. From the moment we arrived, the court has treated her and her family as curiosities and has refused to listen to their concerns and their wishes to be heard. As far as I am concerned, this trial is a farce. It's purely a political game to show the people that the Pretoria Cartel is capable of self-policing, while also avoiding investigation in certain areas of conduct. The accused is no angel, but based on the evidence only we can provide, there is no way you can conclude that he committed this particular crime, and any push to do so makes this whole process even more ridiculous. He should be standing trial for crimes we can prove he did commit, but I understand that would require the court to take a stance in recognising me as a representative of *gamra*, and recognising that a framework for legal cooperation with *gamra* is one thing that's most sorely needed in this whole sorry affair. But I also understand that most people in charge of the court don't want to see that happen. I've had enough of dancing around this issue and pretending it doesn't exist. We've done this for over twenty years and it has gotten us nowhere. I am no longer going to waste my time here."

Robert had suddenly sprung into life. He sat up straight, his eyes wild.

I turned away and led our group in the direction of the door to the foyer.

"I did not kill him," Robert shouted in the courtroom behind me. "See? Even he says it."

A number of people shouted, and the judge rang her bell and called for order.

While I gathered my team around me, Lenka came up to me. Her cheeks were red and eyes wide. "Cory, do you have any idea what you're doing? The cartel, Minke Kluysters in particular, is a very dangerous enemy to have."

"I'm not an enemy of his. I'm willing to talk when they stop playing games with me. I've taken the first step. The next one is up to him."

"It might involve assassins and weapons."

"He doesn't scare me." And then I said something that Amarru could have said. "Our assassins are better than theirs."

The words were out of my mouth before I realised what I'd said. I didn't think Lenka understood the underlying meaning—that of theirs and ours, "theirs" meaning the world where I'd been born and had grown up.

Me, using Amarru's words. These sorts of things kept creeping up on me when I wasn't thinking.

"I'll be fine, really," I said, and she probably didn't even notice my unease. "I have a lot of security with me."

"Good luck."

"I'll try to keep in contact." We might need her later.

And so we marched out of the courtroom, in the company of Reida pushing the trolley and Kita carrying a squealing Idda.

In the foyer, a line of guards were herding people towards the far side. "Everyone out, come on people, leave the building."

"Come on, let's go," I said.

Another group of guards was already coming in our direction from deeper inside the building, and I did not want to be in their control.

Veyada led the way.

While we crossed the hall, Mereeni showed me her reader. "This is the document that Dharma Yuwono has just made public. It outlines all the things he mentioned in his speech, including a lot of ways in which people can get involved. He owns a data distribution company. Their setup is really professional."

"How do they manage to avoid being blocked? Do they block detractors from accessing this information?"

"Not at this level. It's like a regular media hub where people get their information. It covers a lot of other news as well. It's run by Blues so no one in government cares. They're playing the Pretoria Cartel at their own games."

She skipped back to an overview page with one-line news items from all over the world, not only the powerful countries. The hub was called Blue Day.

"Dharma is a Blue?"

"He is. Came from the slums of Jakarta and worked his way up. He's one hell of a smart guy. Inspirational to many."

Inspirational to me. This whole case had taught me one thing: I'd been wrong about how to effect change in opinions on Earth.

All my working life I had assumed that in order to change, we had to convince the ruling order, but as I'd noticed, the harder you pushed for a change, the more they dug in. Maybe it was no longer time to change the minds of the ruling order, but to change the ruling order altogether. Time to abolish this horrible White-Blue system. Time to put the past behind us and move on. Time to engage the disenfranchised. The Age of Enlightenment Mark Two. And who would be better positioned to do that than a president on her last term, who had nothing to lose?

The potential for upheaval in the next year was staggering.

Margarethe was going to need all the help she could get, including mine, including that of all the people around me, and it was up to me, for once, not to turn my back and let Nations of Earth muddle along its own misguided path, but to do the best I could to represent the truth. We'd had two decades of sticking heads in the sand on this issue. Earth's society had become more backward-looking and insular than it had been when knowledge of *gamra* first became official.

Veyada led the way through the protester crowd, most of whom were calmly waiting to file out the door into the forecourt.

My team drew around me to shelter me and the Pengali from the mass of people. An official was yelling through a microphone for people to leave. Others shouted at him. Several people were still chanting. Outside, people were packing up the camp, and sometimes the police even attempted to help.

I could see the hands in the fountain, and the tents and a lot more people. More police and Nations of Earth personnel, one of whom came to me.

"Mr Wilson, the bus is out the back. We will take you to your hotel."

"Thanks, but there is no need. I can make my own way home. It's not far."

"The court has ordered us to see you out of here safely."

"Don't worry about me." I glanced at Evi and Telaris and Sheydu, all of whom looked tense.

"We insist. It's for your safety. The court and Nations of Earth would be hugely embarrassed if something happened to you."

I gave him a hard look. He was a clean-shaven officer with olive skin and brown eyes. He had probably been ordered to collect us. I made my voice as insistent as I could make it. "You can tell your superiors that I have my own security, and rather a lot of it. Thank you for the offer, but we won't need it. Goodbye."

I turned away from him, pushing the trolley.

21

———

T HE NATIONS OF EARTH security guard wasn't happy about me walking off, oh no; that was written all over his face. But I suspected that the presence of an unpredictable crowd—or at least a crowd not unequivocally friendly towards the guards and police—stopped him and his colleagues from using any form of physical threat on me. They might well have been ordered to use any means to keep me under control, but also not to display, let alone threaten me with, weapons.

We pushed through into the crowd, and they stayed behind, talking to each other and into their communication devices.

I stopped at the fountain with the inked hands and called the others around me. "What do we need to know? I want to get out of here as soon as possible without falling under their influence again, without armed skirmishes."

"The others have left the accommodation," Veyada said.

"What? Why?"

"We're leaving, aren't we?"

"Yes, but . . ."

"Eirani and Karana have packed up our rooms and Devlin and the guards have packed up the tech. They're waiting with a bus."

That was a relief. "Can they come here?"

"Apparently vehicles need a special permit to come into the town centre. We're going to have to meet them."

I glanced at Sheydu, who was untangling a set of detonators she had pulled out of her pocket. She gave me a pointed look. *She* definitely didn't think we could get out of here without trouble.

"Who is watching us and where?"

"I'm not so worried about who," Sheydu said.

"Then what are you worried about?"

"Their numbers. They're up there, and up there and there." She pointed to the building to the left and the building to the right of the courthouse. "They're also with the riot police down the street."

"What do you mean 'they'? Tamerians?"

"Can't tell that from here. Just spies. They have vehicles stationed along the edges of the dead zone. There is also a Nations of Earth vehicle waiting for us at the accommodation, and a hover jet at the airport."

"They really want to get rid of us, it seems."

Veyada said, "Amarru says we should make our own way back. She guarantees a safe trip on a commercial flight tonight, but if we want to catch that, we need to get going. The bus belongs to someone from the Exchange register." That was the directory of people, mostly Coldi in various positions and jobs on Earth, that any *gamra* citizen could call on for help. "Some of us know the locality. We should make it to the vehicle as soon as possible."

"I get you, but how do we get out of here without confronting the Special Services guards? I have no desire either to be forced to go with them or to create a fuss."

"We have to divide into groups," Sheydu said. "There will be one or two groups simply walking to the vehicle, which is not far from here, but which will shift according to the projected safest route out of here, and there will be another group of us with the skills to shadow and protect the other groups."

We then discussed who would go in what group. Sheydu said that we shouldn't all use the same route and that it should be unclear where we were going. Apparently, not even the hotel staff were informed that we were gone, so we still held the element of surprise.

I wondered if this level of precaution was necessary, but clearly my team knew a lot more than I did and they thought it was. I could only hope that I would hear about it once we were safe. Meanwhile, we had this awkward trolley that we couldn't move fast and definitely wouldn't be able to run with. And we had Jemiro, who couldn't run at all. There were enough steps and curbs to make me disinclined to take the drum through the streets.

While we had been talking, Evi had flicked through a couple of screens on his reader. He was looking at maps—no, satellite pictures.

Then I remembered something. "How recent are those images?" I asked him.

"The images? This morning. You can see the *police* vehicles around the corner and the tents outside the building."

I also saw something else: the dinghy that the Pengali had used to come here the previous night and we had never returned to the tourist boat jetty. It still lay in the canal at the bottom of the rickety ladder. So we should split up and go different ways, huh?

I turned to Ynggi. "I think we might go for a little trip by boat." I showed him the image. His face lit up. Sheydu gave me a dark look. Somehow our latest adventures always involved boats.

Coldi did *not* like water, and this was true for Sheydu in particular, much as she tried to hide it. She put down her pack, and dug out an object the size of a bar of soap.

"Waterproof explosives."

I feared as much. Hopefully we wouldn't need them.

First we had to get to the water without attracting too much attention. Not all of us were going to fit in that dinghy either, especially not if the *irrka* drum had to come, and there didn't seem to be an easy way to transport it otherwise.

We decided that I would go with the Pengali, because they could believably make the argument that it was the way they had arrived here, and they should take the dinghy back to its owners.

Jemiro should also come, because he probably couldn't run and really needed medical attention.

I wanted Thayu to come. She didn't look well, but like the other Coldi, she only pretended not to mind getting close to bodies of water. She insisted on staying on dry land.

Veyada would come with us.

The others were better suited to making themselves scarce in a crowd since they'd all had that mysterious spy and sniper training at Asto.

"And you're all armed," I added to that.

At that moment, Thayu took a cloth bag from under her coat and pressed it into my hands. I recognised the familiar shape through the material. Damn, the gun. How had she smuggled that into this high-security area? I quickly put it inside my jacket. Then Telaris handed me my body armour.

"Put it on," Thayu said.

Knowing she would not leave me until I did it, I took off my jacket and wormed myself into the armour. It was going to be pretty uncomfortable wearing it over the top of my shirt, but I wasn't taking my shirt off. I looped the gun bracket around my chest and closed the jacket over it.

There.

I hoped no one would ever get to see what I carried under there.

"I wish you would come with us," I said to her in a low voice.

She shrugged. She didn't even argue with me about how the dinghy would be loaded up already, and how they would be more nimble protecting us from the quay, all arguments I expected to hear from her, but she just shook her head.

"Hey, are you all right?" I touched her under the chin, looking into those gold-flecked dark eyes. Her face had lost all the rosy-cheeked complexity it had displayed earlier this morning.

She didn't even answer the question.

I squeezed her arm. "Look after yourself."

She pressed her lips together. Not well at all. A wave of worry washed over me.

"Let's go," I said. "The sooner we're out of here, the better." Jemiro, too, looked like he might collapse any moment.

The Nations of Earth guards and police stood around the perimeter of the forecourt, watching warily, knowing that if something blew up, they'd be vastly outnumbered.

The area hummed with an atmosphere of nervous activity. People were packing, gathering in groups, looking just as keen to get out of here safely as we were. I overheard some talk that the police had ordered the area vacated and that there were groups of riot police gathering in surrounding streets; and according to the satellite imagery I'd seen on Veyada's reader, that was correct.

The amplified voice of a man boomed through the street. He spoke about leaving the area peacefully. That was exactly what

Dharma had told the people to do. The fight would be fought in politics, in information, in the media. If anyone was creating tension here in the street, it was the police.

We pushed the trolley past the fountain.

The paving was a lot rougher here and it was hard to see where we were going because of all the people cramming around us. Many carried big bags.

Someone from the police or the guards was still yelling through a microphone for people to be calm and make their way out of the street peacefully.

"It'd be a lot more peaceful if he stopped screaming," a man next to me said.

We arrived at the steps that led to the street. Several people helped us lift the entire trolley with Jemiro on it. His eyes were half open, and he almost fell off the trolley.

"What's wrong with him?" a man wanted to know.

If only we knew. We needed to get him to the Exchange quickly, because a local hospital would not be able to help him.

Groups of people ran across our path, away from the area to our left where all the noise was coming from.

"What's there?" I asked.

"Tram stop," Veyada said. "People are going home. The *police* demand to see identification."

"Better stay away from those police then."

We crossed the dedicated driverless vehicle road. The section on the other side was paved with cobblestones that made our progress slow and awkward. The hotel trolley was not made for this. One of the wheels was already starting to come loose.

A volley of shouts broke out to our left, accompanied by dull thuds. A smoke canister flew through the air and landed in the waiting crowd. People ran, covering their noses and mouths.

The amplified male voice called, "Please move away from this area. I repeat, please move away . . ."

I said, "Come. It's not far, let's carry this thing."

Between Veyada, myself and the Pengali, we lifted the trolley. It was heavy and awkward to carry, because the only place to hold it were the edges of the platform and they cut into my hands. I couldn't carry my part of the load with just one hand, so I had to walk sideways. People ran around us. Clouds of acrid smoke wafted over the street. My eyes stung with it.

Ynggi started coughing. We had to put the trolley down for him to catch his breath. I couldn't see anything in the street behind us except figures running through the smoke. The forecourt to the court building lay deserted, with debris from the camp scattered around. All the people were at the tram stop where the male voice still ordered people to go home and be calm over the noise of people shouting and thuds that made me think there was a fight going on.

I said, "Ready? Let's cover the rest of the distance in one go."

Just as we had picked up the trolley, three police officers on horses came onto the forecourt.

Ynggi gasped and stopped. "What are those?"

"Those are horses."

"They're so big." His eyes were wide.

"Yes, but not dangerous. Now let's keep going." Before they noticed us with this big thing.

We struggled on and reached the edge of the quay. Ynggi climbed down the ladder first—I don't think he believed me about the horses—followed by Veyada. Abri, Kita and I lifted the drum over the edge into the hands of Veyada and Ynggi. Veyada mainly, because Ynggi was too short to reach.

Just as well Veyada was strong.

They put the drum in the middle of the dinghy, across the seats. Veyada and I managed to wrestle Jemiro down. Veyada half sat, half lay him against one of the benches. He didn't have to say anything for me to know that things were not well. Jemiro's skin had felt clammy and cold. His face was sickly grey and his eyes glazed over.

Then Abri and Kita climbed down.

There was a bit of rejigging as Abri and Kita needed to find space to sit while keeping out of the way of Jemiro, who took up rather a lot of space.

Then Idda chose this moment to come out of her orange jumper that was strapped around Kita's waist and she darted all over the drum.

"Keep her with you!" I said to Kita.

The mounted officers had slowly moved in front of the courthouse in the direction of the tram stop, but when I raised my voice, one of them turned around and noticed me.

He spoke to his colleagues, who turned their animals around.

, sir, what are you doing here?"

"I'm just leaving." Damn it, my off-Earth colonists' accent would give me away, even if they didn't recognise me.

"Can I see your ID, please?"

No, he could most definitely not. I pretended to put my hands in my pocket. I could feel the shape of the gun underneath. Oh, no, they couldn't be allowed to find that, either.

"Sorry, I must have left it in the dinghy. Wait."

I didn't wait for them to tell me to stay where I was, or for them to dismount and come closer or call backup. I half climbed, half fell down the ladder, scraping my shin against the lowest rung. Ouch.

"Go!" I said to Ynggi.

But he was still rearranging the pipes of the drum so that he could get to the engine.

"Go, now!"

Ynggi pushed the pipes aside and jumped. The dinghy wobbled ominously. He pressed the start button on the engine. It hummed to life.

An officer had reached the quayside. From my position, I could see his and the horse's head. "Mr Wilson!"

Damn, they had figured out who I was, too.

I pushed off the ladder as hard as I could. The boat left the quayside with such a jerk that I almost fell over the side. The water looked really dark and cold. "Go, go, go, Ynggi."

He didn't have to be told twice. He turned the dinghy around.

"Stop, Mr Wilson, stop, for your safety!"

Safety my arse. They did not want to let me out of their little controlled bubble.

Ynggi steered the boat along the far side of the canal, back in the direction of the hotel. The officers followed us, but the streets were still full of people and the horses could not walk fast. But that wouldn't matter. They knew where we were. They would call reinforcements who would wait for us downstream.

The dinghy puttered at a speed much too slow for my liking. "Where is this bus that's waiting for us?"

"It's not far," Ynggi said.

"Is there a way we can get there without using the water?" This damn boat was too slow. I wanted to join up with the others. I wanted to see Thayu. I wanted to know where the others were. Before someone used weapons.

"It's best to use the boat," Ynggi said.

We came past the section of the quay where the quayside was low and cafes and a playground was close to the water. Many people sat and walked there, a lot of them belonging to the colourful group of protesters who had been in the forecourt to the courthouse. They cheered and waved when we came past.

I also spotted a number of people running along with us. Not the officers on horseback. I was peering into the crowd, trying to make out who they were—

"Careful!" Veyada called. He pushed my head down as we ducked into a low tunnel. Holy crap. That was close.

We sat in breathless, dark silence as the boat went through a tunnel under a road and back into daylight. Streets were on both sides of the canal here, and were full of people but had some vehicles. Just shoppers going about their business, nothing to do with the protest. We appeared to have lost the people who had been running alongside.

We turned around a corner and went into another tunnel under another road.

As we came out of the tunnel, I became aware of a noise behind us.

There was a boat coming after us.

"How far do we still have to go?"

The other boat, a dinghy with only three people and no heavy instruments, was catching up fast. The men were not in uniform, but didn't look like Tamerians either. Secret agents? They had to be working for the Pretoria Cartel, because Nations of Earth's Special Services would be in uniform, would they? And they would not chase us like this? Or would they? How much had changed over the years that I'd been away?

Oh damn, they were really getting close now. What did they want? Were we police targets now? Why were they chasing us—oh crap, there was another boat ahead, coming towards us.

Ynggi steered the dinghy to the side, where there was a little jetty with another rusty ladder going up to street level. Deyu stood there, looking down at the water.

I was so glad to see her. Thayu, Evi and Telaris were with her. Thank the heavens.

The boat clonked into the jetty. Ynggi jumped out.

I called, "Hurry up."

The Pengali didn't need to be told.

Deyu vaulted down the ladder, landing on the jetty with a big thud, and she and Reida and helped Veyada lift up the drum. Abri, Kita and Ynggi climbed up. Idda was sitting on her grandmother's head, a bright orange beacon ready for target practice. I wanted to nab her off, but I couldn't reach her, not even her tail.

Meanwhile the two boats were coming closer and we really needed to get out of here.

"Come on." I lifted Jemiro under his arms. He barely reacted. The benches in the dinghy were in the way to get him up the ladder quickly. Veyada leaned down from the quay, grabbed him by the arm and hauled him up.

A man shouted, "In the name of the court, don't move."

I turned around and faced the man who had spoken, standing in the closest dinghy. He didn't *look* like a Tamerian. He was European, blond-haired. His companion, of African descent, held a gun.

Really? They were making threats to us *in the name of the court?*

What were these people?

I called out, "Stop this farce and just tell me who you work for. Why are you so keen to control all my movements? Because I might find out something your boss doesn't like?"

Neither of the men reacted to my words, but the African man slowly raised the gun.

"Is your boss Minke Kluysters? Tell him that I don't appreciate receiving threats. Tell him that I have no issues talking to him if he treats me in a civilised manner—"

A crack split the air and a flash of light hit the African's hand. He shouted and dropped the gun into the bottom of the metal dinghy with a clatter.

"Don't come any closer!" Evi called in his strongly accented Isla.

He and Telaris and Amarru's guards spread out along the quay, all of them pointing their weapons at the men.

"Quick!" Deyu held out a hand to me.

I had one foot on the jetty when something flew through the air, landing in the water next to the dinghy. Next thing the world turned into a frothing mass of white, and water sprayed outwards, splashing in my face and all along my side. A big wave made the dinghy rock so much that my foot slipped. I fell, hanging onto the ladder. A strong hand came from above and hauled me up to the street.

Deyu, rescuing me like a drowning kitten. Well, that was kind of embarrassing.

The other boat had overturned and its occupants struggled to get it back upright. A lot of people had come to the water's edge. I could already hear a siren in the distance.

"Come. It's not far," Sheydu said.

She looked smug while closing one of the pouches on her belt. It was empty. Waterproof explosives, huh?

Veyada, Deyu and Telaris picked up the drum between them and took off at such a pace that I had trouble keeping up.

The Pengali—being much smaller than most of us—also struggled. Amarru's guards dragged Jemiro along.

We ran to the corner, and turned left into the street. There was a bus sitting on the side of the road. As we came closer to it, the door opened automatically. It reminded me of Margarethe's bus, but certainly this was a different one.

The drum went in first. Strong hands hauled in Jemiro and we piled in after. I was one of the last ones to enter the plush inside. The driver was Coldi, predictably.

The Pengali were in the first rows behind the driver, panting, wide-eyed. Jemiro was there, pushed into one of the seat, since he could not stand unaided. The rest of the team was there, Eirani and Karana, and Nicha and Ayshada and Mereeni and Reya but . . .

"Where is Thayu?"

Blood draining from my face, I scanned all the seats. I didn't see her. I had definitely seen her just a few moments ago. She had been running alongside us.

Alongside us, while she should have been in front, because she was Coldi, and they were much faster—

And hey, what was that?

Someone crouched between the seats.

Thayu sat doubled over on the floor. He breath was fast, her skin sweaty, her hands trembled. She had undone the fastening to her armour and her uniform. Her fingers were covered in dark Coldi blood.

Damn, no. "Thayu, tell me what's wrong. Where did you get hit?"

She shook her head, her face pale and sweaty with pain. "The child . . ."

Damn—no.

22

I CALLED OUT, "Veyada!"

He stumbled through the aisle, climbing over the drum. Someone must have told the driver that everyone was on board and the bus had started moving.

Veyada took off Thayu's uniform and unstrapped all her equipment and weapons, of which there were a lot. He gave her a bandage and a warm emergency blanket.

Sweat glistened on Thayu's face. To my questions, she would only nod or shake her head. Yes, she was in pain, yes she had been feeling off for a number of days, no, there was nothing I could have done to change this.

I held her hand, while Veyada went to attend Jemiro, who probably needed attention more urgently.

The bus made its way out of the city at good speed. Sometimes it turned into a side street, no doubt avoiding surveillance or police checks.

Thayu looked out the window. Her eyes glittered with tears.

"I'm sorry," she whispered.

"What for? You can't help it."

"I should have been there to help you, but I've just been a waste of space on this trip."

"Don't worry about it." I stroked her cheek.

"We'll try again," she whispered.

"Let's think about you first."

She sniffed. I softly stroked her cheek. I knew she hated appearing to be weak and I didn't want to dwell on it any further. She was much more upset than she let on. I should give her time, after she had herself checked out.

I stroked her hand. "I have you. That's what matters."

We both knew it wasn't quite so simple, and we would, once she had recovered, go back to Lilona in Barresh and go through another set of treatments. Having tasted success, Thayu would only become more adamant that she wouldn't use a surrogate. And I would have my private parts poked with needles again. I understood that the next level of treatment would be more invasive, but I loved her, so I would do it.

Veyada came back a bit later.

"Sorry, there was nothing I could do," he said to me. "She lost the child and she'll be fine. You'll have to try again."

"How is Jemiro?"

"I'm worried about him," he said. "He's still not responsive and he has a very high fever. I have no idea what's going on. I don't know if anyone does, or if anyone can do anything about it."

The undertone in his voice worried me. "Surely you don't think . . ."

"I don't know what to think."

We let Devlin's discovery—that Jemiro Pakiru had died a few weeks ago—hang between us. I didn't know what to think about the implications. Stolen identity, stolen personality—heaven knew, he might be some sort of revived person. A zombie. Whatever they had done to him, he was coming apart. Was there life at the end of this tunnel for him? I had no idea. I felt sick.

"Surely we're not going to take him onto a commercial flight like this?"

"No. I've issued a medical emergency."

"Where are we going?"

"To one of the meet points."

I'd heard meet points mentioned occasionally, but I'd never seen any of them used, nor did I know where they were. All off-world traffic went through the Exchange and the craft remained at the Exchange, but there were some agreed places where *gamra* craft could come in case of emergencies. This was only to transport people to the Exchange if the emergency was specific to *gamra* people. Of course there would be meet points in this area.

"We're still being followed," Sheydu said.

I could only see out the side windows of the bus, and the view out there was of farmland, canals and submerged marsh. I couldn't even see the road in front, let alone behind us.

"What do they think they can achieve?"

She sniffed. "Block our communication for as much as possible for as long as possible."

"But you can get around it, can't you?"

"Some of it."

"Has anything major happened?"

"Amarru needs to talk to us and has news that she needs to share." When didn't she?

But Sheydu was right, my head was still quiet, and we'd long since left the dead zone.

By the time we turned off the main road and went through farmland to a shed half-hidden behind trees, the sun was low on the horizon. I still hadn't seen anyone following us, but I trusted Sheydu and my team on this matter. Did it matter that we were about to meet an Exchange craft, I asked. Sheydu said it didn't, because emergency medical transport was covered under an agreement.

The Exchange craft waited on the other side of the farm shed. It was a standard, Asto-made service craft, with two flight-crew and two medical officers. We informed them of our problems.

They looked after Thayu, who was shivering.

She would have to go to the hospital to make sure the miscarriage was complete and she had no other complications. They took her on a stretcher into the cabin, which had modules that could be moved according to the needs of the patients and the number of passengers.

They took more time with Jemiro. He also came in on a stretcher, but they had attached monitors to him and strapped a mask over his mouth. His skin had gone sickly grey.

I met Veyada's eyes. He pressed his lips together.

"Whatever is going on with him, it's disgusting," I said.

He nodded.

Everyone else came inside. The Pengali's drum went right up front, and Abri, Ynggi and Kita took the seats around it.

I sat next to Thayu in the medical unit at the back, surrounded by screens. Her gold-flecked eyes scanned all the equipment along the walls and even on the ceiling.

Jemiro lay on a stretcher on the other side of the med unit, and the two medical officers, both Coldi and both in light green shirts with a *gamra* blue edge at the edge of the collar, worked over him, even while the flight crew shut the door and the engine hummed.

With a soft shudder, the craft left the ground.

I kept expecting the nose of the craft to turn upwards and to be pressed into my seat, even if I knew that this would not be a high-speed, high-altitude flight. Because of my position at the back of the craft, I could only see a tiny piece of sky, mostly filled with clouds bright orange with the low sunlight.

One of the two med officers crouched next to me.

"When we get to the Exchange, he will go straight into the Emergency Unit. He is not stable, regressing, in fact. Not responsive to our treatments. Do you have next of kin we could contact?"

I met his Coldi eyes and knew it was really bad.

"I have to admit that we're not sure. I presume you have his *gamra* card."

"Yeah. It doesn't check out. It's either been cancelled or there are other issues with it."

Damn. "He's from the Pakiru family of Barresh." But was he, really? "They're fairly well-known." They should be able to confirm with us whether or not they were missing someone fitting Jemiro's description. Why hadn't we checked this out earlier? Because all his qualifications and documentation checked out at the time my team investigated.

I'd *known* about Jasper's reputation. My team had known it, too, maybe even better than I did, and why—

A bank of lights at the ceiling of the craft burst into life. Sound exploded in my head. Hundreds of voices talking over the top of each other, music, other sounds.

"Argh!" I lifted my hands to my head, willing the feeder's reception to narrow.

Clearly, the block on our communication was gone, and everything came in at once.

The noise, the noise.

A single Coldi voice remained. It said, "I need to speak to you. Can you contact me as soon as you can hear this?"

It was Amarru, but the message was a few days old.

I closed the feeder, and I pulled out my reader. Hundreds of messages scrolled over my screen. Most were not terribly important, but there was one from two days ago, from my father, asking where we were and if we were still coming.

———

By the time we had arrived at the Exchange and Thayu and Jemiro had been taken off the craft to the hospital, it was dark outside. I walked up to Amarru's highly guarded and fortified office. The Exchange had just opened and there was a hum of activity through the building.

Amarru's guards opened the door for me.

As I entered the office, I realised that I hadn't been in this room for a long time. Amarru usually came out to meet me.

She sat in an armchair near the window, through which I could see the city lights. She rose as the door shut behind me. "I'm glad you made it out without too much damage."

"Yes?" I was a bit baffled by this. Sure, we'd been watched, but we hadn't been in any great danger at any time, had we? Maybe only at the end with the chase through the canal, or when we went to the beach.

"Your trip has been very enlightening. We don't normally send people into Nations of Earth. We rely on our conventional bugs and trust them to report to us. But it has become apparent that this communication has been much suppressed over the past year. Your trip shows us that our concerns about how suppressed were well-founded."

"So . . . my trip was a spying mission in disguise?"

"Well, let's say we wanted to send people as much as they were keen for you to come."

"I really don't like being used." I felt sick.

"No, but this is an extraordinary time that justifies extraordinary measures. Come. I'll show you something." She opened a door to the side of the room. I'd noticed this door before and assumed that there was a bathroom behind it. The building had been built as a private hospital and, in its original state, many of the rooms had bathrooms attached.

My assumption couldn't have been more wrong.

We entered a darkened large room that appeared to have been formed from knocking out a couple of walls of adjacent suites.

In the centre of the room stood a circular bench that came to life with lights as Amarru approached.

I *had* seen something like this before, only once, when I'd had the privilege to enter Ezhya's nerve centre that he used to communicate with his vast networks of associations.

I shouldn't have been surprised that this existed right here on Earth, but it rattled me, nevertheless. I could already hear the protesting voices in the Nations of Earth Assembly. *We said they controlled us, but no one wanted to believe it, but look at this*. The Pretoria Cartel would be right at the front.

Damn, Amarru. Here was my answer for how much control she had over communication on Earth.

The answer: total control.

Damn, damn.

"What you see here is the completion of more than two hundred years of work. Every time someone uses any electronic form of communication, we can track it." She touched a light point on the screen before her and a projection sprang up. Lines of text—in Isla— scrolled across it.

"Nice." Scary. Absolutely scary. There would be revolt in the assembly once people found out about this. I didn't even dare ask the question: does Margarethe know about this?

I hoped she didn't, in which case a confrontation between Nations of Earth and *gamra* was in the cards if it came out. I hoped that she did, in which case Margarethe's position in the assembly would become untenable if the existence of this network, and her approval of it, became public knowledge.

And then I asked anyway, because I couldn't live with not knowing.

Amarru's reply was, "I didn't bring you here to talk about that."

So—avoidance?

Margarethe didn't know?

"I've brought you here to show you this." She touched another light point on the bench and the projection grew into a ball made of light that hovered in the middle of the room. A very *familiar* ball, with the familiar shapes of coastlines of Earth's continents.

I felt sick, like I had been transported to a conspiracy movie, watching the extent of influence of the bad guys over Earth. She couldn't—I had to—damn, Amarru.

"Look here." She pointed out a dark spot over Western Europe, another over southern Africa and another over eastern Africa. "We've lost communication in these areas. These black zones are growing. This is the work of the Pretoria Cartel. We now know for sure because of your visit. We have not been able to get full coverage of Rotterdam for almost a year."

And now I knew that Margarethe *did* know about this and I felt even sicker.

"Do you know . . ." I cleared my throat. "Do you know that the president intends to hold a referendum about joining *gamra*?"

And oh, *gamra* itself would have something to say about this vast spying network. Coldi had always defended their position that they were *not* attempting to take control of Earth on the sly, and surely one look at this room would put a nail in that coffin.

"I know." She looked up from the seat in the middle of the circular bench. Here she was, a middle-aged woman with grey spiked-up hair who had more influence over Earth than anyone. "These *elections* depend on communication, right?"

Something snapped in me. "No. Amarru, you can't manipulate communication. You can't. That's not how Nations of Earth works and why it was set up. It's not how the court works or how *anything* works on this world!" I breathed fast. "Don't even suggest to me that you're going to do this, because I'm not going to cooperate with it. I will be forced to report it to both Nations of Earth and the *gamra* assembly. Don't do this to me, Amarru. I've trusted you, and—"

She raised her eyebrows at me as if she wanted to say, *I thought you were made of sterner stuff.*

I was sweating under my shirt.

Then she looked down and shrugged. "Well then, I guess you might be happy with this situation." She touched the light point again. Now the vast network flicked off to be replaced with just the previously dark spots around Rotterdam and in Africa. There were additional, albeit much smaller, spots, along the eastern Canadian coast down to the south into the conflict zone of eastern America. All these spots were linked to each other and to threads that came from out of space.

What the hell?

I frowned at her.

She nodded, her lips pressed together.

"What . . . who is that?"

"We can only guess."

"Can I make a guess that it has something to do with Kando Luczon?" In fact, this whole Tamerian thing smacked of Aghyrian influences. We didn't know where the Aghyrian ship had gone and had not been able to locate it. But of course a very old and vindictive mind like Kando Luczon's would not take no for an answer. He'd been denied access to *gamra* worlds, but there were plenty of non-*gamra* ones . . . of which Earth was by far the most populous and influential.

Damn it.

Now we got to the bottom of the issue.

Amarru nodded again, still looking at me. She looked old to me.

The conflict was not Earth vs *gamra* and not even old politics vs new politics, and it had nothing to do with the Pretoria cartel, or the curtailing of off-Earth crime or, heaven forbid, the Zhori clan and their weapon smuggling.

The conflict was two middle-aged women—influential ones but still, only two—against a mysterious force somewhere in deep space, and the battle ground was the hearts and minds of everyone on Earth and possibly at *gamra* as well.

I blew out a sigh. "What now?" Margarethe *had* to win this referendum, or there would be war on a scale *gamra* had never seen.

"I'd like you to stick around for a bit if you can," she said.

"I was planning to take my team for a fun trip to visit my father in New Zealand."

"New Zealand will do." She flicked back to her, our, *trusted* network. There were plenty of light spots in New Zealand. People on the register, who could help us. "I'll get you some tickets so you can go as soon as your female team member has recovered."

———

I went to see Thayu when I came out of Amarru's office. She and the rest of the team were sitting in a bright room at the hospital. Thayu was in bed, but she was drinking tea and her cheeks were pink and her eyes bright.

She smiled at me. "They say I can go. There will be no lasting damage and we can try again."

I thought uncomfortably about the needles and the procedure I'd had to undergo. Ugh. Anyway, we'd face that once we were back home.

I had no idea how much they knew about my talk to Amarru, but we discussed plans to go to New Zealand. There would be time later to bother them with the worrying things I'd seen.

Eirani wanted to know if she was finally going to need the cold weather gear that she had brought.

"It's winter in New Zealand," I said. "That doesn't mean very much, but yes, it may be colder than you find comfortable."

The Pengali sat on the floor at the foot of Thayu's bed, looking at a reader which displayed screen after screen of different kinds of sharks. They would go back to Barresh tomorrow. I made a note to talk to Ynggi in private before he left. I wanted him on my staff.

Eirani had poured me some tea and was sharing around cake when a Damarcian man in a light green hospital uniform came in. He met my eyes and gestured me to the corridor, where he shut the door to Thayu's room before speaking.

"The other . . . person who was with you, do you know much about him?"

"No. He is not usually a member of our group. How is he?"

"Not terribly well, I'm afraid. Do you know anything about the implants he has?"

"Implants? No, I'm afraid none of us know him well enough to know that he has any. What are they for?"

"It will take us some time to figure that out, and I don't think we'll have the time."

"All I can do is give you the details of someone who will know more." *If I could find Jasper's contact details.*

"Is this someone in Barresh?"

"Yes, Jasper Carlson."

"We already contacted him. He claims not to know anything about this man."

What? He would let Jemiro die rather than help him?

"We need to know about these implants before we can touch them. Our medical engineers have looked at it, and they seem to think that the implants are self-destructing and that they are the only things keeping the man alive. We've tried to override the programs, but we're unfamiliar with this technology and may do more harm than good."

He took me to a room a floor down, where a single bed stood in a small room, surrounded by equipment.

I barely recognised the figure in the bed. His face was sickly grey. His hair stringy and thin.

The doctor went on, "We have also contacted the Pakiru family in Barresh. They were quite disturbed about this case. They said their cousin was killed in a fight recently. They sent us a picture of him."

"Is this the same man?"

"It is."

A deep chill went over me.

So, what? Jasper and his cronies had rebuilt Jemiro? Revived him and implanted knowledge into him? As far as I knew, most traditional keihu families farewelled their dead by placing them on a float and letting them be dragged into the ocean by the tidal currents. Were there really people out there who snatched dead bodies to turn them into mindless workers?

They had sent him with us to show how they could create people with skills on demand, and the demonstration had not gone as they intended.

"What do you want us to do?" the doctor asked me.

"Try your best, both to see what is going on with him and to save him. If he's stable, send him to Barresh. If he doesn't make it, send him back to his family."

"They already said they can't afford to pay for it."

"I will." I'd said it before I remembered the dire situation with my accounts.

But, damn it, I was disgusted. This was not how I wanted people to be treated.

He deserved better. His family deserved better.

The doctor asked me for details and declarations before I could go back upstairs. I explained the situation to my team, and they were just as disturbed as I was, in particular Thayu.

"I hope Jemiro comes out of it all right," she said, her voice soft.

Maybe it was hormonal influence, but she seemed more emotional than normal.

"Yeah, I hope so, too." I held little hope, based on what the doctor had told me, but if he did come out, maybe I should give him a simple job in the house.

"You know, I'm always surprised how you manage to think of the small things in the face of much larger problems," Thayu said.

I smiled at her. She was already recovering well from her misfortune, and I would need her in the near future, not just as a partner, but as a colleague and member of my team.

"Sometimes, the smaller problems are the ones that give us hope."

"He talks a lot, but this is true," Sheydu said. "The small problems are the ones we can solve. The bigger ones might solve themselves."

"Or they might not," Nicha said.

"Whether they will or won't is out of our influence." I rose. "We're leaving tomorrow. I suggest everyone get some rest."

Everyone left in pairs. Nicha with Ayshada, Reida and Deyu, Veyada and Sheydu. Mereeni had gone back to Amarru's service. Veyada had not mentioned her and I had not seen him take any time to say goodbye to her, but I reminded myself to ask him about her, because Coldi courtship behaviour mystified me more than ever.

A doctor came and cleared Thayu to leave the hospital. It was also fine for her to come to New Zealand with us.

I contacted my father and made arrangements. He would come to the airport with the bus that belonged to the community where he lived. He was looking forward to seeing us. To be honest, I was looking forward to it, too. Heaven knew when I'd last had a real holiday.

It would be a period of calm before the storm, before we had to sort out with Jasper what was going on, before Margarethe called the referendum and I might have to come back to help her, and before the inevitable upheaval that would follow.

Thayu and I walked to our room hand in hand. No words were necessary for the heaviness in our hearts, the worry in our minds, and the knowledge that whatever happened next, we would always have each other.

———

Thank You

. . . for reading *Ambassador 6: The Enemy Within*. The story continues in *Ambassador 7: The Last Frontier* when Cory faces an enemy with the power to bring down any hope for a fair referendum.

Be a champ and buy Ambassador 7 direct from the author in ebook, print or audio

ABOUT THE AUTHOR

Patty Jansen lives in Sydney, Australia, where she spends most of her time writing Science Fiction and Fantasy.

Her career started in earnest when her story *This Peaceful State of War* placed first in the second quarter of the Writers of the Future contest and was published in their 27th anthology. She has also sold fiction to genre magazines such as Analog Science Fiction and Fact, Redstone SF and Aurealis, before making the move to independent publishing.

Patty has written over fifty novels in both Science Fiction and Fantasy, including the *Icefire Trilogy* and the *Ambassador* series.

pattyjansen.com

BOOKS BY PATTY JANSEN

For a complete list of books, scan the image below with your phone.

Books by Patty Jansen

www.ingramcontent.com/pod-product-compliance
Lightning Source LLC
Chambersburg PA
CBHW031123200726

48286CB00021B/486